I0788942

THE KINGS OF WAYWARD ACADEMY
rebellious rook
BROOKLYN CROSS

THE KINGS OF WAYWARD ACADEMY
rebellious rook
BROOKLYN CROSS

The Kings

The Kings
The Order of Kings (Ord na Rithe)

Kings of the Kings
Last Rank Order (LRO) (Ordú Ranga Deiridh)

For the Deserted, For the Power, For the Blood of the Fallen

Also by: BROOKLYN CROSS

The Kings of Wayward Academy

(Academy/Slow Burn/Slow Build/Why Choose/Mafia - Dark 1-3 Spice 1-4 the dark and spice will progress more as the series continues)

Disobedient Pawn

Defiant Knight

Intolerable Bishop

Rebellious Rook

Queen's Gambit

Volatile King

Vexatious Queen

Fool's Mate

Pucking Snowed In Series of Standalone Novellas

(Hockey/Mafia/Spicy/MF - Spice 2-4 Dark 1-3 - Tie In with Kings of Wayward Academy)

Pucking Snowed In With My Ex

Pucking Snowed In With The Enemy

Pucking Snowed In With The Twins

Pucking Snowed In With Her

California Made Men

(Mafia/MF/Spicy/Crossover with Wayward Academy - Dark 3-4 Spice 3-5)

Protective Phlox

Avenging Azalea

Forbidden Forget-Me-Not

Lost Souls MC

(Motorcycle Club - Dark 3.5-4.5 Spice 3.5-4.5)

Malice

Surrender

Showbiz

The Consumed Trilogy

(Suspense/Thriller/Anti-Hero Romance - Dark 4-5 Spice 3-4)

Burn for Me

Burn with Me

Burn me Down

The Complete Trilogy

WARNING

This book is a Fiction Academy Romance story and is intended for mature audiences only, as defined by the country's laws in which you made your purchase. This book may contain an Irish accent, vulgar language, sexual content including MF, MM and MFM scenes, dark humor, parental manipulation, alcohol and tobacco use, gambling, violence, torture, suspense, Canadian slang and PTSD.

PLAYLIST

BACK IN BLACK - AC/DC
I WILL NOT BOW - BREAKING BENJAMIN
GOOD LIFE - ONE REPUBLIC
IT AIN'T OVER 'TIL IT'S OVER - LENNY KRAVITZ
UPSIDE DOWN - JACK JOHNSON
SWEATER WEATHER - THE NEIGHBOURHOOD
BRUISES - LEWIS CAPALDI
PRETTY BABY -ALEX SAMPSON
PSYCHO - HARDY
LOVE ME BACK - MAX MCNOWN
LOVE FACES - TREY SONGZ
BEAUTIFUL THINGS - BENSON BOONE
FIRE - BARNS COURTNEY
I LIKE THE WAY YOU KISS - ARTEMAS
GUESS - CHARLI XCX
CHIHIRO - DREAMSODA
HOLD ON - DRAKE
FIRST CLASS - JACK HARLOW
NUMB - LINKIN PARK
BE YOUR LOVE - BISHOP BRIGGS
FEEL GOOD INC - GORILLAZ
KRYPTONITE - 3 DOORS DOWN
STARGAZING - MYLES SMITH
DO I WANNA KNOW? - ARCTIC MONKEYS
SECRETS AND LIES - RUELLE
GOING UNDER - EVANESCENCE

A
PLAYER
NEVER REVEALS THE
ACE
HE'S HOLDING,
LITTLE RABBIT

Dedicated to all those who have waited patiently for this next installment in The Kings of Wayward Academy.

I hope you don't smash your tablets and if you do...please forgive me.

Love Brooklyn Cross

Chapter 1

SEPTEMBER 9 – TUESDAY 7:30 AM

Liam

Careening out of the last turn toward the school, I floored it. As expected, the cop, who had spent everyday lurking in the trees, went lights and sirens as he pulled out behind me. Too bad for him, I was already down the driveway of the school and through the gates before he even found the gas.

Just past the guard station, at the first light post, I idled and watched in my rearview mirror. The cocky prick drove right up to the gate, but the guards never budged. Some things had changed since Morrison was fired or forcibly retired, whatever way you wanted to look at it. They no longer had jurisdiction on the property without a warrant. Putting my window down, I hung my head out.

"Better luck next time, asshole," I yelled, flipping Ellis my middle finger. That should do it. Smiling like a grandpa out for a Sunday drive, I continued to the parking lot. Nash leaned against his car, waiting for me. Backing into the spot beside him, I got out and took a deep breath of the fresh morning air.

They couldn't have picked a better location for Wayward. The wilderness was where I preferred to be.

"You almost ran over my foot," Nash grumbled.

"Then fucking move it next time." He was lying, and his miniature rants never bothered me.

"How did it go?"

"Perfect, he'll be fuming all day. I wouldn't be surprised if he camped outside the gate waiting for me." Fuck I wanted a smoke. Instead, I played with the fidget thing in my pocket. I could get away with a few when Nash wasn't around, but even I wasn't stupid enough to light up beside him. He'd set me on fire with my lighter.

"Perfect, let's move the shit over." He opened the back doors of his car as I popped my small trunk. Nash hefted out two black duffel bags.

"How much fucking room do you think I have?"

"Get out of my way. They'll fit. You just need to know how to stuff the bigger one in."

"Are we still talking about the bags?" Nash glared at me over his shoulder, making me laugh. "Come on, that was funny."

"Whatever," he grumbled, loading the first one.

"Does that mean you're still doing the celibate thing?" I dropped the question like a bomb and held back a smirk as Nash glared over his shoulder. The silence that was supposed to intimidate me was all the answer I needed.

"I don't want to talk about it," he said.

"I don't understand this. You're not dating Ren, why aren't you fucking anyone?"

Impressively, Nash managed to get the second bag in, with a couple inches to spare, before he closed the trunk and turned to look at me. "What part of, I don't want to talk about this, did you not get the first time?"

"I don't tend to listen to you unless it's about work. This isn't work, so...what the hell is going on?"

"Relentless fucker," Nash swore, locked his car, and marched for the school.

"Why don't you want to tell me? You tell me everything, even showed me a photo of your father and mother in a very compromising position."

"Don't remind me, I still need therapy for that," Nash said.

He snarled when I grabbed his arm, but it didn't bother me.

"Tell me."

"What the fuck? Why do you care?" I stayed silent. "Are you caving to what Theo wants and fucking her?" Releasing his arm, I looked away. "You are? You pussy."

"Fuck you. I'm at least still having sex, unlike you. She has you whipped, and you can't even admit it."

"Me not having sex has nothing to do with Princess," Nash growled, drawing looks from a group nearby.

"Then what is it?"

"I don't know, okay? Happy now? I don't know. I just...I don't have any interest."

My mouth dropped open, dumbfounded. Nash was a whore with a capital W and proudly got more than anyone else we knew. Most parties meant two and three girls at a time.

"I'm sorry, I don't think I heard you. Did you just say you don't have any interest? Are you sick? Do you have a transmittable disease? Did someone cut off your balls?"

"See, this is why I didn't say anything. I knew you fuckers would go off on me. Okay, not having interest is not exactly accurate. I'm trying something new," he said, glancing around and glaring at the people eavesdropping. "What the fuck are you looking at?" The small group jumped and took off for the school. He rolled out his shoulders. "I'm trying for a healthier lifestyle. Less red meat, more exercise, and focusing on my work, school, and swimming. I'm stepping back from girls and the drama in general."

"Yeah...sure, and elephants with long ears can fly."

"I fucking hate you." Nash crossed his arms.

"If you're not going to be honest, then I'm not sure we're still best friends." I walked away from him, and he swore under his breath.

"What's there not to believe?"

"For starters, you're already a beast when it comes to your health. So much so you could be a science experiment for doctors. You're not quite as good as me, but damn close. Second, this non-interest only surfaced when a certain silver-haired princess came to Wayward. Huh...she actually is a princess. Good call on that. I don't believe in coincidences. Your dick no longer working, and her presence every second of the day is too big of a coincidence."

"There is nothing wrong with my dick," Nash said as we walked into the foyer.

Everyone went dead quiet. You could hear a pin drop, and I bit my lip to keep from laughing.

"Well, as good as that is to know, Mr. Collier, can you maybe save this conversation for when you and Mr. Hicks are in private? Or with the doctor, perhaps." Nash smacked a hand over his face as Dean Henry walked around us to his office.

"I think I hate you," Nash mumbled under his breath at me, and I couldn't contain my laughter. Nash being humiliated was like a blue moon, and you had to take advantage of the situation. "Look, you can believe whatever the hell you want. It's the truth," Nash said as he marched for the cafeteria.

"That's the whole truth and nothing but the truth, so help you, God," I teased, loving this way too much to drop it now.

"Go fuck yourself."

"Oh look, there is your troublemaker now," I said as he grabbed a coffee and a plate.

"Don't care."

"Sure, you don't."

"I swear to god, I'm going to stab you through the eye with my fork if you don't shut up." I snickered, and if looks could kill, I would be dead as he held out his plate for Betty to fill. She knew him well enough now to just put three omelets on his plate and hand it back.

I swiped a couple boiled eggs and an orange juice before following Nash to the table. He was eating like a caveman, shoveling the food into his mouth as Theo, Blake, Myles, and Ren stared at him.

Theo looked up as I got closer, and our eyes locked. Fuck I missed him. Having sex and being in a relationship were very different. A lesson that was painfully being taught. He never stayed longer than a few minutes after we had sex, and there was no hanging out or talking anymore. He didn't tell me when his races were or how he did. We'd drifted so far apart that I could hardly see the shore, and I had no clue how to fix us.

Even though he looked away without so much as a twitch of his lip, I sat down beside him. Meals were the only significant time spent together anymore, and it was driving me insane. I was starved for more, and the person I chose to blame for this was sitting directly across the table.

Popping one of the eggs into my mouth whole, I glared at Ren as she typed away on her laptop. Even the soft clicking of the keys annoyed me. I'd warned her not to try and take Theo from me—a line drawn in the sand—but she wiped it away, not giving a fuck. Now, I daydreamed of wrapping my hands around her throat. I wasn't sure if I wanted to kill her, fuck her as she begged for more, or fuck her and then kill her. All were excellent options.

"Stop it," Theo whispered in my ear, and I bit back a groan as his voice hit in all the right ways.

"I wasn't doing anything," I said, turning my head to meet his glare. Theo's green eyes were livid, the look just as hot as his breath along my skin.

"Don't bullshit me. I know exactly what you were thinking," he said, and I licked my lip.

"Is that so? What am I thinking right now," I asked, and he shifted on the bench. "Well? What do I want?"

"Don't change the topic, you know what I mean, or meant, whatever," Theo said. My whole body got excited when he was rattled.

"And whose fault is it?" I slid my hand onto his leg. "That I may or may not have unkind thoughts?"

"You two do know we can hear you at this end of the table," Blake said.

I flicked my gaze over to Theo's twin and then Nash, who was sitting with a bite of omelet halfway to his mouth, while Myles and Ren stared from across the table.

"Oh no, continue. It was awesome. You just don't have to whisper."

Myles and Nash laughed. Fuck this. I quickly chugged my juice and got the fuck out of there.

"Aw, come on, don't be like that," Blake called after me, but I chose to ignore him.

"How do you like the shoe on the other foot," Nash asked, then laughed. Prick.

Putting space between me and Ren was safest for everyone. Teaching her how to box was going to be annoying enough, so the less time we spent together, the better.

Marching outside, I took the path to the park and swore as I remembered that I'd left my smokes in my glove compartment. This fucking place. One more year and then freedom. It couldn't come fast enough.

"Hey."

Theo's voice made me turn my head, and I rolled my eyes as he marched toward me. Not bothering to stop until reaching the picnic tables, I sat down and pulled the fidget spinner from my pocket.

"What do you want, Theo?"

The argument looming was a waste of breath for both of us, but we couldn't seem to quit each other. We danced around the subject again and again. He didn't understand where my anger was coming from, and no matter how hard I tried, I couldn't figure out how to express what I was feeling in a way that got through to him.

Taking me completely by surprise, he grabbed my face and crushed our lips together. We never kissed in public, and I stiffened with shock. Theo stepped back slowly, shaking his head at me. Silently, he turned and walked away.

"What the hell was that?" I yelled after him.

His eyes were sad as he looked back, and I had no idea what I'd done. "You just proved everything I've been saying."

My hands flew up in total confusion. "What do you mean? I didn't do anything. You kissed me."

"And you stiffened." Theo shook his head. "You didn't even kiss me back."

Wanting desperately to dispute the claim, I opened my mouth and realized he was right. I hadn't. I'd been too freaked out that someone would see us. Shit.

"You're the bravest person I've ever met. So imagine how hurtful it is that when it comes to us, you're scared for anyone to find out. Maybe one day you won't...stiffen. Hopefully, I'm still here."

I jumped up, hands balled, furious that he called me out like this. But there was some truth to what he said.

Theo wasn't the problem. I wasn't embarrassed by him, never

him, but I was brought up in a traditional home. If this got back to my parents...it was a fight I didn't want to have, yet. He was all about needing heirs and passing on the family name. It was worse for me because I had two sisters who would take their husbands' names. There were other ways to have a child these days, but that wasn't the point, I just didn't want to explain my life or lifestyle to anyone, ever. I hated anyone knowing anything about my personal life, not just where Theo was concerned.

"I gave you my class ring, and you practically threw it back at me," I growled. "I was trying, and you shot me down."

Theo spun around and pulled off his glasses, his eyes wild with rage.

"No, you tried to put a second collar on me and make a statement to Ren. Giving me that ring wasn't for my benefit. And tell me, how was anyone ever going to know that you gave it to me? It looks just like mine. But that's the point, right? I'd know, you'd know, but no one else would be the wiser." He poked me in the chest. "That ring, that gesture you're saying was done out of love, was just another way for you to impose control. It was your way of creating a symbol that said, 'I am yours' without you ever having to be vulnerable."

I crossed my arms, my teeth grinding together.

"Next, you'd try to placate me with lavish gifts and trips away to secluded islands that, on the surface, were romantic until you looked closer. Then, you would ask me to move into the penthouse you purchased downtown. You'd want to keep me down there away from your family, making me the perfect plaything. I'm not that. Either you treat me as your partner, or you can fuck off. I'm so tired of waiting for you to open your eyes and see what we could have if you just let go, but you won't. You're scared. Too fucking scared."

He looked me up and down and it was like he'd just folded his hand and left the game after he pushed all his chips into the center of the table.

My heart raced, panic choking me as he stepped back. We stood there staring at one another, neither saying anything until the bell rang, and he walked away.

So many things ran through my mind to say, to call out and tell him, but none of them left my lips.

"Fuck!"

SEPTEMBER 9 – TUESDAY 7:45 AM

R**en**

"Well, that was really awkward," I said as Blake ran his thumb over my hand.

His fingers tightened on mine as we walked out toward Bowfield Hall. Blake glanced down at me, and I knew what he was going to say before he opened his mouth.

"I know. Theo and Liam have to fix their relationship, but it's so hard to stay out of it when they're fighting about me. I did this."

"Pfft. You didn't do this. My brother knew what he was doing when he slept with you. That was his choice, and the reason doesn't matter. What they have going on has been brewing for a while. You just kind of kicked them over the edge and forced them to face it rather than continue to ignore the issues," Blake said.

"I know. Theo said the same thing...I just wish there was something I could do to help. Theo won't talk about it, and Liam can hardly stand being within fifty feet of me. He was glaring at me like he wanted to eat me alive this morning."

"What do you think," I asked Ivy, and her eyes went wide as she took a bite of her muffin.

"Me?"

"Yeah, you." I laughed at the horrified look on her face.

She waved me off. "I'm not the person to ask. Hell, I can't get anyone to want to date me, and the only guy who did date me ditched me after a month. I'm not qualified to puzzle out a four—" She lifted her fingers. "I guess technically five-way relationship if you're counting Liam in by default. That's far too complicated for my brain to figure out."

"Come on, you must have thoughts on the topic. You've seen all of this from the beginning, and you know the guys from before."

Ivy glanced up at Blake and then looked me in the eyes. I smiled, trying to reassure her.

"Blake's not going to hate you or be mad for anything you say."

"I'm the least likely to hate anyone...well, I can think of two people, but aside from them, never."

She sighed.

"Okay...well, to start...this multiple-guy thing leads to so many questions. Like...do you have sex with them all at the same time? That really seems like a hella number of dicks coming for your face. Who do you grab first, or do they sword fight for first right to a hole?"

Oh no.

"I've read some kinky alien romance, and the image of all of them together totally reminds me of it. Each one of the guys with a tentacle poking at you and trying to get in somewhere to pleasure you. I mean, it's hot, don't get me wrong...but still. Oh, and I found this site that sells fun-looking toys if you ever get experimental."

Blake burst out laughing, and I instantly regretted opening this box. Award went to Ivy for finding something that I not only didn't need to know about her but really didn't need to picture. Now, every time a box showed up at the dorm for her, I'd be wondering. Great.

"On second thought, never mind," I said, my face burning up with embarrassment, but knowing it was too late. Once Ivy started down a path, she was like a wind-up toy that would only stop once she was through.

"No, no, I'm seriously curious. Does everyone finish at once, or do they take turns? I don't know how you even consider taking four guys at once. That is a feat all on its own. Is it like the movies where you're coated afterward? Ugh, that would be sticky. That's a hell of a lot of come. The water bill on showers alone must be insane."

I smacked my forehead while Blake gasped trying to draw a breath as he laughed to the point of tears.

"Do they all use protection? I mean, they should. You don't want one of those wiggly little bastards getting you all bun in the oven. That will, for reals, get you some side-eye and start an all-out beef among the guys. Oh my god, can you imagine the tea that'll swirl trying to figure out who the father is? I mean, if you add Nash to complete the group, then we'll all have to say it's his by default. He just gives off those 'I'll kill you otherwise' vibes. Baby, I am your father," she said like she was Darth Vader.

Dear God, what have I done?

"You can stop any time," I said, but she completely ignored me. Her eyes were fixed on whatever planet she just went to with her runaway thoughts. I could feel her building into a full-blown rant that would give me a migraine.

"And then there's the working out. I mean, how do you stay that fit? Who gets to sleep beside you at night? Who do you say good-night to first? Does anyone get jealous? Do you even care? You are the queen of the harem. I guess you don't have to care. Do you all sit and talk everything out all the time? It's just exhausting to think about. Don't get me wrong, they're the Kings, they slay, so I get it, and I'm not saying that if roles were reversed that I'd do anything differently, but...wow."

"Can we steer this back to Liam?"

"Oh yeah, Liam. That's where I was going with this. He's legit fire and a total baddie, but still, he gives sketch vibes that I don't always trust. I think Liam is just salty because he was the straight-up GOAT in Theo's life, and now, he's lowkey pressed and giving toxic energy on having to share what was once all his."

When the hell did Ivy become Gen Z? I'd never heard her talk like that before, and that alone was making my brain hurt.

"Please tell me you're done?"

"Almost. I mean, honestly, if I was Theo, I wouldn't have been vibing with what Liam was putting into their relationship a long time ago. Theo has been super patient. I would've split the moment Liam chose to keep us on the down low for more than a month, let alone over a year. Can you imagine if Blake told you to pretend you were only his bestie in public because he didn't want to admit that he liked you? I mean, hello, red flag, fam. You know?"

Aside from the fact that I made a mental note to keep all questions to myself from now on, Ivy oddly had a point with that last bit.

"She's right." Blake shrugged. "If you told me that you wanted me, but not in so many words, showed me that you were embarrassed to be seen with me...damn, that would hurt. I hadn't even thought about it that way because they've been like that from the beginning. I just sort of assumed that was the way they chose to be."

And just like that, I wanted to punch Liam in the face and hug Theo.

"Why is he being like this, do you know?"

Blake held the door open for me and Ivy as I looked at the schedule to make sure we went to the right room.

"I have no idea. Only me, Myles, and Nash have known until recently when Ivy and a couple others found out about them. But if I had to take a guess, it's his family."

That surprised me. The Hicks family had seemed perfectly nice at Thanksgiving last year.

"They are very traditional. It's driving them insane that Nora wants nothing to do with the family as long as they support Lawrence. She walked away, also hating the whole arranged marriage thing. If they thought something was going on between him and Theo...I can't see it going well."

"Like how bad?"

"I don't know the Hicks well. They kind of keep to themselves. My guess is that they'd start by banning Theo from their home. They might pull their support of the council or try to have my dad removed for Theo corrupting their son. Liam's dad is the largest financial contributor to Lawrence and runs all the imports and exports. It would cripple the flow until a new shipper could be found. All the family businesses are tied into what the council does, so that would mean a major haircut in profits. That would bring a ton of heat to my parents. But that's just a guess. It's not like Theo or Liam ever talks to me about any of this."

"So, he may not just be a selfish asshole, is what you're saying. Great, make it even more confusing. Thanks."

Blake smiled and wrapped his arm around my shoulders. "That's what I'm here for."

Following Ivy, we walked into Women's Literature class. The desks were set out in a circle, meaning less paperwork and more class discussion. I chose my seat and Ivy grabbed the chair on my left and Blake on my right.

"Can I ask why you are taking Women's Literature, Blake?"

"Are you being sexist right now, Ms. Davies?"

Blake leaned in closer, his arm wrapped around the back of my chair, and one sexy eyebrow arched. The bell rang, and everyone quickly filed into the class and sat down. Chairs scraped across the floor, and the sound of pens, paper, and all the other noises that screamed classroom filled me with joy.

"Please, as if. Now, if I asked Nash that question, I probably would've been, but you...never. I'm genuinely curious about what intrigued you enough to take this class as a guy?"

"That is a fabulous question. In fact, I want all of you to tell me what intrigues you about this course," Ms. Stanton said from right behind us.

I cringed and looked back, but she was smiling wide at me. She was short in stature and wearing a bright red dress with black polka dots. Mixed with her thick glasses and round face, she looked like an adorable ladybug in human form.

"Let's start with this end of the class." She looked at her list. "You must be Blake?"

"Yes, Ms. Stanton."

"Great, you go first."

Blake sat up straight and grabbed his necklace, rubbing the pick between his fingers. A nervous habit I'd noticed this past summer.

"Well...I suppose it's because of my mother. My family, like most of ours, is patriarchally dominated. But my mother has always been strong, smart, and extremely creative. My father treats my mother as a true partner and values her insight on every decision made in our household. I think that more men need to be like my father and take a greater and more active role in not only the support of women and their rights but also in understanding the social and cultural influences that women and their writing have contributed to literary traditions throughout the ages. When you think of artists or authors, we always see men front and center and the most revered, but right from the Middle Ages, women in arts have played a pivotal role. Everything from artistic expression, economic subsistence, and even political resistance. There is nothing in our history that hasn't been prominently touched and influenced by a woman. We need to ensure as a society that it stays that way."

The room remained completely quiet as we all stared at Blake. Not one person wasn't moved by what he'd just said. A tear stung my eye as I truly realized what made Blake so special to me. He'd been more open, honest, and vulnerable with me than anyone else. Blake wasn't afraid to admit that he was hurting and trusted me in a way that even Myles still struggled to show despite how much he loved me.

I laid my hand on Blake's as he looked around the room, his eyes wide like he was about to be blasted.

"That was beautiful," I said.

Ms. Stanton took off her glasses and wiped them as she sniffed. "It really was. Very good, Mr. O'Brien, very good indeed. Let's go counterclockwise next."

As the next students introduced themselves and said their piece, I couldn't take my eyes off Blake.

Leaning into him, I whispered, "You have an artist's heart, and I think it allows you to see the world in a way that the other guys don't. That's also why you sometimes struggle to be yourself with them. You don't feel they can ever understand. It makes you far wiser than all of them put together."

He linked our fingers, his smile shining as bright as his school ring glinting in the light pouring in the window. "Theo may argue that."

"Oh, I'm sure he would, but he'll never convince me otherwise."

"I really want to kiss you right now," he whispered, close to my ear.

I cleared my throat as Ms. Stanton looked our way.

"Better not get us kicked out on our first day and after you made such a great impression."

"I really did, didn't I?" I nodded as he sat back, his arms behind his head, looking as proud as punch.

Blake and I shared a similar reason for taking this class. My mother had played such an important role in my life and had fought hard right to the very end.

My hand tightened on my pen. I was going to find out who killed her and why, and then...then, I didn't know, but part of me wanted to kill them.

Chapter 3

SEPTEMBER 9 – TUESDAY 12:30 PM

Ren *Tap, tap, tap.* My pen was like a steady metronome as it bounced off the table. I was supposed to be studying for my Russian 101 class tomorrow, but I couldn't get into it. None of the words made sense. I never struggled like this.

Playing detective was new for me, but here I was, trying to figure out my past like a private investigator. Reaching into my bag, I pulled out the photo I'd found of the Mikhailov family from years before I was born.

I had spent days painstakingly figuring out who every person was, how they were related to me, who was still alive, and how old they were now. Each name was written over a head with the link to my past, yet I was no further along in my quest for answers. No matter how much I dug up, there was always a new dead end.

It didn't help that anything I found that seemed promising was in Russian. I didn't trust the translators after one of the sentences that I put in said, *"I don't have sex with dogs in the winter."* If that was really what the line said, then I wasn't sure I wanted to know more about my family.

"How the hell do I crack this when the people who have the answers are the same people trying to kill me?"

"Such a conundrum you have."

Jerking back, I looked up to see Nash leaning on the back of a chair across from me.

"When did you get here?"

"Long enough ago to see you aren't getting any work done," he said, smirking. "Is this what you really do? Come in here to daydream, but have all the teachers convinced of how hard you work?"

"Funny." I placed the picture down. Nash snatched the photo, and at one point, I would've jumped up and started a fight with him about it.

How things have changed.

Nash's eyes skimmed over the image as mine traced his face. He'd been really strange since he got back from the vacation he wouldn't talk about. It was bothering Myles and Theo that Nash hadn't said a single word. Not where he went, who he met with, or what had happened. In some ways, Nash seemed...more smug, like he was suddenly untouchable, and yet...there was something off.

If I didn't know Nash and his 'I don't give a fuck about anyone attitude' I'd almost say he felt guilty for something. If he really did, that was a terrifying prospect. What the hell did he do that he'd feel guilty enough that he couldn't tell his guys?

"Why are you staring at me? You're burning a hole in my forehead." He looked up and smiled. "I know I'm irresistible, but you used to be better at hiding your interest in getting me naked."

"Well, I see that your fantasizing skills are still in working order." I held out my hand for the photo, but he walked around the table and dropped down beside me.

"You have got to be the most stubborn person I've ever met," Nash said. "Why won't you just admit it? Think of it as a cleansing. It'll feel good to get all those pent-up feelings off your chest."

I rolled my eyes at him.

"Maybe you should take your own advice."

"Maybe I should," he said, and even though he didn't say it was about me, the butterflies went insane in my stomach. We sat in silence until I couldn't take it anymore.

"Myles told me you know this guy," I said, pointing to the little boy of six in the photo.

"Sure, I know Nathaniel. He's not that cute anymore. He's the guy you don't mess with in a dark alley now."

Turning in my chair, I feigned shock.

"Nash Collier, did you just admit you're intimidated by someone?"

"Fuck that." He crossed his arms over his chest. "Just saying you need to know your enemies and your allies and what they're capable of." I laughed, earning a glare. "What? You don't believe me?"

"I do, but you do know it's okay to admit that someone scares you."

"Never. The day I admit that anything scares me is after I'm already in the ground," he said.

"Now that I do believe." I sighed. "Okay, what can you tell me about my cousin? Other than he's scary. Could he have killed my mother?"

"Could he physically...sure. Do I think he did...no."

"Why not?"

Nash shrugged. "Lots of reasons, but the biggest one is that there was nothing for him to gain. Look, when you think of this world we're in, what do you imagine?"

"I'm not sure what you mean?"

"Okay, let me put it to you this way. If we were a game, what game would we be?"

Mirroring his position, I stared into his blue eyes and said the first thing that came to my mind. "Chess."

He smiled, and a wicked dimple appeared on his cheek.

"Yes. It's not a coincidence that we have the nickname the Kings. Now tell me this. What advantage would Nathaniel gain from killing off your mother? A woman who had disavowed her family ties, held no power, was married to a random guy with no pull, and was trying to remain hidden from this world? Your mother's death had nothing to offer Nathaniel that would give him or that side of his family anything other than a headache."

"But I saw that polar bear tattoo. I know I did."

"All the men in the Mikhailov family, including soldiers, have that tattoo. You're talking about thousands of people who have pledged loyalty. If someone was kicked out, they'd cut it off their hand, but if they ran before that could happen, then they'd still have it. Or it could be her father's men. She ran away from her marriage and embarrassed him. It is very possible if he's as vindictive as we've heard."

"My grandfather is still the most likely suspect unless the men were rogue. I mean, your guys wouldn't...."

I almost blurted out the word assassinate and snapped my mouth shut at Nash's intense stare.

"They wouldn't do anything you didn't want," I said, finishing my errant thought. "I was really hoping that wasn't the case and that we'd find something to show it wasn't him. But...there is nothing good in any of these articles."

"That's true, but you still haven't answered my question."

He leaned closer, and I swallowed down the shiver of excitement that had developed where he was concerned. If there was a way to squash an emotion, this was the one I'd dropkick.

"You don't make a move on a chess board randomly. The moves are precise and with distinct reasons for getting closer to the end of the game and taking your opponent down. So the answer to your burning question is...who had something to gain from your mother's death? Or...by killing you. You're not dead yet, but it's not for a lack of trying. I think they were going to kill you both, and your mother knew that which is why she tricked you into the safe room."

That was one way to crush every little fluttery feeling floating around in my body. All the butterflies dropped to the floor, and I looked away. Nash gripped the back of my chair, and it screeched across the floor as he pulled me closer.

"Look at me," he ordered.

My whole body radiated with tension. I didn't want to piss him off. If I did, Nash would just step up his annoying efforts. Turning my head, I met his steady gaze.

"If you really want answers, then the first thing you need to do is come to terms with the truth because you're still living in a dream world half the time."

The fiery rage inside of me was instant, and I narrowed my eyes into a glare.

"What do you think I've done from the second I was locked in the safe room to when I woke up from passing out after watching my mother's murder? You think I've just been pretending she's alive? Maybe if you and Vicky weren't always in my face causing issues, I'd have more time to deal with it."

Shaking my head, I tried to stand, but Nash grabbed my arm and jerked me back down into the chair.

"Let go of me," I hissed.

Nash, of course, did the complete opposite. He gripped the arms of the chair and pulled me so close that my legs were trapped between his, and I was caged in with his hands on either side of me.

"You haven't come to terms with what happened. You've been too busy blaming yourself for a murder you never could've predicted, planned for, or stopped. Do you wish you had died? Do you wish that your mother didn't lock you in that room and they succeeded?"

Tears stung my eyes, and I had to look down to force them not to spill down my cheeks. Crying in front of Nash was humiliating, but he just couldn't leave me alone and tilted my head up with his finger. I jerked my head away from his touch and sucked in a sharp breath as he grabbed my jaw and forced me to look at him. My hands balled into fists. I wanted to hit him. I wanted to do it with every fiber of my being, but I didn't want to be hauled into Dean Henry's office again.

"Let go of me, or I swear I'll scream."

"Then scream. Just make sure it's my name and say that you're coming." Unbelievable, he just didn't know when to quit. "Are you so afraid of saying the words out loud that you'd rather run like a coward? I didn't take Ren Davies for a coward, but guess I was wrong," he said, letting go of my jaw.

"I guess we're both cowards then, aren't we," I snarled and regretted it as he leaned in so close that the only way to keep distance would be to crawl over the back of the chair.

"You going to tell me I have a smart mouth again."

He shook his head, his eyes furious as they drilled holes into my soul. The intensity was as strong as any slap, and my heart tripped in my chest.

Nash was like a tornado. You didn't know when he was coming, where he would show up, or how much damage he would do. It was the equivalent of being picked up, violently thrown around, and then torn in two before you even realized it was happening.

"Say the words," he growled. I pressed my lips together. "Say it, or you'll never be free of the pain. It's just you and me. Say it, say why you hate yourself when you look in the mirror."

"Fine, you want me to say it...." The tears started, and there was no stopping them. "I hate her for not telling me who I am. I hate her for dying after I gave up my childhood to love her and look after her. I hate that she left me alone with a man who can't stand being my father. I hate that I was dumped here like trash. I hate that I have to deal with this world and act like I'm okay all the time when I'm not. And most of all...I'm happy that I didn't die." I covered my mouth. "I hate myself for feeling like this," I said softly. "And you for making me say it."

"Hate me all you want, Princess. But you know as well as I do that you'll never heal or move on until you are honest with yourself." He pushed his chair back and stood. "Nathaniel didn't kill your mother, and neither did his immediate family, but if you don't believe me, I will set up a meet for you."

"You'd do that?"

"I'll let you know the details when I have them." Nash walked around the table as I wiped away the tears. "Princess?" He looked down at me, his jaw firm and eyes as arrogant as always. "For whatever it's worth, I'm happy you didn't die."

What the hell do I do with that? Other than punch him square in the face.

I finished wiping away the tears as he walked away and swore under my breath as he stopped to talk to Liam. They must have been talking about me because Nash pointed in my direction. Fuck. Liam spotted me across the room and made his way over. Great, were all the assholes in my life standing outside in a line waiting to get their hits in?

"Why are you crying," Liam asked as he leaned on the chair across from me exactly as Nash had started.

"Oh, you know, just Nash handing out sweet compliments. I'm simply overcome with shock and joy." Liam raised an eyebrow at me.

"Yeah...sure. Don't play poker anytime soon. They'll take you for all you're...not worth." He smirked.

"Wow, this conversation is about as much fun as the last." Grabbing my bag, I packed up all my books and laptop.

"The Little Rabbit is getting ready to run. If you can't handle some razzing by Nash or me, then you'll never survive this world. They'll eat you like a tiger tearing apart prey the moment you leave the protection of Wayward."

Hanging my head, I sucked in a deep breath so that I didn't murder him. "Did you come looking for me for a reason?"

"Yes, I promised that I'd train you once school started," he said, and I crossed my arms.

"I don't know who you promised, but you don't need to train me. It's no secret you can't stomach being in the same room with me."

"You worried I'll kill you?"

"Honestly, I'm worried that anyone in here could kill me, but no, that's not the reason. Go sort your shit out with Theo, then we can talk."

His forehead pulled into such a deep glare that his eyebrows almost touched. "What does me and Theo have to do with me training you?"

"Everything. One, it's awkward. Two, I know you hate me. Three, it's...awkward," I reiterated.

"But it's not awkward fucking my boyfriend?"

The corner of my mouth turned up. "You really want to fight about this now?"

Liam's jaw twitched, and I didn't think anyone could be more intimidating to deal with than Nash, but Liam was in a league of his own. "No, I don't. But I am going to train you because I promised, and I keep my promises. So, pick a time."

"Fine, Wednesdays. I can do anytime."

Liam laughed. "What do you think you're going to learn one day a week? No, I mean every day. The same time every day, except four o'clock. I can't miss swim practice, or Nash will kill me."

Everyday? I'd rather a hole to hell opened up so I could jump in.

"I don't know...what works for you?"

"Morning, before classes. How's five-thirty a.m. in the gym, Monday to Friday? I'll let you have the weekend. I'm nice like that."

I smiled wide, while inside, I wanted to cry all over again. "Sounds fantastic. Can't wait."

"Uh huh, sure. See you later, Little Rabbit. You better run. You'll be late for class," Liam said.

I glanced at the time and swore as he walked away. Shit, I was going to be late for my first day as Mr. Sharpe's teaching assistant.

Grabbing my bag, I zipped it as I jogged to the door and sprinted all the way across the property. Why did everything have to be so spread apart here?

Great first day, just great.

Theo

Bending over, I pulled up my swim jammers and felt Liam's gaze on my body. He was across the room, but it didn't matter. His eyes felt like a heat-seeking missile and always had the same effect. I could want to run him over with my car or be so hurt that looking at him made my chest ache, and yet...I still fucking loved him.

Maybe Blake wasn't the only one with an addiction problem. Mine just came in the form of a six-two asshole. Ignoring him, I grabbed my towel, tossed it over my shoulder, slammed my locker, and walked out.

A shiver raced down my spine, and even though he made no sound, I knew he was following me. Suddenly, I knew what it felt like to be stalked through the jungle by a predator. Even though I wanted to look back at him, I kept my eyes trained forward, and I'd never been so happy to see Nash's pissed-off face.

"Hurry the fuck up, you're late," he barked.

"Nash, I think I can control my practice," Coach Stevens said, and Nash crossed his arms, the slap of his foot on the damp poolside speaking as loudly as his voice. "But Nash is correct. You're five minutes late, so you'll have to do an extra four hundred meters after practice."

Liam stopped beside me. "Easy," he said.

Coach smirked. "For every minute that you were both late," he said, and I glared at Liam. "We are going to start with an ab blaster workout that will take us to the forty-five-minute mark, and then we will finish with sprints. Theo and Liam you can do the extra at the very end."

"Yes, Coach," we said together.

"Okay, pick a lane, let's go."

Coach blew his whistle, and we took up our usual spots. I dove in, wanting to forget everything for a little while. Swimming hadn't been my first choice of sport when Nash had insisted we all join the team, but now I loved being in the water.

Liam was in the lane to my left and Blake was on my right, but instead of focusing on either of them, I worked on my stroke and found my rhythm. By the time I was done with the opening warm-up, every worry had been washed away and was blissfully somewhere in the pool.

This was the closest I'd get to downtime from now until the end of the year, and every second was precious. Coach blew his whistle again, and I immediately started into the dolphin kick for another four hundred meters before switching directions, pushing off, and streamlining for distance.

The whistle blew again at the end of sprints, and Coach waved us over, a scowl on his face. I glanced at the massive clock on the wall and couldn't believe that practice was already done despite the fact that we were all panting hard. Reaching up, I hung on the edge of the pool.

"Am I leading a geriatric swim class? What the hell do you think this is? A fucking tea party? The first meet is in three weeks, and if you swim like that, you can forget about getting a sniff at the championships. All of you get out of here. Liam and Theo, start your extra laps."

Everyone except the two of us got out of the water. I watched the rest of the team leave and wouldn't have been surprised if Liam had purposely arranged this private pool session with me.

Shit. Fixing my goggles, I turned and pushed off the wall, determined to finish before Liam. Of course, my efforts were futile. When it came to racing vehicles, I could wipe the floor with Liam, but physically, he was a machine and could keep going and going like that fucking bunny in commercials. With each lap, he pulled ahead a little further, and even as I pushed as hard as I could on the final lap, there was no catching him, and I could feel my leg tightening up.

My chest heaved as I grabbed the ledge and looked up at Coach, who was staring at his stopwatch. "That was much better. Bring this effort tomorrow."

We nodded as Coach walked away. Liam glanced at me and then pushed himself up and out of the water like fucking Adonis had emerged beside me with water streaming down his muscled body.

Nope, I wasn't doing this to myself.

"What are you doing," Liam asked as I turned to do another lap.

"What does it look like?"

Pushing off, I loved that I was in the pool alone. There was no other noise than the sound of my body slicing through the water in a perfect rhythm. I swam until I had to get out or drown. My arms shook as I climbed out of the water and collapsed on the deck, staring at the ceiling before I attempted to stand.

Thoughts of dinner and my study date with Ren finally peeled me off the ground.

The locker room was quiet when I walked in and sighed, relieved. My quota of Myles' and Blake's sideways stares and Liam's heated looks was officially filled. Turning on the shower, I stripped and braced my hands on the wall as the hot water rained down on my shoulders and back.

When my brain came back online, all the same questions resurfaced. Was I being too harsh with Liam? Was he right, and Ren had changed me to the point that he didn't recognize me anymore? How the hell did I fix us and keep him at a distance?

The hair stood on the back of my neck a second too late for me to react before Liam pressed me up against the cool tile. I groaned as his body molded to mine, his fingers gripping my hands and holding them above my head, silently ordering me to remain still.

"Fuck you're sexy," he growled against my neck before he bit down hard enough that it would leave a mark. "I can't resist this ass." He rubbed against me, and it became the struggle of a lifetime not to crumble and cave under his touch. He knew what he did to me, and it gave him way too much power.

"Why do you keep doing this," I asked, sucking in a deep breath as his hard cock slid between my ass cheeks. "I'm trying to keep distance between us."

"Is that what you really want? Distance," he asked, an irritating challenge to his tone, daring me to say yes.

"You know what I want," I said, cagily sidestepping around the answer.

Liam chuckled, and the normally sensual sound only angered me. Nothing had changed. If anyone walked in here, he would jump away from me, and not because he didn't want to be caught having sex. It was having it with me that bothered him.

"Get off of me, Liam."

He shocked me when he put a little space between us. It wasn't much, but at least my brain wasn't misfiring. Liam released my hands, and I turned around, hating myself for loving him. For wanting him. For craving his touch as much as I did.

"Why are you doing this to us? You so clearly want me," he said, looking down.

His hungry gaze made me shiver, but I refused to play his game. He licked his lips and reached for my cock, but I grabbed his wrist, stopping him.

"You make me feel like I'm only good for one thing." I shook my head at him and then pointed at my cock. "Is this it? You like my ass and ordering me around? You can go to a private club if all you want is sex or to fulfill whatever fantasies I do."

"That's not fucking true, and you know it," he growled.

I figured he'd storm away like all our other arguments, but with Liam, you never fully knew what he was going to do. He managed to take me by surprise again as he grabbed me and crushed our lips together, pushing me against the wall.

The searing heat melted my fragile resolve, and I grabbed his waist, holding him tightly. He thrust his hips, and our cocks rubbed together while the world faded to nothing but static and him. The water warmed our skin, and his possessiveness came out in a growl as he continued to grind against me.

"Open for me," he ordered against my lips.

This was how he got me to give in every single time. He knew there was no resisting him like this, and as soon as my lips parted, he deepened the kiss. Liam's hands slid around to my ass, and I shuddered as he pulled us so tightly together that it was like he was trying to make us one person.

Breaking the kiss, he rested his forehead against mine, our chests rising as fast as they had after the sprints.

"I need you, Theo. You know that," he bit out aggressively as if admitting any emotion pissed him off, which it probably did.

"Then stop treating me like a dirty secret and give Ren a chance. That's all I'm asking. You don't need to love her."

He closed his eyes and sighed. For just a moment, I thought he was going to agree, but the sound of the locker room door opening burst the bubble of honesty we'd managed to find.

Laughter from what sounded like the football team filtered into the shower area as the guys came in to change for practice. Liam jumped back like my touch burned his skin. And just like that, my hope was crushed as reality punched me in the face.

His eyes locked with mine, and I could see the conflict in his dark amber depths. A rare occurrence to see what he was thinking written all over his face. Part of him wanted to say fuck it and continue, but there was another side. A side that held back and refused to acknowledge who he was and what he wanted.

I didn't give a fuck who knew that I loved him and Ren. I'd yell it from the top of the school if they asked, but Liam just couldn't do it. An air of indifference rose around him like a castle wall rising into place and I was once more on the outside in the cold.

"I guess you just answered your question. Go look in a mirror, Liam. You'll find what you're looking for, and you don't need me to spell it out. You're not stupid, and you know me better than anyone, so you must know what it does to me every time you act like this. Yet, you don't care, at least not enough."

Liam didn't say anything, but his eyes were fierce, the anger in them, his go-to whenever he was uncomfortable.

"Fine, you want me to spell it out for you. Your actions are as painful as if you pulled a gun and shot me. I can't keep doing this. I just can't."

"Fuck," he swore under his breath as the sound of lockers

opening and closing in the changing area got louder as more guys arrived.

Dismissing him and the conversation, I turned and pushed the button on the soap dispenser.

The football team was still suspicious of us and our possible involvement in the death of their old captain, Axel, so we tended to avoid each other. It was safer that way. We didn't need to bring the wrath of the Curators down on our heads by getting into a full-out war inside the school.

I didn't hear Liam leave, but it was as if he'd brought the heat to the room and just as quickly stolen it again despite the hot water. There was so much pain and scarring now from him cutting my heart open again and again that sometimes I wondered if it would ever heal. Was there really anything he could do at this point to rebuild my trust? Who was I kidding? He could do it with a snap of his fingers. That was his power and my weakness.

Liam thought Ren was a disease that had infected us and was destroying what we had, but in reality, his fear was the disease.

I'd been living with the way he wanted things and ignoring my desires, just happy to get his table scraps and make it through another day. Ren had become my cure, the medicine I didn't know I needed. She'd woken parts of myself that I'd suppressed so long ago that I forgot they even existed.

The worst part of all of this was that it was becoming painfully clear that no matter what I did, the barbs of my love for Liam would remain embedded. The harder I tried to tear them out, the longing would only get worse. I was doomed if I did or if I didn't at this point. Leaving him for good would be like ripping my chest open and handing him my heart. But staying with him when he was so obviously embarrassed by me...well, that was a death of another kind, and my soul couldn't take anymore.

SEPTEMBER 9 – TUESDAY 7:03 PM

Liam

Slamming my car door, I smacked my hands off the top of the steering wheel.

"Fuck! Fuck! Fuck!"

Theo was the only one who could make me this insane. I was so tempted to stomp back in there and...and what?

Fuck him, show him who is boss, make him scream my name?

He knew who I was, what I was, what I hated. There were no sweet declarations of love or public displays of affection. The thing I detested most of all was people knowing anything about me. My family hardly knew me, and that was how it should remain, but no, fucking Ren came along, and suddenly he wanted me to prove I loved him. How? What the hell did he want from me?

Starting the car, I drove down through the gates and forgot all about this morning until the cop left his hiding spot, and the red and blue lights flashed. Fucking Nash and his bright ideas. Pulling over, I got my license and registration ready, then quickly sent my irritating best friend a text.

L: The fish is in the barrel.

N: Just don't shoot it.

L: No promises.

N: A.S.S.H.O.L.E

Chuckling at Nash's annoyance, I put my phone in the cup holder and waited for Agent Ellis to say hi. I'd still love to know why he was posing as a cop. Of all the things a Fed could pretend to be for undercover research into mafia families, this was the stupidest one. Yes, he had the power to pull us over, but he was never going to get close to us. We were missing something from the equation, but I'd figure it out. I always did.

The bright light from his flashlight blinded me as he walked up to my window, and for just a split second, I wondered if I could take my anger out on him and stuff him in my trunk, but instead, I smiled.

"Hi there, Deputy Ellis. How can I help you? I wasn't speeding," I said.

Even though I couldn't see his face clearly, there was no doubt who it was. He'd been the perfect little stalker.

"It's Sheriff Ellis now. License and registration," he ordered, and I held them out between my fingers.

"Oh, fancy new title, congratulations. Are you going to answer my question, Sheriff Ellis? There are a lot of sketchy officers around. I wouldn't want to needlessly end up with a hole in my head and become another statistic."

"Why would I shoot you? Do I have a reason to?"

I shrugged. "Just repeating what I see in the news. I have a right to know what I've done. You know, for when I call my lawyer and press charges for harassment."

There was a long pregnant pause, which made me smirk, waiting for him to make the next move.

"I pulled you over for racing this morning and evading police."

"I'm sorry, I don't know what you're talking about. You must have the wrong person. Do you have any evidence of this occurrence? A radar lock or camera footage, perhaps?"

"I saw what I saw." I picked up my phone. "Put the phone down."

"No, I don't think I will." I made it look like I was calling my lawyer and wasn't shocked when he yanked my door open and pointed his Taser at me.

"Put the phone down and get out of the car."

Glancing at the taser and then the sheriff's face, I dropped my phone dramatically into the cup holder and undid my seatbelt. As soon as I stepped out, he grabbed me and shoved me up against the vehicle. If this asshole wasn't a Fed, I really would snap his neck for touching me. But we were playing the long game.

"You think I don't know who you are," he asked.

"I know you do. I just gave you my license. I would hope the sheriff could read. If not, standards have really dropped off from Morrison."

"You think you're funny," he asked, pushing me harder into the car. It took all my control not to fight back.

"I wouldn't say it's my strong suit, no," I said as he turned me around to face him.

"You're Liam Hicks." I cocked an eyebrow.

"So, you can read. That's good. Do you need me to type it into your report for you? I have someplace to be and would prefer not to stand here all night with you telling me my name."

His face twisted with rage, but I leaned against my car in the most unthreatening pose I could for the camera installed in the dashboard of the cruiser.

"I know what your family does. Don't think I'm not watching you. I have eyes everywhere."

"You sound like a creepy stalker. Are you a stalker, Sheriff? Or do you want to get into the import-export business of clothes? We have some top-quality suppliers in Italy. You can't beat their suits."

"We both know that your family is into more than clothing," he said.

"Of course we are. We have a very diverse portfolio."

He smiled. "Diverse portfolio, that's funny." The smile dropped. "Empty your pockets."

The fish was zeroing in on the bait.

"Are you sure you want me to do that," I asked as a couple more cars pulled out of Wayward and drove by slowly. I nodded to the people watching. "Especially now that there are witnesses to your harassing behavior."

"Empty your pockets."

With a sigh, I shoved my hands into my jeans and pulled out everything that I had, which included a small clear baggie with our logo on it. His eyes went wide as he stared at the small amount of white powder. Ellis put his taser away and pulled his gun.

"Open the trunk."

"I'll ask again. Are you sure you want to do that without a warrant?" Red flags should be waving around in his mind, but he would ignore them for the possibility of nailing me with a large amount of drugs.

For me, being a criminal was no different than flipping burgers at a fast-food restaurant, only it paid better. This wasn't just a job. It was our lifestyle and our livelihood. People would say that we were killing people, but so were heart attacks and cancer, and yet they still sold grease and chemical-laden food and cigarettes. Hypocrites, as far as I was concerned.

"I said open the trunk."

"I need my fob. It's in the cup holder."

"Get it, but don't do anything stupid. Wouldn't want you to end up that stat you mentioned."

Making sure he could see my hands, I grabbed my fob and hit the unlock button.

"Last chance to let me go. Once it's open, there is no going back. I will sue you and the department." Gripping my arm, he pulled me to the trunk. "Okay, but don't say I didn't warn you."

Stuffed inside were the two black duffel bags. "Open the bags."

This time, I didn't give him a chance to back out. I opened the bags to show off the neatly wrapped kilos of white powder.

"You're under arrest," he said. Grabbing me, he shoved me up against my car and handcuffed my hands as he read me my rights. The entire time, I smiled.

"Can I call my lawyer now?"

"You may want to call a whole team of lawyers. You're going to need them," he said, walking me to the cruiser and putting me in the back. Most people didn't have getting arrested in their evening plans, but then again, they weren't me. I had to hand it to Nash. This whole setup was kind of brilliant.

Laying my head back against the leather of the seat, I settled in to spend the next few hours in custody until they realized we'd played them for fools. Act like an idiot and get treated like one.

I couldn't wait to get out and laugh with Theo about this. My smirk fell with the thought of the locker room. For a few minutes, I'd forgotten that we were at odds, and of course, the only person that I wanted to share this with was him.

Fuck.

Chapter 6

SEPTEMBER 10 – WEDNESDAY 3:11 AM

Nash

Outside the police station, I leaned against my car in the dark, waiting for Liam to be released. The glass doors allowed me to watch as he signed the paperwork. I couldn't keep the smile off my face. Oh, to have been a fly on the wall when they realized all they had was fifty kilos of icing sugar. Guess I'd have to thank Princess for the idea at some point. That thought sent my brain into overdrive.

She had a breakthrough moment the other day. For just a flash, her guard was stripped away, and under that tough-as-nails exterior, I saw her vulnerable side. The side that fucking Blake and Myles got all the time. It was my fault that she never shared that with me, and the few times she had, I gave her more than enough reason to lock it away in my presence. What the hell did I do with her sweet and emotional personality? Crushed it. Yet...fuck, she swam around in my mind as easily as I did a pool.

"Can I have a cigarette," Liam asked as soon as he walked outside.

"Not a fucking chance."

"I was in jail for you. The least you can do is let me have a smoke. Even inmates get smokes."

"Get in the car and shut up, or I leave you here," I said as I got into the driver's seat.

He mumbled a number of creative profanities as he slipped in beside me.

"When can we pick up your car?"

"They're releasing it from the impound tomorrow. Mr. Howard was pissed that they wouldn't cut it loose tonight. I swear he's going to get the entire division shut down. I did warn Ellis. He can't say I lured him into a trap."

"Fuck, I wish I'd been able to see it. How did it go?"

Liam smirked and then laughed, the sound rare coming from him.

"Oh fuck, that was the funniest shit I've ever seen. Ellis was so fucking arrogant. He was positive that he'd nailed us with a massive load of product. But when he started testing the bags, and they were coming back negative, even the fucking drug dog looked at him like he was crazy. Just before I left, he got a very nasty call from someone he didn't want anyone to know about. You could hear the screaming through the phone before he closed the door. My bet is that it was the mayor or governor. Knowing Mr. Howard, it could be both."

"That's fucking brilliant," I said, smacking my steering wheel. "I'm sure Ellis will be a little more careful with his random searches now. I genuinely love this and may have to come up with another way to make him look like an incompetent idiot." Starting the car, I headed for the exit.

"It was a stroke of genius, man. But I'll deny saying that if you tell the guys."

I rubbed the back of my neck. "It wasn't my idea. Princess came up with it."

"Seriously?"

"Yeah. Who knew the little snow queen would help us evade the Feds?" Flicking on my turn signal, I pulled onto the highway and cruised toward the school.

"Didn't know she had it in her—under that holier-than-thou persona," Liam said with a distinct bitterness in his tone. A glance showed his arms crossed protectively, and his face pulled into a dark glower.

"Still having issues with Theo?"

"Don't want to fucking talk about it," he said.

"Well, that's a yes if I've ever heard one," I said and smiled.

At least she wasn't just under my skin poking at me. Totally different reason, but the fact that Liam was holding strong against her wiles gave me hope that I wouldn't fall prey. There was something about her...fuck, it was annoying.

"Whatever. If Theo wants her and not me, then fuck him."

"Pretty sure that wasn't what he said." I looked at Liam as he glared at me and shrugged. "Why are you looking at me like that? It's true. If you want to hear it that way...well, then it's your prerogative. But we both know the truth."

"It is way too fucking late, or I guess early, to be talking about this shit. Can we change the topic?"

"Sure, I don't care. The new lights got installed yesterday. Nora is whipping the contractors. It's kind of nice not to be the one having to do it all the time and to have someone keeping an eye on them during the day."

"She's great at speaking her mind. None of them will get away with anything. They take even a five-minute unscheduled break, and she will let them hear it and deduct their pay. Great for the building but bad when she was living at home. Trust me."

"I'll take your word for it. We'll need a ballbuster like that for the business. Just feels weird not being hands-on at the helm every day."

"Get used to it. With the number of businesses you inherit once you take over, you'll end up a puppet master pulling all the strings but won't get to visit them often."

I looked at Liam and licked my lips but kept my mouth shut about Mr. Genovese.

Holding back from Liam felt wrong, but there were very strict rules to our deal, and I couldn't do anything to jeopardize what I'd put into place. It was fucking unnerving to place so much trust in such a powerful family. I didn't know them well, and he could crush me with a single call, but anything was better than living under my father's control, even if it meant selling my soul to another family to make it happen.

"What? You look like you were going to say something."

He had that analyzing look in his eyes, and I made sure not to twitch, or I'd give something away.

"Was just going to say something stupid but decided not to be a prick. Take the win," I said and glanced over at him.

His eyes eerily searched my face in the dark of the car. I hated when he used his skills on me, but he nodded and looked away. Either my lying skills were becoming top-notch, or he was letting it go.

We lapsed into silence for the rest of the drive, and by the time we pulled into Wayward, I was thankful to have first period free this morning. Everything was still and quiet when we got to our dorm. It was the only time of day that I didn't mind being here.

"You not coming in," I asked as we reached our room, but Liam continued down the hall.

"Naw, not tonight," he said.

Why he wouldn't just cave confused me, but not my circus.

Myles was sound asleep when I opened the door, and I smirked. That meant there was a high probability that Ren was alone. Walking over to my side of the room, I grabbed the photo I'd printed, the glue stick, and a couple coffee creamers. Liam was nowhere to be found when I slipped back into the hallway.

Getting to Ren's room unnoticed was easy. Unlocking and opening the door without a sound was the tricky part. Ivy was curled up in a ball facing the wall when I slipped inside. I bypassed her quickly and went straight for Ren. She was lying on her side with her hand under her pillow. Perfect.

Walking into the bathroom, I doctored the photo and was so tempted to set up a camera to catch her glorious reaction. Dean Henry might actually kill me if evidence of this got out. I didn't trust him to overlook my indiscretion despite how much he'd helped me.

Heading back out to Ren, I kneeled beside her bed and stared at her sleeping face.

"Are you dreaming of me, Princess?" A small crease formed between her eyes. "Do you want me to crawl into bed with you?"

"Nash," she mumbled. The soft sound hit hard and had me fully erect.

Fuck, I needed to step away, or I really would lay down beside her. Sighing, I pulled out the glue stick and smeared some long lines all over the photo of her sleeping.

It took all my stealthy skills to get it slipped beneath her hand that was hidden under her pillow, but as soon as it felt stuck, I left it alone. Reaching out, I swept a strand of hair away from her face.

"Sleep well, Princess," I whispered in her ear and almost lost it as she said my name again, and it ended with a soft moan. Backing away before I did something that couldn't be taken back, I snuck out.

"Fuck," I said, leaning against the wall, closing my eyes.

Her walls were crumbling around me, but what the hell was I going to do when the truth came out and she found out about Mr.

Genovese and the deal we made? Vicky...god...I couldn't even imagine how this was going to unfold. I was a dead man walking.

Until then, I was going to have fun with Princess. Pushing away from the wall, I wandered back to my room to collapse for a few hours. I'd never been so excited to attend a Russian class before.

SEPTEMBER 10 – WEDNESDAY 4:55 AM

Ren

Strange dreams and restlessness had plagued me every night since getting back from Canada. Worse was the constant appearance of Nash. He randomly popped into my head and took over the scene, just as annoying in dream form as when I was awake. Arrogant, acting like I should want him. There was something seriously wrong with me because the feelings were forming whether I wanted them to or not.

No one in their right mind would willingly choose to be with Nash Collier.

My alarm beeped softly so as not to wake Ivy. It was pure insanity to be up at this hour of the morning, so of course, that was when Liam wanted to train. Reaching out, I hit my alarm and realized that something was stuck to my hand. Panicking, I sat up, trying to make sense of what was attached to me.

Did I leave some of my notes on my bed?

Flicking on my bedside light, I swore before I could stop myself.

"Eww, fuck...oh my god, he didn't actually...."

"What? Is everything okay," Ivy asked, her voice groggy.

"No, no, it's not." Oh my god, this was disgusting. Frantically shaking my hand to get it to fall off wasn't working. It wouldn't budge, and I was left staring at a photo. Not just any photo, it was one of me sleeping.

Ivy walked around the corner while I humiliatingly danced around like a child, freaking out. She stared at me like I'd lost all my marbles, and at this point, that probably wasn't far off the mark. This place was enough to make anyone go crazy.

"I can't get it off. Is his come made of glue or what?"

"What? Did you say come? Whose come?"

"Nashole, the asshole. Oh my god, I need to sterilize my hand, and my bed, and the entire room. What if he did this in here while he watched me sleep? I can't believe he actually did it."

And cue the obscenely mixed feelings about that thought. The fact that Nash would wait until I was asleep, risk getting in here, and then enjoy staring at me while he jerked off was both disturbing as hell and kind of hot. I shook my head.

"Girl, you're making no sense," Ivy said, yawning.

Growling, I grabbed some tissue and held the corner. My hand made a suction cup sound as the picture pulled up, making my stomach roll.

"Eww, it's making sucking noises, yuck, yuck, yuck! I'm going to kill him."

I glared at Ivy, even though she wasn't the object of my rage.

"When we were at my house in Canada, I was texting with Nash and purposely annoyed him. I mean, what was the worst he could do while we were in another country? He threatened that he'd come on a photo of me and leave it under my pillow. Naturally, I assumed it was an idle threat. It's been like two freaking months, and while I'd completely forgotten all about it...well, as you can see, he did not."

Ivy's face scrunched up as she made a gagging sound. I showed her my hand with the photo half hanging off it now.

"I'm going to kill him."

"Why are guys so gross?" Ivy shivered.

"Not all guys, just freaking Nash Collier."

Ivy looked a little closer and did a yuck dance of her own. "It has white streaks. Dear god, how many times did he come on it?"

"Shh...don't make it worse."

Glancing at the time, I bit my lip, closed my eyes, and pulled it the rest of the way off. The feel of it pulling at my skin had me running into the bathroom to clean my hand.

I dropped the photo and tissue into the garbage before turning on the taps and washing my hands ten times before all the stickiness was gone.

"How did he get in here anyway," Ivy asked when I emerged from the bathroom, ready to murder.

"Because he's Satan's son and can walk through walls like the demon he is," I said, drying my hand.

"Please tell me you're not serious?" Ivy looked around, and I smirked.

"No, but it feels like it. Nash has a key from last year when this was mine and Vicky's room. I'd have the locks changed, but I'm pretty sure he'll just get a new key. He seems to be able to threaten or bribe his way into anything he wants."

I quickly got dressed for training, and...shit, now I was running late. Liam wouldn't care what had caused my tardiness, that was for sure.

"Well, they don't call him a King for no reason."

I hit Ivy with a glare as I pulled my hoodie on over my workout clothes.

"Look on the bright side. You can tease Vicky that you've touched his come. She doesn't need to know how."

"Nooo, let's just let sleeping bullying bitches lay. She's kept her distance since she moved back in, and I'd like to keep it that way."

Ivy crossed her arms and shrugged.

"It would serve her right if she found out. She was such a cow to you that she deserves whatever she gets. I hope she ends up having to marry a man five times her age with a limp dick and no money. That would drive her insane and is the perfect revenge," Ivy said, making me laugh.

Grabbing my uniform and school bag, I marched for the door.

"I'm really happy not to be on your bad side. Go back to bed. I'm sorry I woke you up."

"Be careful. I don't trust Liam," she said.

That made two of us.

I hurried out of my room and jogged down the hallway past the domiciles of sleeping people who had no idea what I'd already had to deal with at five AM. Practically punching the elevator button, it felt like it took an eternity to reach me on the top floor. As soon as the doors opened, I darted across the foyer. Yanking the door open, I bolted outside.

"About time."

My heart nearly exploded in my chest as I screamed, dropping all my stuff on the pathway. I stared into the darkness, but there was nothing other than the soft glow of a cigarette.

"Liam?"

He moved like a panther, one with the dark. Even when he stepped into the light from the walkway lamp post, half of his face was hidden by shadows.

"You're running late."

Glancing at my phone, I still had one minute to reach the gym, which coincidentally was in the same building as the pool.

"I have one minute left."

"You wouldn't have made it. I've seen you run."

I glared at him, not taking the bait. Liam just stared, his face a mask of stone.

"I thought you were going to stand me up. You know, too scared to face me alone."

He dropped the cigarette on the ground and stomped it out with his sneaker.

Like a charging bull, all I saw was red. My shoulders straightened, and any of the lingering sluggishness was kicked to the side.

"Why exactly would I be scared of you?"

He shrugged but didn't say any more.

Dropping down to gather my things, I bit my lip to keep from punching him. When had I become so violent? I'd never thought of hitting anyone until coming here. It was this place, with its dark energy and the insanity that lived inside the walls. Especially the guy in front of me and Nash. Both were on my naughty list and I wondered if Santa took requests for coal.

"You like to act tough, Little Rabbit, but you're always one nervous breakdown away from running for the hills again. Aren't you?"

He had his hands on his knees as he bent over and looked me dead in the eyes. Squatting in front of him like this made me feel incredibly small. I swallowed back the fear and stood up, forcing him to do the same.

"No, I'm pretty sure it's you that's running." I smiled and hitched my backpack onto my shoulder. His eyes narrowed into thin slits. "You're the one who can't handle Theo wanting to be treated like a person and not a possession. Big bad Liam is scared of his emotions."

He sucked in breath, his lip pulling up in a sneer, and every instinct told me that I should back off. But I would never back down again, even if it killed me.

"Now I understand why Nash wants to put a bullet...." He held up his finger and made a gun as he pretended to shoot me between the eyes. "Pow, right there."

"Oh, he wants to fire something, but it's not his gun. Nice try, though," I said with my whole heart. *Did I really just say that with a straight face?*

"Axel should've just killed you and saved us all the trouble," he said with such venom that the words punched me in the gut.

My fist connected with his jaw before I realized that I'd even moved. Apparently, Liam didn't see it coming either as he stumbled back from the hit. Genuine shock was all over his face as he rubbed his cheek.

I took a threatening step toward him and snarled.

"Don't ever fucking mention that day to me ever again," I ordered, my hands still balled into fists. "You want me dead, then fine. Here I am, let's do this. I will fight to the death, and I don't care who you are, but that monster's name will not pass through your lips again in my presence. Not ever, for any reason, or so help me, I'll find a way to cut out your tongue."

Liam's eyes were wide, but he didn't give anything else away as he looked me up and down.

"Well, alright then. I'll never mention that day or he who will not be named again," he said, and I took a shaky breath.

It always felt like I was being tested. *Are you smart enough, strong enough, tough enough?* The list was endless...and tiring. How did everyone here grow up like that their whole lives?

The pain didn't register until I relaxed my fist.

"Dammit." My whole arm was tingling, and I would need ice for my throbbing hand.

"The pain is because you hit me hard but wrong. I wouldn't be surprised if you just fractured your knuckle."

The painful pulse radiated up into my wrist, and I squeezed my eyes shut.

"Great, just great."

"Come on, let's go get you some ice."

All the anger that had been in his tone a second ago was completely gone. He stood with his hands on his hips and calmly stared at me, completely unfazed that I'd punched him.

"What about training?"

"You're not going to be much good training if you have a broken knuckle. Now are you? Let's take a look at it and see what we're dealing with." Nodding, I followed him back into the dorm.

Liam didn't hesitate as he pulled me through the cafeteria and veered toward the door clearly marked *Employees Only*. It felt wrong to step through the kitchen door, and I kept expecting someone to jump out and yell that we weren't allowed to be back here. Passing the long workstations and equipment, including knives, I wondered if this was a wise idea.

Liam pointed to a table. "You can put your stuff there. I'll be right back."

Taking in my surroundings, I set my bag and change of clothes down. Everything was perfectly shiny, and there didn't seem to be a speck of dirt anywhere. Gordon Ramsay would like this kitchen.

Bang! A door slammed, making me jump, but it was just Liam. He rounded the corner with a cloth and a bag of ice.

"We need to work on how jumpy you are. I wasn't lying about you sprinting off into the night. A person's nerves can only take so much before something gives," he said, eyeing me.

His eyes were similar and yet darker than Myles'. They were caught between amber and whiskey with gold flecks.

"Hello? Did you hear what I said?"

"Sorry. Um...yes, we do," I said, my neck smarting from looking up at him. Why did they all have to be so tall? "I won't run again, but finding an outlet would be good."

Liam set the ice and cloth down, and I squealed as he lifted me. Holy hell. The heat from his hands traveled through my body as he held my waist, unmoving. And the way he was looking at me did nothing to stop my imagination from running off and picturing being pressed between him and Theo.

Liam slowly let go, but his finger grazed my arm before he held out his hand, and I stared at his open palm. My mind was blank.

"Hand," he said.

Crawling under the table seemed like a fabulous idea. Acquiescing to his request, I looked down for the first time and groaned at the sight of the swollen and very red middle knuckle.

Liam softly probed with his thumbs around the swelling, then manipulated my finger until I winced. He was incredibly gentle, which was confusing considering why we were in here.

"Do you really wish I was dead," I asked, needing to know.

His eyes locked with mine.

"No. I'm sorry I said that." He picked up the cloth and placed it on my knuckles before adding the bag of ice and tying it all in place. "You may or may not have struck the right nerve to set me off."

"I'm sorry, too. I shouldn't have said that about you and Theo." I rubbed my eyes. "I hate seeing you two at odds, and I know you don't believe me, but it's the truth."

Liam sighed and the hair stood all over my body as he gripped the counter on either side of me. His arms flexed under the black t-shirt as he pressed closer, forcing me to lean back to maintain any distance.

"Theo wants us to be together, like the three of us. I'm not sure how that even works without Myles and Blake in the relationship, let alone with them. What I do know is that it's a fucking mess and is most likely going to end in disaster."

"Maybe it will. Maybe it won't. Maybe a meteor will hit the earth today, and we all die. Maybe aliens land and take us all away. There are too many variables to state it's not going to work. Complicated, sure. Impossible...I don't believe anything is impossible if you want it bad enough."

"I don't like the odds, and Theo is a fool to want this."

"Don't insult Theo like that. He is far from a fool, and you know it."

"Regardless, I don't exactly share well, Little Rabbit," he said. His voice raspy and gliding straight between my legs, making everything fuzzy. Men shouldn't have that power. It wasn't fair. "Not unless I'm in charge."

Licking my lips, I fought to push down the fire building within me.

"I don't know how it works either, but I'm willing to try."

Liam's fingers wrapped around my throat, squeezing enough that he was choking off most of my air supply. The only thing I could do was grab his arm to try and save myself.

"Let go of my arm," he ordered, the tone leaving no wiggle room. "Now."

Hands shaking, I dropped them to my lap. Liam moved in so our noses touched, his eyes boring into mine as my heart went wild in my chest. His lips hovered close enough that I could feel the heat and magnetic draw that he naturally oozed.

"Do you really think you can handle me, Little Rabbit?"

The tip of his tongue running up my cheek caused uncontrollable reactions as the sensation shot down my spine. I sucked in as much air as I could through my constricted airway as he drew a line to my ear and then nipped at my earlobe.

"See, the problem is, I don't think you're ready. I don't think you'll ever be able to handle what I can give you. I'm not mean, but I'm not a kind lover, Little Rabbit. I'll push you to your limit and back again, over and over, until you can't take anymore. But you will. I demand complete compliance in the bedroom. If you use that sharp tongue to mouth off, you'll quickly wish you hadn't."

His hand tightened a little more. My mind was screaming, but I managed to remain frozen to the spot.

"I'll never give you hearts and flowers. I'm not going to write you a song or plan romantic weekends away. You'll never touch me in public unless I tell you to. If you're with me, it's either a hot one-night stand or complete submission."

"I think I know why you and Theo are at odds," I choked out.

Liam twisted his head and jerked me closer. Makeup would be needed to hide his handprint. Of this, I was certain, but I stubbornly straightened my spine.

"I can handle anything you do in the bedroom. Go ahead and do your worst. But your rules push everyone away, including Theo. Maybe it's time you learned to bend rather than trying to break him."

His eyebrows shot up, and then he laughed. Liam released my throat, and I sucked in a deep breath. Knowing he would see that as a sign of weakness, I didn't rub at my neck. He pushed back, and suddenly, I knew how Icarus had felt flying too close to the sun. Liam took all the warmth in the room with him when he pulled away.

"Your answer is just so you. Bend...sure," Liam mumbled sarcastically and shook his head. "If you knew anything about me, you wouldn't have given me carte blanche to do whatever I wanted. Even just in the bedroom, that would not end well for either of us."

"I don't understand," I said.

"Exactly. This will never work. We live on the same pedestal but with different ideals."

"I really wish you'd just say what you mean," I said, feeling ridiculous and humiliated.

He smirked and stepped back, and I quickly grabbed his arm. Was this amusing to him?

"Don't do that. Tell me what you mean."

"You really want to know?"

"I wouldn't ask you otherwise. Just a waste of both our time."

He chuckled and rubbed at his lower lip. His whiskey eyes were so intense that one could forget to breathe.

"Do you know what a Dom is?"

"Does Fifty Shades of Grey count?"

I didn't think that Liam could get more venomous, but I wiggled under his disgusted glare.

"Are you fucking with me?"

"No, you asked. Okay, then, what should I look up?"

"You'll know when you find it. As for your hand, it's not broken, but take anti-inflammatories for the next couple days and keep icing it. We'll push training to next Monday."

"I can still train," I said stubbornly, refusing to be shot down again.

"You can't hit a bag like that unless you're trying to ruin your hand. Is that what you want, to not be able to write, or type, or paint?"

"No."

"Then next week it is."

Gripping my waist he helped me off the table.

"I'll do the research," I said.

"I'm sure you will." Liam turned and walked away. "Have a good day, Little Rabbit."

Just like that, he was gone, and I massaged my neck.

Jesus, what the hell was I thinking? Could I handle him and what he wanted to dish out?

The answer was simple...for Theo, I would try. Liam was right. I had no clue what I was agreeing to. Then again, neither did he. He had considered what I said about bending, which meant deep down he knew something needed to change, or he was going to lose Theo forever.

SEPTEMBER 10 – WEDNESDAY 10:38 PM

Theo

This was not on my bingo card for the year, but it gave my mind and hands something to do. Nash wanted to have his next trap set to go in a couple weeks, so I'd volunteered to fill the five-thousand mini-baggies with confectionary sugar. It also got me off Wayward property and away from the temptation of Liam. I turned the page in my molecular biology textbook and continued reading as I filled the next bag. The shit that I didn't want to think about was trying really hard to take up space.

"I never thought I'd see this," Liam drawled, like I'd summoned him.

The baggie that was still open when I jumped went flying and landed right on my textbook and notes. White powder spread everywhere.

"Fuck, do you ever walk like a normal person? Make some fucking noise, would you," I growled, glaring at him.

He, annoyingly, didn't look like he had a care in the world as he leaned against the door jamb.

"I've been here ten minutes watching you. I was tired of waiting for you to notice me," Liam said and stepped into the room.

"Are you stalking me now," I asked, and hated that the thought excited me.

"I will if you want me to," he said, and the hair stood on the back of my neck.

I knew that tone all too well. Standing and walking around the table kept some distance between us without being too obvious. Not that there was anywhere to go in the basement.

"If you're not stalking me, then why are you here? Did Nash send you?" Picking up my notepad, I blew it off and sent sugar into a small billowing cloud. "He's crazy if he thinks I have all of these done already."

"Nash didn't send me. I wanted to speak to you alone."

"So, you are stalking me."

"Sort of, if you want to look at it that way. You're the one who tripped the motion sensor when you came into the room." He pointed to the hidden camera. "I was watching you, too. I do love it when you have that ultra-serious expression. I always know when you're thinking too hard."

"Stupid sensor." Wiping off my textbook and closing it, I stuffed it and my notepad in my bag, all too aware of Liam inching closer. Zipping the bag, I sighed and crossed my arms, locking eyes with him. "You must want something if you followed me all the way out here, so what is it?"

"Like I said, I want to talk," he said, sidestepping the table.

He moved like he was getting ready to pounce on me, managing to stir up all sorts of images of what we could be doing instead of fighting. If only it was that easy.

"Then stay where you are and talk," I said.

"Why do you seem so nervous, Theo," Liam asked, ignoring me and stepping closer.

"I'm not."

"Yes, you are, and you've been a lot of things while we've been together but nervous isn't one of them."

"I'm not nervous, I'm frustrated. I came here for some time alone, and yet, here you are."

"No, I don't think that's it." He took another step forward, and I took one back. Liam had always been relentless, and he followed me until my back hit the wall. "What's the real reason?"

"You're so smart. You can figure it out." I tried to walk around him, but he blocked my way. "Leave me alone, Liam."

"No," he said, pushing me back and trapping me against the wall in the cage of his arms.

"Get out of my face," I snarled.

"No, I'm not going to do that. See, I think the reason you don't want me in here is because you don't trust yourself around me." The decadent scent of the cologne I got him last Christmas filled my nose as my heart raced out of control. "I know you want me," he growled.

"You're right, I do."

There was no point trying to hide it or pretend around Liam. Between his uncanny ability to read people and the fact that he knew me better than pretty much anyone, he would instantly sniff out the lie.

"I never said that I didn't." Dropping my bag, I grabbed his belt and pulled it free.

"What are you doing," he asked, his face twisted in confusion. This wasn't how our relationship worked. Liam gave the orders, and I obeyed.

Yanking open his button and zipper, his hard cock sprang free.

"What does it look like I'm doing?" I wrapped my hand around his shaft, and Liam's body shuddered as I stroked him, teasing the tip with my thumb and his precum. "Isn't this what you wanted?"

Before Liam could respond, I dropped to my knees and expertly slipped him into my mouth. I knew what he liked, how he liked it, and there was no holding back.

"Fuck, Theo."

Liam's voice was reduced to a raspy growl as he fisted my hair. I could picture his face twisted in pleasure, and as turned on as my body was, the same excitement that pleasing him used to bring me was blocked by the ache in my chest. The smoldering remains of what we had were still smoking, but the flame had been slowly suffocated. He'd been stomping on the fire long before I got back from Canada, and there was only so much anyone, including me, could handle before giving up.

My tongue teased all his sensitive spots as I cupped his balls and softly tugged and rolled them the way he'd made me practice until I could do it in my sleep. Up and down, my head bobbed. Faster and faster, my fingers tightened at the base of his balls like a cock ring. Almost instantly, they began to swell with his building need to come. Liam sucked in a ragged breath. His grip on my hair tightened, and I knew what was coming. Before he could force his cock down my throat, I swallowed the full length of him until my nose touched his six-pack.

"Fuck, that's incredible."

Relaxing my jaw, I let him take control and fuck my mouth as hard as he wanted. The deep groan and his body shuddering were a distinct giveaway that he was close. I released my hold on his balls, and he yelled while hammering into my throat.

"Yes. Fuck, so good," Liam growled, stilling as he came.

His cock twitched with the last of his release, and he pulled out, unthreading his fingers from my hair. I sucked in a deep breath, wiped my mouth, and grabbed my bag. Liam staggered back a step, and I stood. This was when I'd normally be filled with pride. A thrill would ripple through my body, but instead, there was nothing but numbness. Liam's eyes were glassy and cheeks a little flushed like he'd just taken a hit as he smirked at me.

Not saying a word, I hooked my bag on my shoulder and marched for the door.

"Hey, where are you going?"

Pausing, I turned back to face him. "I'm leaving."

"But...I thought that...."

"What? You thought that I'd beg you to stay? Maybe take your hand and go upstairs so we could have another round in the bed or shower? Perhaps you pictured bending me over the couch," I asked, stuffing my hands into my pockets.

"Um...."

I snorted, disgusted. "You got what you wanted. This is why you drove out here, is it not? Prove that I can't say no to you and that I'll cave and give you what you want. Put me back in my little Sub box and hope the lid stays on this time. Well, I caved. Congratulations. You win, I lose."

"That's not what...." He stopped and I could see him struggling for the right word.

"Liam, face it. The problem is that no matter what we do, it is always what you want." I shook my head at him. "I can remember so clearly the day you told me that you wanted to be my Dom and that it was your duty to take care of me, that you'd always look out for me. I was so in love with you that I would've believed anything you said, and I did. What I think you forgot to mention was that all of that only applied if what I wanted aligned with what you wanted."

"That's not fair. We've had an incredible relationship until the last few months. There is only one thing that has changed, and that is Ren."

"Don't do that!" I balled my fists. "This is not about Ren. You keep missing the point, and you're not stupid, so I can only assume you're choosing to act like you don't get it."

Liam crossed his arms, his jaw twitching as he clenched it tight.

"This is about how you don't respect me and how you're embarrassed of me. You couldn't run away fast enough yesterday in the shower the second you heard the football team come in." Rage filled my chest, and yet it was as if ice had been injected into my veins. "And that was after you cringed when I kissed you on the bench and claimed that it was just because I took you by surprise." I shook my head at him. "Don't do that. Don't fucking lie to me. I deserve better. The only thing you're right about is that Ren ripped away what was making me blind. And if you still don't believe me...well, I can't say it more plainly than I already have."

"I came out here to tell you that I'm sorry about yesterday."

"Sorry? Do you really believe your hollow words to placate me are what I'm after? That has been your takeaway from everything that's happened between us the last few months?"

I'd fallen into the oldest relationship trap of thinking that I could change him, that I would be enough, or the one to make the difference. That hadn't been the case. If anything, he'd become more secretive, more degrading, and emotionally manipulated me into a box that I refused to return to, ever.

"No, I...." He ran his hand through his hair, and as enjoyable as it was to see Liam at a loss for words, which was rare, it also hurt.

We stared at one another, the seconds ticking by in a deafening silence. It was tearing me apart. Sucking in a deep breath, my hand tightened on the strap of my backpack.

"Liam, the fact that you can no longer read me...let's just say that says more about you as a Dom than it does me as your Sub." I'd hit a nerve as his eyes filled with anger, but he didn't say anything to dispute me. "You know that I love you, but this isn't going to work anymore. I think we should take a break."

He stepped back, his eyes hardening.

"You're breaking up with me?" Shock was written all over his normally unreadable face.

"We both saw this coming, but neither of us wanted to be the one to do it. I'll take the hit."

Turning, I marched out, but every limb shook, the pain and pent-up emotion creating a black hole where my heart had been.

"Theo, don't be like this. You know I love you. Why can't that be enough," Liam yelled after me but didn't chase me down or grab me.

A tear ran down my cheek, and I swiped it away, just like Liam had been doing to me since our very first date. Memories, good and bad, flooded my mind with each step I took away from the toxicity of our past and toward the future I wanted.

"I will always love you...no matter what," I whispered, getting into my car before completely falling apart.

SEPTEMBER 11 – THURSDAY 12:25 AM

Ren

It was late, and I really should be asleep but studying yesterday had been near impossible. Myles and Blake just couldn't be in the same room to study. No...scrap that. They could be in the same room, just not with me. We ended up doing everything except what we were supposed to be doing. Who knew that being tied up could be so much fun?

Sighing, I continued to fill out the assignment from Mr. Sharpe.

It wasn't due until next week, but if I had any chance of beating Theo this year for that top spot, I couldn't start off slacking.

Thinking of Theo made me run through the conversation with Liam again. I hadn't told anyone about it, and Myles and Blake easily believed that my swollen knuckle was from hitting the bag wrong during training. Divulging what we'd yelled at one another or what he had said in the kitchen wouldn't bring us together, but his words had been on a loop in my mind ever since.

A soft knock broke through my absentminded thoughts. Ivy was sound asleep when I glanced over before answering the door. Theo stood there, his red, swollen eyes locked with mine, looking like an apparition haunting the hallway.

"What's wrong?"

He just shook his head, and once more, my heart got a workout as it began to pound hard in my chest.

"Is someone injured or dead?"

He shook his head again and closed his eyes. A tear slid down his cheek, and the fear in my chest ignited into a burning rage. What had Liam done now? Making sure the hall was clear, I took his hand, tugged him into the room, and closed the door.

Theo took off his shoes and sat on my bed as I saved my assignment and closed my laptop. It was crushing me that he still hadn't spoken. He looked like someone had died, and that could only mean one thing if no one was injured—he and Liam had another fight, and this one ended badly.

Flicking off the light, I didn't care if I got into trouble for him spending the night. There was no way in hell I was leaving him alone in this state. I'd never seen him so withdrawn or emotional. This wasn't the same guy who ordered me to get on his motorcycle and challenged me to be better at every opportunity.

"Get under the blankets," I whispered.

To further my worry, he obeyed. No smart-ass remarks or sarcastic comeback. He didn't even mention the incorrect powering down of my computer. Snuggling in beside him, I wrapped my arms around his waist and laid my head on his shoulder. It was only then that I realized that he was shaking.

"Do you want to talk about it," I asked, even though I knew he wouldn't.

"No."

"Is this about Liam?" He nodded, holding me tighter. "Do I need to cut his balls off? Because I'll do it. I'll do it with a spoon 'cause it'll hurt more."

Theo chuckled, but even that sounded sad. "I wish it were that simple," he said, the pain straining his voice, breaking my heart.

"Is there anything I can do?"

"No, the ball is in his court now," he whispered and kissed the top of my head.

Theo didn't speak again, and it was driving me insane. What the fuck had Liam done? He was too fucking stubborn for his own good. Theo would cut off a limb for him, and he couldn't even show a little respect or at least explain himself.

I laid awake long after Theo had fallen asleep, more determined than ever to find a way to force the two of them to see that they were meant to be together. Liam just needed to get out of his own way.

As I watched the clock click over to six, I left Theo's arms and got ready for class. Theo's sleeping face was too much to resist and I reached out to run my finger down his cheek. He was relaxed, and the pain had vanished as he slept, but I knew the moment he woke up, it would be back.

"It's going to be okay. I promise I'll find a way to make this right," I whispered in Theo's ear before leaving to get showered.

Chapter 9

SEPTEMBER 11 – THURSDAY 7:45 AM

Ren

"Ugh, I have to share a locker room with you."

Vicky's snarky voice cut through the chatter as I tied my sneakers the best I could with my sore hand. Why had the dean allowed her to come back for this year? She was a leopard, and there was no changing her spots. What did they think was going to happen? She was suddenly going to turn into a girl guide with a sunny disposition.

"Don't give us all bugs or anything. I mean, you are fucking three guys at once. Who knew that under that uptight exterior was the biggest whore in the room?"

"Takes one to know one, I guess." I stood up straight. "Oh wait... my guys want to be with me while yours run away."

Vicky's nostrils flared, and I couldn't help staring at them.

"Watch out, everyone. It looks like she's going to blow," I said.

Jennifer laughed and then coughed as Vicky turned her glacier stare on her best friend.

"So, you don't deny fucking all the kings?"

"Not all of them." I smiled at her. "At least not yet."

There was a collective gasp at my open reveal, as well as the veiled threat. Vicky knew I meant Nash. It didn't matter that I had no plan to race down that road, but she didn't need to know that. I'd sworn not to start shit, but I never said that I wouldn't finish it.

"You're such a fucking piece of trailer park trash. I have no idea what they see in you, but I can assure you that you can forget about whatever happily ever after you have built up in that head of yours. None of their families are going to approve of you, and soon enough, they will be forced to choose someone...." She walked forward and looked me up and down like we weren't wearing the same gym outfit. "Well...someone that isn't you."

Vicky walked out of the locker room laughing, followed by her minions.

"Why didn't you tell her that you're a Mikhailov," Ivy asked, her voice only loud enough for me and Chantry to hear.

"I could say that I was the daughter of the president or a descendant of Jesus himself, and she would still find a way to turn it against me. Besides, I don't want everyone to know yet. I'm still finding my footing and don't know who from my family wants me dead."

"Good point. She just burns my ass. I'd love to shove her face in a cake, a flavor she hates," Ivy said, making me smile. That was the cutest revenge I'd ever heard. "It should be illegal to have to deal with her before noon."

"How are you doing rooming with her," I asked Chantry, grabbing my water bottle to leave. I looked at her, and she shrugged.

"She doesn't bother me. I'm no threat to her queen-ness, and I'm good and making myself invisible. Most of the time, she forgets I'm in the same room."

"Lucky you," Ivy said. "You know you're always welcome to crash with us if you need a break."

"Thanks," Chantry said with a small smile.

"We better get out there."

The noise of girls talking and balls bouncing greeted us as we opened the door. I groaned audibly as I noticed the volleyball nets set up down the center of the gym. Why did it have to be a hand-coordination sport? Luckily, Vicky was warming up at the far end of the four courts.

Grabbing a ball, the three of us formed a triangle and practiced bumping it between us until Ms. Pearson blew the whistle.

"Gather round," she called out. She always wore crazy-colored socks, and today was no exception. The lime green with pink stripes was blinding this morning. "Alright, we are playing round-robin style. I'll divide you up and the winning teams will rotate to the court on their right, while the losing team remains where they are."

Please, dear God, if you like me at all, do not put Vicky and me on the same team.

"The first six are Ivy, Ren, Samantha, Laura, Bri, and Justine. Go to court six."

I breathed a sigh of relief and walked to the far end of the gym, all too aware of Vicky's eyes on me. She was worse than a over the top, jealous, possessive stalker.

The whistle blew again, and I instantly regretted not taping my fingers as the opposing team served. Laura bumped the ball from the back in a perfect assist, but the second my fingers touched the ball to hit it over, pain shot into my hand and down my arm.

"Shit."

By the time the round was over it was obvious that I shouldn't be participating. I'd tried to defend the last attack with just one hand, and the ball flew wildly into the neighboring court.

"Maybe you should tell Ms. Pearson you can't play," Ivy said as we drank some water and waited to see who we would face next.

"Big yikes. Is one game too much for you," Vicky asked as she walked by. Of course, she was our next opponent.

"Don't do it. Don't let her goad you into playing."

Ivy was right, of course, but Vicky's smug look as she made a crying face had me tossing down my towel and water like a gauntlet.

"You're going to anyway, aren't you?" Ivy sighed.

"Hell yeah, I am."

Taking up the service position, I waited until the whistle blew and served overhand. My finger screamed, making me wince. Not getting the right lift or arc on the hit, the ball uselessly sailed right into the net. Vicky and Jennifer laughed their asses off as my team stared at me. Fuck.

"Nice serve, loser," Vicky said, smirking as we sent the ball over to their side.

"Sorry," I said to my team.

Ivy gave me a sympathetic smile, but all the bravado from a moment ago was gone. She was right. I shouldn't be playing. But if I backed out now, it would be worse than just losing the game.

Luckily, the ball didn't come near me for the next few plays, but the moment I moved into the front center position, Vicky smiled at me. She reminded me of an evil clown, like the one in *IT*.

It all happened so fast, yet it felt like slow motion. Her team served, and Ivy bumped it from the back row, but it went too far, floating over the net like a slow beach ball. Vicky jumped, and even though I saw the spike coming, the ball came back so hard that it was all I could do to get my hands up.

Not that it helped. It pushed through my sore hand like it wasn't even there and cracked the bridge of my nose.

This hurt a hundred times worse than when Myles accidentally hit me in the face. I stumbled back and dropped to my ass as tears sprang to my eyes and blinded me.

"You bitch." I heard Ivy uncharacteristically yell. "You did that on purpose."

Holding my bleeding nose, I blinked and caught a glimpse of Ivy darting under the volleyball net, attacking Vicky. Chaos erupted all around me, complete with screaming and whistle-blowing.

A hand touched my shoulder. "Let me see," Chantry said in a soothing voice.

My hands slowly dropped away from my face, and I could taste the metallic tang of blood on my lips.

"Hurts, and…can't breathe," I said.

"It's broken. I can fix it. Do you want me to?" I nodded, not wanting to wait. "This will hurt."

"I'm fine, just do it."

Chantry braced my nose with her fingers. I winced and closed my eyes like that would somehow prevent the pain I knew was coming. She squeezed and twisted quickly. There was a weird crunching sound, and it hurt as much as the ball hitting my face, but the relief was instant.

"Keep your head tipped forward. I'll help you up," she said, far calmer and more assured than I'd ever seen her. Maybe her calling was to be a doctor. With Chantry's help, I got to my feet. "We need to get the bleeding under control. Can you pinch here?" She touched my nose and then wrapped her arm around my shoulders as I tried to stem the bleeding.

"Where are you going," Ms. Pearson yelled.

"I'm taking her to the infirmary," Chantry yelled back over the madness all around us. "I'll send guards."

I glanced at her out of the corner of my eye. Who the hell was this version of Chantry, and how did we keep her?

"I don't need a doctor, do I?"

We stepped outside, and I immediately rethought my question as the gentle breeze hurt my entire face.

"They need to make sure you don't have a concussion, and we need ice for your nose."

"The blood is slowing."

"Good, we're still going."

"Who are you, and who stole my mild-mannered Chantry?"

She laughed. "I'm good in emergencies. It's sort of my thing."

"You should be a doctor, like a trauma surgeon." She smiled and shrugged.

"Maybe. My family, that's not part of the Yakuza, are pretty much all in the medical field in some way. Doctors, nurses, and even engineers designing medical equipment. My mother is a heart surgeon, so I guess you could say it runs in our blood."

Some guys stared at us as we walked by, their mouths hanging open.

"How bad do I look?"

"You've definitely had better days," she said, and even though it hurt, I laughed.

"Thank you. I needed that."

When we walked into the foyer, I knew that I must look like a walking horror show. Everyone milling around gasped and covered their mouths. Great, just freaking great. Just when I didn't think I could feel more conflicted about a place....

Chapter 11

SEPTEMBER 11 – THURSDAY 7:45 AM

Liam

"What the fuck?"

I blinked, my head throbbing, and was just able to make out Nash in the doorway.

"What the hell happened in here? What the fuck happened to you?"

Licking my lips, I sucked in a gasp as it felt like a spike was being drilled into my brain. Not giving a shit about Nash and his stupid rules, I swiped the pack of smokes off the floor and put one between my lips.

Cold metal touched my forehead, and as much as it hurt, I looked up at him. The barrel of the gun was pressed against my head.

"Go ahead, do it. I'll pull the fucking trigger."

"Then kill me," I said, really not giving a fuck if he did.

Lighting up, I sucked in a breath and sat back on the couch, blowing the smoke in the air. Leaning over the arm of the couch, I spotted my bottle of whiskey and reached for it. Nash kicked it like he was trying out for FIFA. The bottle sailed through the air and smashed into the wall behind me.

"Asshole."

"Have you looked around? It's like a fucking bomb went off," he growled. "What the hell happened?" He wiped his hand along the couch, collected the white powder, and held it up for me to see.

I glanced around, remembering all too well why there were man-sized holes in the walls.

"I used the table to redecorate," I said sarcastically, staring at said coffee table hanging halfway out of the small storage room door. Not a single thing in the room had been safe. If it was liftable then it was throwable. "Just be happy that I didn't decide the entire cabin needed a makeover." Smirking, I took another drag of my cigarette.

He flopped down on the couch beside me and shook his head.

"What happened?"

"You don't want to hear my sob story." He turned his head and glared at me. "Fuck. Fine." Crushing the butt out on the bottom of my boot, I leaned back again and stared at the ceiling. "Theo ended us."

Saying those words out loud was another thousand slashes to my heart. My eyes stung, and I draped my arm over my face to keep Nash from seeing me cry. I didn't cry. Theo had made me fucking cry. Fucker.

"Why?"

"Why do you think?"

"Well, I know what I think, but what do you think is the reason?"

"Oh no, don't go all Yoda on me," I growled. "That's my job, and my head hurts way too much for that shit."

"You look more like Jabba the Hutt at the moment." I glared at Nash even though he was probably right. "Do you want some water," he asked.

"Yeah."

"Come on."

The couch moved beside me. Opening my eyes, Nash had his hand stretched out in front of my face. I was tempted to swipe it away, but there was no way I was staying upright without help.

Clasping hands with Nash, he pulled me to my feet and put my arm around his neck.

"I'm sorry about the room."

"Don't be. I'm going to take the cost to fix it out of your salary, and I'll make sure to add all the upgrades I'd been too cheap to do myself," he said.

I snorted and then groaned as my head and stomach turned on me at the same time. Nash unceremoniously dumped me in the bathroom to throw up and shower. Every part of my body hurt. I hadn't even felt like this after my last twenty-four-hour race.

Theo's words looped around and around like a dark carousel of pain. Pulling myself up off the floor, I stepped into the shower. As the hot water hit my back, it was all I could do to keep the lethal combination of rage and misery under control.

Only the knock on the door broke the loop.

"Hurry up," Nash barked.

Getting dressed was slow and arduous, but I finally managed to get my jeans zipped and hoodie on before walking out to find Nash. He was in the kitchen, and my stomach was undecided if it liked the smell of fried eggs and sausage. He made a couple of breakfast sandwiches and handed them over to me with a bottle of water before making his own. I took a bite as he licked his fingers and waved me to follow him. He pulled my cigarettes out of his pocket.

"What the fuck are you doing," I asked as he twisted them into dust over the toilet bowl.

"You told me that you quit."

"Fuck off. I slipped, so what?"

Nash flushed the toilet and dropped the empty pack into the garbage.

"You think I don't know that you never stopped?" I crossed my arms.

"Whatever," I drawled and then swore as Nash grabbed me and pushed me up against the wall.

"You want to fuck up your lungs, that's your choice, but you will not do it until swimming is over. Yes, I'm making this about me. Don't fuck this up for me, Liam. It's the only good thing in my life."

Words had never hit so hard. The only good thing in my life had walked out on me last night.

"Yeah, okay," I said, and Nash let me go.

"Come on. You can tell me what happened in the car. We need to get to school. I had first period free, but I'm really looking forward to Russian this morning." The way he said it left no doubt in my mind that he had something up his sleeve. "Besides, I don't need a date with Dean Henry this early into the year. We're almost free."

"How did you know I was at the cabin?"

"I didn't, but I checked the camera this morning, and it was pointed at the floor. Decided to check out what the fuck was going on."

"On your own?" He shrugged. "If I have to stop smoking, you need to stop taking stupid risks. What if you arrived and there was a rival gang tearing the place up, or cops found it and had a search warrant to arrest you? Or what if a bear was in the cabin, and you walked in on it ripping shit apart?"

"Fine...I'll be more careful. Now fucking tell me what happened," he ordered.

By the time we reached Wayward, my grease-laden food and the water were gone. Nash got an overview of what went down between me and Theo and what he had said to me. Nash didn't say anything, but he didn't need to. I could see it in his eyes. I'd fucked up. The problem was...I didn't know how to fix it. I had to relook at every moment we'd shared and analyze it from a whole new lens, and what I saw...wasn't good. I'd been a piece of shit to my Sub but worse to the one person I swore I'd never hurt...the person I love.

Fuck.

SEPTEMBER 11 – THURSDAY 11:16 AM

Nash

Focusing on Russian was hard enough, but the empty seat beside me that Ren usually occupied made it nearly impossible. There were very few things that I could count on as regularly as the sun rising, insurance companies fucking people over, and my father being a dick, but one was Ren going to class. Where the hell was she?

I'd hoped she would be in here stomping her foot and glaring at me with that cute as fuck snarl that always got me hot. While she swore she was going to kill me, I would picture yanking her over my lap and tanning her ass. My well thought out plan was foiled, and it was either because she knew that was what I wanted and was purposely staying away, or something bad had happened.

Raising my hand, Mr. Romanovich stopped talking and looked over the rim of his glasses at me.

"Yes, Mr. Collier?"

God, I hated that everyone called me that. It might be my name, but it just reminded me that no matter how far I ran or how much I fought against it, I'd always be my father's son.

"I'm not feeling well and need to go to the clinic," I said. His bushy eyebrows shot up, and annoyance washed over me. "What's my average from last year? Ninety-two percent?" I closed my laptop and stuffed all my shit into my bag. "If you have a problem with it, take it up with the Dean," I said before he could say anything else.

My footfalls echoed in the quiet hallway as I marched away from class. Bowfield Hall was my least favorite of the buildings. There was just something about it that I didn't like.

My stride faltered as I pushed outside and saw Ren walking toward me.

"What the fuck happened?" An unexpected burst of rage ripped through my body at the sight of her face. Her eyes were nearly swollen closed, her cheeks were black and blue, and she had a brace on her nose.

"Ask your delightful ex," Ren said, trying to walk around me, but I snagged her waist and hauled her back. "Nash, I am so not in the mood."

My eyes traced her face, taking in every mark and committing it to memory. I'd seen battered faces before. Hell, I'd seen mine look like this after a round with my father, but there was something about seeing her like this....

"What? No sarcastic comment about how I had this coming," she said, crossing her arms, and that was when I noticed her hand was also bandaged.

"No." My voice was soft, and the defensive look in her eyes began to fade. "Tell me what happened, Princess."

"We were in gym, and Vicky purposely spiked the ball at my face. I'll give it to her. She has a hell of a swing. It broke my nose, but I'll live."

Fucking bitch. Mr. Genovese was the only reason I didn't kill Vicky with my bare hands.

"And your hand?"

Ren looked down at the bandage and shrugged.

"Oh. I punched Liam in the face yesterday morning. He was being a dick and totally deserved it."

My lip twitched up into a lopsided grin. That was my Princess. Feisty as fuck and willing to throw down with anyone.

"Why are you staring at me like that?"

"Just realizing that everyone at the athlete's dinner will think I beat the shit out of you."

She closed her eyes and groaned. "Shit...I really will look hideous. Great."

"No, that could never happen." I cleared my throat. "You should be healed by then. It will be fine."

The stupid words tumbled out before my brain could catch up and shut my mouth. Ren looked down and nibbled her bottom lip. The memory of how those lips tasted and felt had been plaguing my dreams, taunting me to take more.

"Don't think that sweet talk will make me forget the little gift you left for me yesterday. Like seriously...yuck. I can't believe you did that."

I smiled wide. Cue the fantasies.

"Come on. There's no point in you going to class now, and I guess I owe you some ice cream or something."

"Ice cream? You think ice cream will make me forgive you?"

"I can give you another type of cream again if you prefer?" She glared and then winced. "I'm joking...sort of. What do you have to lose? You can't type, and Rambling Romanovich is recapping last year anyway. Nothing exciting ever happens the first class back."

"I'm going to regret this, aren't I?"

"No, never." I shot her a teasing look. She glanced at me as we started walking toward the main hall.

"Did you really come on my picture?" Smiling wide, I shrugged and let her draw her own conclusion. "You need therapy."

Poking her was way more fun than it should be.

"With my parents, that's a given. But you'll never see me in one of those rooms, spilling my guts to some stranger," I said.

"Why? Are you afraid they might never be able to fix whatever the fuck is wrong with you?"

Chuckling, I shook my head.

"Naw, I already know they can't fix me. You just never give anyone that much information about yourself. Every word is a potential bullet that can end your life."

"We really need to work on your trust issues," Ren said as I pulled open the foyer door.

Everyone stared at us, or more specifically Ren, as we walked by. She never glanced at them, and it was becoming clear what intrigued me so much about her. No matter what happened, how hard she was hit, mentally, physically, or emotionally, she always got back up, dusted herself off, and kept going. I felt a kinship with that part of her personality. Not many could handle what she had the way she did.

We walked into the cafeteria, and Liam looked up. He did a double-take before standing and walking over.

"What the fuck? Did you decide to box someone without taking my lessons first?"

Ren glared at him. "No, this was care of Vicky. You are so lucky that I already feel like I've been trampled by a charging moose. Otherwise, I'd kick your ass for whatever the fuck you did to Theo last night." Liam's face blanched.

"What did he say?"

"Nothing, not a single word. He looked like you ripped his heart right out of his chest, and so help me God, Liam, if you do not make this right between the two of you...." She held up her hand as she reigned in her rant. "You don't deserve him. Think about that and how lonely and empty your life would be without him because no one, and I mean no one, will ever love you like Theo does."

"Are you done sharing my dirty laundry with the school," Liam asked, looking around.

"Dirty? Dirty? Wrong choice of word there, Bud. Don't push me. I'll get on the fucking PA and announce exactly what I think of you and your treatment of him to everyone."

Liam swallowed hard. I was loving every second of this and couldn't keep the smirk off my face.

"I need to fix this," he whispered.

"You're damn right you do. This is the last thing I'm going to say on this. Theo told me that he thinks you're embarrassed to be seen with him—to acknowledge what you two have publicly. I don't know why, and you don't have to tell me, but unless the answer is that you'd be shot in the head, there is no excuse. Have you looked at him? I mean, really took a step back and looked?"

Ren cocked her hip, and her skirt shifted, showing off the shape of her ass. I put my hands in my pocket to keep from doing something stupid.

"Yeah, of course I have."

"Really? Well then, you're a bigger idiot than I thought."

It was so rare to see Liam flustered that I was going to soak in every second of this. She held up her finger as she counted off.

"He's the smartest guy in school, don't tell him I said that. He's smoking hot."

I ground my teeth together as a seed of jealousy began to sprout. Not that I could do anything. My deal with Mr. Genovese handcuffed me.

"He rides a motorcycle. I mean that alone...and then on top of it all, he would die to protect you. So the next time you want to be an asshole to him, why don't you try thinking about how lucky you are first?"

"He broke up with me," Liam said so quietly that I almost didn't hear it. "So there won't be a next time. He doesn't want anything to do with me."

Ren threw her hands in the air.

"How is it that you can be so smart and stupid at the same time? If you really believe it's over, then fine. But from where I'm sitting, he wants you to man up, get off your hands, and prove what you keep giving as lip service."

"When did you get so fucking mouthy," Liam asked, and I laughed.

"Trust me she came this way," I drawled, earning a lifted eyebrow from Ren.

"Fine, you're so smart. What should I do," Liam asked.

Ren shrugged.

"Think outside the box and push all your chips into the center of the table or lose forever. Now, I need more painkillers and a coffee. My fucking head is pounding," Ren said and walked away, dismissing us both.

She was growing into her last name. I hadn't met a Mikhailov yet who wouldn't rip your balls off and force you to eat them.

"Coffee?" Liam nodded toward Ren at the barista bar.

"You know...why the hell not."

It wasn't like I could fuck up any more than I already had.

SEPTEMBER 11 – THURSDAY 12:15 PM

Ren

Myles burst into the cafeteria, his face shifting from sweet and loving to murderous when he saw me.

"What in the ever-lovin' fuck? Blake said to prepare myself, but he didn't tell me that I'd be wantin' to kill someone."

He sat down beside me and softly brushed my cheek. I always wanted to press myself into him like a cat. Myles could comfort me with the smallest of touches.

"I'll be fine. It looks a lot worse than it is," I said, grabbing his hand and linking our fingers.

"I'm gonna kill Vicky. I swear it," he snarled.

"You're going to have to get in line," Theo said as he walked up, looking as perfectly put together and in control as that first day I met him.

You'd never know that anything was going on between him and Liam. Well...other than the fact that he didn't look at Liam or sit down in his usual spot.

"Yer not gettin' first crack at the bitch," Myles growled.

Theo crossed his arms.

"Not what I meant. No one is killing her...at least not in the near future."

"Why," Blake asked.

"Because Mr. Genovese just walked into the office, and he did not look pleased," Theo said.

Nash spit his coffee out on the table, choking. *What the hell?*

"You okay down there?" Theo gave Nash a questioning look.

"Yup, just went down the wrong way," he said, wiping up the coffee.

I didn't think I'd ever seen Nash nervous, but it was there in his eyes.

"You're serious? Mr. Genovese is here," Liam asked, and even I shivered as Theo turned his gaze down to Liam.

"Yes, I saw him myself. He looked livid. I'm going to go back out to the foyer and watch the drama unfold. Anyone else interested?"

"Count me in. Anything that humiliates Vicky makes me happy." Blake stood, and we gathered our things before finding a spot to watch the show.

Vicky's screaming echoed around the foyer before they even left the office. Ivy was the first to emerge, and I met her halfway, hugging her.

"What happened? What did Dean Henry decide," I asked as we walked back to the guys.

"I have detention for going after Vicky. But I will happily take the ten days punishment." Ivy crossed her arms. "Mr. Genovese is so calm it's scary."

"What do you mean?"

"When he walked in, Vicky folded in on herself. He didn't even say a word. She looked like a little kid. It was freaky."

"So why is she in there screamin' like a banshee," Myles asked as more yelling filled the hall. "Is she getting expelled for good this time?"

"No, Dean Henry was going to expel her, but Mr. Genovese asked him not to. He told the dean that he would be staying in town until graduation and would keep his daughter from causing any more trouble." Ivy pointed a thumb over her shoulder. "The freakout started when he told her that he was taking away all of her credit cards, her car, and that she had to do community service for the remainder of the year."

"No, shit...Vicky without her credit cards?" Blake laughed hard. "No wonder she is losing her mind."

"This isn't fair!" Vicky yanked open the door, and we all watched as she threw a tantrum to rival any two-year-old.

Vicky turned her eyes in my direction and snarled. "This is all your fault. I'm being punished because you're pathetic," she said, taking a step in my direction.

"Victoria Gabriella Genovese!" Even I swallowed as the man who had to be her father stepped out of the office. Vicky froze. "Do I need to repeat myself?"

Mr. Genovese held an air of authority that Lawrence would pay to pull off. With his midnight black hair and impressive height, he looked like he had just stepped out of a mafia movie or off the cover of one of my novels. Tattoos lined hands that held large silver rings, and his eyes unusual gray eyes were cool as steel as he glared at his daughter's back.

"You are acting like a spoiled child," he said, and I couldn't agree more.

Vicky turned—her hands balled into fists as she stomped her foot.

"But Papa, it's her fault, not mine. She's always pushing my buttons on purpose. All I did was spike the ball. She didn't get her hands up. This is not fair."

His intense gaze shifted in my direction, paralyzing me to the spot. Just as quickly, he snapped back to Vicky.

"Do you want me to continue taking your things away? Treat you like the child you're acting? I'm disgusted by your conduct. Had I known that your mother was allowing you to act like this unchecked, I would've forced you home last year."

"But Papa...."

He lifted one finger, and Vicky's mouth snapped shut.

"Not another word, or the next thing to go will be your phone, then every piece of designer clothing you own, followed by your trust fund." Her mouth fell open. "I will not tolerate this behavior. You will not throw my name around that way and shame me. You'll learn humility starting right now."

He stepped into her personal space, forcing her to look up at him.

"One more call from Dean Henry...about anything other than how well you're doing in classes, and you'll regret the consequences of your actions. Do not test me, mia figlia."

Vicky looked around at the dozens of people holding their collective breath. No one moved or blinked.

"Now, you will apologize for what you've done, and I better be satisfied with your performance, or you will do it again and again until I am."

Vicky looked like she'd rather chew glass as she walked toward me. Mr. Genovese followed like a dangerous shadow. Vicky's mouth moved, but no words came out. Sighing, she cleared her throat.

"I'm sorry for hitting you in the face with the volleyball," she said.

"And..." Mr. Genovese prompted. That one word held so much weight, and even though it wasn't directed at me, my heart pounded harder.

Vicky's misery was bringing me untold joy. She was in full melt-down mode, and if her father wasn't standing behind her, something very different would come out of her mouth. He was delusional if he believed that Vicky would ever learn to be humble or kind.

"I'm sorry that I've bullied you since you arrived. It was wrong of me, and it won't happen again." She held out her hand, and I stared at it like it was a snake ready to strike. "Can we call a truce and try to start over?"

My eyes ping-ponged between Vicky and her father, who was extremely imposing up close. His square jaw and unwavering gaze were as if the covers of *Serial Killers Are Among Us* and *GQ* magazine had merged into a person.

I held out my unbandaged hand and she shook it, but I felt like I'd just made a deal with a shark. At some point, she would get hungry and wouldn't be able to resist biting it off.

"Good, now go wait in the car for me," he ordered.

It was the first time I realized that there were a dozen massive guards with him. I'd been so hypnotized that I hadn't even noticed the army of black suits.

"Papa...." She started, but with one arch of his brow, Vicky pressed her lips together.

Damn, I needed to learn that trick. Vicky sulked and walked away, with guards following.

As soon as she was gone, Mr. Genovese gazed down at me. It felt like he was analyzing me or searching my face for something. Then again, he could've just been taking in the black and blue raccoon mask I was sporting. I was not looking my finest.

"I would like to personally extend an apology for my daughter's treatment of you. I was unaware of the escalation, and I do not condone her behavior. If you need anything, please let Dean Henry know, and it will be handled."

Before I could think of a reply, he looked at Nash, nodded, and walked away. His entourage followed in his wake.

"That right there is who we all aspire to become. He is the youngest recorded Don of Dons, who didn't kill his father to take the throne. I think he's like forty...if that." That was more than impressive. It was scary. "They also say that only one student in every five generations at Wayward will accomplish what Mr. Genovese has. Makes me wonder what he was like at our age," Theo said.

The foyer was quiet. It felt as if everyone was waiting to be told they could speak again. Just like that, another layer of blinders was ripped away.

Wayward allowed us to be teens, but outside the gates, we were the next heads of families. Whether that was in a political ring or the darker underground organizations, knowing it and seeing it were very different things. Lawrence was no example. Everyone, including his son, wanted him dead, and no one trusted him. But the hushed respect around the room was loud and clear.

Mr. Genovese was not just a leader. He was a man who had found a way to live in both the criminal and common world. More impressively than that, he was who other men strived to be, which could easily be seen in the guy's eyes. That made him a bigger target than anyone else but also more powerful.

The iron fist that Lawrence ruled by would only last so long, and at some point, he would fall—most likely in a Machiavellian manner. But from what Theo said, Mr. Genovese lived by a different set of rules.

"Why did he nod at you," Liam asked Nash.

"No clue," Nash said, shrugging, his face completely blank.

I couldn't help thinking he knew more than he was letting on. That was the problem with Nash. No matter how much you learned, he played his cards close to the vest.

SEPTEMBER 11 – THURSDAY 10:11 PM

Nash

Fucking Vicky.

Ren had disappeared with Ivy after Mr. Genovese left, but that didn't stop me from seeing the bruising and swelling in my mind. Despite the show Vicky put on in the foyer, I knew she'd try something again, and part of my deal with her father was to keep her in line. Apparently, going more than forty-eight hours after the start of school before acting out was too difficult. She was going to get me killed, and there was no way in hell that was happening.

Chantry was staying with Ren and Ivy for the night, so it gave me the perfect opportunity to have a private conversation with the thorn in my side. From my position by the window, I watched her car pull up to the front doors. Vicky exited the vehicle, not waiting for her driver to open the door, and solemnly climbed the stairs. The conversation with her father clearly hadn't been enjoyable.

Pulling my knife, I got into position and waited. The shadows gave away her arrival before she unlocked the door. I silently stepped from my spot as she entered her room. Vicky managed a small scream as I fisted her hair and slammed her up against the wall. The tip of my knife was pressed to the side of her neck.

"You just can't keep from being a bitch," I said.

"Nash," her voice came out terrified, which matched her trembling body.

"I warned you. I told you not to go near Ren, and yet, here we are."

"I swear, I didn't mean to break her nose." My blade pushed a little deeper into her skin. "I'm serious. I'm not lying. Yes, I meant to spike it at her, but how was I to know she wouldn't block it like a normal person or get the hell out of the way?"

"I really don't give a fuck what your intentions were. What matters is the result. So this is what's going to happen. You're going to stop fucking my father before he kills you. You're going to leave Ren alone, so I don't kill you. When the school year is done you won't have to see either one of them ever again. Understand?"

She pushed her ass back into my crotch and wiggled.

"Why don't you just say you want me back? I know you do."

"Is that so?"

"It is. Nash, my mother told me that my Papa signed a contract for me. I know that you visited him this summer."

"You know all of that, do you?"

"Yes," she said huskily and rubbed against me again. "I told you that I don't want your father. I've only ever wanted you. I was only with him to piss you off."

"Well, at least you can admit that you were acting like a cunt. Good for you. Do you remember me walking in on the two of you? Fucking disgusting. Did you really think that stunt would work?"

Moving the knife, I folded it up and stuffed it back in my pocket. Vicky turned and faced me, stupidly throwing her arms around my neck.

"I'm sorry. I've missed you so much," she said and kissed the side of my throat. "Please fuck me. Complete the contract, and I'll do whatever you want. I'll be as sweet as pie to Ren. I'll even bring her breakfast in bed if you want." Vicky nipped at my lip and wrapped her leg around my waist.

Pulling her arms off me so she wasn't touching me and pushing her back, I stared into her eyes.

"Nash...please...."

"No. The contract I signed with your father has very strict instructions that I must follow."

She crossed her arms and shook her head at me.

"That means no sex?"

"Among other things, yes."

"But it's just us. He'll never find out." She stepped toward me, and I grabbed her arms, forcing her to keep her distance.

"But I would, and I have too much respect for your father to break his trust. So, no. Not unless you want your contract to disappear. You'll stay away from both my father and Ren. I fucking mean it. Keep your shit in line, Vicky. Find some self-control. You're like a bitch in heat. It's not attractive."

"Fine," she said, rolling her eyes. "I'll do what you say because I know that I won, and that's all that matters. Everyone else will know it soon enough."

She was right. Everyone would know the details soon enough, and that was what I was worried about. I'd painted myself into a complicated corner.

Grabbing the handle, I opened the door.

"Nash?"

"Yes?"

"Thank you for choosing me."

"Just follow the fucking rules, Vicky, or the entire contract will fall apart," I said.

"I will...for you. I promise."

"Fuck my life," I growled under my breath, walking down the hallway.

SEPTEMBER 15 – MONDAY 7:38 PM

Theo

"What year did Einstein publish his theory on special relativity," I asked.

"Easy, 1905," Ren answered.

"What three new fields did theorists experiment in once special relativity was established?"

Ren sat back on the bed while Blake and Myles watched with—what I could only assume was—a mix of boredom and fascination as they kept track of the score.

I held up my fingers as I rhymed off the answers.

"Atomic physics, quantum mechanics, and nuclear physics. That was too easy. Better luck next time," I said as Ren huffed.

She'd only missed one question all night, but one was all it took for me to take the win.

We all jumped as the door burst open, and Liam marched in.

"Are you fucking kidding me," he snarled at me.

"Whoa, what's going on," Blake asked, standing, but I held up my hand, stopping my brother from interfering.

"You'll have to be a little more specific," I said, even though I knew damn well what he was going on about.

Pissing him off and seeing him bent out of shape about it... well, that was just my little revenge. Apparently, I had a petty streak.

He held up a class schedule and waved it in the air.

"You moved all of your classes, so you're no longer in any with me."

"And you felt the need to print it off? Is it so that you could wave it around?"

"Answer the question," he ordered.

"Technically, you didn't ask a question, but yes, I did. We're not together, and you have hardly spoken to me in three days other than to say good morning, so what do you care?"

"You said we were on a break, not done for good. I thought you wanted some space to think."

"Exactly, so putting distance between us seemed logical. How are we supposed to know what it feels like to really be without one another when we live side by side, hang out with the same friends, and are in most of the same classes?"

Liam's eyes were livid. If I'd pissed him off like this when we were still together, he would have fucked me until I couldn't stand and then punished me. All of which I would have happily taken, but me begging him to prove himself hadn't worked, so it was time to shake things up. Liam detested change and loathed being out of control.

Fuck with both of those at once, and you got this, a man on the edge. Now, all I needed him to do was jump.

"Logic...you don't get to make a decision like this without talking to me about it first."

Crossing my arms, I cocked my head and stared at him.

"Oh yeah? And why is that? We're on a break. I don't work for you, and you have no authority over me in any other capacity. I can do whatever I want, see whoever I want, fuck whoever I want...but look on the bright side, so can you."

I swiveled my chair to face the desk, knowing he would lose his mind.

"Did you just dismiss me? And where the fuck is your watch?"

Rubbing at my bare wrist, I didn't bother to look up at him. I felt naked without it, but wearing it would give him the wrong message.

"Yeah, there is nothing else to say. I'm not changing it back...you can leave."

"Um...should we go and let ya talk this out," Myles asked.

"Yes," Liam barked.

"No," I countered.

"Oh, well, that clears it right up," Myles drawled.

"I know what you're trying to do," Liam growled, the sound as alluring as always.

He crumpled the schedule and leaned on the edge of my desk. His shadow pressed in on me even if he wasn't physically touching me.

"And what exactly do you think that is?"

"You're trying to get under my skin and piss me off. Well, it's working. I'm pissed. This is a fucking childish maneuver and beneath you," Liam said.

"Fuck you, Hicks," I snarled, meeting his angry gaze. "You're literally in every part of my life. I can't take a piss without seeing something of yours or you being there right beside me. I'm trying the best way I know how to get the fuck over you. There, I said it. I don't think you want to fix what's going on between us, and I need to find a way to move on."

Pissing him off was only part of the goal, but it ran so much deeper than that. Whenever we fought, the first thing Liam did was go radio silent. I understood that it was part of his personality and that he wasn't actually trying to hurt or manipulate me. At least, I didn't think so, but it didn't matter. It was always me who caved, and deep down, I knew that was what he was hoping for again.

"Liam, I genuinely wanted to give you the space without me around to decide if you want to accept me for who I am. That means the parts you want and don't want. It can't be just about how good the sex is, not anymore."

My voice was calm, but my body sure as hell didn't feel that way. A tremble had started under my skin, and I clenched my hands into fists to keep it from spreading.

"I really think the three of us should go and leave you two to discuss this alone," Ren said, standing.

Both of us turned our heads and looked at her.

"No," we said in unison.

"Okay, then...." She sat down between Blake and Myles.

"If we are going to be in this relationship together, then all of us need to be part of this discussion. Because, like it or not, this is what you've signed up for," I said to the three of them.

"Touché," Ren whispered as she nodded.

I turned my attention back to Liam.

"You know how I feel and what I need. I've been crystal clear and have never lied to you. It's your turn to choose, so choose."

"Fine...fucking fine. You want me to try with Ren as part of your *new you*, right?"

There was no point in answering a question I'd answered a million times already, so I just kept looking at him. Standing up straight, he rolled his shoulders and fixed his stare on Ren.

"Alright, that's the way you want to be, fine. Ren, I can't get to know you the way I need to and give us an honest effort here."

"Um...okay. I don't know what that means," Ren said, standing.

He approached her like a hunter going in for the kill. Even with his hands in his pockets he looked intimidating, but Ren didn't back down.

"It means that this happens on my turf. There are way too many ears inside these walls, and I hate people knowing my business. I want you to go camping with me. Alone."

I burst from my seat.

"Hell no. It's not happening."

"I'll do it," Ren answered as I grabbed her arm and tugged her away from Liam.

"No, you're not going camping with him. I forbid it."

She arched a brow at me. "First, don't tell me what I can and cannot do. Second, why? What's your reasoning?"

"There are a million reasons. For starters, it's way too dangerous to be off school property that long. Look what happened in Canada, and we were followed on our date. And...." I faltered because I trusted Liam. But did I trust him alone with Ren in the wilderness?

"He thinks I'm going to Hansel and Gretel you in the woods," Liam said sarcastically.

"Well, can you blame me? You haven't exactly been her biggest fan."

He shrugged and fixed Ren with a hard stare, silently daring her to say no. He had that challenging glint in his eye, and I was tempted to tackle him, but I wouldn't put it past him that he wanted that all along.

"I'm gonna interject here since I'm supposed to have an opinion," Myles said from the bed. "This is a bad idea. Even before we knew that someone was tryin' ta kill ya, Snowflake, it would be dangerous. If somethin' happens on the trail, ya only have one another to count on, and you'd be a long way out if you go where I think Liam is wantin' to take ya."

Ren paced the room, and I glared at Liam, wanting to kill him myself. He knew that she would say yes. She was too brave for her own good and she so badly wanted to fix what she never broke.

"Ren, don't do it. What's going on between me and Liam started long before you arrived. He's using this to shove my feelings for you back in my face, and in doing so, he's putting your life at risk."

"Think what you want, but I didn't come in here with the intention of making this deal. You've put me in the position of having to come up with an idea that might work. You say you want us all to somehow be in a relationship...."

He held his hands out to Myles and Blake, emphasizing it wasn't just Ren he was concerned about.

"Well, then I need to see if Ren and I can really connect. That's not going to happen with you three assholes kicking around all the time and watching us like a fucking experiment."

"Then be normal for once and go to dinner or something," I argued.

"Yes, because that's so me. When have I ever taken anyone out on a dinner date? I've never even taken you."

"Don't I know it," I growled, and he huffed out a frustrated sigh.

"Why don't I take her to one of the underground kink clubs? How do you think that will go?"

"For fucks sake."

I threw my hands in the air and walked to the window. It was still light outside, and the leaves hadn't started to change yet, but they would with the season as surely as the tide coming into shore and Ren saying yes. She wouldn't be able to help herself.

Turning around, I faced them.

"If she goes with you, then I'm going too," I said, crossing my arms.

"No," Liam said, moving closer.

"Yes," I said, matching his movements like we were in a backward dual.

"No." He took another step, and we were close enough to touch.

"Yes," I growled.

"Theo, you asked me to try. She told me to think outside the box. This is my out-of-the-box idea and my terms."

Walking away from me, Liam stepped up to Ren.

"I need to trust you and connect with you. I have no intention of killing you. So you can take your chances for a single weekend with me, or Theo and I are over for good because I don't see any other way to find common ground. If you choose to do this, and we can hammer out details to make the three of us work, then I promise to put in the effort for the other issues lying between me and Theo." He looked up at me. "Including telling my parents."

My mouth dropped, but I quickly recovered.

"You can't use Ren like a poker chip and toss her into the center of the table. It doesn't work like that," I argued.

"Why not? You did it to me."

The room fell deathly quiet as we glared at one another, and I hated that he was right. I was forcing his hand, but I hadn't done it like this or to be manipulative. Was I really any better? Shit.

"When?" Ren broke the silence.

"The weekend after Nash's dinner in Seattle. The weather will still be good, and it's before my initiation and swearing-in. I have no idea what that will entail. So, what do you say, Little Rabbit? Will you take the carrot? This was sort of your idea, after all."

"I'll do it," Ren said.

"Fuck." I shook my head at them. "This is not smart, not fucking smart, and for once, I really don't want to say I told you so."

SEPTEMBER 15 – MONDAY 8:10 PM

R en

"I'll do it," I said.

"Fuck." Theo shook his head. "This is not smart, not fucking smart, and for once, I really don't want to say I told you so."

"Was it really any smarter for us to go to Seattle," I asked.

He opened his mouth, closed it, and walked to the window again like he might find the answers outside.

"Guys, can you give the three of us some space? I need to talk to Theo and Liam alone."

Myles jumped up and kissed my cheek.

"We'll head next door and annoy the shite out of Nash. He'll love it," he said, making me giggle.

Blake was next, and he ran his hand down my arm.

"Go easy on Theo," he whispered in my ear, and I gave him a reassuring smile.

As they left the room, I turned my attention to Liam and Theo.

"Theo, tell me why you really don't want me to go with Liam. I'm not stupid. There are things you have held back mentioning."

He glanced at me in the reflection of the window before slowly turning around.

"You're not like me, Ren, and that worries me. I don't want to see you get hurt, and what he's proposing is like tossing you into the deep end of a pool, not knowing how to swim."

I actually knew what that was like but had no idea in what context he meant. Scrunching up my nose, I immediately swore and winced. I might not need the brace, but it at least reminded me why I didn't want to move my face.

Walking to the bed to sit down, I folded my hands in my lap and hit Theo with my stare.

"I understand the words but not the meaning. What are you talking about?"

"He means that you're not a Sub. You've only scratched the surface of our lifestyle. It's also what I was talking about the other day when I said we sit on the same pedestal," Liam filled in before stealing Theo's chair.

"But I don't want to be a Dom. I haven't had time to look much up yet, but from what I could find, it's not who I am."

"Maybe not, but you're an alpha personality," Theo said.

"No, I'm not."

"Yes, you are," they said together.

"Well, apparently, you agree on at least one thing," I said.

Having a label slapped on me was annoying and made me feel defensive. When I thought of an alpha, it was the captain of the football team or, hell, even Nash. Annoying, pushy, arrogant, and wanting to be in control of everyone.

"Don't take it as an insult." Liam leaned forward to rest his arms on his knees. "It means you're naturally a leader, and more importantly, people are drawn to you and want to follow you."

"Okay...so why is that a bad thing?"

"What did I tell you in the kitchen," Liam asked.

I sighed as I ran through everything he had mentioned, and then the light switched on in my brain.

"It's your way. You're the one in control," I said, finally understanding, or at least partially.

"Being dominant and being a Dom are very different. For example, you and Nash are dominant, but I'm a Dom. I can't wrap my head around how this would ever work, but it's not just that. There are things I like that Theo is willing to give. I have no clue if you've even tried anything kinky, and I don't do vanilla."

"Wow, thanks for insulting me."

"Nothing wrong with vanilla if that's your flavor, but I'm more Rocky Road." He smirked. "That doesn't mean I'm going to throw you in the deep end. Theo's exaggerating. I wouldn't be doing my job if I did that."

"Okay, so give me some examples."

"Rough sex, for one," Theo said. "And I'm not talking like what I do to you. Liam will make you beg for mercy, and you'll swear you're going to die, and yet it somehow still ends up being the best experience of your life. But it's not for everyone."

That sounded extreme, and I shifted as I tried to picture what he could do to me.

Theo continued, pulling me out of my thoughts.

"Anal, for another. You need to be prepped for that. If not, you'll think you're dying or badly injured. Breath, blood, water, temperature, and role play. Primal which would be just great for you alone in the forest with him. I can't help but see that ending badly. Liam also loves to punish when you're out of line. You'd scratch his eyes out if he really disciplined you," Theo said, like Liam wasn't even in the room.

"Again, with the extremes." Liam glared at Theo. "Do you really think I'm going to start her out, hanging her from hooks and fucking her? Seriously, are you trying to tank any hope of us working? I don't get you."

"No, of course not," he said.

"Theo, you've done all the stuff you mentioned?"

I was genuinely curious about their relationship and not even sure what some of what they said meant.

"Yes, and lots more. Whips, floggers, nipple clamps, vibrators, anal beads, ball gags, shackled to an X and strapped to a swing. Everything that you can ever find on the lifestyle, we have at least tried once. Then, we picked what we enjoyed together and what worked for us. There are some things that even I can't get into, like needle-play and golden showers."

"Key word is tried. We experimented, and if we, one or the other, didn't like it, then we didn't do it again," Liam said, and Theo looked down at his feet.

My knee was bouncing, the nervousness getting the better of me. Alone in the woods with someone who would find it amusing to punish me and push every one of my limits was both intriguing and wholly terrifying.

"The part that Theo is conveniently leaving out is that I took care of him. As rough as I can be, it is my job to know what you can take and when it is too much. To train you to accept things like the toys and be your emotional, physical, and mental support not just in the bedroom but outside of it. I also care for your body with any after-care. My entire job is to bring us both the maximum amount of pleasure without pushing too far. If done right...there is nothing else like it. It's also part of my hesitation to the three of us. I need to be prepared and ready for that level of responsibility."

"I hadn't thought about that. I'm sorry," Theo said, and as the two of them looked at one another, I could feel a bit of the gap between them reduce.

"It's okay. I should've been more upfront with all my concerns." Liam shifted his stare to me. "If I'm going to do this, Ren, then I want to do it right."

I rubbed my forehead and needed to move. Pacing would help me put into words what was going on in my mind. Oddly, it always helped.

"What about what I saw at the cabin? That didn't look unusual or kinky, as you put it."

"That was a mild night, blowjobs and teasing. But even then, our roles remain the same as our more intense experiences. I'm the Dom, he's the Sub," Liam said.

"Then why aren't you both on the same page if this is all so wonderful? If what you do is look after him? Because Theo seems pretty miserable from where I'm standing."

Liam's jaw cracked as he clenched his teeth and glared at me. I thought he wouldn't answer, but he surprised me.

"Because for a Dom and Sub to work, we have to explore and agree on what we want. We laid down all the ground rules and were just fine."

"No, we weren't," Theo injected.

"Yes, we were. You didn't mention one word to me about anything else bothering you until...." Liam stopped talking, but I knew what he was going to say.

"Until I came along. Right?"

Liam held his hand out in my direction.

"See, she gets it," he said to Theo.

"Don't do that. Don't talk down to him." I put my hands on my hips and glared at Liam.

Liam burst out laughing, and Theo smirked.

"And that right there is the issue. What you just did there, Little Rabbit, is why you're an alpha personality."

"So be straight with me. Are you taking me out to the woods so you can hurt me enough that I give up the idea of the three of us?"

Liam shook his head.

"It's not about hurting you. I'm not a sadist, at least not all the time." I lifted a brow at him and immediately regretted it as he stood. "It's about learning what works for us. Finding common ground where we work outside of the three of us, and you with Blake and Myles."

"Why do I keep picturing a Lord of the Flies ending for all of us?"

Theo laughed, and it was good to see him smile.

"Before I agree to anything, I want to know what changed between you two. Explain this to me because I can't figure out why I am causing this rift when Theo said you'd shared girls before."

"I told you, you're not—"

Liam held up two fingers, stopping Theo mid-sentence.

It might not have seemed like much to anyone else, but I could see it now. Liam commanded, and Theo obeyed. They were right about one thing. If he held up two fingers like that to me, I was going to break them.

"I'll explain this as simply as I can." Liam crossed his arms, which added to his already imposing aura. "I am a Dom. Theo was a Sub, but he is no longer. There is a long list of different needs and personalities in the kink community. Theo has realized he's what is known as a switch."

"A what now?"

"A switch. Just the basics for now, or we will be here all night. Theo likes what I do to him and being my Sub, but he also likes to have control. Here is the issue. I need control, I will never give it up. Therefore, no matter how much Theo wants the same, it will never happen with me."

"But he is with me? I don't really remember Theo ordering me around."

"Yes. It can be more subtle than you might think. Tell me, has Theo told you to get on your knees?"

I shuffled, a little uncomfortable with the direct question. Liam walked a little closer, his eyes locked with mine, and the tension in the room notched up with each step he took.

"Has he told you that you're a good girl," he growled, and a shiver raced down my spine.

"Has he ordered you not to fucking come until he tells you to?"

Grabbing my arms, he pushed me back one step at a time until I hit the wall. My heart was in my throat. Was it suddenly hot in here? Liam towered over the top of me, his body so close that I could feel the heat he was giving off even though he was careful not to touch my skin.

"What would you do if I told you to get on your knees and suck my cock?"

My mind went completely blank.

"Liam, enough. Give her a minute," Theo said, and as Liam glanced at him, I was able to take a shaky breath.

"If she can't take a simple order, how would she handle anything else? Like consent to no consent."

"What's that," I asked, cursing my curious mind and the need to understand.

"Basically, it means that you consent to be fucked by me or who I choose, how I choose at any time, whether you like it or not. I could hand you off to six guys and jerk off watching you."

"Oh...I...um...."

Liam leaned in and whispered in my ear, the hair standing on the back of my neck, as he groaned.

"Be very sure you want this, Little Rabbit, very, very, sure."

I had to bite my lip to keep from shaking. The fear I expected, but the inferno in my gut and between my legs, I did not. Holy hell, so this was what Theo saw and why he was so addicted.

Liam stepped back.

"What's it going to be, Little Rabbit? None of this is going to work if we can't get on the same page."

My eyes bounced between the two of them.

"Let me make sure I understand. If we do something and I'm not comfortable or hate it...."

"Then we scrap it. Everything is about mutual pleasure, trust, and respect. I won't force you to do something you're not comfortable with, but I sure as hell am going to push you to your limits."

I licked my lips and decided to take a leap of faith. "Okay, I'll do it," I said.

Liam smirked, the corner of his lip pulling up.

"Well, alright then. We have a date."

Jesus, save me. What was I getting myself into?

Chapter 14

SEPTEMBER 17 – WEDNESDAY 8:10 AM

Myles

Mr. Martelli's bad day was my gain. Class was canceled, and I was on the hunt like a bloodhound for my Snowflake. Spending the day in bed with her was just what the doctor ordered to make me feel better.

My father had blissfully been staying away until today. No clue if it was because Lawrence had him running all over the place or if it was because he was trying hard to find a way to get Devin back. Whatever the reason, I hadn't had to deal with the insane bastard.

My phone felt like it was burning a hole in my pocket, but it was going to be ignored for as long as possible.

Owen's text summons were never a good thing, but the tone of his last text was more erratic than normal. I was leaning into the fact that I was supposed to have class all day, and he couldn't come on the property and force me to leave. The beauty of being eighteen was that I could officially write a list of people who were not to be admitted. I'd marched into the office on day one and handed them my father's name and a picture for good measure.

Dean Henry had taken the information with his eyebrow raised. He didn't say a word before nodding. It was a small thing, but it meant that there was one place on this godforsaken earth where my father couldn't reach me no matter how hard he tried.

"Hey man, what are ya doing," I asked as Blake caught up to me at the elevator.

"Le cours de français est annulé, j'ai donc pensé visiter Ren."

"Ya want to say that again, but in English this time?"

"Oh merde, désolé. Class was canceled. I'm heading up to see Ren." He narrowed his eyes at me suspiciously. "Why are you out of class?"

"My class was canceled, too. Huh, that's kind of weird, isn't it," I asked and stepped into the elevator as the doors opened.

Blake shrugged.

"Maybe Ms. Costa and Mr. Martelli ate the same meal," he said, and my brain conjured an image of Lady and the Tramp.

"Question, why haven't ya used any of that smooth talkin' French on Ren?"

He gave me the cockiest grin.

"Who says I haven't?"

"Fucker...I need to up my game," I swore as he laughed.

"I even sang to her in French."

Annoyed, I crossed my arms.

"Okay, ya can stop now. Yer just showing off. No one likes a show-off."

"Ren did."

"Don't make me toss yer ass out of the elevator," I said, making him laugh harder.

Asshole. How was this jerk, my best friend?

"How are things at home," I asked, wanting to change the topic, and Blake sighed.

"Weird. Ever since Theo and I found Lawrence there acting all shady, it's felt like my mom is different. But I can't put my finger on how. She is still baking up a storm and bugging us to have Ren come over for Thanksgiving this year. Lawrence isn't holding his annual dinner. Something about being out of town. I don't know. Maybe I'm reading too much into it and looking for something that isn't there."

I grabbed his arm before he could unlock the door to his room.

"Nah man, if ya think there is somethin' going on, then listen to yer gut," I said, releasing him.

He opened the door, and we both froze as we stared at Snowflake.

"Sweet Lord, thank you," I mumbled, watching Ren's bare legs swing.

She was lying on Blake's bed, her earphones on, wearing only the blue lace underwear I'd gotten her and a matching tank top. She was watching something on her laptop while dutifully taking notes, and I had to adjust myself. It was impossible not to walk around hard half the day when I was thinking about her.

Blake quietly closed the door, and we snuck across the room. The same shocked expression on Blake's face had to be on mine as we got close enough to see what was on Ren's screen. There, clear as day, was some BDSM porno with a woman tied up in ropes and hanging from a metal grate. She had a ball gag in her mouth while the guy walked around her with a whip in his hand.

It wasn't that Ren was watching porn, which was out of character, or even the type that was on the screen that made me smile. It was the fact that Snowflake was researching what Liam had told her to with as much seriousness as chemistry class. She scribbled fast across her notepad.

Peeling off my school sweater, I tossed it aside and inched closer to see an entire legend with multiple toys and positions sketched that even I couldn't name. There was a giant X in the middle of her page, with a diagram outlining what each part was called and a list of sexual ideas as well as generic terms and questions.

"Now, this is research."

Snowflake screamed and jumped like a scared cat. She slammed the laptop shut and leaped up so fast that I thought she would actually end up clinging to the ceiling. Her silver eyes were as wide as saucers, and her hands were up in a fighting stance.

"Myles...Blake...fuck," she growled and slumped. "I might kill both of you."

"Yer so fuckin' adorable," I said, plucking the headphones off her head and pulling her in tight to my body. Her eyes went from terrified to filled with desire with a blink. "I know a much better way for ya to study," I growled, and her cheeks turned bright red under the healing bruises.

"Do ya want us to give you a little taste of what it'll be like ta be caught by Liam?"

Sliding my hand up her back, she trembled under my fingers. There was nothing sweeter than my Snowflake responding to me like that. I grabbed her neck, and she sucked in a sharp breath that went straight to my cock.

"What do ya want to learn? How about a little degradation? Is that what ya want slut? Ta be our whore?"

"Um...a...."

Ren licked her lips as Blake walked around behind her. She

glanced between the two of us and opened her mouth, but no words came out. Placing a finger under her chin, I made her look up at me.

"Is that a yes, Snowflake?" She nodded. "Say it. Say ya want us to use ya like the little slut ya are."

"Yes. Show me."

Blake nipped at the soft, sensitive skin on her neck, and Ren pressed closer to me. I'd grown used to seeing Blake touch her, and it now seemed second nature to have him in the room and fuck her. It even turned me on to see Snowflake's eyes flutter closed as he toyed with her, his hand snaking up under her shirt to tease her nipples into hard peaks. His mouth moved up the side of her throat as he licked a line up to her earlobe. I gently kissed her lips, careful of her nose and the bruising still on her face.

"Get on your knees and take our cocks out," I ordered.

She hesitated, with Blake still touching her. Grabbing her arm, I tugged her away and smacked her ass hard enough that she jumped and yelped.

"Yer not moving fast enough slut."

Her eyes flared with anger that was mixing with her desire, and I'd just found my new favorite look.

"If yer not able to handle that little smack, Snowflake, then ya better back out now. Liam is going to tan yer ass until ya can't sit down."

"He's right. I haven't seen him in action, but Theo has come home after a weekend away looking like Liam dragged him behind his car. He usually stays in bed for an entire day. I know you really want to do this and feel it will be the thing to fix them, but what if you go through all of this and they still don't work out," Blake asked, and Ren chewed her bottom lip.

"Then they don't work out, but at least I know that I tried all I could first."

I glanced at Blake.

"Look, we're happy to continue. More than happy, actually," I said, pointing to the prominent bulge in my pants. "But why is Liam trying to top ya anyway? He has Theo for that, and you can be Theo's bottom. I'm not understanding this."

She lifted her hands and let them drop.

"He says that he needs to trust me and to feel as comfortable with me as he does, Theo. Even if the two of us on our own is not a regular thing."

"Snowflake, it's yer call. We'll be here no matter what ya decide, but regardless of what Liam says, I think it's a bad idea. So...what are ya wantin' to do?"

She wore her determination like I would pull on a sweater, and she showed it again as she dropped to her knees.

"We continue. You didn't tell me why you're both out of class, though."

"Sluts aren't privy to that information," I said, and I knew that there was a good chance I'd pay for that comment later.

Blake stood beside me, his expression silently asking how far I was going to take this. I lifted a shoulder and let it drop. As far as I was concerned, I'd push until she said it was too much. But I'd be lying if I said it didn't worry me what Liam would do to her alone in the woods. More importantly, what her mental state would be like when she got back. Liam believed in facing your demons and what that would look like...kinda terrified me.

SEPTEMBER 17 – WEDNESDAY 8:40 AM

Ren

Being called slut, whore, and bitch was enraging. It was taking all my willpower not to punch them both. Yet my body still loved their attention and betrayed me at every turn. I was equal parts livid and so turned on that I might combust with the throbbing pressure. They were far rougher than normal, and at first, I tried to shy away from the slaps against my bare breasts that stung my nipples. I was positive that I'd have permanent handprints on my ass from them both.

It also brought up images of being pulled over Nash's lap, and that was another whole layer of issues that I had no interest in unpacking.

"Ah," I cried out.

Myles had my arms pinned over my head and back against the wall with my feet forced as far apart as they would go, just like the girl in the video. He was driving me insane as he alternated between sucking and then pinching or smacking my nipples. The entire time, Blake was relentless with his tongue. Swirling it around my clit and teasing me with his fingers until I was sure that I was going to go insane with the need to release.

"Please let me come," I begged. "Please."

"Ya really think a dirty little whore like you gets to come before us," Myles growled, and the tweak to my nipple sent a zing of electricity through me.

It was all I could do to stay on my feet, with my knees shaking uncontrollably. Somehow found the willpower. My body was soaked in sweat, and every muscle hurt from the constant pushing for more. They had me hold positions I'd never been in before, and the sheer roughness of their assault took my breath away.

Every single nerve ending was on fire, and just when I didn't think that I could take anymore. Myles kissed my cheek.

"You've got this," he whispered.

His amber eyes shimmered with mischief and pride. Digging deep, I nodded that I could continue and moaned as Blake sucked harder.

"Come on his face and be quiet about it. I don't want to hear one filthy sound come out of yer mouth."

Blake's fingers pushed deeper, and I almost screamed but choked it off. Somehow, I didn't even whimper as I came. Hips bucking, my pussy ground against Blake's face. My legs gave out with waves of intense pleasure. Myles let my arms slowly go, and I crumpled in a heap on the floor, panting hard.

"Get on yer knees, and take our come like a good come slut," Myles growled.

I didn't think I could move, but I managed to push myself up on shaking limbs to kneel in front of them.

"Now open your mouth and leave it open."

My boys groaned as their hands flew up and down their hard cocks, and impossibly my traitorous pussy tingled at the sight of them. They each braced a hand on the wall and towered over me, their eyes filled with a dark desire.

The guys and girl in the movie we'd left running began yelling as they came, and it set off a chain reaction.

"Fuck, yes," Blake moaned, and the first jet of his release landed on my cheek. The second went straight into my mouth, and I swallowed it, smiling before opening it again for them.

"Oh fuck, fuck, fuck," Myles growled.

I jerked back as something hot hit me in the eye. It stung like I'd just been pepper sprayed and forced me to snap my lids and mouth closed.

"Shit, sorry, ahhh, I can't stop," he said as more rained down on me until it was as if I'd been coated in hot frosting.

It hung off my nose, chin, and lips while more slid down my neck. There were no words to describe what I was feeling, but there was no way they were ever doing that to me again. My eye hurt, which only added insult to injury.

"Shit, Snowflake, I'm sorry. I didn't mean to get ya in the eye."

"Washroom," I said, gagging when my lips gummed together.

Myles helped me stand, apologizing non-stop. He turned on the shower and then guided me to the curtain. I stumbled my way in, holding the wall for support.

"Do ya want me to help wash it off?" I shook my head. "Snowflake, I'm so, so sorry."

"I'll be fine, but never again," I said and stepped under the warm spray.

It kind of made sense that I'd end up with a swollen come eye to add to my broken nose and bruised cheeks. This was not my week.

SEPTEMBER 17 – WEDNESDAY 9:00 PM

Nash

The club was almost ready for our grand opening. A final push to completion included refacing the outside of the building and resurfacing the shitty, cracked, and overgrown parking lot. Our budget had been blown, much to Liam's dismay, in order to draw the attention of the right clientele. Not that it mattered now. I could've purchased the entire street and not made a dent in the money from Mr. Genovese.

"I have to hand it to you, Nora. You have incredible taste," I said, stalking from one room to the next.

Each offered a new experience depending on personal preferences.

"Oh, a compliment from Nash Collier. Whatever shall I do?" She smiled, pulling on her coat.

"Don't get used to it," I said from behind the bar.

The massive slab stretched across the entire lower level. Its surface was a sleek black and silver with red lights installed beneath. The glow gave this place a dark and gritty feel while remaining classy and upscale.

"I wouldn't dream of it." She grabbed her purse and looked around. "The final touches will be done this week. There were a few things that I thought of after, but totally fixable. As soon as the outside is done you can open for business."

"Excellent. I'm aiming for a Halloween grand opening."

"Flashy and a huge party night, great idea," she said.

"So, when are you moving in?"

"Not for a few weeks. I told them to concentrate on everything else first."

I'd always liked Liam's sister, but we were never close. I should've known that, just like her brother, we'd find an easy rhythm. She was his female version and almost as good with numbers. What the hell did that family drink?

"See you later, Nash. I trust that I can leave you to lock up." Nora winked as she walked to the door.

"Get the hell out of here."

"Going."

The door opened, and the temporary bells jingled like Santa's fucking sleigh.

Bending down, I tore open a box of custom black bottles. Unfortunately, I was still waiting on my liquor license. Some palms would need to be greased, but we should be set before the kickoff. If this place did well, then the plan was to open a second club in Seattle, and then who knows. Skies were the limit. Our alcohol was coming in from a few different distilleries in the area. Some of them were owned by families loyal to the council, while others were independents. This allowed me to build relationships with some of the smaller families from the ground up.

Loyalty. That was the key to all my plans. Mr. Genovese had told me I needed to cultivate a base that preferred working with me without attacking anything they had in place with my father. It allowed neutrality until the time was right. I'd spent every available night meeting, wining and dining the heads of families, signing contracts, and laying the groundwork for my future.

Mr. Genovese, a man I hardly knew, had laid out a blueprint for success. In a couple days, he made me feel like family, gave me logical business advice, and more trust than my father had in all nineteen years of my life.

Those damn bells sounded again.

"What did you forget this time?"

"So, this is where you've been spending all your time and money," my father drawled. His voice was thick with sarcasm, and I slowly stood up to face him.

"How did you find it?"

"Please...I know everything," he said, glancing around and it wasn't hard to read the criticizing expression written all over his face.

It took everything I had not to tell him just how wrong he was, but I kept that shit locked down.

"Well, you didn't know for almost a year, so...I guess your moles are slacking." His annoyed glare found me at the bar.

"You missed the meeting with the new adventure capitalists that I arranged."

Straight to his point then.

"No, I didn't. I never intended on going."

He narrowed his gaze at me, his dress shoes echoing on the shiny new floor at his approach. My knife felt heavy in my pocket, reminding me that I had it, just in case.

"You'd insult our investors that way?"

I shrugged.

"Why not? You did when you stood me up on purpose to fuck Vicky on your desk. Do you not remember that? Or maybe it was the night you were tied up and being whipped by my mother. It's hard to keep your social calendar straight."

"Watch your fucking tone with me," he growled.

"No, I don't think I will. You made it clear that you weren't going to hand over the reins of the family, company, or council to me. How did you put it? I was nothing more than a disappointment, and you needed to make more heirs. Something like that, wasn't it?"

Grabbing more bottles, I set them up on the shelves behind the bar, already picturing what it would look like with the mirrored background and LED lighting.

"Did you really think I was going to hang around and beg for whatever scraps you tossed down? Or let you humiliate me by forcing me to call Vicky mommy?"

Happy with the placement, I faced my father and his furious glare.

"I told you that would never happen. I meant it."

"You'd rather work a bar for the rest of your life?"

"It's a club, not a bar, and no, I have much larger plans. This is just the beginning."

He put his hands on the new bar top. A quick glance down, and I was tempted to cut off his fucking fingers that were leaving prints behind.

"And where do you think you got the money to pay for all this? You owe me."

"Are you referring to my trust fund?"

"What else would I be talking about? I know you cleaned it out."

"I did, but it was just a loan. I don't want one penny from you. Every cent has been returned. You didn't know that," I asked, not able to keep the sarcasm from my tone. "I thought you knew everything."

He straightened to his full height, trying to intimidate me, but there was a thread of worry in his arrogant façade. His mind was running, desperately attempting to figure out how I had managed to get that much money. I smiled, ready to deliver my final blows.

"I also cut you a check for my car, truck, and everything else I own. You can check with your accountant. He took the payments and cashed them already." I snapped my fingers. "Oh, and here is something else you didn't know. I've moved out, and no, I'm not telling you where my new place is. I don't want people I don't like dropping in unannounced."

"You fucking piece of shit," he snarled, his hands curling into fists. "You will always owe the council."

"You're right, and I already have that arranged."

"What the fuck are you talking about? I didn't sign any deal with you," he said.

"You didn't? You might want to check what you signed regarding the new bus line. Seems the council, including you, signed off on my company's ownership. I've already secured our route with safe passage from California. Which took some work, considering Owen and Devin are at odds with the Mikhailovs. I'll shave fifty percent off the top for the muscle to keep our route free from issues, pay the drivers, and cover any maintenance on the buses, and my cut. The council gets the remaining fifty percent." Leaning back against the wine fridge, I crossed my arms. "That more than fulfills my obligation to the council of the normal thirty percent. Can't argue with that...actually you could try, but then you'd just look like a vengeful, greedy old man who went back on his word to stick it to his son in a family dispute of your own making. You would look like someone that no longer has the council's best interests at heart when I so clearly just want to help everyone prosper." I laid my hand over my heart.

"You son of a bitch," he growled, looking like he might actually try to leap over the bar.

"In most cases, that would be taken as an insult, but this time you're correct. My mother is a bitch."

"You'll pay for this, son."

"First, I don't know why you're pissed off. I've managed to stand on my own, without your money and have reimbursed every dime you've spent on me other than food. That's hard to quantify, but since you did help create me, the least you can do is put in for the food I ate over the last nineteen years. Second, you're the one who told me you had no intention of having me take over as head of the family. You got what you wanted. I won't challenge you for the crown, and you can give it to whatever kid you manage to conceive at your age. Lastly, don't call me son again. You've never been a father to me. I'm a man now and don't need your approval."

He smiled, but there was no warmth or humor in his eyes.

"Alright, Nash, you want to swim with the big fish in the pond... so be it, but I promise you'll regret humiliating me like this."

"Just be sure not to burn yourself while you're focused on revenge. The council may not be happy if that happens." I smirked. "I'm proving to be quite the asset."

My father was predictable when it came to his fears. His first move would be to circle the wagons and ensure that all the prominent families were on his side with no intention of canceling contracts with Collier Enterprises. Then, he would try to bring in more money for the major shareholders to make them happy, but to do that, he would need to take the company public. That was what I was after.

If you couldn't take on the head of the snake, then you started at the tail and worked your way up.

"Take care, Nash."

The jingle of the bell was more ominous this time as the door opened, but fuck that felt good.

"You too, Dad. I'll be waiting," I whispered to the empty room.

SEPTEMBER 18 – THURSDAY 10:15 AM

R^{en}

> R: What the hell do you mean you're thinking of dropping out of school? You have like 9 months left, and then you never have to see the inside of a high school again.

This was not the message I was expecting when I texted Lizzy this morning. Thankfully, I still had some time before Russian class started to get to the bottom of this.

L: I know, but it's not that simple.

R: It is that simple. What is going through your head?

L: You wouldn't get it, and don't talk to me like you're my mum.

Taking a deep breath, I tried not to act like the worried parent that she accused me of being, but it was hard. I hated being so far away from her, and this was not like Lizzy, not at all.

R: Sorry, you're just taking me by surprise. Why wouldn't I understand?

The bubbles came and went a few times before she finally responded.

L: I'm failing all my classes.

R: How is that even possible?

L: See, this is why I haven't said anything to you. We can't all be geniuses, you know.

R: I didn't mean that. I just meant that you always got decent grades, so what's going on? Maybe I can help.

L: No, just stop. It's my decision, not yours. You can't make this all better.

R: Lizzy, please let me help you. Whatever the reason is, we promised to get through everything together.

L: Like how we got through you being shot at together and then having to go on the run? You mean like that? Because I don't remember you giving me a heads up about any of that.

R: That's not fair.

There was a long pause and no bubbles. Was that it? Was she done talking? My heart hurt to think that something had happened to her, and she was choosing to deal with it alone. Lizzy was smart and had such a bright future, but if she dropped out, that would all disappear. What was so bad that she couldn't talk to me, her best friend, about it?

L: Look…Boo. I love you. I really do, you know that. But I just can't deal with this right now. I'll talk to you later. Xoxo

R: Lizzy, talk to me. Please.

R: Lizzy?

R: Pleeeeeease

Dammit! I wanted to toss my phone across the classroom and then fly to Canada to find out what the hell was going on with the person I trusted most in this world. She'd always been there for me, and now she needed me and wouldn't tell me what had her so willing to throw her life away. This helpless feeling was becoming way too familiar.

"Don't you look chipper this morning," Nash said as he sat down beside me.

Perfect timing. A little verbal sparring with Nash was just what I needed to get my mind off Lizzy. I turned my glare on him, and he narrowed his eyes as his brow pulled together.

"What the hell happened to your eye? It's all red."

Of course, he'd notice that.

"Nothing, I got something in it."

If Myles or Blake told him what happened, I was going to kill them both. Nash did not need any more ammunition.

"That was a hell of a something. Are you sure you're okay?"

The mortification was inching higher.

"Yes, I'm fine."

He leaned closer.

"It kind of looks like pink eye. Maybe you should go see the nurse."

"Oh my god. It's not pink eye," I yelled, and the two girls just walking into the otherwise empty classroom looked over.

"Wow, touchy. Forget I said anything."

Nash turned away and pulled out his computer for class.

"I'm sorry, I'm fine. It's just that I hate everyone looking at me like I'm some science experiment gone wrong."

He snorted.

"Oh, we all know what happened, but I get it. So, you're really not going to tell me what you got in it?"

"No."

"Fine," he mimicked my voice, and a sarcastic smirk tugged at the corner of his mouth.

I really wanted to ask if he already knew, but that was probably what he wanted. Then he could trap me into telling him. God dammit, I hated that anytime I said a word to Nash about anything, I had to think about it six ways to Sunday. A thought occurred to me as I drummed my fingers on the table. Nash seemingly was able to accomplish whatever he wanted, but would he do something for me?

Turning toward him, I moved closer and kept my voice low.

"Nash, do you have contacts who are good at finding stuff out?"

"Depends. What are you trying to find out?"

The gleam in his eye said that this was going to cost me. Reminding myself that this was for Lizzy, I swallowed my pride.

"Something is going on with my friend in Canada. She's always been a B plus to A minus student, and today...she suddenly says that she's thinking of dropping out of school."

He shrugged.

"Okay. It happens all the time. She could just be struggling with senior year and wants out."

"No," I said, shaking my head. "You don't understand. It's not like her to make rash decisions. She had plans and goals and was focused on going to college. You don't wake up one morning and decide you don't want any of that anymore. Something happened. I know my friend like you know your guys. Please, I wouldn't ask you unless this was extremely important to me."

He sighed and leaned back crossing his arms as his look turned devious. Within seconds, my pulse began to race.

"Text me her name and where she lives. I'll see what I can do, but...you have to do something for me."

Shit, I knew it. "What do you want?"

"Our club is having its grand opening Halloween night...I want you to come as my plus one," he said.

Would wonders never cease? I forced myself not to smile or say thank God.

"You thought I was going to ask for something sexual, didn't you?"

"What? Noooo, not you," I said, with the biggest bullshit smile.

Nash snorted in disbelief but didn't say any more. I really needed to stop this flirty stuff with him. It was leading nowhere good.

"Thanks for doing this."

"Don't thank me yet." We looked up as Mr. Romanovich walked in. "You may not like what I find."

He had to say that, didn't he? Now, my mind was running non-stop, picturing the worst of the worst. It had to be something terrible. There were very few things on my mental list bad enough to make Lizzy quit school. If someone had hurt her...they were going to see my newfound mean side.

SEPTEMBER 18 – THURSDAY 12:05 PM

Ren

Trying to be discreet, I peeked up at Nash again. We were on the path leading to the main building for lunch after Russian class. He glanced down before rolling his eyes.

"Out with it, Davies, what do you want now?"

"Who says I want anything else?"

He stopped and crossed his arms as he waited for me to crack.

"I know that look. Most girls give it to me when they want my cock. But this is you, so what are you trying not to ask?"

Did it bother me that he knew me so well? I chose not to look at that too deeply.

"Fine."

Grabbing his arm, I dragged him over to the benches, away from prying eyes.

"Okay, I was wrong. You do want my cock," Nash said, sliding his arm around my waist as he sat down. In a single, smooth maneuver pulled me between his legs. "Not where I would've picked our first time, but I'm easy," he said, and I shivered at the raspiness in his voice.

"Don't I know it?"

My voice was laced with sarcasm, but the eyebrow raise told me that he had picked up on the hint of interest that I couldn't help. Fuck.

While my mind still held up and waved red flags like a marching band, my body had other ideas. I didn't trust myself with Nash and quickly stepped back out of his reach. Each flag had a very good reason to never get into bed with him. Myles and Blake had both called me slut yesterday, and I was starting to believe it. It was imperative for my sanity that I get these errant thoughts of Nash under control.

"Before you get off on another tangent about our nonexistent sexcapades..." Nash smirked at me but remained quiet. "I want to ask you about Fiona, and saying something in class seemed like a bad idea. I've asked Myles a dozen times, and he says he can't say what happened and to trust him. First her, and now Lizzy, I just...I need to know."

He looked around and crooked a finger at me. Shit.

I stepped in close enough for him to touch me again before he whispered. "My rule is I don't do or say anything without something in return." He caressed his fingers down my arm. "Are you really sure you want to ask another favor already?"

Crossing my arms and staring into his blue eyes, I knew this was a bad idea, and yet, I was going to ask anyway.

"Okay...what do you want now?"

He patted his lap, and my eyes dropped down following his movements. This wasn't helping the rapidly spreading rush of warmth I was fighting.

"I don't understand."

"Myles has never invited you to sit on his lap? He's slacking, and I'm thoroughly ashamed of him," he teased, and that evil glint was back in his eye, making me squirm.

"You want me to sit on your lap?"

"Yes."

"Right now?"

"Why not?"

"In front of everyone passing by?"

"Can't get anything past you."

His snark was grating on me, and I rolled my eyes.

"Shut up. If I do this, do you promise to keep your hand out from under my kilt?"

"I promise nothing when you're the one who needs something from me," he drawled and licked his lower lip.

This was a really bad idea.

"Forget it," I said and turned to walk away.

Nash didn't let me get far. I squealed as he pulled me back, and I ended up in the exact position I hadn't wanted to be in...sitting in his lap. My arm naturally wrapped around his neck, and all I could hear was the whooshing of my blood in my ears.

It was impossible to ignore the almost angry, sexual energy that was always around Nash. His body was hot when we touched, but that didn't stop me from shivering. Nash's eyes were trained on the open buttons of my blouse. God, it felt like he was touching me, and I couldn't help wiggling.

"That's better, Princess. This is how you ask me for a favor from now on," he whispered.

If it weren't for his hands holding me in place, I would've leaped up and ran for the hills. At least, that was what I tried to convince myself.

"Fuck, how do you always smell so good," Nash groaned, burying his head in the side of my neck.

My mouth ran dry, and I sat frozen on his lap like a deer caught in headlights.

"We can't do this," I said.

"Do what? We're just sitting here," he said, his breath seductively fanning my ear.

"You know exactly what I mean and what you're doing." I glared at him with zero effect.

As hard as I tried, my voice just didn't sound pissed off or annoyed. Any other day, I'd smack him and walk away, but my defenses were down, and he had found the tiny crack in my armor. He was also the one who had ordered Myles not to tell me a damn thing, so he'd probably planned this exact scenario. What I really needed was a Nash repellant, like bear spray, but stronger.

"Just ask your question, Princess," he growled as he stared into my eyes from inches away.

Nothing wanted to work right. Not my mouth, my body, or even my brain. It was as if someone had come along, grabbed all the different colored wires, and scrambled them up, short-circuiting everything.

"I should just go."

His hands tightened.

"No, you should tell me what you want from me."

"I...I...I can't think with you doing that."

I pointedly looked at his hand, resting on the bare skin of my thigh and sliding ever so slowly up and down. He smirked.

"Princess, I thought you weren't susceptible to me," he challenged with his fake shocked expression.

"I'm not."

"Then, you wouldn't mind me doing this," he said, inching his hand up a little higher. My breath hitched. "And this wouldn't bother you either."

Dropping his head to my neck, he growled like an animal against my skin, sending a vibration through my body that had the last of my resolve falling away. His fingers squeezed a little tighter.

"No...of course not," I managed to mumble, but even I called myself a liar as I gripped his shirt, not caring if I wrinkled the once perfectly pressed fabric.

"Fuck you make me hard, Princess. So fucking hard. I should spank you again just for that."

My pussy clenched, and I shook my head, trying to rid the hormonal haze that surrounded us. Nash was having none of that, and I gasped as his hand slid all the way up my kilt.

"We need to stop this," I argued, even as he pushed my thighs further apart with no resistance.

"Do we? Tell me why?"

There were a thousand excellent reasons, and not one of them came to mind other than adding him to the group would be like dropping a bomb in the middle of all my happiness. Although Myles and Blake kept teasing me like they expected this to happen. This was all too much. It was messing with my head.

"Nash...."

"Yes, Princess?"

He teasingly ran his finger up the front of my panties, and the surrounding noise and why this shouldn't happen was quickly fading away.

"Nash, please...."

"Careful, Princess, you keep moaning my name like that, and I'll start to think you want me."

"You always have to ruin a moment, don't you?"

I shook my head and smoothed out his wrinkled shirt.

"I have a talent. What can I say?" He moved his hands so I could stand.

Glancing around and fixing my uniform, I tried to calm my racing pulse. He actually seemed a little disappointed.

"You really are trying to kill me, Princess."

A smart remark was on the tip of my tongue, but I managed to hold it back.

"I have no idea what you mean. You pulled me onto your lap, but if you want to blame me and it will get me my answer, then fine, blame away."

"Fuck, you're a trip," he growled and adjusted his pants. *Don't ask me how I managed to keep my eyes on his.* "Fine, but if you want an answer, you need to promise that you'll never mention her by name again. Call her the red-headed wonder. I really don't care, but

never mention her name...for all our safety," he whispered, but it was
an order.

The conspiratorial tone had me looking around to see who might
be listening.

"Okay, done. Never again."

"She's fine," Nash said as he stood, forcing me to step back or be
in his space all over again. One *Close Encounter of the Third Kind*
with Nash was all I could handle in a day.

"That's it?"

"What else do you want to know," he asked, turning to walk
away.

"That is such a guy answer," I grumbled, shading my face from
the bright sunlight that hurt my eyes but felt wonderfully warm at
the same time.

Nash chuckled. "What else do you need to know? She's alive,
isn't that enough?"

"No, far from it. Where is she? How did you make that happen?
Is it just her or her whole family? Will your father kill Myles if he
finds out? Will Owen find out and what will that mean?"

Nash stopped walking, forcing me to stop as well. He waited for
a group to pass before lowering his voice.

"You don't need to know any of that."

I was going to murder him in his sleep. That was all there was to
it. Balling my hands, I opened my mouth to spout off, but Nash cut
me off.

"But...I will give you a few details. Just remember, the more you
know, the more you're at risk."

"Understood."

"She's here in the States. It was all staged with the help of a few
families loyal to Myles's mother. They hate Owen and suspect that
her death was no accident. The rest of her family is in Bulgaria
because no one would ever look for them there, and they will help

when it's time to make the final push for control. That's all I'm telling you."

Before he could march off again, I grabbed his arm. Nash stared at my hand before his gaze darted up to mine. He didn't say it, and he didn't need to. The look in his eyes clearly said that if I didn't drop my hand, he was going to drag me into the bushes and finish what we started on the picnic table. Letting him go, I crossed my arms to avoid the temptation.

"Where in the States? Can I speak to her?" Nash rubbed the back of his neck. "Please. I feel partially responsible for this happening. If I'd never met Myles, then she would still be safe."

"Guilt is a weakness," he said. "Don't let it cloud your judgment on what's actually important."

"Maybe, or maybe it helps us make better choices in the future."

His lip twitched.

"Fine, she's in California, staying with your extended family." *What the hell?*

"What? But...but...."

Nash rolled his eyes and his shoulders.

"Relax. First of all, I would bet my life that it wasn't them who killed your mom. Second, Nathaniel owed me a favor, and to keep her safe, she needed to not only be in a location where no one would look for her but with a powerful family hard to attack. Now, I'm going to go and jerk off since I'm still hard, and you won't lift that skirt for me. So unless you've changed your mind and you want to get on your knees, shoo, little princess, shoo." He flicked his fingers at me like I was an insect.

"Asshole," I growled.

"You love it," he shot back as he kept walking.

You'd think by now that I'd be used to the random comments that came out of nowhere, but no. The worst part was the scene playing out in my mind.

"Nash?" I called after him as he veered right at the fork that would take him to the parking lot. There were some things you just had to have the answer to, or in this case, some things that I needed to hear out loud even though I knew the answer.

"Yes, Princess," he said with a heavy sigh.

"Why did you tell Myles not to tell me that?"

He smiled wide.

"Isn't it obvious?"

I cocked my head, keeping my expression neutral.

"Because then you'd be forced to ask me. And if there is one thing that I love, Princess...it's watching you squirm when you need my help." Smirking, he stuffed his hands in his pockets and wandered off, just missing Myles as he poked his head out the front door.

"Are ya all good? I was startin' to wonder what was taking ya so long," Myles said, softly kissing my cheek.

He looked up and noticed Nash leaving. Then those gorgeous amber eyes were on me. Myles lifted a brow.

"Yeah, I'm okay. Nash was telling me about F...um...our red-headed...Irish...friend."

Myles laughed. "Did ya just call her a rif?"

My cheeks flamed hot as he continued to laugh. "It was all I could think of."

"Ya know, it's actually kind of genius. Anyone listenin' would think we're talkin' music. Good job, Snowflake." Myles linked our fingers together and rubbed his thumb over my skin. "I'm glad ya finally know that was weighing on me. Come on, I'm starvin'."

Chapter 17

Liam

Despite being a skeptic by nature, Nash had never given me a reason to question his decisions until recently. He was hiding things...big things...life-altering things. I could sense that shit a mile away.

He still refused to talk about his summer trip. That was when I really started to worry. It was too short to be a real vacation and too long to be a simple meeting.

He saw someone and there were negotiations involved before he returned. Whatever it was and whoever it was with was only a guess at this point, but I had my suspicions. If I was right, and it was Mr. Genovese, then why was he keeping all of us on the outside for so long? Was it because we wouldn't like the deal he made? That thought bothered me the most. I was the numbers guy, evaluating the risks with an ace up my sleeve for every scenario. It was normal for us all to have our secrets but not for Nash to shut us out completely. If Nash continued to keep me on the outside, I would lose my ability to plan for emergencies or contingencies. We'd always been tight-knit, and I was his right hand, so his secretive behavior was adding to my already foul mood.

"Do you really think this is a smart idea having them here?"

I nodded toward the small group of guys that Nash had me pick out of the recruits. There were six in total, mingling with Theo, Blake, and Myles, but the two standouts were Rory and Cory. *Fuck, that was funny.*

They were the soldiers that I'd found to be the most dedicated and had brought countless pieces of information forward to help us. Through background checks, being followed off and on, and personal devices duplicated, there hadn't been a single oops, leak, or concern. That didn't mean that including them in a major meeting was a good idea.

"Do you not trust them," Nash asked as he ran a hand down the front of his suit.

"I trust them as much as I do anyone except you, of course. But this is a huge step."

Nash looked over at me, and I had to give it to him. He had dressed the part. The black tailored suit and new tattoos on his hands gave him a similar vibe to other heads of family.

"Do you trust Theo?"

Pressing my lips together, I crossed my arms, not wanting to discuss Theo right now. He was on the other side of the room, and the new lights that Nash had installed in the club kept him half in light and half in shadow. It suited him, and my craving for him threatened to steal my sanity.

As addictive now as he was the first time that we were roughhousing, and I saw him as more than my friend. Theo's blond hair was perfectly styled, his green eyes bright and full of unparalleled intelligence. Under the crisp suit was a bad boy that very few knew about and a body that could keep me hard for days.

"Yes, I do," I finally answered when Nash continued staring at me.

"And his opinion?"

"Of course. What is this an interrogation?"

Nash raised an eyebrow and smirked. "Very touchy subject, apparently."

"Can I punch you? It'll make me feel better, and maybe some of the touchy will leave my body."

"Maybe after the meeting. The point that I was trying to make is that Theo felt it was time we brought a few more into the inner circle, and I agree. So why are you second-guessing the decision?"

Turning to face Nash, I leaned against the wall.

"Because I'm not sure I trust your judgment lately," I said, and his face turned to stone. "Don't give me that look. You're keeping secrets."

"I've always kept secrets."

"Yes, but not big ones and not from me. Our mutual trust is what has always allowed me to do my job flawlessly. I've been cut off at the knees, Nash, and I don't fucking like it," I said.

"Are we still talking about us?"

"Don't deflect or make this about Theo." Nash looked away and sighed. "Do you deny it?"

"Would you believe me if I did?"

"No."

"Then no, I don't deny it. But that doesn't mean I can tell you anything." He locked eyes with me. "Yet...I will soon."

"Answer me this, and all you have to do is nod your head. Does it have to do with Mr. Genovese?"

"Fuck, I hate you sometimes," Nash growled, confirming my suspicions.

"I knew it. You were squirrely when he was at the school, and you didn't say a single word about what went down with Vicky. That's not like you. You normally would've danced and rubbed that shit in her face."

He scoffed. "Squirrely? I didn't even move, and who the hell says I didn't rub it in her face? Just because you didn't see it happen doesn't mean I didn't."

I smiled and rolled out my shoulders.

"Fine, be defensive. I felt the vibes coming off you. I'm in tune with your aura. Does that make you feel better?"

"Don't ever fucking say that to me again," Nash ordered, making me laugh.

Theo glanced over, and my heart rate doubled with just the one inquisitive look. Fuck me.

"You can't say a word, not a single fucking word. I mean it, or everything we've been working for will fall apart. Just trust me."

"Understood, and you will tell me all the details soon, but Nash...." I waited until I had his full attention. "Don't keep shit from me again. I need to know what we are up against at all times, and I'd never, not for anyone, break your confidence."

He gripped my shoulder and nodded as the door opened and our guest arrived.

Louis Kessler. I wasn't sure that getting into bed with a psychiatrist from Ashen Springs, Florida—who also had shadier dealings—was a smart move. But he did own the only shipping docks not already tied to a mafia family or a cartel. To date he hadn't partnered with any organization like ours, and no one knew why. That gave us a distinct advantage if Nash could pull this off.

SEPTEMBER 23 – TUESDAY 10:21 PM

Nash

Fucking Liam. I glanced at him as we went over to greet Mr. Kessler. He was going to pester the shit out of me for more information about what I had cooking with Mr. Genovese. It was an issue for later. Right now, my head had to be in the game.

Smiling, I held out my hand. "Welcome, Mr. Kessler. I'm happy you were able to adjust your schedule to make it this evening."

Just like Mr. Genovese, I expected him to be older. Mr. Kessler looked to be in his forties with chestnut hair and dark eyes that held the same arrogant intelligence as Theo. He wore a dark grey suit and, surprisingly, only seemed to have brought one guard with him.

His handshake was firm and direct, just like his stare.

"Mr. Collier, please call me Louis. Unfortunately, I won't be able to stay as long as I would've liked. There is an issue with one of my businesses that needs my personal attention."

"Call me Nash. I'd prefer to keep this informal."

"Nash it is."

"Well, let's get to it then. I don't want to hold you up."

Raising my finger, Nora brought over a tray with two glasses and a bottle of double malt scotch from Whitley Distillery.

"I see you did your homework on me," Louis said, unbuttoning his suit jacket and sitting down in one of the lush chairs.

"What kind of a host or businessman would I be if I didn't research those I intended to get into bed with."

Louis's lip twitched, a subtle hint of amusement.

"Interesting phrasing. I'd love to know why you chose it. But since we are short on time, I will get right to the heart of the matter."

Leaning forward, he poured himself three fingers before doing the same to my glass. He held it out for me to take. "Are you even old enough to drink?"

"I think when we are soon to be discussing regular shipments of alcohol and guns, having a drink is the least of my worries."

He smiled wide. "Touche." He took a sip and glanced around. "I know why you want to speak to me. It is the same reason the heads of all *unique* enterprises want to speak to me. You want access to my docks." Louis took a sip and sat back in the chair. His henchman stood directly behind him with his hands neatly folded. Liam had taken up a similar pose but at my shoulder.

"You are correct, I do."

"And what makes you think that I would say yes and assume all of that risk...for you? When I've turned everyone else away."

Nora arrived with a tray of finger foods, and Louis happily took a napkin and some puffed pastries before she came to me. Taking three, I popped one in my mouth. Damn, I had to give her credit, she came through again. These were incredible and worthy of the company at the meeting.

"I'm not like the others you've spoken to...and turned away. I'm sure that you have done your homework on me as well."

"I have, and I must say that your father is quite the interesting man."

"That is one way of putting it," I said, barely managing to hold in a laugh.

"And how would you describe your father, Nash?"

Smirking, I popped a second pastry into my mouth and made sure to keep eye contact as I thought of how best to answer.

"Are you asking me as Louis Kessler, the business capitalist, or Dr. Kessler, the psychiatrist?"

Each word, answer, and question was another move on the chess board. All we needed was a little timer to signal our opponent's turn.

"As my son Micah would say, I'm afraid you never get just one or the other."

"Very well." I sat my drink down and slid to the front of my seat, gathering my thoughts. "My father is a monster. There is no sugar-coating that or making it more politically correct. He disrespects those who support him, he is untrustworthy, and I have seen the inside of a hospital more than once because of him."

Louis's features softened. "I'm sorry to hear that, I've known a few men that were the same."

"I'm not looking for pity. I just want you to understand that I'm not my father. I'm a man with a moral code and ethics, and I have strived to put together the needed backing and financial security to crush the snake."

"Then why do you need me?"

This was the second condition of my deal with Mr. Genovese. He needed a new port for his goods, and I promised to deliver untapped, safe passage. Probably wasn't the smartest move at the time, but I wanted to prove to him that I could bring to the table, not just take.

"Because I need a location not under federal scrutiny that can handle the quantity of shipments arriving. I also would like to use Whitley Distillery as cover, which only makes sense with my latest endeavor." I gestured toward the bar and the bottles on display. His eyebrows raised.

"Is that so?"

"Mr. Kessler, this is what I know." I ran my thumb over my bottom lip. "You refuse to deal in party favor pharmaceuticals, so I promise never to disrespect your generosity by bringing them through your dock. You don't want someone trying to take over your properties or the area that will one day belong to Nikolai's heir. Yes, I know who he is."

I took a sip of my drink before continuing.

"You prefer to deal with straight shooters and are fascinated by contentious family dynamics. That is more of a personal hobby for you, but it does draw you to those like myself. My family is...dangerously toxic at best, and I've been beaten to within an inch of my life so many times that I can't count the hospital visits anymore. Despite that, I am not like my father, and despite the abuse, I'm still smart, ambitious, and sleep through the night."

That was a bit of a stretch. I couldn't remember the last time I slept more than three hours straight.

"You have reservations but were intrigued enough with me to take a call and then enjoyed our conversation enough that you made time to fly here from Miami."

"Okay...you have me on all of that. But it doesn't explain why I would take the risk with you, Nash. You're obviously intelligent and have motivation, but you are still your father's son, and how can I trust you will be loyal to your word?"

Standing, I waved over the rest of my guys, who had been lingering far enough away to give us privacy but close enough to eavesdrop.

"Each of these men has a different cause. But there is one thing that unites our families, and that is the terror brought to their doorsteps by my father. They are loyal to me, not because I beat them into submission, but because they know I am loyal to them. I will keep my promise to look out for them, which is something leaders do and what I want to be. Just because we don't hold down the nine-to-five doesn't mean we should not live by a code of ethics. You respect that. You're willing to take a chance on that."

I walked around my men, who looked like perfect *James Bond* replicas, and stopped when I got back to Liam. He looked at me, and I knew that he would lay his life on the line for me at any time as I would for him.

"But the thing that most interests you is family and what you can leave behind for them when you are gone. It is why you want to work with me and why you walked through those doors. I've crunched the numbers, and we can double your income in one year. Triple it in two, and based on the growth projections, you will be doing fifteen times the business by the end of five years. No one else can give you that without eventually needing to take control of your enterprises and area, which I don't want or need."

Theo stepped forward when I pointed to him with a folder and held it out for Louis to take with him. He flipped open the cover, scanning the numbers and locations where the money would flow.

"Obviously, we'd still need to speak on logistics for safe transport and to remain blissfully off of the Fed's lists. But...I'm sure that we can come to an agreement that will make us both happy and feel secure in our decision to work together," I said, patiently waiting for his response.

"And you have the clients and resources already in place to deal with this much product movement," Louis asked.

The tiniest rush of excitement flowed through my body at the subtle undertone of respect that came through in the question.

"I not only have the resources, but it would only require a single phone call to start tomorrow."

Sitting back down in front of Louis, I gave him a few minutes to think it over.

"Tell me something. I understand that you already have a major and much larger company at your disposal for imports. Why use me?"

"Because I need a location not tied to any other family. That creates complications."

"Such as information getting back to your father?"

I smirked. "For one. Yes."

"I have to say that I'm titillated by your thoroughness and eye for detail. I have one final question." I opened my hands and sat back, silently telling him to ask whatever he wanted. "How do I know that this is not a setup? Life is never too good to be true, and this Nash seems too good to be true."

Liam placed a plain brown envelope in my waiting hand. I held the inch-thick wad of papers and photos out to Dr. Kessler.

He pulled out the first few pictures and stared.

I knew what he was looking at, and none of it was pretty. Myles beaten to a bloody pulp with the word WORTHLESS carved into his stomach. Letters from families begging me for my help and others pledging their allegiance. Photos from my time in the hospital and the report of Lawrence killing Mya and my unborn son.

Louis glanced up at me and then around at all those who had been harmed the worst by my father's touch and influence.

"He is a poison, and I'm the cure. In that envelope, you will also find incriminating evidence to humiliate my father or put us all behind bars for what we are and plan to do. That is my gift to you. A token of my respect, but also a show of good faith. No one other than you has seen the extent of abuse that's been hidden for so long. Help me, and I promise that I will hold up my end of the transaction. You will not find anyone more loyal or hardworking."

Louis looked around again, his eyes pausing on Myles and then my face before he stood and buttoned his suit jacket. I followed his lead and waited for him to speak. He held the file and envelope under his arm, and I noticed that there was pain in his eyes. Like a memory of something or someone that had nothing to do with me, but whatever it was, it seemed to sway his decision.

He held out his hand. "You have a deal, Nash. I'll have the paperwork drawn up for you to sign, and I look forward to the part that I'll play in cutting off the head of your snake. Have a good evening."

Once the bells sounded that Louis was gone, I sucked in a deep breath as the guys cheered and, one at a time, pulled me into a hug. It was happening. The *castling* had begun.

SEPTEMBER 24 – WEDNESDAY 1:03 AM

Theo

Oh fuck, I was in trouble—yanked out of sleep as a muscled leg wrapped around mine and a thick forearm pulled me back into a body that I would know anywhere. Liam. His touch was encoded in my mind and every fiber of my being, like he'd managed to crawl under my skin and become one with me.

"What are you doing in here," I whispered, my voice hitching as he bit down at the base of my neck and began to suck. Liam was marking me, and instead of pushing him off, I groaned and gave him more space.

"I can't go without you," he said, and I shivered as he nipped at my skin. "I will give you whatever you need, but I can't lose you."

Turning my head to look at him, the sliver of moonlight coming through the window made his eyes glow an unearthly shade of gold. "You mean that?"

"I've always meant it. I just don't know how to prove that you've never embarrassed me."

"So, you deny that I embarrass you?"

"Of course, you don't fucking embarrass me. I don't even know where the fuck you got that idea. I...I'm private and don't like anyone knowing anything about me, you know that, but if you want me to send out a public announcement, I will. Just stop pushing me away. It's killing me."

"What about Ren?"

Liam shrugged, and I had to bite back the gasp as his hand drifted down my abs and wrapped around my cock. My back arched off the bed as he ran his hand up to the crown, teasing me before gliding all the way down.

"I'm going to go away with her. I'll attempt to connect like I promised. But if it doesn't work out with me, then I'll concede without argument that she will be part of your life. My only condition is that when we are spending time alone, it's just us. She doesn't come up, and you don't push me to try again. When we have time carved out for the two of us, you're mine," he growled and cupped my balls, making me moan for him.

"You want to compromise?"

He shifted us so that his body blanketed mine, pressing me into the mattress. It felt completely natural to move my arms up my pillow and over my head, allowing him to grip my wrists and trap them. His touch was searing, and the feel of his cock rubbing against mine had my heart pounding out of control.

"It's not a traditional third situation. Then again, the entire relationship is already overly complicated with Blake, Myles, and, at some point, Nash." He paused for dramatic effect. "We both know that's inevitable." I nodded. "If you want to spend time with her, I won't fight it or make your life difficult, and as I said, I will try...."

"You just can't make any promises," I finished for him.

"Yes, that too. But that's not what I was going to say."

Liam flexed his hips, and I couldn't deny that I'd yearned for him like a starving person for a scrap of food.

"I love you, Theo. I always have, and I'm sorry for every shitty thing I've done to make you feel like you're not the most important person in my life. I would sell my soul to keep you."

Despite everything else I was feeling at the moment, shock won out as the top emotion. Liam hardly ever opened up, and he certainly didn't apologize. Not without conditions on the end of it. Words like 'but' always accompanied his asking for forgiveness.

"You fucking made me cry, asshole."

"Well, you did have your head shoved so far up your ass that you couldn't see what you were doing to me."

His face grew serious, and with each beat of my heart, it felt like he was digging deeper into my soul.

"You're right. I was happy not to rock the boat and just keep things the way they were. I lost touch with who I am, who you are, and who we are together. I needed to hear it, but more than that, I needed to feel it." I glanced over at the other side of the room. "Blake's not here. He's with Myles in Ren's room."

"And you know that how?"

He smiled. "I may or may not have orchestrated it."

"Devious," I teased and thrust up with my hips. Our sweet moment ended as his eyes darkened. Liam attacked my mouth like it had been years since we were separated. Settling into my bed, I melted under his demanding touch that silently ordered me to hand myself over to whatever he wanted.

He growled at me and reared back. No one pulled off the deep, raspy sound like Liam, and I shuddered as it traveled all the way through my body.

"You're mine, Theo, and I will do this thing with Ren, but I swear to God if you ever threaten to leave me again for someone else...no one will ever find their body."

Instead of being pissed or terrified, I tugged my hands-free and wrapped them around his neck. He made me as crazy as the statement he'd just said. Our movements became frantic, desperation clawing at us both.

"I'm yours," I groaned against his lips, and he shivered.

"Fucking right you are," he said, rubbing himself against my shaft. I was ready to come after being so unbelievably pent up from the lack of his touch. Liam slithered down my body like a snake, flicking his tongue over my nipple, making me jerk against the pleasure.

"Say it again. Who do you fucking belong to?"

Liam disappeared under the covers, his teeth nibbling at my abs as he neared my cock.

"You," I said, grunting when the flat of his tongue licked my full length. "Fuck."

"Are you sure?"

"Yes," I said without hesitation this time.

"Say it louder," he ordered, slipping my cock into his mouth.

My eyes rolled back in my head.

"I'm yours," I said again, but it wasn't any better as he began to suck, stealing the last of the logic in my brain.

"You can do better than that," he growled.

When did it get so fucking hot in here? It felt like he'd set fire to my skin. I kicked the blanket off, needing to see him. Those dark whiskey eyes looked up at me as he swallowed me all the way down into his throat.

"Fuck, fuck, fuck."

I knew Liam's rules and I wasn't allowed to move or come until he gave his permission. This was delicious torture that always ended with a soul-shattering orgasm.

"That's not what I asked you. Should I stop?" Liam pulled his hot mouth off my cock.

Panic, pure blind panic.

"No, please don't stop."

"Then fucking yell as loud as you can," he snarled, squeezing my shaft.

I moaned, but no words came out as I held back my release. The eruption was so close that droplets of come dripped from the head. They landed on Liam's hand, and he licked them up.

Sucking in a deep breath, I yelled. "I'm yours."

Liam smirked.

"That's more like it."

He gripped tighter, and a throbbing started in my cock, making it swell. It wasn't painful in the traditional sense, but the over-whelming desire for a release that was just out of reach had my head thrashing from side to side. He swirled his tongue around my sensitive tip until I was reduced to a whimpering mess, but he wasn't done pushing me. Liam sucked me like his life depended on it. I swore, fisting the sheet in an attempt to maintain some composure.

"You want to come?"

"Yes."

"Will I ever need to remind you who you belong to again?"

"No! I'm yours. I'll always be yours, forever."

"Very good. You deserve a reward."

His voice was so gravelly with desire that it sounded like he'd gargled with whiskey and sandpaper. Liam released the pressure on my aching cock.

My body quaked as I tried to remain still.

"You can move and come now."

Digging my fingers into his messy hair and thrusting up into his mouth, a roar tumbled from my lips as I came. Liam never missed a beat, and even as my body froze with the intensity of being sling-shotted out into the stratosphere, he sucked and swallowed.

"Fucking incredible," I said, flopping back on my pillow completely spent.

But we were just getting started. God help me because I'd let him do whatever he wanted, whenever he wanted, for the rest of my life.

SEPTEMBER 24 – WEDNESDAY 1:33 AM

Liam

Nothing brought me more joy than seeing him like this. When Theo was completely and thoroughly satisfied, something undefinable happened inside of me. He gave me a gift that millions would never have and that was a connection so deep our souls entwined.

I palmed my cock as his chest rose and fell in a steady rhythm. Opening his nightstand drawer, I grabbed the lube and smirked. Theo's eyes fluttered open, and his gaze locked on my cock just in time to watch me squeeze a healthy dollop out before tossing it back in the drawer. He licked his lips and started to push himself up.

"What are you doing?"

"I was going to roll over," he said, and I shook my head.

He looked startled. Taking him while I could stare into his spring-green eyes was not normal for us, but that was going to change. How far I'd fallen that my Sub thought I didn't care. That was never happening again.

The bed creaked as I kneeled between Theo's outstretched legs. I kept my gaze locked on him as I pushed his knees up. I teased him for a few minutes to get him ready before I pressed my cock slowly into his tight hole. No matter how many times I fucked him, he was always incredibly tight. I was groaning and panting by the time I got all nine inches inside of his ass.

"Fuck yes," Theo groaned and shuddered under me.

Holding still, I let him adjust. Not that either of us needed much time, but it also gave me the opportunity to do something I hadn't before. Gripping the back of Theo's neck, I drew him up to my lips. Our tongues lashed as I released all the frustration that had built since the cabin and put it into the kiss.

"You never break up with me again," I ordered through swollen lips, and his green eyes shimmered back at me. "And I promise never to make you feel like you need to."

"Then you have a deal."

"Fuck me," I groaned, pulling almost all the way out and slowly pushing back in.

Bracing my arms next to Theo's head, I never looked away. Picking a pace that was as agonizingly perfect as it was tortuous. No more needed to be said between us. Every touch was a conversation.

Gritting my teeth, I held on until Theo was a writhing mess beneath me, his fingers digging into my shoulders and his face twisted in pleasure. Sweat trickled down my back, and my arms burned, but it had never felt so good to push myself. As his panting turned into desperate pleas, I knew he was close again and picked up the pace until I was ruthlessly pounding into him.

Just as he was about to come, I released my tightly wound control and allowed myself to enjoy the moment. Hanging onto Theo's reins gave me extreme satisfaction, but the minutes of complete abandon felt even sweeter.

"Fuck yes," Theo yelled as he came.

His cock kicked as his release landed on his stomach. And that was all it took for me to come with him. I didn't stop moving until every last drop had been spent, and then I collapsed in a tangle of limbs. I kissed the mark I'd made earlier and couldn't believe that I'd almost lost him.

"Shower," I asked, and Theo nodded.

He stopped me as I started to push myself up, and I searched his face.

"I love you, Liam. I always have and always will. Even when you're being a thoughtless, stubborn, pompous asshat."

I chuckled and kissed him before climbing off the bed.

"Have any other adjectives you'd like to call me," I asked as we got to our feet.

"I have many."

That made me laugh. Fuck, I'd missed this. One day, one week, or one year, it made no difference any time spent without Theo felt like an eternity.

SEPTEMBER 27 – SATURDAY 9:03 AM

R*en*

"Okay...enough already, let's go," Nash yelled from his car.

With an exaggerated sigh, Myles stopped kissing me.

Blake, Theo, and Liam were heading to Ethan and Ella's house for the weekend while Myles was checking Lip out of school to spend some time with him. Myles was still avoiding their father and might've had an ulterior motive. He wanted to go alone to see if there was a way to prevent Lip from being allowed to leave with Owen.

Everyone was busy, which was great, but it also meant that it left me awkwardly alone with Nash. When I first thought of getting Nash tickets to the dinner I had assumed that someone, if not all the guys, would volunteer to come along, but I was wrong. At the sound of his window going up, I got a glance at his mischievous eyes before the dark glass concealed my view.

"Was this a good idea," I asked Myles under my breath.

"Nah, it's definitely not. But it doesn't change the fact that it's the most thoughtful gift he's ever received, and ya kinda have ta go. Besides, you'd hate yerself for not going. He's just being a melter 'cause he's nervous, but don't expect him to admit that."

A piece of my hair whipped across my face, the wind a steady force the last few days.

"And I do trust him to keep ya safe."

My safety wasn't exactly what worried me.

Nash had so easily thwarted my defenses on the bench the other day. The whole interlude was still front and center in my mind, but I nodded to reassure Myles that I was good. My imagination was another story.

We had no buffer, no schoolwork, or anything else to distract us from being alone together. Nothing but the open road for a five-hour drive and a fancy dinner—where I was essentially his plus one, which was normally reserved for a partner of the intimate variety. To end the night was an equally awkward hotel room stay. He had proclaimed that the room had two beds, but I really didn't trust Nash, to be honest. And to finish the weekend, another long drive home.

"Try to have fun. Yer doing a really sweet thing," Myles said, kissing my forehead. "Even if he doesn't deserve it."

Myles picked up my overnight bag and the wrapped painting, then placed them gently in the tiny trunk before closing it tight.

Lizzy and her mum had done me a solid. Once my house was no longer crawling with police, they'd gathered my personal belongings and anything they thought might have sentimental value and shipped it to Ella. Among the items was the last of my mother's original works that no one had ever seen. I was using one of the five pieces for Nash. If he ever truly understood my sacrifice and appreciated it... well, it was hard to know much of anything when he came to Nash.

"I'll see ya when you get back, Snowflake."

"Give Lip a hug for me," I said.

"Not a chance. I don't need him lovin' ya any more than he already does," he teased, giving me a wink.

Myles turned to follow the path to the parking lot, and I...well, my attention was on the shiny black sports car. Swallowing the lump in my throat, I got in beside Nash.

He shot me a glare and snapped.

"You're late. We agreed to be on the road by 8:45, and it's now 9:15."

I placed my hand on his. He stared at it and then at me, blinking like I'd completely stunned him with the light touch.

"Do you want me to stay here, and you can go alone?"

"No."

"Then let's not start the trip fighting. We will still get there with hours to spare." As soon as he nodded, I removed my hand. "Good, I didn't want to have to kill you and dump your body at the side of the road if you continued to be an asshole."

Nash smirked.

"You could try, Princess," he said, but he smiled and pulled away from the curb.

"How did you get permission to get me off the property," I asked as Nash slowed for the gate and gave a two-finger salute before it slid open.

"It's me, I could get you off anytime."

He glanced at me from the corner of his eye, and I knew for certain that this was a terrible idea. It had been two minutes, and my body was already on fire. What the hell was a whole night going to look like?

"Are we still talking about the property?"

"Take it however you want. It'll always be true."

"Uh-huh."

I rolled my eyes and crossed my arms. Most people would think that it was a defensive maneuver, and they would be right, just about the wrong thing.

"Wait a second. Does that mean I never had to wear a costume or get in the trunk of Blake's car if I was going with you?" He shrugged and smirked. "Son of a...."

It was tempting to tell him to let me out, and I'd walk back.

"How was I supposed to know you'd act all crazy to get off the property? Besides, even if I had told you, we both know you never would've asked for my help."

There'd never been a truer statement.

Nash turned on his car's sound system, and I laid my head back, letting myself get lost in the music. He had a much broader range of songs in his playlist than I would've thought.

Unable to help myself, I cracked my eyes open just enough to starc at his hands on the steering wheel. They were freshly tattooed, the ink still a rich black that stood out against his skin. The one on his right knuckles read MINE, and I quickly pressed my lids closed again as my imagination heard him growling that in my ear.

This was such a stupid idea. He'd been chipping away at me for over a year, and spending so much time together over the summer hadn't helped. Knowing that I should keep the door slammed closed in his face and being able to do it were very different concepts.

"What are you thinking about," Nash asked.

My eyes opened as my brain raced for anything that wasn't him.

"Mr. Sharpe."

Nash's head snapped in my direction, his face going from casual to murderous in zero point two seconds flat.

"Not like that, gross."

"Then what do you mean?"

Sighing, I sat up straighter.

"I'm in his AP psychology class, and last year, he asked me to be his TA. At the time, I was flattered and excited. But I have no idea what I am doing or what he wants from me. I thought he'd at least have instructions or a plan for me to follow."

Nash tilted his head and stared at me. I pointed at the road, and his lip twitched before he looked forward again.

"He hasn't told you anything?"

"Nope. He threw me in the deep end."

Nash smiled, and I pointed at him.

"Don't even go there. It was a poor choice of words in current company, but you know what I mean."

"Has he hit on you?"

My jaw dropped.

"No...why? Do you think he only asked me to get in my pants? I have a lot to offer in a TA position. I'm tied with Theo in the whole school." My hackles were up now.

"Relax, Princess. I didn't mean that you weren't qualified. But just because you have what it takes doesn't mean he doesn't have other reasons for asking you. Two things can be true at the same time."

"Fine, but he hasn't hit on me."

"Okay, what has he done?"

"Nothing, that's the point. He leaves me alone with students needing extra help, but there is no guidance. On day two, he left quizzes on his desk without a word. I didn't touch them because I would never peek at someone else's work, and the next class, he practically yelled at me for not grading them. How was I supposed to know that he wanted me to do that? It feels like he is setting me up to fail. I just can't figure out why."

"There is another option."

I stared at his face and realized, despite his dickish behavior, that I valued Nash's opinion. That was a terrifying thought.

"Maybe he's doing it to see how quickly you'll figure it out on your own."

"Why? Where is the benefit in that when I'm not doing what he needs?"

"Because the outside world is more like the deep end of the pool with sharks than it is the shallow end with a flutter board. If you can think ahead, plan as if anticipating his needs, then you'll be much further along than if he just handed you a list to check off," Nash said, and then shrugged. "It's what I'd do."

"Shit...I've been failing a test I didn't know I was taking." I smacked my forehead. "Of course, why didn't I see that? It's so obvious. Sink or swim, it's the oldest lesson there is. Thanks, Nash."

Smiling and feeling so much lighter, I squeezed his arm.

Nash looked at my hand and then into my eyes.

"Unless you want me to pull you over here to sit on my lap, remove your hand."

For a moment, I wanted to see if he'd actually do it. Instead, I dropped my hand to my lap as an awkward tension filled the car. Trying desperately to distract myself, I studied the cars in the side-view mirror.

"Nash?"

"Yeah?"

"I think we're being followed." I spun in my seat to look out the small back window and watched the two black SUVs. Icy fear trickled down my back like a cold rain shower, making me shiver.

"We are," Nash said.

Why was he so calm?

"And you're not worried?"

"No," he said, smirking at me. "Stop panicking, Princess. Do you really think I'd take you off the property without protection? That's our escort."

"Escort? Since when do you have guards in black SUVs?"

He shrugged. "I'm making more enemies and allies daily. It was time. Besides, like I said, I wasn't taking you anywhere without an added layer of protection. I'm cocky, not stupid."

"A little heads up would've been nice. You just gave me a heart attack," I grumbled, and yet I felt a lot safer. Damn, Nash was always jumbling every emotion into a confusing mess.

"I could've warned you, but then I wouldn't have gotten to see that adorable panicked look."

"You're such a jerk."

"Guilty as charged."

"Can I ask you something?"

"You don't have to ask if you can ask me questions, Princess. I think we're way beyond that bullshit."

"It's called being polite."

"Fine, don't be polite with me," he said.

I licked my lips, and a thrill traveled through my veins. If anyone at school did what he just told me to, they would end up with their face shoved in a locker or far worse.

"What do you want to know, Princess?"

"Has your father said anything about my dad?"

A deep and gnawing pain just wouldn't let up whenever I thought about him. Neal Davies, the man who raised and loved me until life got too hard. There was still a chance that he was my biological father, and I'd refused to talk to him. I had every right to protect myself from what he was putting me through at the time, but it had never crossed my mind that it might be our last conversation.

Nash ran his hand through his hair, and I sat up a little straighter.

"You know something, don't you?"

"Lawrence hasn't said anything, but...." He looked at me and shook his head. "I wouldn't hold out too much hope that he ever comes home to you."

I covered my mouth and bit back the sharp sting of tears.

"Please, Nash. If you know more, just tell me."

"All I know is that the last time I saw him, and it was just a glimpse, he and Lawrence were talking, and he was in rough shape. He hadn't shaved in days, his hair was greasy, his shirt was dirty, and he was acting wild. I haven't seen him since."

"So, your father was the last person to see him?"

Nash's eyes were as hard as I'd ever seen them when he looked at me.

"No."

"But you don't even know what I was going to say."

"Bullshit. You were going to ask to speak to my father, and the answer was, is, and forever will be, no."

"Nash...." My hands balled into fists.

"No."

"But...."

He growled and smacked the top of his steering wheel before locking eyes with me. The rage there was equal to him smacking me, and I pressed myself as far away as I could get.

"This is exactly why I didn't tell you. What are you going to do?"

My mouth moved, but nothing passed through my constricted throat.

"I'll tell you what you'd do. You'd want to meet with my father. Then you'd beg him to tell you what he knows exactly like you just did with me. But instead of just getting information you don't like, he would only tell you under conditions. What conditions? You might ask. Well, Princess, I'll tell you," Nash snarled, his hands squeezing the wheel so tight that his knuckles had turned bright white.

"He would find a way to use your newfound family name against you. Anything from blackmail, forcing you into marriage or getting you pregnant, to turning you into his sadist toy, you name it, he'll do it."

I'd never seen Nash this worked up, his body was shaking with the rage that was stifling in the car.

"And while you sell your soul to save a man that Lawrence may or may not know his whereabouts, he will lead you on and slowly break you down until there is nothing left of the person you are now. There is no negotiating with terrorists. Believe me, my father is a hostile enemy looking for a way to destroy us all, but you... with you, he would take extra pleasure in crushing. So, No. Never. Don't ask me again, and if you ever try to meet him on your own...just don't. Do you think that's the life your mother wanted for you? Or the exact life she was trying to hide you from? That she died protecting you from?"

The tears ran freely as he watched me, his words cutting deeper than any blade.

His eyes softened, and he sighed, turning away. I took a shaky breath, and like a pin had touched the balloon of tension, it burst. Nash suddenly reached out and grabbed my hand. I tried to tug it away, but he held it tight until I stopped fighting him.

"I didn't tell you that to hurt you. But you don't seem to understand who you're dealing with. My father is something born from hell, and he will not stop until he's sucked the last bit of life out of you, and as much as you think I don't care...."

He locked eyes with me, and my heart tripped in my chest.

"I don't want that to happen to you. I'll kill him first. You can't meet with him. You need to stay as far away from him as possible."

I nodded, the fat tears clouding my vision, but I held back the sob that clogged my throat. Biological father or not. Dead or not. None of that mattered if Lawrence had him or knew where he was. I'd never see him again. That was what Nash was telling me. Even begging for his life wouldn't work because you couldn't beg for mercy from a man who had none.

My soul ached as I silently grieved the loss of my dad, the second parent in a year. As angry as I was, I truly didn't think he knew who he was getting into bed with until it was too late. By then, the snake was already swallowing him whole.

"I'm sorry, Princess," Nash said, squeezing my hand.

Even though I was stuffing the emotions deep down inside to process later, it was as if Nash had tossed me into the water again. This time, he saw me struggling but wasn't going to save me. No one could. I couldn't speak, or I would lose the bit of composure I had maintained. Instead, I nodded and looked away, keeping my eyes trained on the world as it passed by.

"Have you thought about what you want for your birthday," Dad asked as he helped me with the final details of my sandcastle.

My drawbridge was giving me trouble. "That's not how birthday gifts work," I said, looking up at my dad. The sun was really bright at the beach, and I held my hand up to be able to see him.

He chuckled. "Who says that's not how they're supposed to work?"

"It just is."

"Really? Is this the Ren Davies' birthday rules," he said, adding the last turret to the castle top.

"No," I said, wiping my hands off and watching the sand fall and disappear as it joined the rest of the beach. "Everyone knows the rules. You don't ask the person. You have to think of something special."

He smiled. "I must have missed the memo."

"What's a memo," I asked, wiggling my toes in the warm sand and loving the feel of it under my feet.

We didn't come to the beach much because it was so far to drive, but Mum had someone buying art from her here, and they decided to make it a family adventure. Unfortunately, Dad and I hadn't seen Mum much since we arrived. She'd been so busy. Everyone was always busy and never not busy at the same time. It wasn't fair.

"A memo is a letter from a higher power that tells you what is

required for, say, your job or, in this case, your birthday." I giggled as he tickled my foot.

"Daddy?"

"Yeah?"

"Can we do this for my birthday, but have Mommy here and not working," I asked, doodling designs into the sand.

"But it will be cold for your birthday," he said, and I shrugged.

"I just want us to be together." I looked up at him. "Please, Daddy."

Standing up quickly, he grabbed me. I squealed, laughing as he tossed me over his shoulder. "That's all you want? No ice cream?"

"Okay, ice cream, too," I said, kicking and screeching as the cold water touched my skin.

Dad laughed, and I knew that it wouldn't happen, it never did, but it didn't stop me from wishing for it anyway.

"Princess?"

I jerked awake and gasped. Blinking, I realized I was crying and quickly wiped away the tears before looking at Nash. We weren't moving.

"We're here," he said softly. "You okay?"

"Yeah, just wishing for a time machine."

His lip curled up. "Don't we all."

Chapter 20

SEPTEMBER 27 – SATURDAY 6:00 PM

Nash

The lights in the sitting room were dim as I finished adjusting my tie and slipped on my Rolex. Ren was still in her bedroom, and the time to leave was ticking closer. I looked down at my freshly tatted hands. Hands that screamed I no longer fit into this world. No matter how hard I tried, I'd never be just another athlete. There was blood covering them, and it didn't matter what pool I swam in. It was never coming off.

"Are you ready," Ren asked, her voice still holding a lilt of sadness.

I'd put that grief there and would do it again. Not a single word that I spoke was untrue. The first thing she would've done when we got back was try to arrange a meeting with my father. That could never happen for so many reasons, but most of all, because what she found would only break her. If there was even the smallest chance to shield her from some of that pain, then I'd be her villain.

After fiddling with my cufflink to avoid seeing the pain in Ren's eyes, I turned around to face the temptress.

Everything in the room froze. Time stood still, and there was nothing but Ren. It had been the same at my disastrous birthday party. She had stepped into yet another version of herself, so far from the student at Wayward that my mind couldn't connect that they were indeed the same.

Ren smoothed her hand over the dark blue material that matched the clearest coastal waters and shimmered like the moon on the ocean's surface.

What the fuck was wrong with me?

I didn't compare people to shimmering water or lose time when girls were around. Shaking my head, I stepped closer, but with each stride, the foreign thoughts spoke louder.

"You have great taste. Everything fits perfectly," Ren said.

Stopping in front of her, I licked my lip and could still taste her on my tongue. Her soft silvery grey eyes glanced up at me from under her thick lashes, and...fuck. I was in so much trouble.

"I had help."

Needing to touch her, I reached out and skimmed the back of my knuckles down her cheek. Goosebumps rose all along her skin, and she shivered. Running my hand around to the back of her neck, she gasped as my grip tightened. Those intoxicating eyes of hers widened, and her breath hitched as I lowered my lips to hers. At the last second, she looked away, turning her head. My mouth grazed her cheek, but I didn't care while I breathed in her decadent scent.

Fuck my life, why did she always smell so good?

"We can't keep doing this dance, Nash."

Her chest rose and fell, and her pulse thumped under my fingers, screaming that she was suffering from a similar issue. She was as drawn to me as I was to her, and there was something so incredibly satisfying in knowing that I'd managed to get under her skin.

"Maybe not, but you smell so fucking good," I whispered in her ear. "Why did you come with me today?"

"I told you that I have to be here," she said, pushing against my chest to create some distance.

Ren couldn't look me in the eyes, and that alone told me there was another reason. And even though I shouldn't, because it would lead nowhere good, I was going to find out why.

"So, you said, Princess."

Conceding to her need for space, I stepped back before I ripped that enticing dress off and fucked her against the wall. When she still wouldn't look at me, my eyes settled on the necklace she never took off. The charm I'd given her last Christmas still hung from the delicate chain.

"Can you please not call me princess in front of anyone tonight?"

Ren opened her clutch and looked inside like there might be something interesting to see.

"No promises, Princess," I teased and held out my arm.

She hesitated, but only for a moment. I would take it as a win and sign that maybe tonight wouldn't be completely awful.

The short drive to the event was quiet. We were quiet. With each stoplight and turn that brought us closer to the event, a new seed of self-doubt settled in my stomach.

The museum was completely lit up like a Hollywood event, red carpet and all. As we waited in the valet line, I stared at the front of the large glass building, wondering if I had imagined this whole thing. If it wasn't for the massive banners announcing the banquet, I would think it was a possibility.

"Are you okay, Nash?"

Ren touched my hand, and I snapped out of the daze.

"Yeah. Just can't believe I'm actually here. It probably seems stupid to you. It's just a dinner, after all," I said, driving up to the next open spot.

"No, Nash. This is important to you." She smiled, and my heart hammered. "Don't forget the painting in the trunk, it's our ticket in."

The valet opened the door for Ren and helped her out. It was tempting to leap through the car and break his hand for touching her. I sucked in the sudden burst of rage and got out as he came around to open my door next.

"Touch her again for any reason, and I'll break every single one of your fingers," I whispered as I towered over him. "Understand?"

"Understood," he said.

"Very good."

Smiling, I hit the trunk button and then stuffed a hundred into the stunned man's pocket.

Ren already had the painting out and was closing the trunk when I walked up beside her. I nodded toward the plain brown paper rectangle she was holding.

"Are you going to tell me what's so special about this painting that it got us in here?"

She took my offered arm, and I was very aware of the guys looking our way. Without even trying, she commanded space and attention. Ren may not have grown up in our world, but she held herself like she did. Nothing seemed to intimidate her, and when it did, she didn't let it show.

"I'll tell you once we're inside," Ren said and politely thanked the porters at the doors.

The museum was buzzing with the energy of the occasion, and it was hard not to get swept up in the excitement. We stepped up to the sign-in table, and the woman working it smiled at us.

"Name?"

"Nash Collier and Ren Davies."

She looked down the list before crossing off my name.

"Here you go," she said, handing us two small baggies containing what looked to be informational cards, a few gifts, and a schedule for the night.

Floor signs directed us to Brotman Forum, where the dinner was being held. We followed them until Ren stopped and pointed toward an escalator.

"We're early. Can I show you something first?"

"Sure. What are you up to?"

Ren gave me a small smile but remained quiet as we moved to the upper floor. The voices below echoed faintly as we stepped off and walked down the marble corridor.

Art had never really interested me, maybe because no one in my family cared or maybe because I didn't have the eye for it. Whatever the reason, I didn't understand what was so special about the pieces we passed or what made them any different than if I threw a can of paint at a canvas and called it art.

Ren tugged my arm to a stop, and I focused on the three paintings in front of us. Each had their own light as if setting them apart from the others. Ren gazed at the wall with a deep sadness in her eyes despite the small curve of her lips.

"What is it? What's wrong?"

"Nothing."

She turned to face me, and I still couldn't read her properly.

"You asked me what was so special about this." She held up the rectangle and then nodded toward the wall. "Those were painted by my mother."

My head snapped back to the wall, and this time, I zeroed in on the little placard that read *Illianna Davies*.

"I recognized Mr. Paval's name because he was a regular customer of my mother. This is one of five pieces left that I own. She painted these before she died and never showed anyone. I bartered this painting for the tickets."

She looked at the wall again, and a single tear rolled down her cheek.

"Here, it will be loved and cherished forever by those who appreciated her work." She wiped away the tear. "It was a good deal," she said.

No one, not a single person in my entire life, had ever sacrificed something so precious to them for me. The guys would lay down their lives, sure, but this was different. Ren hardly knew me, and I certainly hadn't been the nicest when she arrived. Yet it was a mysterious Canadian with white hair and a vicious tongue who freely gave of herself without asking for anything in return.

My thoughts were all jumbled together, and I couldn't get out what I wanted to say. Cupping Ren's face, I guided her back to me and kissed her. This might be a horrible idea, but I didn't care as I poured every last ounce of what this meant to me into her. Ren moaned softly, and I had to pull away or we were going to get arrested for sure.

"Thank you," I breathed against her lips and then licked the sweet flavor of her gloss off mine.

"You're welcome."

"Ms. Davies?"

Ren turned around, and I glanced over her head, ready to kill whoever had just interrupted us.

"I thought it must be you when security mentioned someone had come this way."

"Mr. Paval, it's nice to see you again. Yes, I wanted to show Nash my mother's work," she said, trying to step away from me.

She looked over her shoulder at me and lifted a brow when I grabbed her hip to stop her. It took more effort to release her than she would ever know.

"You look absolutely divine this evening, and I must say you're the spitting image of your mother," he said, lifting her hand to kiss.

I clenched my jaw as his lips touched her skin.

"Thank you, you're too kind," Ren said. Turning to me, she smiled. "May I introduce you to Nash Collier?"

"By all means. After all, he is the reason I'm getting my hands on something so special."

It was a good fucking thing he was talking about the artwork. He held out his hand, and I clasped it, shaking a little harder than needed.

"Nice to meet you," I said.

"Likewise. Ms. Davies has spoken very highly of you, and I have to say your trial times submitted so far are incredible. Keep it up, and the next time you hear from me will be with an offer to join the national team."

"That is the goal," I said, all too aware of how he glanced at my hands and the tattoo on the side of my neck.

"And, here you go."

Ren held out the package to Mr. Paval, and he smiled like a kid a Christmas.

"May I open it?"

Ren laughed, and it was so good to see her smile. She lit up the room brighter than any of the pieces hanging from the walls.

"Yes, of course. It's yours now. Out of everyone who loved her work, I know you'll appreciate this piece the most."

I'd never seen someone tear off paper so gently before, but when he pulled out the canvas, even I stared in awe. It was a close-up painting of a girl on a beach, building a sandcastle. Even though the young girl's hair was black, there was no mistaking the muse. Ren's silvery eyes were captured perfectly as she smiled at her sandy creation. You could easily see each tiny paint stroke that had been used to create the masterpiece.

"Oh my god," Mr. Paval said. He took off his glasses and wiped away tears. "I can see why she kept this one out of sight. It would have been fought over, but never should be. I'm not sure I can accept this. It is so personal to you," he said, confirming my suspicions.

But Ren shook her head.

"No, keep it. This is where her work belongs. Not wrapped up and hidden away. Knowing how much you and so many others will enjoy it makes my heart smile. It feels like a part of her is still alive and out there in the world."

"I will cherish this forever," Mr. Paval said, holding out his hand for us to follow him. "We better go. The banquet is about to begin."

It was oddly satisfying when Ren automatically looked for my arm. This time, I laid my other hand on top of hers as we walked.

When I felt Ren's stare on my face, I looked down. As our eyes locked, I didn't know who was in more trouble, her or me...or maybe we were both drowning.

Nash

I thought I had a handle on this life, but tonight, it was laughing in my face. We enjoyed an amazing four course meal including a salmon dinner before mingling and introducing ourselves to everyone and anyone with sway in the industry. Ren and I had laughed and sipped alcohol-free champagne all night. I couldn't stand alcohol-free beverages, but it tasted like the best drink of my life tonight. I'd even been called up to the stage and handed an award for the fastest time submitted for the 200m butterfly. This was the path to everything I'd ever wanted, and yet...the highlight of my night had nothing to do with the event but with who had come with me.

Fuck, Myles. I could kill him and kiss him at the same time, and that was not an image that I ever wanted in my head. He'd said from day one that there was something unique about Ren, and the fucker was right. I'd been fighting it for months, would still deny it if asked and yet, I had no clue what real jealousy felt like until this moment.

Her smile was completely captivating, and many people—too many of them men—wanted to be in her presence. While many had come up to chat with me, it was impossible to ignore Ren. It was as if a caged feral animal resided in my chest every time someone shook her hand or looked at her with more than a friendly glance. The blatant eye fucking from some of the men was enough to make me thankful that I couldn't bring a gun into the event. It would've been a bloodbath, and there was no rational explanation for the sudden burst of emotion. The only thing I'd been able to come up with was the fact that she'd made this possible.

"So, do you only race the 200," the national team coach, Mr. Richards, asked.

All I need to say is no, I swim several. But instead, my mind is on my hand, and my hand is on Ren's hip.

Taking a sip of my drink to give my brain a few seconds, I cleared my throat. "No, I also race the 400 individual medley and the team medley. But the butterfly is my strongest stroke."

"I'd be interested in seeing you compete in person, Nash. When is your next meet?"

"This Thursday and Friday, actually. Wayward is hosting against other prominent clubs and schools in the area. It will be a two-day event and is a qualifier," I said.

"If you'll excuse me. I need to use the ladies," Ren said and slipped away from me.

The heat from her touch remained despite her absence. I looked over my shoulder as she walked away, and the swaying of her ass had me itching to get out of this suit.

"Your girlfriend is quite lovely," Mr. Richards said.

My head snapped back in his direction. If he was looking at her ass...I didn't care who he was. He was a dead man. Luckily for him, he was looking at me.

"How long have you two been together?"

"What does that matter?"

"Just curious. If you make the team, you'll be required to travel quite often. It can put a real strain on a relationship."

I ground my teeth but forced a smile, hating the probing into my non-existent relationship.

"I'm sure we will be fine. We've been through some very rocky waters already and are stronger for it," I said, only half lying.

"Very good. I'll look into the event this week and see if I'm able to work it into my schedule. Have a good evening, Nash."

Mr. Richards held out his hand for me to shake, and I returned his gesture. As soon as he turned to leave, I wheeled around and followed Ren.

Stepping out of the banquet hall, I searched for her. This place was too fucking large. Letting Ren out of my sight was an awful idea. Fuck.

The plaque on the wall pointed me in the right direction, and I marched down the corridor. Just as I reached the women's bathroom, Ren walked out, but she was looking down into her purse.

"Jesus Christ, Nash," she said as she came a breath away from running into me. "What are—"

Grabbing her by the waist, I pushed her up against the wall and snarled at her.

"What are you doing? Are you insane? Don't answer that. I know you are. Let go," she whispered, but her eyes were hard and murderous, and there was no saving me tonight. I was lost to whatever magic she had used to ensnare me.

"Don't ever leave me," I growled, feeling as out of control as I sounded, which scared the fucking shit out of me.

"Have you completely lost your mind? I didn't leave you, I—"

Wrapping my hand around her throat, she gasped a moment before I kissed her. I'd been thinking about it all evening. Just like the night of my party, she was defensive at first, but with each second that ticked by, the hard shell she kept firmly in place broke away. With a moan, Princess opened her mouth and placed her hands on my chest. She was melting beneath my touch, but it wasn't enough. I had to have her. I ravaged her mouth, not giving her a second to think until we were completely breathless.

"Let's get out of here," I whispered against her cherry-flavored lips while I stole the tiny mint she was sucking from the tip of her tongue.

"I know it's almost over, but what about the banquet? Don't you want to stay until the end?" Her voice was breathy as she spoke.

"No, I don't care. Let's go."

Taking her hand, I couldn't get us out of this place fast enough. I handed the valet my ticket when we reached the booth seconds later.

"Nash...."

Pulling Ren closer, I placed a finger on her lips, and for just a second, I thought she might bite. My already uncomfortable pants became unbearable as I pictured her doing just that. What the fuck was wrong with me?

"Just don't," I ordered, and she sucked in a seething breath that turned me on even more. "Please," I added, and shivered then she nodded.

The rev of a motor announced my car. Ren slipped inside. Her eyes locked with mine as I held her door. I practically ran to get behind the wheel. The hotel wasn't far, but it felt like it took forever to pull up out front.

We hadn't said a word since we left the museum and remained quiet as we walked through the lobby. The moment we stepped into the elevator, it was over. I couldn't take it anymore. A tiny yelp left Ren's lips as I all but attacked her against the mirrored wall. If we plummeted to our deaths, I wouldn't have even noticed. Not that it mattered. I was already falling down another hole, one that was equally terrifying.

Yanking up her dress, I finally got my hands on her ass and groaned into her mouth. Ren's arms wrapped around my neck, and I pulled her up my body.

"You're making me crazy," I said, breaking the kiss as the elevator stopped. I glanced over my shoulder at the couple waiting to get on with their mouths hanging open. "Take the next one," I ordered, and they nodded as the doors closed, and we continued our ascent to the top floor.

My hands roamed all over her body. A body that had haunted me every fucking night for months. I had her bra unclipped before carrying her out into the hallway. There was no need to be modest. We were in the only room on this floor.

"Grab the key," I said, and she slipped her hand into my suit jacket pocket to pull it out. The beep of the key letting us in sounded like a gift, and a gavel dropped at the same time.

Kissing the side of her neck, Ren moaned and arched into my hold as she ran her fingers through my hair. I inhaled and shivered as her scent filled me. How many times had I been minding my own fucking business, and this scent would hit me. It had somehow seeped into all my clothes, my pillowcase, and everything else I touched.

A very small part of me knew this was a bad idea. But the roar of need coursing through my body like smoldering lava in my veins wasn't letting me think straight.

"Tell me to stop," I said, even as I walked toward my room. "Please, Princess. Order me to stop, or I won't," I said, but Ren remained quiet. "I can't stop myself, and I don't want to." I halted at the foot of the bed, giving her one last opportunity to tell me to go fuck myself. "Tell me to leave, and I will. Do it, Princess, and save us both."

Instead, Ren kissed me, and whatever interlocking pieces there were inside my mind that held a semblance of sanity broke apart.

Ren

"Tell me to stop," he said. I knew we were heading to his room—he hadn't been lying about the separate beds—and yet I couldn't come up with a reason why we shouldn't do this.

"Please, Princess. Order me to stop, or I won't," he growled, the desire thick on his tongue. I opened my mouth, but no words came out. "I can't stop myself, and I don't want to," he said, his voice losing more composure as we stopped at the foot of the bed. He stared into my eyes, giving me one more moment to think, but what had been building between us was beyond thought. "Tell me to leave, and I will. Do it, Princess, and save us both," Nash said, his lips just touching mine.

His body shook, and the hard muscles of his shoulders flexed under my fingers. Instead of telling him to stop, I kissed him. That was when all rational thought that I'd been clinging to fell away, leaving me freefalling.

"You're a fucking siren," Nash snarled.

I didn't know what he meant by that, and at the moment, I didn't care. I only needed him closer. My lips were sore from his ravenous kiss, but I wanted more. I wanted it all. Stopping this from happening was like trying to stop a ship from sinking with a bucket.

Nash moved his mouth to my neck and bit me like a goddamn vampire. His groan of pleasure was so erotic that I held him tighter as the sound raced through my body until I was nothing more than a panting mess. His teeth grazed my skin back up to my lips, and then he locked eyes with me.

No life vests would be thrown. I was sinking into the blue of his eyes and letting him pull me under. I was so tired of fighting this, so tired of denying what had kept me awake at night.

"Are you wet for me, Princess?" Grabbing a handful of my hair, he yanked my head back, and I gasped. "Tell me."

"No," I lied, and he chuckled.

"Liar. I would bet my life that you're dripping for me."

"Not a fucking chance," I said and glared at him.

He smirked. This was us. This had always been us.

"I swear I'm going to fuck you until you're screaming yes this time, Princess."

"You can try."

Nash dropped me on the bed. I screamed as I landed with a bounce. My throat ran dry as he tossed off his jacket and then ripped his shirt off like it was pissing him off as much as I was.

I tried to push myself up the bed, but he snatched my ankle, trapping me like an animal in a snare.

"Where do you think you're going, Princess?" I licked my lips. "What? No sharp answer," he asked as he slowly undid the strap on my heel and tossed it away. He made quick work of the second one, but when I went to move backward, he shook his head at me.

"You did this to me," he accused and pointed to the massive bulge in his dress pants. "It's what you've been doing to me every fucking day. You're relentless."

"That's always been a you problem."

"Not tonight, it's not. I gave you the chance to run, and you didn't take it."

Nash dragged me to the very edge of the bed. He was terrifying like this, but I only wanted him more. He was right. I had my chance, and I didn't take it or want to change my mind now.

"Take my cock out." Nash wasn't amused when I sassily rolled my eyes. He gripped my jaw, fingers pressed tightly, just shy of painful. "Don't you dare give me that fucking look, or the first thing I'll do is fuck this mouth of yours. Take...my...cock...out."

I ran my tongue over my bottom lip and ate up the dark look in his eyes as he watched.

"Okay."

My tone clearly said only because I wanted to, and it earned me a snarl. I kept my eyes on his, not needing to look to undo the black leather belt. He was most likely going to use it on me tonight if I kept pushing him. That was when I knew he'd broken me because that sounded like a great idea. Just the thought made my cheeks tingle where he'd spanked me.

As soon as his belt hung free, I traced the outline of his dick with my fingers. Nash growled and released my face so I could see what was waiting for me. My insides were out of control. My heart pounded hard, matching my pulse and the throbbing between my legs.

"Don't fuck with me tonight, Princess."

He shook his head at me, almost pleading. I reached up and released the clip in my hair, and it fell around my shoulders in loose waves.

"What will you do to me if I keep pushing?"

"Fuck this," he said, and his voice was deeper and raspier than before.

I squealed and tried to dart away as he whipped the leather out of his loops, but he still managed to catch me with one arm. My ass could already feel the belt even though he hadn't touched me with it.

"Where are you running off to?"

Nash quickly wrapped my wrists like I was a calf at the rodeo and hauled me flush against his body. His mouth was relentless on my neck. If I hadn't been a puddle already, I was now. My legs shook as he towered over me and filled me with a passion that seemed to have always been there and was just waiting for me to let go to ignite.

"Are you going to keep testing me?"

"I didn't know I was."

He sat down and dragged me over his lap. I knew it was coming, and I wanted it all. Nash's hand cracked against my ass. I jerked forward, causing me to rub against the hard cock pushing into my stomach.

"You're an asshole," I hissed, and he smacked me again. "I hate you," I moaned.

"Liar," he growled, giving my ass three more smacks before yanking me to my feet. My ass was throbbing and heat radiated between my thighs.

Nash kissed me, his tongue invading my mouth and stealing my breath away until my head was light. When he let go, I stumbled and sat down on the bed. He stripped off the rest of his clothes while I eyed the cock that now bobbed in front of my face.

"Do you like what you see?"

"Maybe, maybe not." Yeah, I was a liar.

Leaning over, he forced me to lay back. I tried to wiggle away from him, but he followed, crawling onto the bed like he was stalking me.

"Why can't you admit that you want me?"

"Why can't you," I bit back.

"I think it's obvious that I do," he said, sitting back on his knees.

Like a cat with a toy, I watched his hand glide up and down his shaft. His abs flexed as he squeezed harder, and the final marble in my brain rolled out the door.

"I want you," I said, finally caving into the three words I'd sworn would remain locked away forever.

Nash's control slipped at my confession, and whatever I'd been fighting between us was stripped away as quickly as my dress. The wild look in his eyes as he grabbed the fabric and tore it in half should've been terrifying, but it only made me hotter. He somehow made me feel the same level of desperation that was in his touch.

My strapless bra was whipped away, and I cried out in pleasure as he sucked my nipple into his mouth and tore a hole in my lace panties. He settled between my legs, and I loved feeling his weight pressing into me. The heat from his skin made me shiver. There was no gentle teasing before he shoved a finger into my pussy and groaned into my mouth. He thrust in and out, teasing me and pushing the climax that was right there on the edge even higher.

"You're not a good liar, Princess. This pussy is soaked. Have you wanted to fuck me all night?"

"Yes. Oh god, yes, more," I cried, churning my hips as my pussy clenched around his finger.

"You're going to get me killed," he said, shaking like he was still trying to hold himself back.

Wrapping my tied hands around his neck, I whispered in his ear. "Fuck me. I want you."

That was it. The last of Nash's control snapped completely. Somehow, his blue eyes took on another level of intensity that shouldn't be humanly possible as he grabbed my hips. The tip of his cock teased me as he nudged at my entrance.

"Yes," I said. "Please...Nash."

The world stopped or maybe spun on its axis as he thrust his massive cock into me in a single go, rubbing over my G-spot. I screamed and bucked up with my hips as I came all over him.

"Oh, fuck me. That feels incredible," Nash said, pulling back and sliding in much easier and deeper this time.

"Oh fuck...I'm a dead man," he growled. I had no idea who he was referring to, but if he thought Myles and the guys were going to care, he was wrong. "So fucking tight and wet. I want you to come again."

Holding my hands above my head, he completely covered my body, his hips pumping faster. I wrapped my legs around his waist, and he snarled at me, his face twisted in pleasure. I savored the look and craved to see him lose himself. To know that I made Nash feel anything, let alone lose control, was something I didn't know I craved until now.

Meeting him thrust for thrust, I loved how he swore and braced his arms to hover over me. Keeping my wrists trapped, he picked up the pace until we were bouncing with the force of his movements.

"Such a sweet fucking pussy," he said and pounded into me so hard that he physically stole the air from my lungs as he ripped the orgasm from my body.

"Nash...yes...fuck, I'm coming," I yelled before I came so hard that it made the first climax feel like a teaser. My eyes rolled back in my head as my mouth hung open, and my pussy clamped down around his relentless thrusts.

"Fuck," Nash roared as I came. "I can't hold back. Feels so good." His movements became completely erratic. "Fuck, fuck, fuck...you're mine," he growled, and those two words alone set off a chain of climaxes in my body like fireworks.

"You're fucking mine, Princess," he said, crashing his lips to mine with a guttural sound that made me shudder as his body froze. With each pulse of his cock he swore. He jerked one last time and then went quiet. His mouth was still on mine as we stared into each other's eyes, but I couldn't read him.

"You're mine, Princess." I nodded, not trusting my voice to work properly.

He untied my hands and tossed the belt away, but I knew that if I pushed him, he wouldn't hesitate to use it on my ass next time.

We were still breathing heavily when his cock twitched inside of me, and I gasped at the sudden movement.

Nash clenched his fist and held his knuckles in front of my face. My eyes darted over the word even though I already knew what it said.

"What does that say?"

"Mine."

"That's right. You're mine, Princess." Nash's voice was rough, like he'd swallowed gravel and smoked a pack of cigarettes. It was the sexiest thing I'd ever heard. "Do you understand me?"

"But what about—" Nash cut me off.

"No." He shook his head. "You can fuck them all you want. Love them all you want. But at the end of the day, you're mine. Now say it."

"I'm yours," I whispered.

Nash kissed me like he had at the museum. So much more than just need was in his touch, and I tasted something far sweeter on his lips, but neither of us said the words.

"Roll over and get on your knees. I'm fucking you again." He gripped my throat, constricting my airway, but not enough to scare me. Nash licked my bottom lip before biting it and sucking it into his mouth. "And this time, I want you to scream my name until you can't anymore. I want all of Seattle to know who owns this pussy." I nodded again. "Now tell me who you belong to."

"I'm yours."

"Good girl, Princess."

Chapter 22

Ren

My eyes fluttered open, and I couldn't deny that I loved being wrapped around Nash. I never thought this would've happened, but last night had been scarily perfect. Like seeing a whole new Nash. My leg was slung over his, my arm hugged his waist, and my head was on his chest over his heart. Every single muscle hurt. I'd thought the other guys had put me through my paces, but Nash...acted like it was a competition to see if he could make me pass out from pleasure and exhaustion. He had almost succeeded, almost.

We slept, gripping one another, and for the first time since I'd met him, I felt this undeniable connection. He was still Nash, still demanding and everything else that was him, but it was different. It felt different, like a ray of sunshine breaking through a hard torrential rain.

Lifting my head, I looked up at him and smiled.

"You're awake," I said, and his eyes found mine. The smile slowly faded from my face. "What's wrong?"

"This was a mistake," he said and pushed himself up. All my happy thoughts and fluttery feelings crashed to the ground. "A huge fucking mistake."

"What do you mean it was a mistake? You definitely didn't act like it was a mistake last night."

He walked over to the minibar and yanked it open. Grabbing a bottle of water, he cracked the lid and chugged half of it before tossing it down in front of me.

"Act is the keyword in that sentence. Get your clothes and get out. We need to leave. I have shit to do and can't waste any more of my time hanging around this room with you."

A slap would have hurt less. My heart raced but for a whole new reason than it had last night.

"Are you joking with me? If so, it's not funny, Nash."

"Does it look like I'm fucking joking?"

I gripped the sheet to my chest and stared at his angry face. What happened in the last few hours? Leaving the bed, I moved to reach for his arm, but he jerked it away.

"Don't fucking touch me. I told you this was a mistake. I never should've brought you with me."

"I'm the reason you're even here," I bit out.

"Yeah, thanks for that. Really fucking stupid to give away one of your mother's painting. Too bad you can't get it back. Now, get out of my room."

His words hit right where he was aiming...straight through my heart.

"What the hell is going on, Nash? This isn't you."

He stomped toward me, and in my haste to back up, I tripped over the sheet and landed hard on my ass. Nash bent over and glared at me with so much hatred that I flinched.

"This isn't me? It's been me since the day we met. Did you actually believe I caught feelings for you? That we were going to go away together on a romantic getaway, and I'd suddenly fall in love? How fucking delusional are you?"

"No...but...."

He put his hands on his hips.

"But what? You're so gullible. You haven't learned a fucking thing about our world. We use people, Princess. We move pieces around on the board to get what we want. I already told you that. I saw you staring at me with those big grey eyes, wishing you could get in my pants. You were just too stubborn to let me fuck you and get it out of both our systems. So, I pushed a little more, acted concerned, befriended you, offered to help you, and waited. You broke just like I knew you would." He shook his head at me. "You even screamed my name."

Tears stung my eyes, but there was no way in hell I was giving Nash the satisfaction of seeing me cry. Gathering the sheet, I stood and walked around, picking up the remnants of my dress, shoes, and anything else that I could find before heading to the door.

"What? You got nothing else smart to say? Going to go off and cry to the guys now? Oh, boo-hoo. Poor little Princess got her feelings hurt. Don't worry, I'm sure Myles will eat it right up and console you."

As much of an asshole as Nash could be, I'd never seen him be purposely cruel, not like this. But like he said, maybe I was blinded, wanting to see a shred of good in him so much that I allowed myself to live in this fantasy world and not see what was right in front of my face the entire time.

Stopping in the doorway, I looked back at him and had no idea why he was doing this. There were a dozen possibilities, but none of them mattered, and it didn't stop the pain trying to tear my heart out. The voice in my head had called me a fool so many times, and each time, I came up with an excuse. But the voice was right. I was a fool for ever letting my guard down, for ever believing him, for giving up the one thing he so obviously wanted.

Nash had lured me in, one hour at a time, like I was his greatest challenge, and like the fool I was, wanting to believe the best in everyone, I caved. I fell in love with him and handed my heart over on a silver platter for him to destroy. That was on me.

He warned me when I first arrived that he would fuck me, that I'd beg him to do it and that was all he wanted. I should've continued to believe those first words, but I didn't so here we were. Now, he was happily gloating about tearing my heart out, but I wouldn't let him see that.

"Say it, Princess. Yell at me. Tell me I'm a fucking asshole." He crossed his arms and smirked. "Do your worst."

I kept my voice calm and sucked back all the emotion that was threatening to break free.

"Bravo, it's been quite the performance. You're right, you had me convinced that you cared. I guess you won, pulled one over on me and got everything you wanted and more. There's nothing else to say other than congratulations."

I looked around the room, remembering every little detail of last night, wanting to commit it and the pain to memory as a lesson. I'm not sure what he thought I was going to say, but he seemed confused by my response. Once again, that was a him problem.

With my head held high, I walked across the large suite to the second bedroom, managing to calmly close and lock the door. The shaking began the moment I shut myself in the bathroom. Tears streamed down my face as I stepped into the shower.

Covering my mouth to stifle my sobs and to keep from completely falling apart, I let myself bathe in the agony. I soaked in each word like a stab wound so that I'd never let it happen again. Shame on him for what he had done, but it would be shame on me if I ever believed him again.

I'd grown stronger this past year. No strangers in masks, Vicky, or the likes of Nash Collier were going to destroy me. Nash and others like him thought my generosity was a weakness, but they were wrong.

One day, he would see that, and by then, I would be gone.

Nash

I glared at her, pissed at the world, but mostly myself. My feelings didn't matter. Sleeping with Ren could cost me not only my life and my boys but any deals I had in the works. I'd put my future on the line and then let emotion get involved. What happened last night could unravel it all. She needed to stay the fuck away from me.

"Bravo, it's been quite the performance. You're right, you had me convinced that you cared. I guess you won, pulled one over on me and got everything you wanted and more. There's nothing else to say other than congratulations," Ren said, her voice cold and void of any affection. Even her eyes were flat and gave nothing away.

I followed her and watched as she quietly slipped into her room. The subtle click was like a hammer being cocked while the gun was to my head. Fuck. Fuck. Fuck. Slamming my door, I banged my head on it and wanted to trash the whole suite. Instead, I marched into the bathroom to shower.

The water was frigid when I stepped under the spray and leaned against the wall. Closing my eyes, all I could see was Ren's smile fading as I yelled at her and the cool blanket indifference that she'd wrapped herself in before leaving the room.

"What the hell did I just do?"

Two hours later, I was on the couch, still waiting for Ren to come out. Glancing at her door for the millionth time, I ran through what I would say. My knee bounced until I finally gave up and walked over.

"Ren?" I knocked. "Princess...look, I'm sorry. I...shit. I'm a fucking asshole, just let me explain."

There was no response. Not a fuck you or a go away. Putting my ear to the wood, I listened for any movement. Nothing.

"Princess?"

Panic overrode every other emotion. I grabbed the handle, expecting it to be locked, and terrified of what I might find on the other side. But it opened wide. Her bed was still perfectly made, and nothing seemed out of place.

"Ren?"

Marching into the bathroom, I knew she wasn't there, but I had to check and flicked on the light. The walls were wet, but everything of hers was gone. A hint of sparkle caught my eye on the way out and I bent over to pick up one of her heels from last night in the garbage.

"Fuck," I said, pulling out my cell.

N: Where are you?

It showed read, but she didn't respond.

> N: Answer me, I know you're there.

> Princess: Home.

> N: Home like Canada or home like Wayward? And how the hell are you heading home? It's not safe to be alone.

> Princess: Safer than being with you, and I'm not alone.

Rage burned in my chest as I stomped over to my bag and swiped it off the floor.

> N: Who the fuck are you with?

If she was with some guy and he touched her...I was going to rip him into tiny pieces. Which I realized was fucking ironic considering what I'd just said to her.

> Princess: Nash, leave me alone. You made your point crystal clear. I got the message. Now get mine. I don't want to talk to you.

"Fuck!" Swearing all the way to the elevator, I got in and decided to call her instead. It rang before going to voicemail.

> N: You didn't just send me to VM?

> Princess: Leave me the fuck alone, Nash. I mean it.

> N: Answer the phone.

I dialed again, but this time, it went straight to voicemail, and I almost threw my phone across the lobby. Charging outside, I handed the valet my ticket and looked around, trying to think like Princess. If

I was her, what would I do? My eyes scanned the parking lot, and I swore. The guards. The black SUVs were gone. Oh, fuck my life.

The third attempt was the same, and when she did it again, I called Mr. Genovese's head of security, Marcus.

"Nash, I wondered if you would be calling," Marcus said, picking up on the second ring.

"Is she with you?"

"She is," he drawled.

"Where are you taking her?"

"To the academy as she instructed. I must say, I'm a little confused. What happened with Ms. Mikhailov that made her want to leave your presence and so swiftly?"

I didn't have to see him to know he was calling me a prick and smirking.

"It's a misunderstanding. If you pull over, I'll pick Ren up and take her the rest of the way."

"No."

"What do you mean, no?"

"It's a simple enough word to understand, but I'll clarify for you. I don't answer to you. I answer to Mr. Genovese, and I've already informed him that there was a change in plans."

My heart galloped out of control. I was so fucked.

"He instructed me to take Ms. Mikhailov wherever she wanted to go. Not only that, but we are nearly halfway back, so no, we are not pulling over and waiting almost two hours for you. You've dug this hole or made your bed. Take your pick of saying...either way, you can lie in it. Have a great day, Nash." The phone clicked dead.

"Fuck, fuck, fuck!"

"I'm sorry, sir. I didn't mean to take that long. Your car was blocked in," the valet said, his face terrified.

"Not you. A business deal just went sideways," I said as I passed him a hundred.

He nodded, took the money, and couldn't get away from me fast enough. I jogged around the front of the car and tossed my bag on the passenger seat as I slipped behind the wheel. Damage control was the only thing on my mind. Of all the things that I thought Ren would do, this was not one of them. Then again, I wasn't really thinking at all when I pushed her away.

"Fuck my life, Princess. You have no idea what you've just done," I said, pulling out of the hotel. "If Mr. Genovese finds out I've dishonored my contract, I'm as good as dead, and everything will disappear with a snap of his fingers," I said out loud like I was talking to her.

Not that she'd care what happened to me after what I'd said to her. Why would she? I wouldn't if roles were reversed.

Instead of asking for space—which she probably would have given me because she was fucking perfect—I verbally kicked her in the teeth. Yelling to vent some of my frustration, I slammed my hands down on the steering wheel as rage and panic mixed into one volatile cocktail.

I fucked up and broke my word. Which meant no more backing from Mr. Genovese. No more taking over and killing my father while remaining in control. No more Mr. Kessler, and no more deals with Nathaniel or the Mikhailov family. Hell, I could lose my guys for what I just did. I had to fix this with her, but how? My mind was blank, the sadness in her grey eyes needling my mind.

"You need to keep your head screwed on straight. Stop panicking," I said. Why the fuck was I still talking out loud? It didn't stop the fear. Even more concerning than everything else combined was if Ren was serious when she said she never wanted to see me again.

An old ache surfaced, and unlike all the other times, I couldn't shove it down. My body shook as I tried to suppress the pain. I'd fucked up once, and it had cost the person I loved their life. I couldn't fuck any of this up again, I just couldn't.

Like a house of cards, one wrong move was all it took for everything to fall in around me, and I had no one to blame but myself.

Theo

"Mmmm, this is so good," Ren said, licking her fingers and giving me ideas as I watched her tongue slide up a digit before she sucked it into her mouth. "How did you get grumpy, Mrs. Edwards, to let you bring food in here?"

Blinking away my dirty thoughts, I cleared my throat. "Would you believe she is a huge cat lover? She has like ten of them."

Ren stopped eating the piece of fried chicken and stared at me.

"Please tell me this is going somewhere kinky?"

I laughed hard and loved to see the smile on her face. She'd been trying to act like nothing happened when she was away with Nash, but a cavernous void had opened between them.

They'd always fought and poked at one another. Hell, they even flirted, but this was different. Ren actively went out of her way to avoid Nash. She did it casually and thought she was being smart about it, but Nash was acting just as cagey. Combined, all the signs were there.

Something had happened, but neither was talking.

"No, nothing kinky. At least, not that I know of. Anyway, her cat was sick the other day, and no one on staff could cover for her. I offered to look after the library so she could take her cat to a vet appointment. I have keys from late-night studying, and she knows I'm a stickler with the books and rules, so her precious books would be safe."

Ren's eyes filled up with tears. "That's so sweet."

Shifting closer, I touched her chin and made her look at me. I searched her face, but she'd gotten so much better at hiding what she was feeling.

"What's wrong," I asked, running my thumb over her cheek. "It was nice of me, but not tears worthy. Tell me what's going on."

"Nothing, it's just so touching. Don't mind me. I'm just overly emotional, you know us girls," she said, and I shook my head at her.

"Don't do that. You know as well as I do that you're never emotional unless it's for a good reason, and...how damn sexist of you," I teased, making her smile.

"That was pretty sexist of me. Good thing I'm a girl."

I kissed her lips softly and could feel the soft tremble coming through the light contact to mine.

"What did Nash do?"

She looked away and poked at her dinner.

"What makes you think he did something? We're fine. Just

another typical week dealing with the annoyance that is Nash Collier."

"You keep saying words, but they are all lies. Why are you lying to me, Ren?" She dropped her fork and rubbed her forehead. "Give me something. I can't help if I don't know what's going on."

"You can't fix this. It's just Nash being Nash and me being me," she said.

"You're going to have a great career in politics," I teased, nudging the triple chocolate brownie toward her like a bribe.

"I don't want to talk about it." She shrugged but broke off a small piece of the brownie and started nibbling on it. "I went to Seattle with thoughts, feelings, and expectations that, looking back now, were stupid." The soft grey of her eyes held a new layer of pain when she looked at me. "I was wrong, and I need to just get over it. Nash is who he is, he always will be, end of story."

"Did he hurt you," I asked as she blinked away the tears shining in her eyes.

"No more than he always has," she said, but I didn't believe her.

"I'm not great at this like Myles or Blake. But I'm here for you, you know that, right?" She nodded. "You know we love you?" She nodded again. "Are you protecting him?" She shook her head, but a half second of hesitation said enough.

He'd hurt her. Nash said or did something to change their entire dynamic while they were in Seattle. If I found out what it was and he purposely crushed her, I was going to make him hurt.

"Come here," I whispered, pulling her to my side and linking our hands together.

"I'll be fine, I promise. Just need to process and work through my feelings on everything."

"Like how I needed to process when I came to see you after the fight with Liam?"

"Sort of. It's hard letting go of something you thought was real but never was. Like clinging to a fantasy that was as real as unicorns.

What you and Liam have is special, but Nash and me…it's not even in the same game, let alone ballpark."

Closing my eyes, I kissed the top of her head.

"Want to try and beat me in a game of Strip Jeopardy?"

"I'll take hell yes for five hundred," she said, making us both laugh.

I stood, and Ren looked up at me.

"Where are you going?"

"Strip Jeopardy," I smirked. "I'm kicking everyone out of the library and locking the fucking door. Because you're going down, and then I'm going down on you." Her cheeks flamed a vibrant shade of red. "You're going to look so sexy laid out with textbooks all around you."

"You have strange fantasies, Theo O'Brien."

"Tonight, you get Murk." I winked and walked away, yelling that there was a gas leak and everyone needed to leave.

Maybe Liam would have more luck with Nash because it was obvious that Ren was staying tight-lipped about Seattle.

Liam

"I know what you're trying to do," Nash said, holding up his drink. "You're trying to get me drunk and then take advantage of me. I always knew you liked my ass."

I sipped my scotch. "Guilty. It jiggles a little when you walk."

Nash looked insulted and even stared down at his lap like he could see his ass. "It doesn't jiggle." I smirked. "Whatever, it doesn't. I know why you're really doing this anyway."

"Enlighten me."

His scowl darkened. "You want to know what happened last

weekend." He pointed at me. "Don't think I haven't seen you staring at me with your disturbing looks."

"Disturbing looks?"

"Yes, that one. The one that says you're staring into my brain and picking me apart. You really should be a psychiatrist. You'd kick ass at it."

"I'll take it under advisement." I stared at him for a moment, and the far-off, distraught look in his eyes said it all. I waited until he put the glass to his lips—because I was a jerk like that—before I spoke. "I don't need to get you drunk to know you fucked her," I said, and Nash started choking.

He coughed while I grabbed his glass and refilled our drinks. "Fucker."

I shrugged. "You probably deserve it for something."

Snatching his scotch, he stood and walked over to the bar and stared up at the bottles. This place had gone from a rundown piece of shit to a club with sexy lounge vibes and all the high-end services to bring the customers and cash rolling in. If I could only convince him to let me hold high-stakes poker games downstairs, we would make our investment back in no time.

"Was it any good?" I took a sip and watched as Nash turned around to face me.

He smirked. "Indescribable."

"That good?"

"That good."

"That seems like an exaggeration. Are you sure it wasn't because your dick felt like it had been cut off from water and finally got a drink?"

"No," he said and looked down into his glass. I shook my head.

"You actually like her, don't you? Like really like her."

He chugged the two fingers I'd poured for him and walked back over to flop down in the leather chair.

"It doesn't matter."

"Let me guess, you had a full-blown meltdown. We both know you can't handle any emotion, let alone something close to real. So, you got all up in your head and took it out on her. You probably said something stupid and hurt her. You hurt her bad enough that she doesn't want to talk to or see you ever again."

Nash screwed up his face as he stared at me. "Were you fucking there? Did you hide under the bed and watch it all from your creepy stalker position? Did you at least get to jerk off while you watched? Fuck me."

"I did squirt a little. She screams well," I said, and he grabbed one of the hundreds of pillows and threw it at me.

Nash sobered, the internal conflict alive and well. "I really fucked up. I had good reasons, but the shit I said to her...I can't take it back with a sorry. I don't know if this can be fixed."

"That bad?"

"Worse."

"I've never known you to roll over and play dead before." He squeezed the glass, and I thought it was going to be the next thing flung at my head.

"I'm not."

"Then what do you call this." I held my hand out toward him. "She's avoiding you, so what? She's been trying to avoid you for a year now, and it's never stopped you before." He sat there, staring straight ahead like he was watching a movie only he could see. Sitting back, I rubbed my bottom lip as I thought. "You know she loves you, right? It's so obvious when she looks at you."

He cringed and pinched the bridge of his nose.

"Trust me, if she did, she doesn't anymore. I'd hate me forever."

"I don't know what to say 'cause your go-to is poking at one another, and that's not going to work. What you really need is a way to apologize."

"I might as well wish for a miracle," Nash said before emptying the rest of the bottle into our glasses.

He was already well on his way to having a buzz—I glanced at the glass. "You not planning on training tomorrow for the meet?"

"Why?"

"Okay then, forget I said anything." I sighed and leaned forward to rest my arms on my knees. "I have to ask...."

"Must you?" He groaned.

"Yes."

"Fine. What do you want to know?"

"Do you want to fix things? I don't want to hear anything other than yes or no."

"It's complicated."

"No, it's really not. Choose what you want. Life and death are on the line," I said, and he rolled his eyes at me.

"Yes, but I can't. Not right now. Trust me, it's better if she stays away from me because I don't know if I can control myself."

"Interesting. Well, that leads me to question two. Is this going to blow back on us? Do I need to start looking over my shoulder and working out a way to keep us safe?"

He stared at me for so long that I was ready to pick up the phone and call everyone I knew for an emergency lockdown.

"It shouldn't."

"But there's a possibility?"

"There's always a possibility, Liam. But in this case...I think I have the situation under control or I would've looped you in that we had an issue." Nash shifted and rested his head on the back of the chair, staring at the ceiling.

"I'm going to state the obvious here, but I feel I have to fucking say it." Nash rolled his head in my direction. "If you care for her in any fashion and wait too long...you may not get a chance to fix what you broke. Even a partial fix now is better than none at all."

"I know, but I have to evaluate all the risks while my father is still in play. Whether I like it or not," Nash said and closed his eyes. I hadn't seen him like this about a girl since Mya, and I never thought I'd see it again.

Nash might not be able to say it or was too scared to admit it out loud, but he loved Ren. Whatever he said to her was eating him alive. But I knew my best friend well enough to know that by the time he got his head out of his ass, it would be too late, and for once, I couldn't let it happen.

OCTOBER 01 – WEDNESDAY 1:00 PM

Ren

My hand moved over the canvas. The bold, contrasting colors captured the image better than I ever could've imagined. I swayed and hummed to the song on my playlist, loving the early birthday gift from Myles. My earphones wouldn't hold a charge anymore, so he got me this amazing baby blue set. He really didn't need to get me everything in blue, but the little snowflake stickers Blake had put on them looked amazing.

Swirling my brush around the red, I touched up the trees, loving the fall vibe. The trees always looked like they were on fire to me. It truly was my favorite time of year, and nothing else felt right. I'd started a portrait but found myself daydreaming of things I was trying really hard to forget, so I switched to this serene landscape instead.

It had been so long since I could take over the art room and find my peace. I'd forgotten how much I missed this. Raising my arms into the air, I wiggled and turned in a circle as I sang, using my paintbrush as a microphone.

"Cause when I'm in a room with you, that missing piece is found."

Opening my eyes, I screamed as I spotted Nash leaning against the counter, staring at me. His mouth was pulled up in the smile that had suckered me in, along with so many others.

I pushed the headphones back so they hung around my neck as I glared at him.

"Oh, don't stop on my account," he said.

"Yeah, no. I'm not doing this." Marching across the room away from him, I tossed my brush and palette into the sink. I'd circle back when he was gone to clean them.

"Princess," he called out as I pushed through the door and out into the hall, where there was at least a smattering of students and teachers in classrooms. I knew he would follow me because he couldn't leave well enough alone. "Ren, listen to me."

"No. I have no interest in anything you have to say to me. Not now, not ever. Just leave me alone, Nash," I snarled at him as I marched outside.

He grabbed my arm, and I twisted in a move he'd taught me to break his hold.

"Don't touch me," I hissed at him as I continued down the path.

"Then talk to me. You don't understand, and I want to try and explain."

"I'm pretty sure I understand. You were very clear. Everything you've ever said was nothing more than an act to have meaningless sex with me. I was an idiot for believing you might actually care, and oh yeah, I'm a mistake...no...a huge mistake. Did I leave anything out?"

"Ren...."

"What? No Princess? I guess you can cut the nickname, too, right? Just go away, Nash. You've managed to ruin my day off and the one place I find real happiness, so yay for you. Oh, and if you're worried that I'm going to say something to the guys, I won't. Your dirty secret is safe, but I'm pretty sure they already know you're an asshole."

He genuinely looked upset standing there. But that was the problem. I had no idea what was real or fake anymore, and I didn't have it in me to wade through it right now. When he just stared at me, I turned and walked away.

"I'm sorry."

I wheeled on him and stormed back. My hands balled into fists. "You're sorry? What exactly are you sorry for?"

"All of it. Everything I said."

"Saturday night or Sunday morning?"

"Um...."

"No, that's not how this works. You didn't just make a smart-ass remark or a stupid joke. Hell, you didn't even act inappropriately and embarrass me. That's child's play in comparison to what you did." I laughed, but it didn't reach my eyes. "You targeted me, Nash."

"It wasn't like that."

"No, see, I'll tell you what it was like. I gave myself to you, against my better judgment, and warning bells, and numerous flags. I stared into eyes that I finally trusted after a year of believing you were the worst human possible and thought I felt something real between us."

"I felt the same."

"Bullshit, you don't feel what I did and do what you did. You told me once that you strive for peace, but I don't think that's true. I think you love the drama and the chaos. You wouldn't know what to do without it. But I'm not like you, and I hate it. I'd managed to carve out a corner piece of happiness and stupidly thought that you were part of it. But you just can't stand to see me happy, and I don't know why. I don't know what I've done to you, but it's like you feed off my misery. Then again, you are Lawrence's son, so I guess that apple didn't fall far, did it?"

He crossed his arms and looked away, and I glanced around at the crowd, trying to hear our showdown.

My lower lip trembled, but I still refused to give him a single tear. Composing myself, I lowered my voice.

"You didn't just hurt me. You tried to break me," I said with my hand on my chest. "I opened up to you. I literally gave away a piece of my heart to a man I barely knew so you could have a shot at your dream, and you found a way to make me regret it. You chose to thank me for my kindness by making me feel the lowest I have since my mother died."

Shaking my head, I took a step back.

"So no, you don't dictate when we speak, how we speak, or anything else. I know you struggle with listening, but I really want you to hear this...don't look for me, don't talk to me, and don't try to apologize for something that you're not sorry for. Just leave me alone."

"I can't do that," he said, grabbing my arm as I turned to leave.

This time, when I spun around, I slapped him across the face. My palm stung, but I'd never felt anything so satisfying in my life.

Nash's head turned to the side, and he touched his cheek. He looked at me with eyes full of the same possessiveness I'd seen Saturday night. I didn't understand him, and I didn't want to keep playing his games.

"You're mine, Princess. You admitted it. You gave yourself to me. I've claimed you, and I'm keeping you."

"Claimed me? I'm not a dog at the pound. You can't claim me.

You're delusional if you think that. I never belonged to you and will never, in any capacity, be claimed by you."

I jerked my arm away just as Vicky came prancing up the walkway, her face all smiles.

"Oh, trouble in paradise. I guess you finally told her," Vicky said, and Nash glared at her. "Thank God, it's been so difficult keeping the secret to myself."

"Not now, Vicky," he growled.

Despite not really giving a shit what these two had cooking, I couldn't seem to stop my curiosity. Who was I kidding? I was a sucker for punishment.

"Tell me what? I'm done disputing paint colors," I said.

Vicky paused but wouldn't be derailed now that she was racing for the finish line.

"Well, Nash didn't want to make it public yet," Vicky said, and I just knew she was going to say they were back together.

"Not now, Vicky," Nash said and grabbed her arm.

He started dragging her away, but apparently, we both suffered from the same affliction. Her eyes lit up with malice that I felt to my bones as her lips curved into a maniacal sneer.

"Nash signed a contract with my father. We're getting married after graduation."

A sharp ringing started in my ears as I stared at them, my eyes bouncing from Vicky's overly happy face to Nash's furious one. They were talking, but I couldn't make out a single word.

Like cocking the hammer on a gun, it all clicked. The nod from Mr. Genovese to Nash, him telling me I was going to get him killed and practically begging me to kick him out of the room. I was the mistake, but not for the reason I thought. This was so much worse. I fell in love with the guy contracted to marry the one person I hated in this world, the Wicked Bitch of the West. It definitely explained the sudden influx of money for the club and the guards. He told me he had fixed the problem with his father and Vicky, but this never crossed my mind, and yet...it should've been my first thought.

The pain was so sharp that I looked to see if I had been shot, but for some reason—that I'd never be able to explain—I laughed. I laughed so hard that tears rolled down my cheeks, and I gasped for air.

When I glanced up, the two of them were looking at me like I'd lost my mind. Maybe I had because I sat down on the grass as the bursts of hysteria slowed and then started back up.

"Why the hell are you laughing," Vicky finally asked, her arms crossed and toe-tapping on the bricks. I tried to answer, but nothing logical came out. "Fine, whatever. Laugh all you want, but by this time next year, I'll be Mrs. Nash Collier."

"Vicky," Nash growled, and she looked at him. "Not a fucking word to anyone else, or I call your father right now."

Vicky looked like she was about to throw a fit. "Fine, not another word," she spit out, then shot me a glare before marching off with her nose firmly in the air.

Wiping the tears off my face, I looked up at Nash. He was rubbing the back of his neck and muttering under his breath. On some level, I pitied him.

Pushing myself up, I dusted off my coveralls and gave him my best fake smile.

"I hope you two will be very happy together. Have a great life, Nash."

"Ren?" I glanced back. "I...."

"Save it for someone who cares."

"Fuck," Nash yelled as I walked away, needing to put as much distance between me and Nash Collier as I could.

Chapter 25

OCTOBER 02 – THURSDAY 8:10 AM

Ren Myles and Blake were relentless with the questions about Nash, but I didn't say a word about what happened between us or what I'd learned about him and Vicky. It wasn't my secret to tell, and if he didn't want them to know, then he would have to deal with the fallout. Everyone knew that we'd argued, it was far too public with Vicky showing up for people not to know, but she seemed to be keeping her mouth shut as well. I still couldn't believe it, and yet...he didn't deny it.

"You okay? You're off in space," Ivy said, and I looked between her and Chantry who wore an equally worried expression.

"I'm fine. Just didn't sleep well last night. It's nice of the dean to give us all an extra long weekend so we can watch the meet," I said, smoothly changing the topic.

"Yeah, it's rare that they allow this big of a sporting event on campus. They have to take so many extra precautions that they only offer once every two years. Same with all the sports," Ivy said as she flicked the navy and gold striped scarf over her shoulder.

"You do know that it's hot at the pool, right," I asked.

"I know, but I didn't have anything else other than my uniform in our school colors." She spun the two ends, and I smiled. "And I wanted to show school spirit."

The lineup of buses parked in the lot and all the way down the driveway was mindboggling. Each one had a sign in the window with the school's name and image of the mascot.

"They really go all out," I said as I looked at the food trucks. My stomach growled even though I'd already eaten breakfast.

"Sure do. For a couple of days, we get to feel like normal kids," Ivy said and pointed. "There's the cotton candy truck," she squealed with excitement. Chantry and I giggled at her exuberance for spun sugar.

There was a buzz in the air as soon as we got close to the pool. Groups of people in team tracksuits were huddled together, and I quickly realized that there were more than just my guys and there were girls. I didn't realize the swim team was so large.

"I didn't even know our swim team has girls," I said, and Ivy nodded.

"Yeah, there are like thirty people total. The coach has them divided so they train separately."

"How did I not know this?"

Ivy and Chantry shrugged as we stepped inside the building. No matter how much time passed, the overwhelming scent of chlorine would always remind me of Nash.

"Wow, it's insane in here."

The normally dead-quiet hallway hummed with voices. My mouth dropped as we entered, and I stared at the packed bleachers running the perimeter of the pool. Extra corner units had been erected, so there was seating all the way around. They'd also brought in a waist-high wall that the crowd had to stay behind. The school's championship banners hung overhead while navy and gold valances with large ribbons and sparkly streamers draped from window to window. Music was playing, adding to the background noise, and I suddenly wanted to run back outside. I'd always found this Olympic-sized space too big, but today it felt small and almost claustrophobic.

"There's room over there." Ivy pointed to a small space that would just fit the three of us.

Volunteers wearing fluorescent green shirts were everywhere, with clipboards in hand and stopwatches around their necks.

We quickly weaved our way to the spot Ivy had pointed out just as the first set of swimmers stepped out onto the deck. The crowd went crazy, and I would've sworn we were at a hockey game. Ivy jumped up, swinging her scarf like a mad woman. There were so many people that I couldn't even see who was there. Myles had said they were starting with the youngest age groups and working up.

Ivy flopped down beside me, her face glowing with excitement. "You have to get into it. It's so much fun. We get chanting at each other, too, especially for the team medley. You'll see."

I glanced at Chantry, who laughed.

"You look horrified," she said.

"I think I'm just in shock. This is not what I pictured with the words swim meet." She giggled again.

The first race was a heat of girls, and I had no idea what I was cheering for other than the girl in lane three was ours and we wanted her to finish first. For each race, they announced the distance, stroke, and then each athlete individually. The energy never died down, and I knew the moment when Myles stepped out onto the deck for the first time.

Down the bleachers, a group of girls were screaming and chanting, "Team Myles." I recognized the blonde who had been following him around at the lacrosse practices. She had a whole section wearing white T-shirts blinged out with *Team Myles* across their chests.

Getting up, Ivy grabbed my arm. "Where are you going?"

"I'll be right back."

The poor girls froze when I walked down to their row. They were all tense and seemed prepared for me to scream at them. Instead, I smiled.

"You don't happen to have an extra T-shirt, do you?"

The ringleader smiled so wide that it looked like her face would split. She dropped the banner she'd been waving and dug around in a bag before handing me a T-shirt.

"Name's Alex," she said.

"Thanks, these are amazing."

Taking my new shirt, I went back to my seat. Ivy looked amused but confused. I peeled off my hoodie and pulled the t-shirt on over my tank top.

"Now that's much better team spirit," she laughed. "I'm surprised you're okay with all of them drooling over your guy."

I shrugged. "I know who he loves. Besides, the day that I'm as insecure as Vicky is the day I need to reevaluate my life. What they did was sweet, and I just got a kickass shirt out of it."

The bejeweled letters sparkled when I moved around.

Myles glanced over and smirked before he got that super serious look on his face and stepped up to the block. Like all the other races, the crowd didn't make a noise when the swimmers were in position. The buzzer sounded, and I jumped from the bleacher with everyone else, screaming as Myles and his competition cut through the water.

He'd told me that he normally swam the backstroke but had added a second one this year. This had to be it because I was positive this one was called the freestyle. He was in the lead when they somersaulted, pushed off the wall at the end, and started back. But there were two guys quickly closing in, and I screamed like crazy, cheering him on. When they touched the end everyone got quiet.

"Please hold while we confirm the touchpad results," the announcer said.

Myles pushed up out of the water, and I had no idea why I'd never been into this sport before. Holy hell, I couldn't take my eyes off him. He'd pulled off the tight cap and goggles and stood staring up at the electronic display over the pool as he waited. His muscled body was nothing but streams of water that accentuated every delicious cut and dip. The dark tattoos stood out among the other competitors, while the thing that Myles called a jammer left nothing to the imagination.

The results flashed and Myles had come in second. The winning school was across the way, and they jumped up, cheering. He shook hands with the other guys, and so it went. Blake finished first in his individual, and so did Liam, but Theo came in third. Nash took first in the butterfly, and as hard as I tried not to watch or cheer him on, I couldn't help it. I blamed it on the enthusiasm of the crowd. I still didn't understand the heats, but I knew that they had to swim the same stroke more than once, and each time, the groups were whittled down to the best of each, like a round robin.

"Are you hungry," Chantry asked.

"Famished," Ivy said.

"Yeah, I'm starving," I said, realizing that hours had passed.

"Why don't you stay here and save our spots while Ivy and I get some food for all of us?" She nodded to the deck. "We don't have anyone specific to cheer for," Chantry said as if expecting me to argue.

"Okay. Bring me whatever. I'll eat anything at this point."

They'd no sooner taken off when someone tapped me on the shoulder. I expected it to be Vicky, but when I turned, I blinked and then composed myself.

"Coach Richards?" I held out my hand, even as my stomach flipped with the instant reminder of Saturday night and all that was amazing before it wasn't.

"Ren, it's great to see you again," he said, shaking my hand. "Nash is killing it. He's crushing his times like a man possessed."

Smiling and nodding, I'd never wanted to step out of a conversation so badly in my life.

"He really is. He's been training extremely hard. Nash wants to be on the national team more than anything," I said, knowing the intense schedule he kept.

"I'm excited to see the team medley. Tell me, do you think he has the dedication it takes to compete at a higher level? He'll be traveling all the time and spending months away from home."

I honestly had no idea how Nash would handle that with everything else, and it was no longer my problem. Hell, it technically never was. One night together didn't make us a couple, no matter how I felt.

"That is a question only Nash can answer. But what I do know is that you won't find anyone more passionate or hardworking." I looked at the pool and the teams beginning to file out to cheers. "The pool is his peace," I said.

Richards smirked before nodding and pointing at my shirt.

"Who's Myles."

"My other boyfriend," I said with a big smile. "I have four. You can never have too many these days." The slack-jawed look I saw before I turned around was priceless.

I felt eyes on me and should have known it was Nash. My heart raced faster, but I managed to stay composed and act unfazed as I looked away. It wasn't in me to toss him under the bus or make him look bad with Richards. Regardless, nothing had changed, and I still couldn't find it in me to forgive him.

Some pain you just couldn't easily sweep away.

OCTOBER 02 – THURSDAY 5:33 PM

Liam

Nash hadn't taken his eyes off Ren since she started talking to some guy in the stands. I didn't recognize him, but Nash had turned into a statue the moment he spotted the two of them together. Stepping up beside him, I nudged his arm.

"You look like a creeper," I said, and he turned his head to glare at me. "Who is the guy?"

"Coach Richards, the US National coach. We met him at the banquet, and he mentioned trying to fit in a visit."

"That's great that he's here to see you. So why do you look like someone took the jam out of your donut? You think she'll talk trash?"

Nash's jaw twitched. "Did you just quote Snatch to me?"

I shrugged. "Thought it was appropriate."

"You're an idiot, and I don't know."

"Sure, you do. It's part of why you feel guilty," I said. I loved playing the part of Nash's conscience. There were very few things more satisfying than watching him seethe as I picked at emotional scars. But somebody had to do it because his morals had packed up years ago and hitchhiked out of town.

"Have I told you today that I hate you?"

"Not yet, but the day is young, and pointing out your flaws is one of my favorite pastimes."

Nash shook his head and mumbled profanities under his breath.

"No, Ren wouldn't do that. She'll probably be her annoyingly perfect self and talk me up."

"Yes, how dare she be nice, what a bitch move. We should definitely take her out back and shoot her," I drawled, allowing the sarcasm to drip like sweet honey from every word.

"If you're purposely trying to rile me up for this race, it's working," Nash growled under his breath. "And whose side are you on anyway?"

"I'm on the side of logic, and you're not staring at her because you're worried. You're staring because you can't believe that you fucked up this bad. Ren in your bed could've been your prize tonight, but instead, you're still trying to figure out how to grovel for forgiveness."

"I don't grovel to anyone for anything," he said, turning his back on Ren.

"Not yet, but after everything you said about her...." I sucked air in and shivered to annoy the shit out of him. "I can't wait to get her alone for the weekend. Wonder what she'll let me teach her in that tent?" Ren was already packed and ready to leave right after the meet if I wanted. It was impressive.

Nash got in my face. "Shut up. I mean it."

"Alright, under one condition. The school is on fire with speculation of what happened between you, Ren, and Vicky yesterday. Tell me what happened?"

"Is this really the time? We're about to race. I need to stay focused, and you're not helping."

The clock was right above us.

"We still have ten minutes. Besides, you've been racing pissed off all day and swimming faster than ever, so what harm is there?"

"I really don't think I want you as my best friend anymore," Nash said, walking away.

I followed him, loving getting under his skin and making him itch like a rash.

"You agreed to marry Vicky, didn't you? That's why you don't want to tell us."

Nash stopped and looked around before he faced me, his arms crossed.

"First, stop doing that reading me thing. It's fucking disturbing. Second, I did make a deal with her father." My eyebrow raised at the phrasing. "No, I can't tell you any more than that, so let the rumor mill run their mouths. I don't care."

"So, let me get this straight. You made a deal with her father. Vicky's involved, but you're not going to tell me exactly how? What the hell do you have up your sleeve? A joker?"

Nash smirked. "More like a royal flush."

"Oh my god, save me," Myles grumbled as he walked up, and the conversation died.

Nash had given me lots to consider. I'd figure it out. I always did.

Myles's eyes were wide. "They just won't stop."

I looked over his shoulder. "Who? That group of sophomores?"

"Don't look. I don't want them to think I'm talking about them," he said.

"But you are talking about them," Nash countered.

"Fine, I don't want them to know I'm talking about them. Better?"

"Myles! Myles! Myles! Myles!" The cheering got louder, and I smiled as Myles pinched the bridge of his nose. He looked like he wanted to crawl into a hole and disappear. Myles plastered a fake smile on his face as he turned and waved. The one girl in the front looked like she fainted.

"You didn't fuck them, did you," I asked.

Myles whipped around so fast. I was shocked he didn't give himself whiplash. He poked me in the chest, and I looked at his finger.

"Balls ta that. Have ya lost yer mind?"

"Figured it was worth asking. They do seem a little obsessive. Look on the bright side. They gave Ren a T-shirt. Now she can lead your little harem."

"Get ready," Coach yelled, waving us over.

This was our last heat of the day, and I was taking Theo's place. He was pretty sure he strained his hamstring during his first race and had been lagging all day. Not wanting to screw up the team event, Theo stepped down. If it hadn't been for Nash swimming out of this world in the qualifying race, we wouldn't have moved on. Luckily, the freestyle was my fastest swim. As long as the boys gave me some extra breathing room, this race should go our way.

We walked over to lane seven—the lowest we'd started from in forever—and I glanced at Ren as she clapped and yelled along with everyone else.

"Well, here we are again," Sabastian from Hawking Shores said as his team stepped up beside ours. "Hope there aren't any untimely deaths this time. It was a real shame to hear what happened to Austin," he said, and Myles snarled under his breath.

Nash took a step in Sabastian's direction.

"Hopefully, there won't be any false accusations. It would be a real shame if what happened to Austin were to happen again."

"Are you admitting to something, Nash?"

He cocked his head and smirked as he lowered his voice, so only a few of us could hear him.

"No, never. We're nothing more than upstanding and concerned citizens of the community. But cheaters are not well-liked, and karma is a real bitch. So, if I were you...." Nash's voice lowered to a hard growl. "I'd want to make sure nothing like that ever happened again. You know, for safety purposes."

Sabastian stepped back and smiled. "We don't need to cheat to beat the likes of your team, Collier. They've been holding you back all day."

"We'll see," Nash said, but as he turned and looked at us, we all knew what was at stake. This piece of shit was going to get his ass kicked in a humiliating fashion.

"We will. We will rock you!" The crowd roared, drawing our attention away from Sabastian and the guys from Hawking Shores. It was so loud that you could feel the vibration through your feet.

Myles was already in the water and set. I double-checked my cap and goggles before lining up to go last. A hush spread, and I looked left and right at our competition. Our long-standing rivals, Hawking Shores and Meadow Grove, were in the lanes directly on either side once again. These were the challenges we lived for, and this race would be tough.

"On your marks."

Buzz

The calm of the moment before erupted into mayhem as the stands went crazy, and we yelled at our teammates. Myles was a strong swimmer, and by the time he was at the halfway mark, he'd pulled a full body length ahead of everyone else. The second he touched the wall, Blake was off, and my adrenaline started pumping.

I was naturally calmer than most and kept my heart rate under control—a useful skill at the poker table.

Blake hit the wall and Nash was gone, but Meadow Grove had caught up to half a body length, and Sabastian's team was right behind them.

"Shit, that sucked," Blake said as Myles helped him out of the pool, and I got set.

Nash was on fire today. He could've been pitted against anyone in the world, and his times would've stood up. He pulled ahead again and then some.

My muscles tensed as I prepared to spring and counted down in my head. Three, two, one. Pushing off, I sailed through the air and watched the blue water disappear behind me. Most swimmers loved that first entry into the water, but I loved this part. For the briefest second, you were flying. I could hear the crowd and see my lane. My skin tingled with the anticipation of gliding into the water.

The entry was perfect, and the thrill hit. This might not have been my sport of choice when we first started swimming, but I'd grown to love it. Now, feeling my arms slicing through the water as I powered forward was something only swimmers could understand. Turning at the far end, I pushed off the wall and was just rising to the surface when someone grabbed my ankle.

Sucking in water as I was jerked down, I put my hand over my mouth and coughed, trying to push the liquid out as I turned to see who the fuck was holding me. It was one of the guys from Hawking Shores, but one look at his face told me that this was no prank. He was freaking the fuck out and in full panic mode.

He could drown us both if I didn't act quickly. I got my ankle free and signaled for him not to grab me as I wrapped an arm around him. We surfaced in a rescue position just as the lifeguard arrived beside me. I coughed the rest of the water out of my lungs but refused to hand him over. It would just slow us down. There was a whistling sound as he gasped for air that I could easily hear since the crowd had gone deathly quiet.

"What's wrong," I asked, pulling him backward to the pool's edge. The lifeguard was lifting the lane dividers out of the way for me.

"Can't...breathe...asthma," he wheezed.

"Do you have an inhaler?" He nodded. "Do your guys know where it is?" He nodded again.

"Asthma attack," I yelled. "Get his inhaler." Sabastian ran off to the locker room as we reached the edge.

"Name?"

"Trey."

The lifeguards pulled Trey out of the water, and I rested at the edge, watching as they tried to keep him calm. He turned his head to look at me. I climbed out and grabbed his hand but didn't say anything. My eyes locked with his, and I purposely took deep, exaggerated breaths, keeping a firm grip on him. As I hoped, he copied me, and the panic lifted some, his eyes a calmer.

"Here," Sabastian said, handing the paramedic who had joined us the inhaler. Once he got the medication into his system, Trey began to breathe normally again. Clapping started, and people chanted my name, but I didn't care for the recognition. That wasn't why I saved his life.

"Thanks, man...I owe you one," Trey said, releasing my hand. His voice was still shaky and uneven, but there was no more wheeze.

"Don't offer that unless you mean it. I just might take you up on it," I said, smiling.

"Seriously, I freaked out. Anything you need, just ask," he said slowly.

I held out my hand as we got to our feet. "Name's Liam."

"Trey Walton, " he said with a quick shake.

"We need you to come with us to check you over," the paramedic said.

Trey rolled his eyes but went with them as I filed his name away. If he was related to *the* Waltons, he was a good person to owe me a favor.

Chapter 27

Ren

"Are you sure you want to do this," Ivy asked as I laced up my hiking boots. She seemed a lot more worried now than when I first told her I was going away with Liam.

"Do you think this is a bad idea?"

With an exaggerated huff, she sat down on her Care Bear blanketed bed. She said it was her favorite, and she couldn't sleep without it. The pouting face, coupled with pigtails, really suited the kiddish comforter.

"Every time you leave the property, something bad happens. Sprained ankle, Blake's OD, shoot out, you name it. It's not exactly a great track record. What if a poisonous snake bites you or Liam kills you?"

"Wow, that is quite the leap from a snake bite to murder," I teased, smiling at her. Finished with my boots, I stood up, grabbed my jacket, and shoved my arms through the sleeves. Clearly, Ivy needed some reassurance. Sitting down on the Care Bear comforter, I placed my hand on hers.

"I understand where you're coming from, but I can't live my life in constant fear. There are only a few months left, and we'll all be forced to leave anyway."

"Can't I just wrap you in those little bubbles and lock you in an underground armored bunker."

"Are the guards hot?" I tried not to snort but was unsuccessful. "I need hot guards in that scenario. I mean I have gotten used to being pampered by three men," I teased, with an exaggerated tone. I fanned at my face and batted my eyes.

She nudged my shoulder, laughing. "Stop it, I'm being serious. I have two whole friends in this world, and you are one of them. If something happened to you...."

Ivy looked at me when I squeezed her hand.

"Nothing is going to happen to me. You saw Liam yesterday. He saved a guy on a rival team because it was the right thing to do. He's not going to hurt me."

At least not the way Ivy was envisioning. The rest...well, that was still questionable based on the lessons from Myles and Blake. I had to tell them to knock it off before I killed them both.

"I really wish I had your courage."

"Is something more going on?"

Ivy lifted a shoulder and let it drop.

"Zigzag and his new girlfriend were at the meet yesterday. They didn't see me, but they were kissing by one of the buses."

"I'm so sorry," I said, wrapping my arm around her. Ivy laid her head on my shoulder. "So what do you want to do? Do you want me and Liam to take him with us so we can leave his body in the woods?" That made her laugh. "I'll do it."

"I'm sure you would, but no. I just don't get it. No one has ever been interested in me except for him, and we couldn't even make it a whole semester. And don't you dare say, 'It's not you, it's them'."

"Can I be honest?"

"Oh no, I'm not sure I want to know."

"I don't think you're going to find your person at Wayward. Most of the guys already have arranged marriages. You know what happened to Myles when he refused his father's pick. He was beaten so badly that he had to hide in his room for a week. I know not everyone is like Owen, but you get what I mean. From what I can tell, people are just having fun, nothing serious."

"Except you."

Well, I couldn't argue with that.

"We all know I'm an oddball. Don't compare yourself with me."

"Zigzag and I just clicked, or I thought we did, until he found a preppy, rich girl. You know he got in because he was thrown into juvey for hacking the Defense Department's servers. And I'm here because my dad...well, you know my dad. But you're right. Everyone here is from a rich, powerful family, and I have nothing to offer. Hell, my father is not even Sheriff anymore. I'm just a freeloading nobody."

"I didn't mean it like that," I said.

"I know, but it's the truth." She looked so sad, and all I wanted was to wrap her up in a hug and not let go.

"It's their loss. Money will not buy them happiness. You are beautiful, funny, and sweet. Trust me, Zigzag will regret making that choice one day, and by then, you will have found the right, Mr. Ivy Morrison."

"I did kind of meet someone." Ivy blushed as she bit her lip and looked around like there might be cameras in the room. God, I hoped there weren't any, or they were getting a hell of a show lately.

A sharp knock announced Liam before I could find out more about this mystery guy. Giving Ivy a quick hug, I stood up to answer the door.

"You're giving me all the details when I get back," I said, smiling.

Liam leaned against the wall, looking like he just came from a spa instead of spending another whole day in the pool. He was completely decked out in hiking gear and equipment, including the massive pack on his back and a knife in a sheath at his waist. *Wow* was the only word that came to mind as I stood there stupidly staring at him.

"You ready?"

"Sorry...yeah, can you help me with my pack?"

Nodding, he stepped into the room.

"Wow, you look like one of those survivor guys. You know, the ones they set loose in the wilderness with a few tools and a camera? Are you going to do any rock climbing," Ivy asked excitedly.

"No, we are not," I answered for him. "There is no way I'm going up or down a rock face, and you can forget about that insanity of sleeping in a tent on the side of a mountain. That is pure craziness," I said as Liam lifted the pack and put it on my shoulders.

"Oh, that's a shame. That was exactly what I had planned for us. I even brought you a piss cup and barf bag."

"You didn't...did you?"

Horror filled me as I pictured us suspended hundreds of feet in the air in a swaying tent. I mean, who came up with this stuff? Were two guys super drunk and one guy looked at the other and was like, *"You know what would be super fun? If we didn't tent on top of the mountain, but on the side of it. Then we can worry about plummeting to our deaths all night long or forgetting and getting out to pee when we're half asleep. Won't that be ten times more exciting?"* Like seriously.

Liam smirked. "No, not really. At least not this trip."

"Well, if he's talking about another trip, he's probably not going to kill you," Ivy said, and I shook my head at her.

"That's what you think," he growled at Ivy, and her face paled.

I grabbed Liam's arm and tugged him toward the door before Ivy decided to send Dean Henry and the Curators after us or something.

"See you in a few days," I said to Ivy and then promptly closed the door before she could ask anything else.

"This way," Liam said, heading for the back staircase I'd used a few times.

When we got outside, he picked up a light jog and went straight to the forest. The very narrow path would've been nearly impossible to see unless you knew where it was. My bag bounced slightly, and it didn't take more than ten minutes to wonder why I'd wanted to do this.

"We'll walk once we reach the main trail," he said as if reading my mind.

There was no point asking how far that was, because there was no way I was telling him that I was tired and needed to walk.

"Are you going to be good to train on Monday?"

"Do you ever not think about working out?"

"Do you ever stop thinking about schoolwork or beating Theo?"

"Good point," I said as we popped out of the thick brush and found a crushed gravel path.

Liam slowed to a walk, and I sucked in a deep breath.

"So where are we heading?"

"Worried?" Liam looked down at me with an expression caught between indignant and mischievous.

"No, I just like to know. It's always good to know. I can guess. We are on the path heading toward the one that I took last year."

The corner of his mouth tugged up. "Correct."

"I prefer it out here," I said, looking around at the tall trees. Blake would be all over the different birds and their calls. It felt like we were walking in a chorus of different birdsongs. "People and I don't seem to get along."

"I would have to disagree with you."

I snorted.

"I don't dislike or hate you, Ren. I don't trust that this can work. This could very well destroy friendships. I'm not the enemy. If anything, you're the enemy coming into my group of friends and my relationship. But...." He put his hands up as if warding off an argument. "There is no blame, it just is what it is. Complicated." I eyed him suspiciously. It was comments like this that really confused me about Liam. "You don't look like you believe me."

"More like you confuse me. You are all over the place. Maybe Theo isn't the only one struggling and making things...complicated?" I playfully nudged his arm. He grunted at me but didn't dispute the thought. I was taking that as a win in my column.

We fell into a comfortable silence, our matching footfalls breaking the quiet of the slowly darkening forest. We still had a few hours until we would stop for the night, and that was what worried me. Liam wanted to connect and get to know me, but I didn't know what to say or do to make that happen. Now that we were out here, I felt pressured to find something to bring us together. Sex wasn't the answer. Sure, Liam was hot, but physical attraction only went so deep.

Liam returned my playful nudge, and I looked up at him.

"Don't overthink things. We're just out here to have a good time. Whatever that looks like."

"Theo warned me that you have a freaky ability to read minds, but I didn't believe it."

Liam's laugh echoed off the trees, the deep, rich sound blanketing me in a warmth that made me smile.

"Did he now? What else did Theo say? No, wait, let me guess...."

The tension faded like the slowly setting sun. We laughed and teased one another, and I realized that when we put our hypothetical swords away, we weren't that different. In fact, I felt hope that Liam and I would be more than the rivals we were when we stepped onto the trail to parts unknown.

Chapter 28

OCTOBER 03 – FRIDAY 7:40 PM

L iam

The night was perfect. You couldn't have asked for a better fall evening. The sky was clear of all clouds, leaving us sitting under a blanket of stars. The fire was crackling, but Ren refused to sit closer or ask for a blanket despite shivering. She thought I was difficult to figure out, but she was just as big of a mystery.

Ren was alluring with her stunning features and silver hair. She wrapped herself in a layer of permafrost, but the warmth of her heart was impossible to hide. It was a protective shield from the world, but there was no doubt that when the time came, Ren would stand up and fight.

There was nothing about her that was pretentious or fake, and she didn't take herself too seriously. I'd poked at her ten different ways already and she never got angry, always giving back as good as I gave. She was quick on her feet with a sharp tongue and didn't seem to have an ego. I couldn't understand that. I had never met anyone who truly didn't give a shit what people thought of them until her.

Was this what drew everyone in? Well, everyone but Myles. He was a love-struck pup the moment he laid eyes on her. But Blake, Theo, and hell, even Nash were all drawn to her like a moth to a flame. I had viewed her as nothing more than a threat. Worming her way into the group and obliterating us from the inside. Destroying me and Theo. But now...now, I didn't know what to make of her, and that was a new experience for me.

Ren glanced at me a few times before pressing her lips together and looking away. For as alpha as she was, there was a timidness there that would be irresistible in the bedroom. Ren was a conundrum.

"Okay...I'm just going to ask it," Ren said and wiped her hands on her jeans. I took a drink to prepare myself for Ren's questions. "Are you going to come in my eye?"

Water spewed out of my mouth and into the fire. I wasn't expecting that and started laughing so hard that tears were streaming down my face, and I couldn't see a fucking thing.

"What the hell have you been watching?"

Ren glared at me.

"You told me to research, not what to research or where."

"Fair enough. So, what the hell are you talking about? Why would I come in your eye?"

Ren's face turned a wicked shade of pink. "Myles and Blake thought they could educate me on your lifestyle."

My jaw dropped as I stared at her. "Please tell me you didn't listen to a single word they said?"

"Said...they didn't say anything. They demonstrated. Myles smacked me and called me slut. He came all over my face and got me in the eye and...stop laughing," she said, but I couldn't.

My stomach hurt, and I rolled off the log, howling with laughter, picturing it in my head. The blind leading the blind and trying to make her blind at that.

"Stop it," Ren said, nudging my foot but chuckling. "Are you telling me that everything they showed me was wrong? Am I going to have to kill them? I am aren't I?"

It took me a minute to speak as I gasped for air, but I managed to climb back up onto the log.

"Wait, wait, wait...when your eye was red, was that because...."

"Yes," she growled, and the hysterics started all over again.

"Oh my god. That is the funniest shit I've ever heard." Wiping my eyes, I looked over and Ren was shaking her head and pinching the bridge of her nose.

"I was going to kill them if they called me their come slut one more time."

"Stop, I can't take anymore."

"It's not funny. I thought...I thought I was finding a way to make you like me. I'm such an idiot. Why did I listen to them?" She stood up to walk away, but I blocked her path. "I feel so freaking stupid."

"Don't. I should've pointed you in the right direction. That's on me. But...you get an A for effort," I said, snickering, then laughed as she punched me in the arm.

"Jerk."

Sobering, I stared down at her. There it was again, open honesty. I tipped her chin up with my finger, and she shivered.

"We need some ground rules." She nodded slightly, her eyes going wide as my mouth ghosted over hers. "You never...ever...under any circumstance...ask Myles and Blake about anything to do with the lifestyle. In fact, it's kind of like fight club. The first rule of the lifestyle is never take instruction from someone not in the lifestyle. Understand?"

"Yes," she whispered, the word sounding like candy to my ears.

Brushing my nose against the corner of her mouth, I drew a line across her cheek. Goosebumps rose along her skin, but she didn't shy away from me.

"Tell me why you agreed to do this," I breathed softly next to her ear and loved how she shuddered.

I might not be able to understand her outside of sex, but I was picking up on all of her subtle cues when I touched her. Fuck Theo because she was just what I loved.

"I love Theo, and he loves you. If us being together makes him happy, then I want to try."

"I believe you," I said, nipping Ren's ear, and she moaned.

"Will you ever listen to them again?"

"No," she answered quickly.

"No, Sir," I said.

"No, Sir." Her voice was so soft and breathy that if I hadn't been so close, I wouldn't have heard it, but it was perfect for her.

"That's a good Little Rabbit," I growled, and she swayed on her feet. Taking a slow step back, I stared into her glassy eyes and smiled. She didn't move or pull away from my finger still holding her chin up. Dropping it, I watched her blink like she was clearing away a fog. "That's how you teach a lesson. Do you see the difference?"

"Yes," Ren said, and I lifted a brow. "Yes, Sir."

"Good." Walking back to the log, I sat down and picked up my water, keeping an eye on her. Ren bit her bottom lip and eventually wandered back like a wary animal. Her nickname was perfect. She reminded me so much of a rabbit. She'd just gotten a taste of a sweet carrot and was curious enough to look for more as she sat down, closer to me this time.

"I don't understand. What about all that stuff Theo said about how I couldn't handle you? And everything you said?"

"We'll build up to that. You need to know that the lifestyle is about mutual trust, respect, and pleasure. If any one of those is missing, everything falls apart. And yes, I might have been trying to push your buttons in the kitchen to see how you would respond."

"You really are a jerk." Ren shook her head, and I chuckled.

"Not as much as Nash."

Her face fell, and she looked away. I watched her closely, wondering if she might admit what happened in Seattle.

"No, not as much as Nash."

"If that's the case, then why did you sleep with him?"

Her head whipped in my direction, anger brimming under her skin. "He told you?"

"No, but you just did."

She rolled her eyes. "Son of a...."

"Look at me for a minute."

Ren crossed her arms defensively before looking at me. I reached out, grabbed her, and tugged until she gave up and let her arms fall. Sliding my hands down to hers, I held them. Anxiety was pouring off her in waves.

"I'm not judging, but why haven't you told the guys."

"Trust me, I've thought about it."

It was another truth. Ren just wasn't built to lie. A pro for us, but a con in this world. No wonder Lawrence hit her. He wouldn't have liked anything she'd said about him.

"What would it accomplish other than turning everyone against Nash? That's not what the Kings need, even if I never want to see his face again. I'm not after destruction, Liam."

She looked away, but not before I saw the devastation Nash had caused. Dumbass had no clue. If he wanted to fix this it was going to be a lot harder than I originally thought.

"Okay…I won't say anything." She flicked her gaze at me, and I cupped her chin, forcing her to face me. "I promise."

"If they ever find out, then they'll be pissed with both of us. Why would you want to take that chance?"

"Because you're right. They'll go after Nash, and despite recent events, we need him." Tracing her cheek with my thumb, I sighed before letting my hand drop. "I'm going to tell you something because…we are up here as a trust and bonding exercise, but this can never get back to Nash."

"Are you going to try and convince me that he's actually a sugar-coated teddy bear, and this is all a big misunderstanding? Because if so, I call bullshit," she sassed, and my cock twitched. Shit, she had a certain, je ne sais quoi.

"No, but that's quite an image."

Nash would shoot me if he found out I told Ren about this, but it was worth the risk if it closed the gap between them. Whatever deal he'd made with Vicky's father, there was no way he would go through with it unless he had a way out. At least, I fucking hoped so. I'd never bow down to Vicky as Nash's wife.

Reaching into my pack, I pulled out my silver flask and two metal cups. Pouring some in each, I handed her one. "Sip it. Don't take it as a shot," I said as she put it to her lips. "It's sixty-year-old scotch."

Ren looked down. "Who takes sixty-year-old scotch camping?"

"Someone intelligent."

She smirked and took a drink. Ren made a face like she was pleasantly surprised by the flavor as she swallowed. When her tongue peeked out to clean the remnants, I grabbed her chin and kissed her hard, taking us both by surprise. I licked the bold flavor off her lips, sucking the bottom one into my mouth to get it all. I really did like how she opened for me with a small moan. Ren would be easy to train, but if I told her that, she'd smack me, which made her so much more interesting than I initially believed.

"You taste good," I said, letting her go.

She looked a little less defensive now as she smoothed down her hair, sipped the drink again, and cleared her throat.

"So, what did you want to tell me about Nash?"

"He has many reasons for the way he treated you. But...the one that made him lash out in such a volatile manner is what I'm going to talk to you about."

"I'm not sure there's anything you can say that will excuse what he said, but I'm all ears."

"Nash was in love with a girl. I know, shocking," I said as Ren's eyes went wide. "Her name was Mya. Her family was typical middle class, but her father had done a few favors for Lawrence, so the payouts allowed her to attend Sacred Heart. Nash met Mya at one of the joint events, they hit it off, and I'm sure you can guess the rest."

"How long ago was that?"

"Over five years ago now, they were fourteen the first time they met."

Ren cocked her head as she looked at me, and I could see the wheels turning. "I'm not sure why you're telling me this."

"Relax, I'm getting there." I poured her a little more scotch. "As I'm sure you can imagine, Lawrence wasn't happy about Nash dating someone with nothing to offer the family. But they were only fourteen, puppy love, so he didn't really pay them any attention until two years later when Nash got her pregnant."

"What? Nash has a child?"

"No."

Standing up, I took my drink as a shot and let the liquid burn down my throat.

"They aborted, or she lost it?"

"No."

I dropped my eyes to hers, and she gasped.

"No."

"Yes. Lawrence wanted to teach Nash a lesson. He made Nash

watch as he killed Mya's family. Then, had Nash taken away as he killed Mya and their unborn child."

"Oh my god," Ren said, covering her mouth. Tears filled her eyes, and in that second, I knew I'd done the right thing. She needed to understand the scars to understand the man.

"He's never been the same. He blames himself for her death, hates his father, but most importantly, he's never, and I mean never, let anyone back in...until you." Ren gazed up at me, and I nodded. "Nash is fucking terrified that if he lets you in, something will happen again. Mostly that his father will find out and use you to crush him."

I sat back down and wrapped my arm around Ren's shoulders.

"He loves you, but he may never admit it or ever be able to let you in all the way. I'm not telling you this so you'll forgive him because I don't think you should, at least not without him begging for forgiveness. Nash needs to really dig deep and fight for what he wants. If that's you, then he'll prove it."

"This is a lot and heavy. I feel terrible, and I can't say anything. Do the other guys know?"

I nodded. "Yes, but they can't know that you know, or it will get back to him. I'm better at keeping secrets."

"I'm not sure that's a selling feature. It's kind of like saying this car is fantastic, but it has a speed regulator on it."

"Oh...I like that reference. But it's the truth. So, before you write Nash off forever, I need you to understand the fear and wound that is under the rage you saw. He's not mad at you. He's mad at himself for opening the door to feelings that he swore he wouldn't have again. Think about it like this. He wasn't wearing you down over the last year, it's the other way around. You got under his skin, and now he's lost."

"And what about the marriage to Vicky," she asked softly, confirming my second suspicion.

"I can't answer that one, but I know he doesn't want to marry her. If he did sign a contract for Vicky, he'd have a plan to get out of it. Take of that what you will, but I thought you should know."

Ren rested her head on my shoulder like she had the night of Myles's initiation. She was quiet for so long that I thought she'd fallen asleep with her deep, even breathing.

"Thanks for trusting me, Liam."

"You're welcome, Little Rabbit."

OCTOBER 04 – SATURDAY ASS CRACK OF DAWN

Ren

Liam had completely obliterated the images and expectations he'd put into my head. For all of his proclamations against dinner, flowers, and sweetness, I'd seen a softer side. Mind you, we didn't have an audience out here, and I knew from his argument with Theo that he valued his privacy. Oddly and very unexpectedly, I agreed with him.

With his foam roll on the ground and my sleeping bag as added padding, Liam had zipped us into his wider and extra warm one. I wasn't sure if it was extra warm because of the quality or because of Liam. That was a total lie. It was him. He hadn't tried anything, and I wasn't sure if I was insulted or relieved that he wasn't using sex to connect. I really did hate all this relationship stuff sometimes.

"Why do you always think so hard," Liam asked, holding me tighter, and I smirked.

He'd remained on his side all night, cuddling me. The few times that I'd woken up, I either startled him, or he never slept because he had whispered in my ear, telling me to go back to sleep. No one, not even Myles, had ever woken up when I was having a nightmare unless I screamed.

"I wish I knew," I answered softly into the darkness. "Do you know what time it is?"

"The ass crack of dawn," he whispered, his breath fanning my neck.

"That's a very precise time," I said, and he chuckled.

Liam had a way about him that sent shivers racing all over my body, even when he was doing absolutely nothing. I'd noticed it before and assumed it was just my nervousness, but I wasn't nervous right now. I was happily soaking in his warmth and didn't want to move, but there was no chance of sleep for me now.

"You're not going to sleep anymore, are you?"

"How do you do that? I need to know."

"Learned it. My dad's the same way. When I was a kid, I had to be able to read him and be better than he was to lie to him or ask for something."

"Maybe that's what makes you a great Dom," I said, and I could feel him smile against my neck.

"Who says that I'm any good?"

"I think we both know who. You don't need me to tell you unless you're trying to stroke your ego."

"Maybe don't use the word stroke," Liam growled low as he

pressed closer, and I stiffened when I felt his cock against my ass. "You're interesting, Little Rabbit."

"How so?"

"So tough and ready to protect those you care about, but still so shy about your sexuality. Why is that?"

My mouth moved, but no words came out. I wasn't sure how to answer.

"I honestly don't know," I said, relaxing as Liam ran his hand down my side, over and over, like he was soothing me into accepting more than just holding still. My eyes fluttered closed.

"Do you like that?"

"Yes."

"Tell me how it makes you feel," he whispered in my ear. If anyone was capable of turning someone into a puddle without even trying, it was Liam.

"Relaxed. Comfortable. Safe."

Liam kissed my neck, and I sighed, suddenly craving a whole lot more.

"We better get up and head out. We have a very long day of hiking before we camp."

He unzipped the sleeping bag and got up. I couldn't see him moving around in the dim morning light, but I tracked him nonetheless.

"I feel your eyes on me, Little Rabbit." The sound of his zipper announced he'd put on his jeans. "And you're not ready."

"Says who?"

"Says me, and in here...I rule."

I glanced around. "We aren't exactly in a bedroom."

"Any place I choose to have sex with you is the bedroom," Liam said and then laughed. "I can feel your need to argue with me but don't bother. You're only pressing because you like the challenge. But if we move forward with our relationship there will be no arguing with my rules. Unless you want your ass tanned." He opened the tent and stepped out but poked his head back in. The early morning haze turned him into a silhouette. "You like your oatmeal hot, with cinnamon and brown sugar," he said.

"How? Never mind...I don't want to know," I said, dumbfounded.

"Two oatmeals, coming right up."

I slumped back down in the sleeping bag and stared up at the roof of the tent. Before we went to sleep, Liam explained more about the lifestyle, some of his rules, and how we would work up to the intense forms of play. It still seemed terrifying, but there was a certain appeal that had my heart racing. Could I let myself go? Trust him to have complete control over my body.

"I don't hear you getting ready," Liam said, and I made a face at the side of the tent. "Don't think I didn't see you making faces at me."

"Okay, you're officially sus," I said, and he laughed.

"I get that a lot."

Sighing, I tossed the sleeping bag off.

OCTOBER 04 – SATURDAY 5:03 PM

Liam

Little Rabbit thought she was alone, but like any good hunter, my prey was right in my sights. She'd snuck off while I gathered firewood to get a fire going. Maybe she thought she had enough time to bathe before I was done. No such luck, and this was a big no-no for many reasons.

Luckily for her, she wasn't trying to hide from me. I found her trail easily. We were near the spot where she'd fallen in last year, but instead of the stream, which was a mile in the opposite direction, I'd taken her to one of the area's hidden gems.

These hot springs weren't on a map and were warm rather than hot. Perfect for bathing or relaxing sore muscles after a long trek, which I'd done many times before. Ren stood naked at the edge, her toes just touching the turquoise water. The silvery strands of her hair blew around her face with a gust of wind, and she hugged herself, shivering.

I wasn't blind to her stunning and unique beauty, but I preferred to judge people by their actions. She took a graceful step forward, so the water swirled around her ankles. Ren could easily play an elf in *The Lord of the Rings*. All she needed was some pointed ears and a bow and arrow. I couldn't explain why that image was a total turn-on, but taking her to a Cosplay suddenly held a whole new appeal.

Ren looked around, some instinct sensing me. She didn't know it yet but she was already caught. My Little Rabbit waded into the spring until she was up to her waist and then bent backward to wet her hair.

Slipping from my hidden vantage point, I stripped off my clothes and prowled down the slope behind her. Staying alert for any sign that she knew I was there as she washed her body, I silently sunk into the water. Ren never even flinched. If I had been a mountain lion or another stealthy killer, she would be dead in seconds. What I was after was far less deadly but maybe just as terrifying.

She was humming as she used the small bar of biodegradable soap I'd supplied. Smiling, I slipped under the surface and swam around in front of her. Her humming stopped, and I knew that she felt my presence. She stepped back toward the shore, and I grabbed her ankles. Ren screamed bloody murder and tried to jump back, landing with a splash.

Grabbing her before she was completely submerged, I lifted her by her waist.

"You fucking, fuckity, fucker...you knobend. I swear to fuck. You should take a really long walk off a short-ass plank. Fuck, fuck, fuck," Ren swore, making me laugh hard. Easing her down my body, she looked like she was going to take a swing at my face. Instead, she kept swearing like a well-groomed sailor. "I should punch you again but my hand just healed."

"Well, now, isn't that the most adorable freakout I've ever seen."

"You are a dead man, Hicks. I swear I just had a Jaws flashback and thought I was dead," she said with her lips pursed and arms crossed.

Lowering slowly until I was on my knees in the water, I guided her legs around my waist. Ren tried to hide the effect it had on her, but her body couldn't hide the truth as she relaxed in my arms.

"I'm not sure where a great white is coming from in here. I thought you knew everything." Teasing her was too much fun.

She growled and tried to pull away, but I kept a firm hold on my wiggly rabbit.

"I'm rethinking murdering you."

Ren had a fiery side and grit that the others weren't utilizing, but I loved it.

"No, you won't."

"Fine, you're right. I'm not exactly into murdering people, so you're getting off easy. But trust me, I'm all stabby in my mind."

Laughing, I tugged her crossed arms apart, and she bit her lower lip.

"Put them around my neck," I ordered. With her reluctant compliance, I drew her flush against my body. "Where's my soap," I asked, kissing one of the snowflake tattoos on her neck.

"I squeezed that slippery little bastard so hard that it shot out of my hand. You're on your own if you want to find it."

"Knobend and slippery little bastard. You have some very interesting choices of swear words." I said, running my fingertips down her spine, loving how she arched closer. "You're very different from

Theo, but I like it," I said and smirked as she lifted an eyebrow at me. "It's how you respond to me."

"How am I different?"

I gripped her ass, and she squeezed my hips, looking down into my eyes.

"Like that. You're more sensitive. You feel my touch as deeply as you do your emotions." When she ran her lip through her teeth, I knew she wanted to kiss me. But she held off as per our talk last night.

"Do you want me to kiss you?"

"Yes." I narrowed my gaze. "Yes, Sir." My lip curled.

"Do I scare you, Little Rabbit?"

"A little." I waited, and Ren's cheeks turned bright red. "Sir," she tagged on.

"Let's see if we can fix that. Be a good girl and lean back for me."

Releasing my neck, she did as I said, and my hand followed her movement up the center of her chest. Pausing between her breasts, I watched her take deep breaths, silently begging for more as her thighs clenched. I licked my lips. Ren had no idea how naturally sensual she was, and I planned on working the timid out of her until she had the fire and attitude to take whatever she wanted from this world.

My hand snaked around her throat, and she flinched like she might grab my arm. Even when I applied enough pressure to make it hard to breathe, she obeyed. I pulled her up, locking eyes, and nipping at her bottom lip.

"Why do I scare you?"

"Because I find you hard to read. I never really know what you're thinking. You say you don't want me dead, but I also know you lie well enough to convince hardened criminals that you're telling the truth. So, how am I supposed to know what is fake and what is real?"

"Are we still talking about me or Nash?"

She looked away. "You're a lot alike," she said.

"And you don't want to be hurt again?" She turned her head and peeked up at me from under her thick lashes. "Unfortunately, this life will continue to try and rip you apart until there is nothing left. The brighter you shine, the more people will want to tear you down." Her eyes darkened with restrained passion. "I promise that I won't purposely hurt you, and as much as Nash and I are the same, we are also vastly different."

"You could rule," she said, and I smirked.

"I could, but I don't want to. That must seem strange, considering everything you've learned about me. But moving pieces around, making alliances, and signing contracts—while watching my back for a knife—is not who I want to be."

"Then who do you want to be, Liam Hicks?"

"I want to be the one who stops the blade before it sinks into Nash's back...or yours."

"Oh...um." She looked surprised before she lowered her gaze and sighed. "Can I ask you to please stop bringing him up...at least for the rest of our time out here."

I smiled. "Done, he won't come up again. Pray tell, Little Rabbit, do you think you can trust me?"

She licked her lips. "I want to."

"Let's do a trust exercise. Take a deep breath."

Ren submitted, and I pushed back into the deepest part of the spring, sinking under the water. My feet still touched the sandy bottom, but my Little Rabbit stiffened like a board as soon as we were fully submerged. She was terrified.

Releasing her throat, I cupped her cheeks and kissed her, commanding her to relax. I waited until she reciprocated before pushing up and letting her take a breath. I did it again and again until she didn't tense at all, even when I pushed the limits of her air.

Floating back into the waist-deep water, I licked the droplets off her lips.

"Stand for me."

Ren shivered in the quickly cooling air, disentangling her legs and standing. The water ran down her body like strands of diamonds. I stood to my full height, and her eyes flicked down to my cock before she lifted her chin again.

Circling her body like a shark, I ran my hand over her skin before grabbing her wet hair in my fist. A sharp gasp left her lips as I pulled her head back until she was forced to look up at me. This time, I didn't just kiss her. I conquered her mouth, claiming it, and her, as mine.

"You're testing me, Little Rabbit," I growled when I pulled away. Confusion clouded her eyes. "I'm going to need a priest for even thinking about the things I want to do to you."

"Does that mean you want me, Sir?"

Fuck. I loved how that word sounded rolling off her tongue.

"Yes, but there are two things we need to get out of the way."

I unfisted her hair so Ren could stand. Appraising her body, I envisioned teaching her to embrace her alpha personality while being the best fucking Sub in the bedroom.

Scenes of fucking her with Theo danced behind my eyes. Ren would scream in pleasure as we filled her. Our cocks would rub together as she dug her nails into our skin and came on us. I shuddered at the visceral imagery.

"I need you to know and understand that I fucking loathe the idea of you sleeping with anyone but myself and Theo. It physically hurts me to think about it." I let that statement hang in the air between us. "It's taking a huge effort on my part to set aside my hatred of any other male touching your skin. So, please be mindful of that. I also realize that Myles and Blake were in your life first. They love you, protect you, and you won't let them go even if I demand it, so I won't."

"Good, because I won't. I love them as I love Theo, and I don't turn my back on those I love."

"Do you think you could love me?"

Stopping in front of her, I slowly rolled the hard buds of her nipples between my fingers. She moaned and swayed slightly. My body's reaction was instant, and I savored the ache in my cock at denying my need.

"I do...as long as you understand that my stance on them will never change. Don't try to manipulate or guilt me because it won't be them I cut loose." The don't fuck with me in her tone was hot as hell, and I liked it. She had the same look in her eye the day she punched me.

"Alright, the guys are non-negotiable. But I have a non-negotiable condition of my own."

"What's that?"

"You're going to wear a collar." Her eyes went wide, and I could tell she was going to argue, so I shook my head at her. "This is not like a dog collar. It's a symbol that you're mine. If we go places where there are others from the community, it announces that you are not to be touched or approached unless I give them permission."

"I can't picture wearing a collar at school."

"It'll be custom-made of platinum and blue diamonds. No one at Wayward will be the wiser. I promise that it will be as beautiful as you. But, as long as we're together, you're never to take it off. Not for anything."

"Why doesn't Theo wear one?"

Her sass was unparalleled.

"Who says he doesn't?"

I could practically see the gears running in her head as I moved behind her. Twisting her long hair up out of the way, I wish that I already had the delicate piece of jewelry on her neck.

"Haven't you noticed the diamond-encrusted watch that Theo always wears," I asked, nipping at the soft skin under her ear.

"No, I didn't realize."

Ren tilted her head to the side, allowing me to suck on her neck. She whimpered, silently begging for more. I hadn't planned on marking her, but once I started, I didn't want to stop. Slipping my hand between her thighs, I ran my fingers over her clit and pussy lips loving how she quivered like she might collapse.

"This collar is not about control. It's different than leading you on a leather collar for the night. Like the ring that Myles gave you or Blake's necklace, it's a symbol of our relationship. In the lifestyle, it signifies your position with me, which is vital when we go anywhere." Licking a line up her neck and stopping to kiss each of the snowflakes, I pictured clipping my collar around her dainty throat. "It's important to me," I whispered in her ear.

"Okay."

"Okay, what?"

"Sir," she moaned as I teased her.

"Such a good girl. Such a wet pussy. From now on, I want your pussy ready for me at all times, and I will be checking to make sure you are."

"Yes, Sir," Ren said, and I pressed my cock between her ass cheeks.

"Do you know what that means?"

She shook her head, and I let the lack of formality go because she'd already learned and accepted far more than she even realized.

"You'll find out," I chuckled against her neck and pushed the tip of my finger inside her. She pressed back into me.

"Don't move until I tell you," I ordered.

"Yes...Sir," she panted as I pumped deeper until I was fucking her with my finger and memorizing every tremble of her body.

There was a delicate balance to this process that was lost on most, and I had to be extra cautious with my Little Rabbit. She was only here because of Theo and if I pushed too hard, too fast, Ren could easily get frustrated and walk. It was my job to take control and find the sweet spot that would have her on her knees with just a look. I already had a test in mind for when we got back to school, and the throbbing in my cock intensified.

"You want me to fuck you out here in the wild. Hard and fast like a goddamn animal. Don't you, Little Rabbit?" I growled, and she practically melted. "Make you come on my cock, over and over again."

"Yes, Sir," she groaned as I picked up speed.

"Good girl."

Ren whined when I pulled my finger out, frustration written all over her face. I turned her by her shoulders to face me.

"Next rule...." She held perfectly still. "Don't sulk or brat out with me. I will haul you over my lap, and I don't care where we are. Test me in public, and you'll quickly find out I have no problem putting you on your knees to suck my cock in front of everyone. Understood?"

My rabbit swallowed hard. With my hands under her ass, I lifted Ren until she wrapped her legs around my waist, and I was pressing right into her heat.

"Answer the question."

"Yes, I understand, Sir. No brating."

Grabbing the back of Ren's neck, I kissed her hard and thrust up, swallowing her intoxicating scream.

"That's my good fucking girl," I growled against her lips as I began fucking her. Going until Ren was close to exploding and then I stopped. She was not happy.

"Don't glare at me like that, Little Rabbit."

She was fighting her nature for me while her pussy steadily gripped my cock. Holding off was becoming more difficult. I craved this moment. It was what I lived for and why I enjoyed being a Dom.

"Oh fuck," Ren screamed as I started fucking her again.

Her nails dug into my shoulders, and my jaw twitched as she bounced like a goddamn goddess. I didn't stop this time as she got to the edge and instead pushed her over. Ren's walls tightened around me as she arched back, frozen in the throws of her release.

"Oh my god," she panted as she collapsed in my arms.

Wading over to some large rocks, I slowly set her on her feet and pointed.

"Bend over," I growled. Ren complied but slowly, and as soon as she had her hands on the rock, I slapped her sexy ass.

"Ahh!" Ren scowled at me over her shoulder.

"Don't hesitate, and what did I say about glaring at me?"

Smacking her other cheek, she moaned before growling back and wiggling her ass in the air. I spanked her again, and she jumped but hung her head.

"You like it, don't you?" She hesitated again. Smack. "Don't lie to me."

"Ahh fuck," she cried. "Yes, Sir," Ren yelled.

Using some of the warm water, I gently massaged her reddening cheeks before grabbing her hips and teasing her again. I caressed every inch of her before dipping just the tip of my cock into her heat. My Little Rabbit was shaking with need. It was delicious fucking torture, and by the time I thrust into her, she came again right away, soaking me and testing my control.

Grabbing her hair, I pulled, and her back arched. "Next time, you wait for permission to come, Little Rabbit," I snarled in her ear, and her body quaked all around my cock. "Be a good girl and come again."

"Oh god...." Ren mumbled, making me smile.

Gripping her hip, I wrapped her hair around my fist and fucked her hard. The water sloshed around us as I closed my eyes and soaked in her screams of pleasure and the sound of our skin slapping together. Holding off on my release until she was ready to come, I tugged on her hair.

"Hold it. Don't you dare fucking come, Litle Rabbit. If you do, you'll be out here all night with my cock in you. I can fuck you for hours, non-stop. Are you going to test me?"

"No...Sir," she wailed.

It was exquisite torture watching the sensations wracking her body. Smirking, I released her hair and dug my fingers into her lush ass.

"Come for me," I said.

Ren screamed as she came, and I relinquished my tightly spun control, unraveling completely. Time was irrelevant as the world narrowed down to the feel of our bodies writhing together in pleasure. With a growl, I pulled out and jerked my cock fast, coming all over her ass.

"Fuck...."

Milking the last drops from my cock, I stumbled back. Now that I'd gotten a taste of her, I didn't know who was in more trouble tonight, her or me. But as Ren turned around and slid down the rock into the water, panting, I felt the shift I'd been waiting for since I agreed to try.

I was all in, and my Little Rabbit had just clasped her collar around her neck whether she could see it or not.

Chapter 30

OCTOBER 04 – SATURDAY 8:22 PM

Nash

My father's office was the last place I wanted to be today. Myles and I had been summoned, and neither of us had any clue as to why. It was tempting to tell him to go fuck himself, but that would be playing my next move too soon. I still had to attend his stupid cult meetings, and if this was about an issue with the business, then I needed to know, even if I hated the fact.

"Do ya have any idea what this is about," Myles asked as he walked in.

"No clue. Have you heard from Liam," I asked, pouring a glass of water from the bar in the corner.

"Naw, but Theo said he wouldn't call unless there was a problem," he said, sitting down in one of the leather chairs.

Leaning against the bar, I knew I shouldn't ask, but the urge was just too strong.

"And you're really okay with Princess being alone with Liam in the woods doing whatever?"

Myles leaned over the coffee table and picked up the marble pawn off the chess board and twirled it in his fingers.

"Sure. I already told her that I don't care if she wants all of us. Just no one outside of the Kings."

I laughed. "Me included?"

The little piece paused, caught between two fingers, as he looked up at me.

"Of course, as long as yer not thinkin' of cuttin' us out. Then we'll have a problem 'cause Ren's mine."

I chugged my water and set it down, never more thankful to hear my father stomping down the hallway, putting an end to the conversation. Lawrence walked in, swearing under his breath, and slammed a folder down on his desk.

"We have a problem," my father said. Myles and I looked at one another.

"Meaning?"

Lawrence sat down, opened his bottom drawer, and pulled out whiskey. He poured himself a full glass and left the open bottle on his desk. By midnight, he would be drunk, and anyone near him would be screaming and sorry they'd come across him.

"Meaning...Owen is causing issues." He hit Myles with a hard glare. "Your father has gone rogue."

Myles stood. "What are ya sayin'?"

"He isn't taking Devin's capture well, so I've been keeping him extra busy. Giving him more responsibility, but he's been unorganized, distracted, and erratic. That I can handle, but he just slaughtered the entire Kilroy family at the business meeting I set up."

"What the fuck," I growled, my hands balling. "They are one of our biggest supporters back home."

"Don't you think I fucking know that?" My father loosened his tie and gulped down a mouthful of whiskey. "Everything is in chaos. Rumblings have already started that I set this in motion. That I'm trying to take over and families are turning against us. I need you to stop this, Myles."

"Me? What the fuck do ya think I can do?"

My father stood and stomped around the desk. "He'll reach out to you. I know you don't care, but you are his son and heir."

Myles laughed. "Ya must be jokin'." Lawrence glared at him. "Did ya see what he did to me last year?" Lawrence's jaw twitched, and I knew that he did. Fuck I would place bets that it was my father who put the idea in Owen's head. "Or what he's done to me my whole life? He din't see me as his son, and I'm the last person he'd call for help or anything else."

"Call it a hunch. But I know he's going to reach out, Myles, and I want you to take the call."

"And say what?"

"Whatever you can to lure him back here, and then you're going to kill him."

I laughed, and Lawrence looked at me.

"You think this is funny?"

"Yeah, I really fucking do. How many times did I tell you that your attack dog was insane and that he or Devin would turn on you?" I touched my jaw where he'd hit me for saying that to him. "Remember how you answered me? Now the chain has broken, and you want us to put your dog down." I chuckled. "Fuck you. You have men and contacts all over the world. Clean up your own mess."

I marched for the door.

"Nash, this affects everything. All our families. Ethan, Ella,

Emmett, Bridget, Lip, Nora, all of you. If we don't work together to stop Owen from doing more damage, they will come for all of us."

He was right, and worse than that, this would get back to Mr. Genovese. Instability with the families in Ireland would make our alliance rocky.

"Fuck," I growled, pointing at him. "Fine, we'll help. But you own it right now."

"Own what?"

"Admit that this is your fault."

He ground his teeth, but he couldn't intimidate me anymore. Lawrence was many things, but stupid wasn't one of them. He needed us, but he wasn't getting any cooperation until he ate crow.

"This isn't the time for a power struggle, son," he said.

I shook my head, following him to his desk. When he sat down, I pressed the tips of my fingers into the polished wood. It would drive him crazy that I was not only touching his desk but that I'd smudge the perfect shine.

"This isn't about power. No one other than Myles will know. You want our help, fine. We'll clean up your shit, but you're giving me this first. Admit right now that I warned you this would happen and that Devin is a traitor. You refused to believe it and punched me. You were wrong, and I was right."

He sat back in his chair and chugged the rest of his drink.

As if on cue, Myles's phone rang. "Shite, it's him."

"Answer it, Myles," Lawrence ordered.

"No, don't," I said.

Myles didn't move, making my father scowl.

"Now or never, Father. Say the words."

He snarled at me, his eyes snapping with rage that, at one point, would've terrified me.

"Fine, you were right about Owen and Devin, and I should've listened to you. I'm sorry I hit you. There? Happy?"

Nodding, I looked over my shoulder at Myles. "Answer it."

Myles hit talk and then put it on speaker.

"Hey, Da. I didn't get back to ya 'cause school's been busy."

"Din't trust 'em."

"Who?" Myles looked at me.

"Lawrence, he's a lyin' prick."

Myles laughed. "You just figuring that out? I could've told ya that fecking ages ago."

My father's eyebrows raised.

"Listen to me, son. I know ya won't believe me, but we need to stick together."

"Da, what the hell is going on?'

"He's a liar! He's gonna take it all. He's after it all," Owen ranted like the lunatic he was.

"Da, I don't know what yer talkin' about. But yer my da. What do ya need?"

Lawrence gave him a thumbs up, and I wanted to roll my eyes at him—like Myles needed his approval.

"He knows who she is. He's made deals, Myles, deals to steal all our power."

I looked at my father and cocked my head. Owen was talking about Ren, but did that mean my father knew she was a Mikhailov all along? If so, what was his endgame? No, scratch that. I knew his endgame.

"Shite, I need to go." Sirens wailed in the background, and we could hear Owen running. "I'm gonna fix this for us, son. I'm gonna fix it all."

"No, Da. Da. Fuck, he hung up."

"You did good, Myles. He wants to believe you. If he thinks he still has you on his side, he'll call back again. Get him to tell you a place to meet and take care of this. If you do that, then I'll support you taking over for your father. I'll make sure the other families know you stopped the threat."

Myles nodded. "Do ya know what he meant? What "she" is he talking about?"

Lawrence shook his head. "No, I have no idea. Your father is delusional. I don't know what he's thinking about anything right now."

I looked at Myles. "Can you wait for me outside? I need to talk to my father for a minute."

Myles walked out and closed the door. I wheeled on Lawrence, but he held up his hand like he was trying to dismiss me.

"I don't want to hear whatever it is you're going to say. You already humiliated me tonight."

"You humiliated yourself," I growled back.

"How dare you."

"You want to go, old man? I'll take you right now." He didn't move. "Didn't think so. Who was he talking about? And don't give me the bullshit you just gave Myles. I know you better than he does. You were lying, and I want to know what the fuck is really going on before I lift a finger."

He sighed and took forever to answer, but I wasn't budging.

"When Owen started to show signs of cracking, I pulled strings to have his assets rolled into Collier Enterprises. His homes, cars, and bank accounts were all seized, but I didn't let him know. I still allowed him full access, so he was none the wiser."

"Well, obviously, he found out somehow."

"Obviously."

"And the "she" he was referring to?"

He placed his hands on the desk, tapping his fingers. "I'm going to level with you, son. I never planned on marrying Vicky."

He opened a drawer and pulled out a folder, then tossed it on the desk. Picking it up, I opened the file and stared at the marriage contract. I lifted my eyes to his.

"Ren? You plan on marrying Ren? She's a nobody. Why would

you want to do that?" I knew exactly why, but I needed him to think I didn't have a clue.

He stood and grabbed his glass and the bottle.

"She's not a Davies. She is a Mikhailov, but the family ties between her dead mother and the family are...tense."

I shook my head and slammed the folder down.

"This is why you're keeping Neil locked up downstairs. You needed him to sign this."

"Yes. He has signing authority for her now and he was being difficult. Fucking unloyal if you ask me after all I've done."

"How long have you known about this?" I turned, following his movements. I didn't trust him as far as I could throw him. But he walked over to the couch and sat down.

"Does it matter?"

"It all matters."

"Always so difficult, Nash. I've known for a few years. I've been biding my time. First, I tried negotiating with her mother...but the fucking woman wouldn't hear of it. She flat-out refused to talk to me and said that she wanted her daughter to make her own choices. Stupid, bitch."

Fuck, I didn't know if I wanted the answer, but I had to ask.

"Did you have Ren's mother killed?"

He chuckled. "Do you think I'd need useless Neil if I had? No, the woman was dying of cancer. It was killing her for me. Why interfere with natural selection?"

"You bastard. Ren loved her mother," I said, and he narrowed his eyes at me. I crossed my arms and shook my head before I overplayed my hand. "Your crassness never ceases to amaze me."

"Yeah, well, one day when you take control of all of this...and you will, despite what you say to me. You know you still want it. Sometimes not giving a fuck is necessary, and some people are worth more than others. It's that simple."

"So, are you planning on keeping her father locked up forever?"

He snorted and poured himself another glass.

"No. I have a feeling Ms. Mikhailov won't agree to the marriage, not that I have an issue with tying her up and fucking her, but she's smart."

I swallowed hard and forced my body not to give anything away as I pictured pulling out my knife and slitting his throat.

"Neil is simply my leverage. I don't believe his loving daughter, no matter how angry she is, will be able to stomach what I'll do to him if she doesn't spread her legs like a good girl and give me the child I want."

He smirked.

"Keep judging me all you want. This is a good move, and now you can have your girlfriend back. She's not a bad lay."

Turning, I stomped to the door and whipped it open.

"Oh, and Nash...." I stopped moving but didn't dare turn around to face him. "I trust you won't tell anyone else who she is."

I left and couldn't get out of the house fast enough.

Myles was leaning against his car, waiting for me.

"What did he say?"

"He knows who Ren is," I said, and Myles's face paled.

"What's he going to do?"

I shook my head. "Nothing good."

He glanced up at the office window and then locked eyes with me.

"Then we'll have ta stop 'em." Myles held out his hand, and I opened mine. He dropped the black marble pawn into my palm. "Never underestimate the power of a pawn."

Chapter 31

OCTOBER 05 – SUNDAY 2:22 AM

Myles

A heavy hand clamped over my mouth, jarring me from sleep. It took a second for the fog to clear, but when it did, I recognized my father. He looked and smelled like he'd been living on the streets like a rat. Dirt and sweat coated his face and only accentuated the crazy look in his eyes, but it was the blade at my throat that had my attention.

"Shh," he said, and I nodded as much as I could. He moved the knife and sat on my bed. I slowly pushed myself into a sitting position, wishing that either Nash or Liam were here. Then again, who the hell knew what he'd do if they were?

"Da, what ya doing here? How'd ya even get in?"

He snorted. "I was here for me senior year. Ya think I dinnie know all the ways ta sneak off and meet up for a party or a shag?"

Gross. That was news to me. I thought Devin was the first of the family.

I glanced around for a weapon of any kind, just in case. "What's going on?"

"Where is she?"

"Who?"

He pointed the knife at me, and I held my hands up. "Din't ya feck wi me."

"Tell me who."

I knew who he was after, but Nash was right when he said we needed to look as oblivious as possible. The insanity written on my father's face was more than I'd ever seen before. He'd always been cruel, but this was...different...unpredictable and definitely more dangerous. I never thought that was possible.

"That white-haired cunt," he growled, and I almost leaped at him despite the knife in my face.

"She's not here."

"Lies," he growled, his hand shaking. "I know yer in love wi the wee bitch." If he called her one more name.... "Ya cannie protect her. We need ta use her."

"Da, we broke up," I lied. "She doesn't want me no more, she used me, and I fekin hate her." Saying that tasted like battery acid on my tongue. I wanted to cut the thing out of my mouth, but it worked. His eyes lit up. "I'm serious. I'll show you her room if you want. She left for a retreat with the school. She's gone for the week. Fuckin' good riddance if ya ask me."

Please, God, forgive me.

"Aye, I 'member those." Wayward had all different kinds of

retreats. Not that I ever participated, and he knew nothing of Ren. I could've said anything, and he couldn't argue it.

"Shite."

He lowered the knife, twirling it in his hand like I'd done with the chess piece. I looked away, hating that I'd picked up any habit from him.

"We need her, Myles." He turned toward me again but kept the blade pointed down. "Ya need to bring her to me, son."

"Why? Yer still not makin' any sense. What does Ren have ta do with Lawrence?"

He burst up off the bed and stomped across the extra-large dorm room and back again, mumbling to himself.

"He's tryin' to destroy us. He's gonna take it all, but I can take it back. I just need the girl."

My father's obsession with Ren was dangerous for her but also him. Even if I didn't want to help Lawrence, I'd never let my father lay one finger on her. Fuck, I wished I had my gun. My pen was on my desk, and moving slowly, I picked it up and tucked it up my forearm out of sight.

"Don't ya see, son. If we have da girl, we have da power."

He grabbed my shoulders, and it took all my willpower not to stab him in the eye. I needed to keep a clear head if I wanted him dead and a future with Ren. If I killed him...I might not live to see another night. There was no telling what the Curators would do for killing someone on school grounds, and I couldn't take the chance of never seeing Ren again.

"Okay, tell me what ya want me ta do, and I'll do it."

He pulled me into a hug. My da hadn't hugged me since I was a wee lad. I held perfectly still, half expecting him to shove the blade into my back. Stepping away, he smiled, a shimmering of tears in his wild eyes.

"We'll beat em' and when we get yer brother back, we'll be a family again."

I nodded but still felt a knot in the pit of my stomach at the mention of Devin. Lawrence said Owen had started to fall apart after Devin's capture. Would he be like this if something happened to me? No. Who was I kidding? He would go on as if I never existed. I'd probably never know the reason why my father was so indifferent toward me, but it didn't matter. He was a dead man.

"As soon as the group gets back, I'll text ya," I said.

"I knew I could count on ya, son." He walked to the door, and a thought occurred to me.

"Da." He looked at me with his hand on the handle. "Whatever ya do, don't go see Lip. Lawrence figured ya'd try and has men there waitin'."

"How do ya know that?"

"Nash. He mentioned it when he got home from visiting Lawrence last night. He said his father was livid, and it had something to do with yer trip to Ireland. That's all I know, but he said that he was covering all the places you'd go. Seeing Lip was one of them. I guess he figured ya wouldn't try to see me." I lifted a shoulder and let it flop down. "Ya know with us normally arguin' and stuff."

He nodded, and I could see the wheels of chaos working in his psychotic mind.

"Aye, he does know me. You'd turn on Nash like that? Ta tell me this."

"Like ya said, no matter what, blood is thicker than water. Yer me da. McCoys look after one another," I said and put conviction behind it.

"Ya did good, son. Let me know when da bitch is back," he said and slipped out of my dorm room.

I yanked on my hoodie and sneakers before grabbing my phone. Following the slippery bastard, I ran down the stairs to the back exit. I pulled up Nash's number, and he answered like he'd been waiting for the call.

"What's up?"

"My father broke into our room."

"What? You fucking kidding me?"

"No, I'm following him. If I can figure out where he's staying, we can get him tonight," I said, pushing outside.

It was quiet, and I worried that I had missed him, but then a shadow darted into the trees. Running for the spot where he'd disappeared, I bent down and checked the ground. There was a set of boot prints heading toward the road. That had to be him.

"Don't, Myles. He's too dangerous to go after by yourself." Not bothering to listen, I ran along the overgrown path. "Fuck, Myles. Stop, we'll get him. I'm on my way."

"You'll be too late. Gotta go."

"No—"

Hitting end before Nash could finish, I stuffed the phone in my pocket and skidded to a stop. An engine started, and a beam of light cut through the trees. I bolted in that direction, sprinting as hard as I could, and reached the edge of the forest as a car disappeared around the bend in the road. Fuck, fuck, fuck.

"No one threatens my Snowflake," I growled and returned to the campus.

I would find Owen and kill him, and then we would take care of Lawrence.

Nash was pacing by the back door when I walked up the path.

"How the hell did ya get here so fast? I thought ya were at the cabin." I stumbled and landed on my ass as Nash clocked me hard enough that I saw stars. "What the fuck was that fir?"

He squatted down beside me, his eyes furious.

"I got back early and went to the pool. Don't ever ignore a direct order again."

I rubbed my jaw. "He fuckin' threatened Snowflake. I couldn't just let him drive off without trying to stop him or get a license plate."

Nash shook his head at me. "What fucking good would that do

us? It'll be stolen. He's probably going to dump it tonight. And, he's certifiable at the best of times, you don't go after someone like that alone. Who knows what the fuck he'd do."

"Aye, fuck, yer right." I pulled my knees up and wrapped my arms around them. "I can't let him hurt her, Nash."

"And we won't, but I can't question if you'll follow orders, Myles. Your dick is not your brain. Start using the right head to think."

Standing, he held his hand out and hauled me to my feet.

"Did ya have to hit me so fuckin' hard?"

"Did it knock some sense into you?"

"I don't like ya."

"I get that a lot. I've learned to live with it." He nodded toward the door. "Come on, you can tell me exactly what he said, and we can make a plan."

Nash was right. I needed to keep my cool. But it was far more difficult with my da than it was with anyone else. Owen pushed a button in me, one that would end his life, and the sooner, the better.

OCTOBER 06 – MONDAY 6:02 AM

Ren

"Left, left, right, right, right, right. Grab the bag. Left knee, again, again, now right. Good."

Liam stepped back, letting go of the punching bag while I leaned over, panting.

"You're better than I thought you'd be," he said. As I rolled my eyes up to him, I knew he was purposely trying to piss me off. Our weekend away had provided fresh insight into Liam Hicks and how he operated.

While we were alone, he was talkative, funny, and scary smart, especially at reading people. The domineering side of him was nothing like I'd been expecting, and I had to admit it was incredibly hot. Liam's training was all I needed, and there would be no more BDSM porn or Myles and Blake shenanigans.

After keeping me up all night, we had hiked the rest of the way to the cabin. Liam and I had made breakfast and ate while we waited for Theo to bring us back to Wayward. All I could think about was passing out for a whole day while Liam had looked like he could run a damn marathon. My brain and body were so tired that I hadn't been able to add one plus one, and I hardly remembered passing out once I got back to my room.

"I see you silently sassing me," he said as he smirked and walked away. "And no, you won't kill me. But I will fuck that attitude out of you if you keep it up." An instant inferno that had nothing to do with the training erupted inside of me.

"That wasn't sass. It was annoyance," I said, staring at the massive bonsai tree tattooed on his back.

The highly intricate tribute to nature stretched across his shoulders all the way down to his hips. It suited his steady and calm personality. Unlike the other guys who loved their full tattoo sleeves, Liam was more reserved. Along with the tree, he had a row of symbols on his chest that I thought might be Gaelic and an ace of spades playing card on the underside of his right forearm.

Liam grabbed the water bottles off the ground and walked toward me. I cleared my throat. The look in his eyes told me he didn't believe a word coming out of my mouth.

"Are we done for the morning?"

"Yes, you had a long and arduous workout this weekend already. We need to build up your stamina," he said. Liam's eyes reminded me of cinnamon and held a sexy edge that had me licking my lips.

"Are we still talking about the same thing?"

He stepped in a little closer, forcing me to look up to keep eye contact with him.

"Life is one long and very hard training session, Little Rabbit," he said, but each word was dipped in something sweet and sexual. I tried, I really did, but I just couldn't keep my mind on anything that didn't involve getting him naked.

"Can I take these off," I asked, holding up my boxing glove-clad hands. I desperately wanted to change the topic before we ended up on the mats in the corner. "They feel so strange, like really thick padded mittens."

"In a minute." Liam put the water to my lips but didn't let me drink.

"I'm sorry I silently cursed you out," I said, and gave him a cheeky smile.

"You do love to push limits, don't you, Little Rabbit?" Chuckling, he tipped the bottle up and let me take a few sips before setting it aside. "Give me your hand." I held out the glove, and he pulled on the lace, loosening it enough that he could pull it off and drop it to the floor. I stretched out my fingers, testing it. I felt kind of badass with the black wrapping he'd put on my hand and wrist.

"This reminds me of Rocky," I blurted out.

"What does?"

"All of this. The wraps, the gloves, the sweat. The song won't stop playing in my head," I said and hummed *Eye of the Tiger*. Liam smiled as he finished unwrapping my hand.

"I think you have a ways to go before you're ready to start punching slabs of beef in a freezer," he teased.

"I can get the other one," I said, reaching for my left glove, but Liam grabbed my wrist.

"What did I tell you?"

"You've told me many things in the last couple days. Can we narrow it down slightly?"

"What is my job?"

The gears in my brain whirred as I thought, but when he raised an eyebrow, it clicked.

"To take care of me. You do know that I don't need you to take care of me all the time, right? I can take off my boxing glove," I said as he worked at undoing the lace and then tugged it off. He dropped it to the ground, and I yelped as he snagged me around the waist and hauled me against his hard, muscled body.

Even before he spoke, I melted and wiggled in his hold. But then he whispered in my ear.

"It's not about the glove. It's the act of caring. Do we need to have a lesson? It's never too early to learn new things."

I wanted to run away and drop to my knees at the same time. There was no doubt that he'd chase after me. Liam was fast and could run circles around me for days. I would be caught like a rabbit in a snare. Maybe even hung by my foot. Why did that seem so hot?

"Answer me, Little Rabbit. Do you need a lesson?"

"No, Sir," I whispered.

"Are you sure? I don't mind teaching."

"Yes, I'm sure, Sir," I said, and he slid his hand down my back until it rested just above my ass, the heat spiking my already raised heart ratc.

"You're breathing hard, Little Rabbit. Is something wrong?" Liam growled, and I wanted to touch him. But as soon as my hands came into contact with his chest, I knew that I was in trouble.

"You tricked me," I breathed, and he chuckled. His no-touching-unless-invited rule was going to be hard to follow. Liam touching me whenever he wanted seemed slightly unfair if you asked me.

"It's not a trick when you know the rule. It just means you broke it with knowledge and couldn't control yourself." Stepping back, he ran his finger along the edge of my chin and tilted my head up to look directly at him. "But...I'm going to overlook it because you caught your mistake. Next time...you'll be screaming the gym down."

Again, like everything else he said, his words caused a conflicting jumble of feelings. My brain was stuck on my need to avoid being pushed around. My body, however, was ready to submit as all my muscles quaked, and I felt instant excitement between my thighs.

"Do you need something, Nash," Liam asked, yet he never looked in his direction, and I hadn't even noticed him. Smirking, Liam released my chin, and just like that, he was back to normal. He flowed in and out of the different sides of his personality so smoothly that it was hard to keep up.

"I'll go," I said.

"Actually, Princess. I'm here to talk to you."

Swiping my gloves off the floor, I marched for my bag and began unwrapping my left wrist.

"We already had this discussion, Nash. Nothing has changed."

"Liam, give us a few minutes," Nash said.

"No, that's not necessary," I said, but Liam had already grabbed his stuff and was walking to the door. Shit, no matter what, Liam was Nash's number two. Without even thinking about it, I'd put him in the middle of our fight.

Liam looked at me. "I'm going to hit the showers."

His eyes quietly asked me to hear Nash out while promising a punishment for what I'd done. I nodded. Now that I knew him better, it felt good to understand how Liam and Theo could stare at one another and then just agree. I swore he was telepathic.

The silence in the gym was deafening.

"You wanted to talk, so talk," I said, my voice echoing in the cavernous space.

"I need to speak to you about something important. But before I do, I want to apologize again."

"You say you want to apologize, but do I want to listen? No, I don't. I'm not ready."

The remorseful look on his face and what Liam had told me about Mya weakened my resistance to his charms. I hated how he affected me. My heart just wasn't ready for the next battle with Nash

Collier. I stuffed my gloves and towel in my bag and marched for the door, but Nash blocked my path.

"Get out of my way, Nash."

"No, you need to hear this."

He blocked me again when I tried to step around him and it felt like last year all over again. Nash had made me feel beaten down. That was what I hated. I'd always gotten back up from a knockdown. It was who I was, but he made me want to hide. Under a blanket, away from the world and all the bad people in it, just like I hid from monsters when I was a little girl.

"Nash," I growled with frustration. He grabbed me by the shoulder and spun me around, pushing my back up against the wall. "I hate you. I swear, I hate you so much."

"Then hate me. But my father knows who you are, and he's made it very clear that he's after you," Nash said.

My mind went blank, and I shuddered like a bucket of ice water had been dumped on my head.

"Did you tell him?"

"Fuck no," he said. "I'd never do that to you."

"I don't get you. You're here, then there." I pointed like he was actually moving. "You like me, then hate me. You want to fuck me, then you order me out of the room. You care, then I'm a mistake the next second. I can't do this. You're giving me emotional whiplash. I wish I'd never gone with you to Seattle."

"I'm glad you did," he said, and I pushed his hands off my arms.

"Sorry if I don't believe you. And as far as your father goes...so what? I knew he would be after me at some point. Maybe not for who I am, but your father is an asshole. You didn't see the way he looked at me the night of your birthday party. If all those guests weren't in the house...well, let's just say I have experience with that look."

Nash's jaw twitched, and I had to look away before I caved.

"The way he ordered me away from all of you was weird. I knew he was up to something, this just makes sense. I assume he wants me to marry him, but he can forget it. It's never happening. I'll kill him first or die trying."

"That's what I'm afraid of. He's still going to try and he's not just going to get down on a knee and hope you say yes."

Nash had a point. Treating Lawrence like an annoying fly was a mistake. But him wanting me and getting me to sign a contract were two different things. Unless....

"Shit, he'll hurt someone I care about. One of you, my dad, or my friends back home, won't he?"

Nash sucked in a deep breath. "Yes."

I closed my eyes, and Nash cupped my cheek, but I smacked his hand way.

"Stop doing that. I don't even understand why you care."

"Because I fucking care, okay? I don't want to see him hurt you," he growled, grabbing my upper arms again like he just couldn't stop touching me.

He held me firmly in place to keep me from pulling away.

"Don't make me kick you in the balls. I'll do it. Let me go, Nash."

"Fuck!" He roared and slammed his bare fist against the cinder block wall. "I'm sorry. I'm...I fucked up. I care and I don't know how to say sorry in a way that you'll believe me."

"Nash...you slept with me while you were contracted to someone else. There is nothing you can say that will ever make that better. I believe that you're sorry. I can feel that you are, but what you don't get is that I lo—. Fuck you, Nash, just fuck you."

I'd managed to suck back the word before I said it, but the shocked expression told me he knew what had almost slipped out. I looked away, needing to get away from him.

"Princess, there's so much more going on," he said, his hands loosening as the rage in him began to calm.

"Then trust me enough to tell me. You want to prove that you didn't just take advantage of me, then tell me what the hell is happening?"

His jaw twitched, and his brows pulled down in a dark frown.

"I can't...yet, but...I haven't even told the guys. I can't for safety's sake, but as soon as I can, I will."

"So you say. I don't know what to believe anymore, Nash," I said, wanting to take a hot shower and get to class. I needed a normal day, whatever the hell that even meant now.

"It's the truth. Look in my eyes. I would tell you if I could, but I can't until all the pieces are set."

"Am I one of the pieces on your chess board, Nash?" He ran his thumbs over my cheeks, but I gripped his arms, and he stopped.

Sadness coated him just like violence floated around him. "Everyone is a piece on the board, but it doesn't mean that I want to use you or purposely hurt you."

"I'll think about it, but Nash...fuck," I swore as the tear I promised myself would never fall slid down my cheek. "I don't know if I can ever really trust you again."

He placed his forehead against mine, and I just wanted to pretend he'd never said all those hurtful things, and my heart broke all over again.

"Tell me what I can do, Princess. Name it, other than telling you everything because I can't. I won't put you or the guys at that much risk. Whether you understand or agree with it doesn't change the fact that I couldn't live with myself if something happened."

"Then I don't know. This whole Vicky thing...I don't know if you could've hurt me more. You made me look like an idiot, but worse, you turned me into an adulterer. You made me the other woman. I deserve better."

Nash dropped his hands, and I stepped away from the temptation of his touch.

"Didn't Theo make you the other woman to him and Liam without talking to Liam first? Isn't that the same thing?"

"That's not fair, and you know it."

He sighed, stuffing his hands in his pockets. "Feels like you're holding me to a higher standard than everyone else, Princess."

"Maybe I am." He locked eyes with me, and I shrugged. "You're the king of the Kings. You should be holding yourself to a higher standard."

Nash looked away, and the same uncomfortable silence fell like a thick blanket between us.

"What about my grand opening," he asked.

"I don't think I can go with you.

"You gave me your word."

"That's low."

Nash shrugged. "I have the information you want, and you gave me your word. I don't always play fair to get what I want, and I want you to come with me. Not Vicky, you."

I crossed my arms so I didn't beat him to death with my bag.

"Fine, I'll still go with you, but not because I want to. Let me make that clear. Now, you said you learned something about Lizzy?"

"She's moving to Toronto. I think her father is there," he said.

"Toronto? But...that doesn't make sense. She loves Alberta. Are you sure?" He nodded. "Okay, but why move, drop out of school, and lie to me? Something is missing."

"You may want to sit down for this next part," Nash said, and the look in his eyes had me walking over to the closest bench and sitting down.

"What? What's happened?"

The terror of what could've happened was choking me. Every horrible thing, all the way to her dying, was crossing my mind, and I gripped the strap on my bag tighter.

"Your friend is pregnant."

OCTOBER 08 – WEDNESDAY 12:50 PM

Nash

The sound of clicking keys and ringing phones was non-stop. I'd been staring at the framed photo of Wayward's construction for the last twenty minutes while waiting to speak to Dean Henry. My mind filled with questions as I sat idle. How much did the people who work here know? Were they privy to all the dirty secrets or completely oblivious?

The door to the dean's office opened, and a girl stepped out. I recognized her but couldn't have told you her name to save my soul. Tears ran down her cheeks as she left.

"Nash," Dean Henry said, leaving his door open in invitation.

Two years of never being in this office and then Ren arrived. Now, it felt like a second home. Pushing myself up, I wandered in and shut the door behind me.

"Coffee," he asked. I nodded.

"Are you going to make me cry, too?"

"I doubt there is anything that I can say to make you cry," he said, filling two mugs from the pot in the corner.

"That is probably true."

Dean Henry was a methodical man. Sitting down, I couldn't help noticing that he always did everything in a specific order. Every time I was called into his office, he offered me coffee. Cream first, then the coffee, followed by one cube of sugar and twenty stirs per cup.

"So, I understand that you had a productive summer," he said.

"Thank you for pointing me in the right direction. I found a business arrangement that I believe will work out quite well," I said, watching him.

Dean Henry intrigued me. Who he worked for...well, that intrigued me even more, what I wouldn't give to find out more about the Curators.

"I'm still not sure why you are helping me."

He looked at me from the corner of his eye before tapping the spoon on the second mug and setting it aside.

"Life is full of mysteries. Some are worth understanding, and others are never answered."

"Is that your way of saying you're never going to tell me, so stop asking," I said, and the corner of his mouth tugged up.

"Yes, precisely."

The dean sat down and placed the mug of coffee in front of me. I sniffed it before taking a sip, and Dean Henry stared at me over the top of his glasses.

"What kind of coffee is this? It's very good."

"For a second there, I thought you were checking for poison," he said. "If that were the case, I wouldn't use a poison detectable by sniffing."

My eyebrows shot up before I stared down into my mug. "Should I be checking for poison," I asked, eyeing the liquid suspiciously.

"Trust me, Nash, if I want you dead, it won't happen in my office. The paperwork would be a nightmare."

He reminded me of Mr. Genovese. Under the calm demeanor was a man far darker than I ever imagined.

"The coffee is from Peru. A special roast brought in just for me." He sipped his coffee and set it aside. "So tell me, to what do I owe the visit? And please refrain from anything to do with your genitalia." I closed my eyes, and he chuckled. "I couldn't resist."

"Funny, that was actually very funny." I sat back with my coffee. "I need to talk to you about two things. The first is that Owen McCoy snuck onto the property early Sunday morning. He made it to mine and Myles's room, but only Myles was there. He was held at knife point." Dean Henry's eyes remained unreadable.

"Why didn't you come to me right away?"

"Why didn't you already know? I thought you had eyes everywhere, at all times?"

Dean Henry eyed me as he smirked. "I did say that, didn't I?"

"You did, and you also promised to make sure we were all safe. I personally don't care if my father sneaks on the property. If he comes to hurt me, I'll make sure he never leaves, and you can do whatever the hell you want with me. But this is Myles. I'm not sure if you know the abuse he has suffered, but he is really shaken."

"Myles asked me to ban his father from the property, which is why Mr. McCoy didn't use the front gates. He'd already tried and was turned away. Myles didn't tell me why he wanted his father barred. We normally stay out of family business. But, if Mr. McCoy snuck on and say hurt Myles, we now have recourse to make it our business."

I nodded and then narrowed my eyes at him as a thought occurred to me. "You purposely allowed him to sneak on so you could set this in motion? You're hunting him aren't you?"

"Do I seem that devious to you?"

"Honestly, yes." He laughed, and I wasn't sure what was eerier, the smirk or his laugh. "And is this moment just another test to see if I'll come to you with information?"

"I can see why they like you, Nash. You're smart."

"Who are they?"

He smiled again and didn't answer. It was official, he set my teeth on edge. I kept expecting a trap door to open, and I'd end up in some room with a real secret society, unlike the games my father played.

"I will ensure that Mr. McCoy doesn't get on the property again." He leaned a little closer. "What was the second issue you needed to discuss?"

"Next week, the swim team is in California for a meet," I said.

"I'm aware. What of it?"

"I want Ren to come with the team."

"Absolutely not. I let her leave with Mr. Hicks for the weekend. But I won't allow her to venture further than the immediate area around the school."

"If you were aware that Ren left, then you most certainly knew when Owen snuck on the property." Dean Henry's lip twitched. "Unbelievable. He could've killed Myles."

"That wouldn't have happened. Mr. McCoy was under surveillance the moment he touched school grounds. Nash, you have your chess pieces and reasons for doing what you do, and I have mine. But unlike you, I have rules that must adhere to and protocols that Wayward and the Curators hold sacred. Getting involved in Mr.

Collier's or Mr. McCoy's issues is out of my scope unless they make it my scope. Do you understand me?"

"I do, but that's a hell of a dangerous game to be playing with our lives. You don't know what Owen is capable of," I said.

"Nash, this is a dangerous world. I'm very aware of what Mr. McCoy and Devin are capable of just as I'm aware of what your father is capable of, but personal vendettas outside of these walls is not Curator business. Whether I want to interfere or not does not matter. Curators do not interfere in any family drama unless it touches this school. We are not your personal bodyguards. So as much as I would love to simply write an order to have Mr. McCoy senior wiped away, that is not in my scope of duties, or choices."

"Is there ever an exception to these rules?"

Henry was quiet as he sat back in his chair, his finger tapping on the top of the coffee mug he was holding.

"There has been a few exceptions made over the generations, but they are exceedingly rare. It is a whole process to have an exception made, we do not simply point and say that one is an asshole and has done terrible things therefore he or she must die. By that premise almost all the families in this school would be dead already."

I shook my head and sucked in a deep breath.

"Fair enough, I guess. Seems ridiculous to me to have so much power to stop evil and just sit on it."

"I know it must seem that way to you."

Henry took a sip of his coffee while I thought about what he'd said. It really did feel like a tightrope walk of when to get involved, and even if I didn't like it, that didn't mean I didn't understand it.

"Now as far as Owen is concerned. The rules were explained to Owen by the guards when he showed up the first time. He has now violated them by sneaking in and speaking to Myles on Wayward property."

"I get it. I don't like it, but I understand what you're saying. Is there someone actively hunting for him right now?"

"I'm glad that we understand one another, Nash, but that is not a question I can answer. As for Ms. Davies, I cannot let her leave."

"But we can't leave her here. If you know everything, then you know that her life is at risk. Even inside these walls, she isn't safe."

"And what makes you think she will be with you? My understanding is that you are not on speaking terms, or did I hear that wrong?" I ground my teeth and wished I had his moles. They seemed to be endless. Maybe checking under the bed wasn't a bad idea.

"We are working through some things," I said, and he smirked.

"I see. Nothing more than a lovers quarrel," he said, his lip lifted, calling me out.

"Look, make fun of me all you want. I want her with the team. I can't focus on the meet if I am worried about her safety. Besides, I think it's time she met her family. The Mikhailovs have expressed a desire to reconnect, and Ren is wanting to meet them. She is just a big enough pain in my ass that she will try to go on her own."

Dean Henry removed his glasses and pulled out a handkerchief. He stood and walked to the window, cleaning them while staring outside. "This is a very difficult situation, Nash. You're putting me in a terrible position. I accept your argument, but the truth is, Ren is still far safer behind these walls."

"I thought you might say that. There is only so much risk you can take before your rules or keeping students safe are broken. But... what if the responsibility was no longer your issue?"

"Meaning?"

Reaching into my pocket, I pulled out a sealed envelope and placed it on his desk. Walking over, he picked it up and turned on his desk lamp and shined it through the envelope.

"Now who's looking for poison?"

The dean didn't respond as he opened what I'd given him and pulled out the paperwork. He took his time reading it over before sitting down and stamping each page. When finished, he filed it in the bottom drawer of his desk.

"Well, you've backed me into a corner. How do you see this playing out? Only members of the team are allowed to travel." He folded his hands and leaned back in his chair. I'd stepped on his toes and, in a way, gone above his head, but it needed to be done. Leaving Ren here was too risky.

"Team manager. We don't have one currently. Ren is smart, always on time, and great at organizing. Coach can utilize her, and we can keep her safe."

He stared at me unblinking for so long that I wondered if he'd fallen asleep with his eyes open. "I want to make this clear, Nash. I don't like this. You're removing my ability to pull authority over anyone who attacks you, so if something happens, you can't look to me for help. You've nullified my power."

"I haven't for the rest of the team, just Ren, so by your measure if the bus was attacked, then you'd still have authority to go after those individuals. And, are you talking just for this trip or ever again?"

"You do love to split hairs," he said, but didn't deny my claim. "And, no. On Wayward property, Ren is still our responsibility, and that will never change. But from here on out, unless you remove this order you've given me, the moment you take her off the property, you can't return and ask for help if "shit goes sideways"," he said, making little air quotes with his fingers. "Do you understand?"

Fuck, I hated this so much. "Yes, I understand."

He stood and buttoned up his suit jacket. "Then I will make it happen with Coach. You can show yourself out."

I stopped at the door and turned. "I didn't do this to undermine you. I do respect you and appreciate what you've done for me. I'm also not trying to pull one over on you or the Curators, and want you to know that. I'm doing what is necessary."

"I understand that you needed to make a move, but be careful that you don't have so many pieces in play that you unknowingly put yourself in checkmate with pieces you didn't see coming. The board is always in flux. Good day, Nash."

Once outside of the office, I stood there for a minute, breathing deeply. What was he trying to tell me? Everything with Dean Henry was a riddle. What pieces did I have in play that worried him? What pieces didn't I see that I should be scared of? I hated that he made me question my every decision. Fuck.

OCTOBER 08 – WEDNESDAY 1:20 PM

Ren

Blake's hand grazed my leg, and I jerked out my day-long daze.

"What's going on," he asked, and I shook my head.

"Just can't focus, and I hate it. My mind is swirling around every thing but learning Russian. The stupid thing is, I would know more about my family if I could read it, but nothing is sticking. Feels like I've got a mental block or something. Everytime I sit down and try to learn it starts, and no matter what I do the words all jumble together." Tossing my pen down, I crossed my arms. "I'm sorry for wasting your time."

"Spending time with you is never a waste. But I do have to get to class. Do you want me to walk you to the library?"

As tempting as it was to get out of my room for a bit, it was too easy to get distracted by all the books in the library.

"No, I better force myself to study while it's still quiet. I love Ivy, but she's a talker."

Blake leaned in and hovered his lips over mine, putting the proverbial ball in my court. It was an invitation he always offered, and I'd never refuse. I kissed him deeply—what I wouldn't give to keep him here with me all day.

"I'll grab us dinner after class. Tell me what you want, anything, and it's yours," he said against my lips.

"So many things to choose from. Do you like spicy food?"

"I like anything hot and spicy when you're involved," Blake teased and winked. "But, yes, I do. Myles, not so much."

"Caribbean then. Surprise me with your favorites."

"You've got it."

He kissed me again before grabbing his laptop and bag and heading for the door. Blake opened it, and Nash was on the other side with his hand poised to knock. Ugh, a showdown with Nash was the last thing I wanted right now.

"Hey, man. We're getting Caribbean food for dinner. Do you want anything?"

"Jerk chicken, perhaps," I called out, and Blake laughed.

"Funny, but no thanks. I have to hit the club tonight," Nash said as he stepped around Blake.

"If you change your mind, let me know. See you later, Ren. Love you," Blake said and disappeared. Nash stood there staring after him before closing the door.

"I'm busy, Nash."

Flipping the page in the textbook, I stared at the practice phrases, willing them to make sense. I felt Nash moving around my room, tainting my safe space with his essence. It drove me insane.

"What?"

The asshole laid down on my bed. *Jesus, give me strength.* With his arm over his eyes, he looked way too damn relaxed.

"Earth to Nash. What are you doing in here?"

He rolled his head in my direction, and his ocean-blue eyes locked on mine. The devil himself wasn't as tempting to me as Nash. I wanted to hate him, but not loving someone was easier said than done.

"Next week the swim team is heading out of state for a meet."

"Okay, good luck. Have fun."

"We can't leave you here alone. It is far too dangerous, so you're coming with us," Nash said, and I chuckled.

"Are you serious? This is the most secure place I could be. Why would I go with you?"

Not that I minded traveling with the others. It sounded fun if I was being honest. But there was no way in hell that I was signing up to sit on a bus with Nash for five minutes, let alone however long it took to leave the state.

"Us," he corrected. "And because Owen snuck in here on Sunday and put a knife to Myles's throat." *What the fuck.* My hands started shaking, and I stood up, needing to move around so I didn't explode. "So, Myles didn't tell you. He probably didn't want you to worry, but Owen came here looking for you."

My head was spinning, and my stomach churned. That demented bastard came looking for me and had gotten close enough to hurt Myles again. If he touched one hair on Myles's head....

"Does Dean Henry know," I asked.

Nash nodded. "I just left his office. He's making the arrangements for you to travel with us as the team manager."

"Team manager? What do I know about managing a swim team? I can't even swim."

"You don't need to know anything. Coach will tell you what he wants, and the rest of the time, you'll be with us."

Pacing the room wasn't helping, and I dropped down into my desk chair again. Nash sat up and ran his hand through his hair. Memories of what it felt like running through my fingers surfaced, and I quickly shut them down.

He shifted closer. I should've slid the chair away, but I didn't and instead crossed my arms to keep my hands firmly to myself.

"Look, there's another reason that I want you to come."

He licked his lips, and my heart pounded harder. Even when he was looking me directly in the eyes, it felt like he was undressing me. I sucked my bottom lip into my mouth and bit it to remind myself of the fact that he was engaged to Vicky, of all fucking people.

"Okay, and what's that?"

"We're going to California. I've put a call into your family. They really want to meet you, and the red-headed wonder you were asking about is very excited to see you."

"You did that for me?" Stunned was an understatement of how I felt.

"I promised that I'd set up a meeting for you and your family. I'm not very good at saying sorry, but...."

For the rest of my life, I would swear that I had an out-of-body experience and no control over my actions when I jumped from the chair, grabbed his face, and kissed him. The spark between us was, as always, right there at the surface and burst into a roaring flame. I knew I'd need to douse it again later, but not right this second.

From one heartbeat to the next, Nash's shock dissipated, and he groaned into my mouth. Wrapping his arms around my waist, he yanked me down onto the bed. Nash pressed me into the mattress as his lips almost painfully devoured mine. There was no explanation for the effect that Nash had on me. I'd fought it for so long, but now...now I knew what we were like together.

I gasped for air as he broke the kiss.

"I still hate you."

"Good," Nash growled, his hands gripping mine over my head. "I want your hate. You should stay away from me," he said, kissing a line along my jaw to my neck.

Nash sucked on the sensitive spot under my ear, and my eyes fluttered closed. I twisted my head to give him more room as my entire body shook. My heart and head battled between not allowing this and wanting it at the same time.

"Fuck, you make me insane," he growled, his teeth grazing my skin.

"You're an asshole. Stop coming into my room."

"I am an asshole," he said. Nash's breath fanned my ear. "And because of that, I'll...never...stop...coming...in...you."

He flexed his ass, grinding into me. I was so close to tearing the clothes right off his body. It was a good thing he had my arms pinned.

"I think you mean my room."

"No, I mean you."

My heart stopped. Panting, I glared at him.

"Why can't you just leave me alone," I whispered.

"I'm trying, but you're a fucking witch, Princess. What the hell kind of spell have you put on me?"

"I can't do this again."

Lies, all lies. It didn't matter what words came out of my mouth or how much I wanted them to be true. He could be happily married to Vicky, and I would still crave his touch, his scent, and the taste of him on my lips.

"You broke my heart."

"I know." He looked down. "I know, and I wish I could take back every word."

"But you can't, and...why her? Why Vicky? Of all people...."

Looking away from him, I closed my eyes.

"It's com—" Nash started to speak, but the door opened, and we looked over to see Ivy standing in the doorway.

"Oh god."

Ivy's eyes were wide, and she was gaping like a fish. There was an apple in her hand halfway to her mouth. She turned around, turned back again, bumped into the wall as she turned away, and hit the door as if she was a stuck Roomba.

"Oh, dear god, I'm sorry. Don't kill me." She faced us but with her eyes closed. She was adorable in such a weird way.

"Ivy, it's fine. Nash was just leaving," I said.

He let out a frustrated sound and a couple of curses but pushed himself off me.

"This discussion is not over."

"Yes, it is. We can't do this again. I told you I hate you."

"I know, but I don't care."

His tone made me shiver. Snatching my chin, he pressed his lips to mine and nipped at my bottom lip. He stared at me for an extra beat before turning to leave, and I knew he was going to continue to push things with us. But why? Yes, I just kissed him, and yes, we had chemistry. He came here with a sweet gesture, but I didn't get why he couldn't leave me alone. I'd never be his mistress. He could forget about that.

"Nash?" He looked back at me. "Thank you for setting up the meeting."

He nodded, shot Ivy a dirty look, and walked out.

I flopped back down on the bed, trying to reign in the frenzied chaos that he evoked. I'd never felt more out of control in my entire life than when he was around me. If I was a computer, then he had infected me with a virus that was slowly eating away all my defenses, leaving behind code that I couldn't read. Nothing made sense.

"I'm really sorry."

Ivy was still standing near the door, looking completely out of her depth.

"No, I should thank you. I can't be alone with him. I don't trust myself, and as much as I want to kill him...ugh," I said, holding up my hands in a choking position to demonstrate to Ivy. "He just... ugh," I growled in frustration.

"So...you never said. Does this mean things went well in Seattle? You haven't talked about anything. I just assumed nothing eventful happened or it was terrible." Ivy walked over and sat in my chair while I curled up on my side and looked at her.

"I caved," I said, and Ivy gasped.

"You and Nash...you know...." I nodded. "Wow, you really did take them all."

Groaning, I rolled onto my back and covered my face. "I had a weak moment."

"What I just walked in on seemed like more than just a moment," she said and bit into her apple.

"It was a mistake." I looked at her. "I need to stay away from him, Ivy. I never thought I'd ever say that about him, but...."

"I get it. I'll do what I can to help." She smiled and took another bite of her apple, making me hungry. "Sooo, can I ask how it was?"

"It was incredible and horrible. I never should've gone to Seattle with him."

"I'm so confused."

"You and me both."

She was trying to work that out in her head, but I just didn't have it in me to explain it all right now.

"What about the Queen Bitch?"

"Nash wants me to trust him, and he says he has a plan. I don't know if I can. It seems I don't know much of anything anymore. I always thought school was supposed to make me smarter, but this place...this place has only made me feel like I know nothing at all."

Grabbing the stuffie that Myles had given me, I rolled onto my side and held it to my chest.

God, I miss my mum.

Chapter 35

OCTOBER 10 – FRIDAY 2:00 PM

Theo

I thought my nerves were tested when Liam took Ren camping. Turned out that I was worried for nothing, but this...this really could blow us up, and I felt sick to my stomach. Ren grabbed my hand under the desk, and I tried to take a deep breath. We could've been anywhere because whatever Mr. Sharpe had said was lost on me.

"Class, please continue reading and answering the questions. I'll be back in a few minutes," Mr. Sharpe said.

Translation: *I don't have any more in the lesson today, so I'm going to the staff room to get a coffee and stay there until class is over.*

Ren waited until Mr. Sharpe left before turning toward me.

"What's going on? You look ill."

"I feel ill."

"Did something happen with Liam? I thought the two of you were better than ever since we got back from the camping trip."

Ren's face darkened like she was ready to take on the world to try and save our relationship. She made me smile. It felt amazing to say *our* and know that it meant the three of us. Blake and Myles were with Ren, but I didn't consider them part of what I had with Ren and Liam.

"It's not anything like that. You know when you're so sure that you want something, and then when the moment arrives, you realize that it may not be what you really want? You know that saying be careful what you wish for?"

Ren squeezed my hand a little tighter. "Theo, what's going on?"

People had started talking all around us, but I shifted closer to make sure no one else could hear.

"I'm going over to Liam's tonight for dinner," I said.

"Okay...you do that all the time."

"Yes, I know, but this is different."

"Are they serving food you don't like," she teased, smiling at me, but I was too scared to laugh.

My stomach rolled. "I need to call this off," I said.

"Call what off? The dinner or the relationship?"

My eyes snapped up to hers. "The dinner. I can't let him go through with this. If he tells them about us, they'll probably order Liam to stay away from me."

"He won't listen. Liam has a mind of his own, and he loves you."

Ren flipped to the next page in the textbook, completely unfazed. It was fucking annoying when all I wanted was to scream.

I was normally the calm one. Things like dinner didn't get to me, but I had hardly slept a wink, couldn't eat, and now was practically shaking from the nerves.

"You can't know that."

Ren typed away on her laptop, fingers flying over the keys even as she turned her head and looked at me.

"I'm confused. You know Liam better than anyone else, and yet, I can confidently say, from the time I spent with him, that he would destroy anyone who really tried to come between you two. I got off easy because it was what you wanted until...well, we finally found some common ground."

"If that's what you want to call it," I said, smirking.

Her cheeks turned pink, and I knew that look. Liam had a way of embedding himself in your brain like an earworm. Thoughts and memories popped into your head at the most unexpected times. I'd been there more than once. Taking off my glasses, I rubbed my eyes and groaned.

"No, I don't think he would leave. But I don't know what's worse. Liam being disowned and still choosing me while knowing that I'm the cause for a huge rift in his family. Or he follows his family's wishes and drops me or maybe even us."

"If he drops you, I drop him. We have an understanding. It's a package deal either way. You are the glue."

My heart swelled, but I crossed my arms. "That makes it even worse. I need to cancel this dinner. It's too soon. They're not ready."

"They aren't ready, or you're not ready?"

I glared at Ren, but she just sat there quietly, staring at me. Jesus she was so much like Liam. What the hell had I done to myself? Well, at least I was consistent and had a type.

"Just be honest with yourself. There's no right or wrong answer, but don't cancel because you're scared. If Liam is ready to tell them, shouldn't you support him?"

"You're really annoyingly wise sometimes, Davies." Ren snorted. "Then maybe both. I don't want him to have to choose between us and his family. But I also don't want us skulking in the shadows and pretending in front of them all the time. I'm tired of acting like we are just friends. Not looking at him in certain ways, avoiding touching him, or accidentally saying anything that alerts them to our relationship. But this...these options now that I'm sitting here with the knife over my head...I'm not sure what I was thinking."

"You were thinking that you love him, and you're tired of hiding it. We're about to graduate. What if Mr. Hicks signs a contract with another family because he doesn't know how you two feel?"

"Or what if he runs out and signs one because we tell him how we feel?"

Suddenly, running off for a couple of hours with Ren on the back of my bike seemed like a great idea. I needed to be free from any of these decisions for a little while longer.

"What do you think I should do?"

"Do your parents know?"

"Yeah, my mom brought it up while we were away last Christmas. We were sitting on the beach, and she turned to me and started signing her heart out. She said that she knew and just wanted me to stop sneaking around and talk to her. I didn't know what to say."

"Well...if Ella figured it out, what makes you think the Hicks haven't and just aren't as forward about it?"

Ren lifted her shoulders and let them fall.

"Look, here is the bottom line. I can't help you with this part. The risks are real, so you need to be ready for anything. But you two grew up together, and you've told me a ton of times that they love you like family. If they really love you, then they will find a way to get over their hang-ups. Only you know the answer to what you can live with and what you can't."

Reaching out, she grabbed my hand again, and I took a deep breath.

"But you already know the answer. You just need to stop second-guessing yourself. It's not very Theo O'Brien or Murk of you," she said teasingly, but she was right.

I didn't panic. I came up with plans.

Straightening my back, I cupped her face and kissed her hard before smiling. "You're right. I know what I need to do."

OCTOBER 10 – FRIDAY 7:22 PM

Liam

The roar of Theo's Ducati announced his arrival before he sped into the driveway. I tracked him on the black motorcycle as he pulled up, and my mouth was dry when he parked and climbed off in his suit. It brought me back to the day he got his bike, and I was seeing Theo for the first time all over again. He removed the matching helmet and tugged at the cuffs of his sleeves before running his hands through his hair. My heart stopped as he looked up at me. He'd left his glasses off and his sharp green eyes cut into me as a devilish grin tugged at his lips.

I was leaning against the wall, trying to act casual, like this was just another dinner, but we both knew it was a lot more than that. He opened the compartment in the seat, and I smirked as he pulled out my father's favorite brandy.

"Getting a little late in the year to be taking the bike out, isn't it?"

Theo smiled, caressing the sleek machine, and my pants were suddenly snugger.

"Polly gets lonely if I leave her without being touched for too long. So, I promised to ride her hard until the first snowfall."

"You still talking about the motorcycle?" My tongue teased over my bottom lip, and my body tensed as he walked toward me. Theo picked up on it and lifted a brow at me as his eyes roamed freely.

"That depends on what you'll do if I say no."

There was no way I could go inside without touching him first.

Theo stepped in close enough that I could feel the material of our suit jackets brushing. The challenging heat in his eyes pushed me over the edge. Like we'd rehearsed a dance, I took a step to the side, and Theo shifted until his back was against the door.

"Fuck, you look good," I said, placing my hand beside his head and pressing closer. Theo groaned. The sound was as seductive as if he'd spouted off a dozen dirty things he wanted me to do to him.

"You drive me crazy. You know that, right?"

"No more than you do to me," Theo answered, each word dripping with sexual tension. Fuck, we had to get through this dinner, but there were other things I preferred to be doing with him.

Taking a deep breath, I shuddered.

"Touch me."

With no hesitation, Theo wrapped his hand around the back of my neck and kissed me like it was our last time.

Desperation laced his lips, and fire licked through my body, making me hard all over. We were both panting as I broke the kiss, but I kept my forehead against his.

"It's going to be okay," I said.

"Are you sure about that?"

"Yes, but right now, I really just want to drag you around to the back of the house and finish this."

"I thought you liked the agony of waiting," he teased and nipped at my lip, but I pulled back before he could get me.

"Oh, I do...just think about how much trouble you'll be in by the time dinner is over." Smirking, I stepped away and loved that he had to adjust himself. "It's good to have you back," I said, and he cocked his head as he looked at me.

"I wasn't the one being a dick. Admit it, you like her. I was right about Ren, and it pisses you off."

"You're a little too cocky tonight. I'm really going to enjoy punishing you later."

He chuckled. "Not as much as I will."

"Fuck me. Let's go before we never make it off the steps."

"One day, you'll admit it to me, I promise."

Theo turned around and opened the door. Rolling my shoulders, we stepped into my parent's house and were hit with the scent of a home-cooked meal. Theo grabbed my arm before we walked into the dining room.

"Wait...who called this dinner?"

"Does it matter?"

"Yeah, it kind of does. Do you know what this is about?"

I shrugged. "Best guess is my initiation and being officially sworn in tomorrow."

"Oh shit...I...."

"You didn't forget that tomorrow is my birthday, did you, Theo?"

"No, it's not that. I've been so preoccupied with the thought of this dinner and us that I forgot about whatever insanity Lawrence has in store for you. How could I forget that?" He ran a hand through his hair again, his eyes filling with a different worry.

"Don't worry about it. I can handle whatever he throws at me. Trust me." I didn't say it outloud because Theo would tell me that I'm being arrogant, but Lawrence didn't scare me. Maybe he should, I'd seen what he could do. But, when I looked at him, all I saw was a pathetic man, with self-esteem issues and an affinity for depraved kinks. The rest was nothing more than a cover to hide his inadequacies.

"Are you boys out there," my mom called out.

"Come on."

Theo took a deep breath and nodded, letting the mask of friendship fall into place. My mom smiled as we walked through the entryway.

"Theo, you get more handsome every time I see you," she said as she kissed his cheek.

"Mrs. Hicks, you are ravishing this evening," he said, and my mom blushed.

Her face lit up when he reached into his suit jacket and pulled out a single red rose. It was her favorite flower, and typical of Theo to remember something like that.

"A beautiful flower for the true head of the house," he said.

"I heard that. Are you hitting on my wife," Dad asked, walking in, and we chuckled.

"Emmett, you leave Theo alone. He was brought up right. When was the last time you brought me flowers?"

I laughed at the horrified look on my father's face. Theo held up his hands and laughed.

"Hmm, I think we better sit down and eat before I get myself into any more trouble," my dad said, sitting down at the table.

"Sir, I brought this for you," Theo said, holding out the brandy. No matter how many times my parents told Theo to call them by their names, he never did. My dad nodded, studying the offering, and then looked up at Theo. I could tell he was reading him, and I changed the subject before he could start an interrogation.

"Are Nora and Sienna joining us," I asked.

"No. Nora is still being stubborn," Dad grumbled.

"I wonder where she gets that trait from," my mom said, taking her seat.

"Don't start in on me again. I have explained many times why things are the way they are. Besides, as far as marriage goes, the Mallory boy was a perfect match."

"For Nora or business," Mom asked.

"Why can't both things be true?"

My parents glared at one another as Theo sat down beside me.

Nora and her decision to separate herself from the family was a hot topic. I was hoping to use it to my benefit, but I held that card back for now.

"What about Sienna?"

My mom was the one to answer and turned her head away from my dad with a huff.

"She is at a friend's house for the night. We thought that might be best for the conversation about tomorrow," Mom said.

"Good, because there is something I want to talk to the two of you about before we eat."

I felt Theo's eyes on the side of my face and the tension in his body as if it were my own.

"And it can't wait until after dinner? The lamb is done. I can just go grab it and—"

"No, this can't wait. It's something I should've told you a while ago," I said. My parents glanced at one another. I could read them as well as anyone, and they had no idea what I was about to say, but they were worried it had something to do with Lawrence.

"This sounds serious, son."

"It is, and I'm not sure how you'll react. As much as I hope you'll still love me and give me your blessing, I need you to know that I'm prepared to walk away from the family just like Nora."

Dad sat back in his chair, hands on the table like he was bracing himself for the news.

"If this has anything to do with...."

I held up my hand. "It has nothing to do with Mr. Collier." They both relaxed. "No, this has to do with me. I won't be choosing or signing any marriage contracts with whichever families you have picked out."

"Who says that I have anything negotiated?" Dad crossed his arms, and I copied his pose. "Okay, fine, I had a few irons in the fire. What the hell is it with our children? I blame you, Bridget. They have too much dreamer in them."

"Me?"

A fight was brewing, and I needed to head it off.

"Stop. It's no one's fault. I'm in love with someone, and I can't marry another just to bind businesses together. It's not me."

My parents wore matching shocked expressions.

"You love someone? We didn't even know you were dating anyone."

Theo shifted beside me. I glanced at him, but his face was blank of all emotion despite the nervousness he radiated.

"Who is she? Can we meet her? Oh my god, this is so exciting. Are you telling us now because things are heading toward marriage?"

"Mom, please stop."

I waited until they were both focused on me again before taking a deep breath and grabbing Theo's hand on the table. They looked at our hands, then our faces, our hands again, and I watched as they pieced it together on their own.

The room was deathly quiet, with the exception of our breaths. No one moved as we stared at one another. I'd just dropped the equivalent of an atomic bomb on them, and how they responded would determine the rest of my life.

OCTOBER 10 – FRIDAY 7:45 PM

Theo

The seconds ticked like loud clicks in my head. Ten, twenty, a minute. The four of us stared at one another in what felt like a silent standoff. The grandfather clock sitting in the corner was the only thing to break the silence as the pendulum slowly swung back and forth as if it, too, was waiting to see what happened next.

Mrs. Hicks was the first to blink. She burst into tears, and all the nervousness that I'd managed to push down stormed to the surface, making me feel ill all over again. Liam's hand tightened on mine even though I hadn't moved.

"But...but...."

She looked between us, and I could see the shock registering. I swallowed, waiting for the blow-up. Mrs. Hicks didn't like surprises. It was widely known, but I still hoped that she would smile and be happy.

"I'm never going to have grandchildren. First Nora, now you, and I'll probably be long dead by the time Sienna is old enough," she wailed, her face twisted in anguish. "All I ever wanted was a full house," she cried and got up from the table, walking out of the room while her sobs carried through the house.

Mr. Hicks looked at the swinging door where his wife had just disappeared and then turned his attention to us. He sat back and rested his elbows on the arms of his chair, reminding me of a king on a throne. He didn't say anything, and I couldn't tell by his face what he was thinking. At least he hadn't screamed at us to get out of his house. I remained hopeful that at least one of Liam's parents was going to accept me...us.

We all winced as plates clattered and what sounded like metal pots crashed together. Mrs. Hicks stormed back in and dropped a massive platter with a rack of lamb down in the middle of the table.

"Bridget."

Mr. Hicks tried to get her attention, but her hysterical crying only got worse as she walked back out again. He waved his hand in her direction.

"I love your mother, you know I do, but...she can be very dramatic," he said, just as Mrs. Hicks walked in with the bowl of potato puree and a plate of veggies.

"I am not dramatic! Did you hear what he said? None of our children want to get married, carry on our bloodline, or...who am I supposed to spoil? It's my job, my one job, and...."

"Technically, Liam hasn't said anything yet."

Mrs. Hick's face went a violent shade of cherry tomato, and she screamed like a banshee. She swore in Gaelic before dropping the two dishes on the table, making the plates and cutlery bounce.

"Don't you dare give me that shit, Emmett, or so help me, you'll be in the spare bedroom."

He smirked. "Which one? I kind of like the one with the jacuzzi."

"Ah!"

I was pretty sure that Emmett was a dead man. Mrs. Hicks appeared ready to jump on him. Instead, she stormed back out. Her tears were like a tap that wouldn't shut off now that she'd turned them on.

Emmett remaining ultra calm while Bridget cried was not what I had expected. I glanced down at the table to see my watch peeking out from under my suit jacket sleeve and couldn't imagine taking it off forever. The few days I hadn't worn it were too long as it was. I'd never felt so naked.

"Don't mind your mother. She processes...loudly. She had a similar moment when we were informed of our marriage contract, the day of our wedding, the moment she found out that she was pregnant with Nora, and then again with you. There's more, but you get the idea." He sighed and linked his fingers together on the table. "Let me start by saying I don't care that you two want to be together. What I care about is the tradition of marrying families together to strengthen bonds and bottom lines."

"Does that mean you only cared about what mom's family could do for you when you married her?"

Mr. Hicks smirked. "We grew to love one another. But ours wasn't a marriage based on love. So, Theo, tell me what you bring to this alliance?"

"That's your first question," Liam said, and Emmett shrugged.

"Like I said, I don't care if you want to marry a purple dinosaur. What makes this union more profitable than the others I've begun lining up? If you two are this serious, then I want to know what he brings to the table?"

"I'm not some breeding stock to be sold off to the highest bidder," Liam growled, but if Emmett was fazed, he did not show it.

Instead, he laughed before his face turned serious once more.

"Yes, you are. You all are and don't fool yourselves into thinking otherwise. I was, your mother was, and our parents were before that. In this world, we marry to increase our financial holdings or to create a bridge with another powerful family for protection. That's how we stay alive generation after generation. You, of all people, should know that, Liam. So, I'll ask again...Theo, what do you bring to this union?"

"Nora left because of this exact reason," Liam said, fuming and about to explode "Do you want me to leave, too?"

Emmett smacked his hand down on the table, and I grabbed Liam's arm.

"You're not leaving. We're not leaving," I said, and Liam turned his raptor gaze on me.

"You don't have to answer this question, at least not tonight," Liam said. "We came for dinner, not a business meeting."

"And yet, this is a business issue. You dropped it at the dinner table, so now you get to either discuss this or leave," Emmett said.

"Our relationship shouldn't be considered business," Liam said.

"Liam, he's right. We could've waited until after dinner, but we brought it up, and your father has a valid point."

Liam sucked in a deep breath and crossed his arms but didn't argue. I could tell by the look on Liam's face that he wasn't so sure this was a good idea.

"I want to answer," I said. My talk with Ren earlier had prepared me for this very moment. Liam wasn't the only one that could read people. The only thing I could think of that Mr. Hicks valued as much as passing along his name to an heir was money and business connections. So I'd prepared everything that I could think of.

Turning to Emmett, a calm washed over me. I'd been terrified until this second, but now that it was finally out there, I could breathe better than I had since I first started worrying about this night.

"Mr. Hicks, I am a massive asset that you've already utilized without realizing it." He narrowed his eyes.

"How so?"

"The paperwork that you just had Truform Steel sign, who do you think wrote that contract?"

"That is the most ironclad contract I've ever seen," he said.

"Exactly, and if you think that is good, then imagine how exceptional of a lawyer I'll be when I graduate from Harvard. I've already been accepted. Yes, my father signed off on it, but he didn't change a single line." Emmett sat back, and I could see the astonishment in his eyes. "I don't need to tell you that we are always in need of top lawyers, but how about a lawyer who will also be co-owner of an investment banking firm?"

"Co-owner with who?"

I looked at Liam. "We're small right now, but with a little more capital, it'll be a thriving business."

"That is a cutthroat industry. What makes you think you can handle those sharks?"

Liam smiled. "Have you seen me at the poker table? I will eat them and use their bones as my toothpicks."

Emmett looked between the two of us. "You've put real thought into this and have been planning for some time. So, you're serious? This isn't some whim to get out of a marriage arranged by your parents."

"We have, sir. You also know that I'll end up with half of my father's law firm, O'Brien, O'Brien, and Spector, as well as the construction business my mother built from the ground up. This isn't what you were planning, but you haven't met anyone more dedicated to succeeding and being the best than me."

He rubbed at his chin, his shrewd eyes trying to cut through me to see if I was telling the truth. I'd gotten used to that look from Liam.

"I want to see numbers, but...I will say that I'm impressed so far. That's enough business talk until after dinner. I should go check on your mother."

"No, let me," I said, standing.

Squeezing Liam's shoulder, I followed the muffled cries. They were much softer now, but when I walked through the kitchen door, Bridget was standing at the counter icing a cake.

"Mrs. Hicks, may I speak to you for a minute?"

She jumped a little, and to my surprise, she didn't whip the cake at my head.

"Sweetie, you know you can call me Bridget," she said. "I'm sorry. I'm a mess." Grabbing tissues, she dabbed at the tears. "I'm not angry, despite what it looks like." We walked over to the small table with two tall stools in the corner and sat down.

"You're allowed to be upset. We sprung this on you without warning." Laying my hand on hers, she smiled.

"I think I knew all along that you and Liam were more than friends," she said. "You share a closeness that only comes with intimacy."

"Are you disappointed?"

She shook her head. "No, and yes. No, because I love you like my own, you know that. Ella and I raised the two of you together, and I have memories of you sitting on the same blankie playing with toys. Well, you wanted to play. Liam kept trying to steal them."

I smiled. "But you wanted grandchildren?"

She nodded. "It's selfish, really, but I just always pictured the house full for generations. Nora and Emmett are barely speaking, and I have no idea how to fix that. Sienna is only ten. I pinned all my hope on Liam. I think I'm suffering from empty nest syndrome. Most of the time, it's just me in this massive house. Emmett works all the time, and...." She wiped away more tears. "I'm sorry, I feel so greedy. Some people never have what I do. I should be thankful for what the good Lord has given me already. I just need a little time to wrap my head and heart around the changes coming."

"Well, I can't guarantee where we'll live, but we're definitely having kids."

"You are?" Bridget's eyes brightened.

"We are?" Liam was lurking in the middle of the kitchen after doing his impression of the Invisible Man.

"Yes, we are," I said, ignoring his wide-eyed expression and turning my attention back to Bridget. "Don't give up on that dream."

The tears were instant. "Really?"

Standing, I gently helped Bridget to her feet and wrapped my arms around the woman I'd known for my entire life. I smiled when Liam hugged his mom from behind, making her laugh.

"I love you boys so much."

"We love you too, Mom," Liam said.

"You know Lawrence isn't going to like this," she said.

Liam and I shared a look over her head.

"What am I missing," she asked, looking back and forth between us.

"Let's just say that there is more we need to discuss with Dad," Liam said, and Bridget chewed her bottom lip.

"Please tell me you're not planning anything dangerous. I couldn't live if something happened to either of you."

Liam gave his best reassuring smirk and wink. "We wouldn't do anything to get in trouble, would we, Theo?"

I laughed and shook my head. "Nope, never."

"Now I know you're both lying."

"What the hell is going on in here? Dinner is getting cold, and I'm sitting out there alone with my thumb up my arse," Emmett complained.

"Don't swear at dinner time. You're right. Let's go eat before it's completely ruined."

Liam tugged my arm, and I stopped as his parents walked out. "Kids?" He whispered. I crushed my lips to his and felt him shudder.

"Kids," I said and walked out of the kitchen, leaving him to follow.

Making it past step one with Emmett and Bridget was huge, but shocking Liam silent was just as sweet as the icing on the cake.

OCTOBER 10 – FRIDAY 11:05 PM

Liam

Confident, intelligent, and commanding—all words that described the man who owned my heart and made my cock hard. I knew Theo was smart and could conduct himself like he had thirty years experience on any topic and he was certainly capable of commanding a room. But knowing it and seeing it...were totally different things.

We'd both grown and changed over the years, but in the last four months, I had been fighting a significant shift in our relationship. Change wasn't easy for me at the best of times, but the changes in Theo felt like too much. He was my constant, and despite our dynamic in the bedroom, he was my fucking rock.

When my father had demanded to know what Theo brought to the table, I'd been ready to follow in Nora's footsteps. Fuck him, we would strike out on our own. But Theo had taken charge and ordered me to stay. I wouldn't have gotten to experience this if I had let my dominance get the best of me.

The four of us sat around the table talking and laughing like we always had, but now...the underlying tension about who we were to one another was gone. My father was busy talking about new deals while Theo thumbed through an arrangement that had Dad concerned. It took Theo all of ten minutes to read the document and point out the issues. When he handed the paperwork back, it was as good as scribbling his name across a marriage certificate.

My father had agreed to draw up a contract for us. Now, we just needed to figure out how that worked with Ren. My guess was that nothing would change. She didn't seem like it would bother her, but that was our next big conversation.

"We really should get some sleep," I said, standing and buttoning up my suit jacket out of habit. In reality sleep was the last thing on my mind and couldn't wait to get Theo naked.

"Why so soon?"

"My initiation and oath swearing are tomorrow. You didn't forget, did you?"

Mom and Dad looked at one another before my father stood and picked up his glass.

"Why don't we take this conversation to the cigar lounge? I'd like to have one." That was code for, *we need to talk.*

Theo glanced up at me from his seat, and we shared the same worry. What was so terrible about tomorrow that it required a cigar lounge discussion?

"I'll look after the dishes," Mom said, taking the plates out of Theo's hands as he picked them up. "Go on, shoo, go talk."

"Thank you for another fabulous meal," Theo said, and I could see my mom melt as he kissed her cheek.

"Oh, stop, get out of here before I start crying again," Mom said, and I hugged her before following Dad down the long hall to the room across from his office.

As soon as we walked in, Dad closed the door and opened his

cigar box. He picked out his favorite and poured another drink. "Have a seat."

"How serious is the challenge that you need to talk to us privately?" Theo and I sat down in two of the four leather chairs and waited for him to speak.

"Honestly, it depends on how you view it." Dad wandered over with his cigar smoldering between his fingers and his brandy in the other hand.

This room suited my father. He'd designed it in dark woods with glass-door cabinets that displayed the bottles of brandy, scotch, and whiskey that he'd collected over the years. The furniture was dark brown to match the wood, and the walls showcased massive oil paintings of racehorses at the track. As far as I knew, my father had never gone to the races, been a gambler, or even rode a horse, and yet famous thoroughbreds such as Secretariat, Seabiscuit, War Admiral, Northern Dancer and even Man o' War graced the walls.

"There is no gathering to attend tomorrow."

"What?" Theo and I said together.

"Lawrence is away dealing with an issue in Ireland. We all know you can run circles around any mental, physical, or emotional challenges."

"Okay…I'm sensing a but," I said.

"You are correct. You'll still need to make your contribution in some manner and prove your loyalty before you're sworn in."

I glanced at Theo, and he seemed just as confused as I was.

"What does Lawrence want me to do?"

"Not Lawrence. Me. He has left it up to me to choose your initiation trial."

Staring my father in the eyes, I slid forward in my seat, trying to gauge what he might deem an appropriate contribution. Killing and assaulting people wasn't his style.

"I came up with the perfect balance of what you can do and what will keep Lawrence happy, and more importantly what will keep all the other council members happy."

"Well, don't keep me in suspense. What is my task?"

"You'll play poker."

"Lawrence wants money? Easy. How much?"

"Five million, and you have two weeks."

My father stood and polished off his drink before stubbing out his cigar. He casually walked to the door and looked back at us.

"And son...I didn't set the timeframe or the punishment if you don't succeed. I suggest you succeed because you won't like what Lawrence does if you fail. Good night."

OCTOBER 12 – SUNDAY 1:15 PM

Ren

My pencil slid across the page in little strokes as I finished the details on the outer edges of my sketch. I'd stared at the blank cream-colored page for an hour until it felt like it had sucked me into the endless flat void. Then, my hand moved on its own as the image clear in my mind.

Myles was finished first. The mischievous glint in his expression was perfect. I could almost hear him say, *Hello, Snowflake*. Next had been Theo, with his helmet under his arm and the arrogant arch in his prominent brow as he challenged me to argue with him. Blake followed, oozing the kindness that embodied everything he did. He was looking down, his messy hair falling over his forehead as his fingers strummed the strings of his guitar. I'd struggled with Liam at first, but then I drew him from behind. He looked over his shoulder at me with his tattoo proudly on display and a don't test me smirk, curling his lip.

Nash stood in the middle with the rest of his guys. His arms crossed as he glared at me like it pissed him off that I was even drawing him. I'd thought of doing something decorative, but my hand just wouldn't cooperate when I tried to fill the space in the center.

"Wow, that's beautiful!"

My coffee tipped over as I jumped up, screaming. I grabbed my sketch pad so none of the god's nectar got on the image. Pulling off my headphones, I glared at Ivy, who I loved but wanted to kill for scaring me. She was supposed to be visiting her dad today, so I hadn't expected anyone until later.

The guys were in the pool putting in an extra training session before we all left for California. I could've gone to watch, but staying the hell away from Nash was my latest self-preservation mission. Who the hell was I kidding? It had always been my mission, but I'd slipped and fallen in the deep end. Now, I needed to remain away from the pool, or Nash would drag me back under.

Fucking Nash. Fucking Vicky. It made me sick that I understood her obsession. Having anything in common with Vicky was an all-new level of hell.

"Oh my god. I'm so sorry," Ivy said and ran into the bathroom, returning with a roll of paper towels. "I didn't mean to scare you."

"It's alright. I didn't hear you come in." Tossing my sketchpad onto my bed, I helped clean up as Ivy apologized non-stop. "What happened to your visit?"

"Dad is starting work for Nash this week. It kind of feels like trading in Satan for his underling as a boss. But he needs to work, and Nash paid for him to go to rehab."

She held out my trash basket for me to toss in my dirty paper towels.

"Anyway, he's the new head of security at Nash's club. With the opening in a few weeks, I guess he had things to take care of today. No idea what that means, and honestly, I'm scared to ask."

I felt that statement in the very fabric of my soul. I hated being in the dark, but I'd never sleep at night if I knew the details of what the guys did for their families. At least, I hoped I wouldn't. The night I slept soundly, knowing I'd committed multiple felonies, would be very dark indeed.

"Working for Nash is an upgrade from being Lawrence's whipping boy. Lawrence is sick and twisted. Who knows what he made your dad do? Nash has his faults, but I can't picture him ordering your dad to do the deplorable shit Lawrence finds amusing."

"That's true. Do you want to head down and grab another coffee?"

"Sure, I haven't eaten yet today and probably should before Myles scolds me."

Taking off my headphones, I laid them on the bed and pulled on my sneakers.

"So, you never did get to tell me about this guy you met." I nudged her arm. "I've seen you smiling and texting someone. Tell me about him."

Ivy's face lit up as she smiled. "Okay, but you can't tell the guys who it is."

"That sounds mysterious. Fine, I won't tell them," I said, smiling. A girly conspiracy that didn't lead to death or destruction was just what I needed.

"It's Sabastian from Hawking Shores, you know, the captain."

On second thought, it could lead to murder. "Ivy...."

"I know, I know. Nash and the boys don't like him, and he hates them. But Ren...he's hot and funny, and he wants to take me out on a date. A real date, like dinner or something."

"God, I hate to do this, but...has he asked anything about the guys?"

We stepped into the elevator, and Ivy crossed her arms as she glared at me.

"No. Why? Do you think that's the only reason he's interested in me?"

"Of course not. You are incredible and a catch. It just seems weird. They exchanged words when he was here for the meet. I'm not a big believer in coincidences anymore," I said, and Ivy shook her head at me.

"You can't look at anything without wondering if there is an angle or a conspiracy theory. I know you've had a shit time of it, but not everyone is trying to find a way to cause havoc for you or the Kings."

I rubbed my face, "I know, but...Ivy, you have to admit that there's a possibility."

She put her hands on her hips.

"No, I don't. He didn't even know that I knew the Kings personally until a couple of days after we started talking. I can't believe you want to stomp all over my excitement like this."

The elevator doors opened, and Ivy marched out. The worst part was that she wasn't wrong—at least not about the conspiracy stuff. I looked at everyone differently.

What was their motive for talking to me? Were they trying to get information on one of the guys? Did they plan to kill me? Did they have a Lawrence in their family who wanted to get their hands on me? As much as I hated that my mum kept all of this from me...I got it. This life...the looking over my shoulder for the knife coming, was tiring.

Jogging after Ivy, I grabbed her in a hug and forced her to stop walking.

"You know I love you, and I want you to be happy. That shouldn't have been my first thought. You're right, and I'm so sorry."

Releasing her, she turned and looked at me. Her eyes still held some anger but had softened.

"I hate that you might be right and that you put the thought in my head. Now, every conversation I'll be looking for hidden questions and motives."

"God...I'm so sorry, Ivy. Don't think that. You're right. He wouldn't know you have anything to do with the guys. Can we just pretend that I never asked? I'm sorry I opened my mouth."

Her gaze flicked up to mine, and her big eyes filled with a spark of hope again.

"I mean it. You're freaking incredible, beautiful, and I love you to bits. He sees it too, and about damn time someone gets their head out of their ass to notice. Now, tell me all about the hottie from Hawking Shores. I want to know everything."

"Well...."

Ivy started gushing all about Sabastian, and as much as it pained me, I knew I had to tell Myles. He could look into him and keep it quiet unless there was an issue. God...it made me sick to my stomach to think about breaking her trust. I already had one friend ignoring my texts and calls. I didn't want to lose Ivy, too.

Grabbing a fresh coffee, I treated myself to some of the warm chocolate chip cookies on the tray. Who the hell could resist these?

"Yeah, so we have a lot in common. More than I ever thought we would. The best part is that his parents aren't insanely rich. He got into Hawking on a scholarship. Anyway, do you think we can go shopping this week?"

I popped one of the warm cookies into my mouth and moaned. They were trying to kill us with these. I could eat the entire tray.

"Apparently, only Ella or Nash can take me off the property. Don't ask me how that was arranged, but he's not taking us shopping, I'm sorry. Also...I leave on Monday to go with the swim team to California."

"What?" Ivy's eyes were wide as she grabbed my arm. "How the heck did you manage that?"

"It's a long story, but...." I looked around and lowered my voice. "My cousins are there, and Nash made arrangements for me to meet them."

Ivy's jaw dropped.

"Are you sure they aren't the ones from Canada who...you know...."

I shook my head. "No, I'm not. But Nash says it wasn't them."

She crossed her arms and narrowed her eyes into thin slits.

"You are putting an awful lot of trust in Nash's word. Is that safe after how he hurt you? You haven't told me what happened, but you can't deny it after the other day."

Sighing, I looked down at my shoes. "There are some things that I'll never trust coming out of his mouth. But with this...I do. It's complicated."

"That seems to be you in a nutshell lately."

"Tell me about it."

We laughed as we walked across the foyer and waited for the elevator. The doors opened, and my smile fell as Vicky and Jennifer stepped out. Of course, the Queen Bitch couldn't just walk by, Nope, she needed to get a rise out of me.

"I was thinking pink, white, and black. What do you think Ren?"

Ivy and I shared a look before she shook her head, not knowing what Vicky meant either.

"Pink, white, and black for what?"

"Decorations. For the wedding, of course. What do you think?" She smirked, but it was more of a snarl, so I smiled.

"Oh...well, that's a good question," I said, stepping around her and getting in the elevator. Holding the door open, I tapped my cheek, pretending to think. "Vomit green suits the two of you best. Maybe pair it with shit brown."

"Bitch," she hissed.

"Maybe, but...." I waggled my finger between her and Jennifer. "I'm pretty sure Nash ordered you not to say anything, or he would cancel the whole arrangement. Oops, it would be terrible if someone accidentally told him that you're opening your very loud, annoying mouth and spilling the news." Her face paled. "Don't worry, Vicky, your secret is safe. I think you two are perfect together. Truly, well suited."

I waited for the door to start closing on her before shoving my hand in the gap, forcing it to open again. I chuckled at Vicky's confused expression.

"Oh, I almost forgot...did Nash mention that he's taking me to the Halloween party? You know the big grand opening that is so special to him? Seems strange that he neglected to mention that to his...." I mouthed, *fiancé*.

Vicky balled her hands as she made a high-pitched squealing sound like she was a nuclear plant about to meltdown.

"I don't believe you."

Shrugging, I let the elevator close.

"I don't care what you believe. Ask Nash yourself," I said as Vicky's face turned an alarming shade of red before disappearing from view.

"Damn girl, you've gotten vicious," Ivy said.

Even though she was smiling, and I knew she meant it as I compliment, it hit worse than anything Vicky ever said. I didn't want to be known for my viciousness. That wasn't me...was it?

"I guess I know what happened now," she said, and I nodded. "Don't worry, I won't ask any more questions."

The elevator opened, and Ivy stopped as Zigzag stood up from the couch in the little sitting area.

"Ivy, can I talk to you," he asked.

"Do you want me to stay?"

"No, I'm fine. Thanks, though."

Nodding, I left them alone and went back to our room, nibbling on my next cookie. I didn't know how the kitchen staff managed to get the perfect ratio of chocolate to cookie and made them so chewy. I already wanted to go down and get more.

Opening the door to my bedroom, I froze. Nash sat on my bed, holding my sketchpad.

"It's rude to look at someone's work without asking first," I said.

"It's...really damn good." He looked up at me and...*nope*. I couldn't be in here with him.

I turned around, but the door didn't even get a chance to close before he caught me in the hall and hauled me back inside the bedroom with a hand over my mouth.

He had the audacity to groan when I bit his finger.

"Nash, let me go," I mumbled as he spun me around and pushed me up against the wall.

His leg was between mine, and my hands were locked above my head.

"Nash...." I scowled, but it didn't deter him. He kissed me, but I refused to open my mouth.

"Open for me, Princess," he whispered and licked at my bottom lip. "You taste like sex and chocolate on my tongue. I want to fuck you with this taste in my mouth. You're delicious."

"I told you that we are not doing this again. Are you hard of hearing?"

"Oh, I'm definitely hard. You're mine, Princess. That means I don't give a fuck. I'm not letting you go."

"I think your fiancé, who just asked my opinion on wedding decorations, would disagree," I said, rolling my eyes and fighting the urge to submit to him.

"Fucking Vicky," he growled, and a shiver raced down my spine.

There was no stopping the moan as he kissed me again. He was hard and demanding while I was putty in his hands. Everything with Nash was wild. He made me frantic for more, and fighting it felt like a losing battle, but I had to try.

Nash broke the kiss, and I thought my heart was going to run out the door.

"I can't do this, Nash. Please."

"And I can't stop wanting you. One of us will win this battle of wills, Princess. I'll bet on me any day. I can still feel your pussy wrapped around my cock as you slept," he said in my ear. "All. Night. Long." He rubbed against me, and my body shuddered. "I'll have you again."

"That sounds like a threat," I said, and he smiled.

"It's a promise. I know you lay awake at night and think about me."

I didn't respond, and he pushed back, giving me space. He nodded toward the sketch and pulled up the sleeve on his arm.

"Don't forget this tattoo," he said.

Annoyed, I looked down. The bag of cookies fell from my hand as I stared in shock, unable to form a coherent thought. *Princess* took up the entire underside of his forearm with decorative lines, Celtic symbols and a lily with vines. It wasn't there when we went away, I was sure of it. The tattoo was dry and no longer raised and the rich new design stood out against his skin. That could only mean he had it done as soon as we got back.

"What...what did you do?"

"You're mine, Princess. Get used to it."

Nash bent and grabbed the cookies off the floor. Smirking, he pulled two out and popped one in his mouth.

"You ignored me when I told you to stop me." Nash ran his thumb over my bottom lip, his eyes penetrating right through me. "You didn't take the out I offered, and now...well, now I'm keeping you."

"I thought you meant sex, not marking your body with my name or nickname. And I never agreed to more than that one night," I stammered, flustered and feeling lightheaded.

I moved away and had just cleared the door when it suddenly opened with a bang. Ivy and I screamed at the same time as she stared at Nash standing in front of her.

He smirked at me. "See you later, Princess. Thanks for your cookie," he said, his eyes never leaving mine. My body flushed hot. He walked out as confident and unfazed as I'd ever seen him.

What the fuck did he have up his sleeve?

Chapter 38

OCTOBER 13 – MONDAY 6:00 PM

R**en**

"Anyone else lovin' this show," Myles asked, and the rest of the bus laughed.

No one was trying to hide that they were mesmerized by the fight outside as they pressed themselves up against the windows like a bunch of children. I was trying not to watch, but Vicky's tantrums were impossible to ignore.

She'd marched outside when the fancy coach bus arrived. Not wanting to be involved in her drama with Nash, I got on and parked myself in a window seat near the back. Some of the other team members stared at me, probably confused by my presence, but as long as Coach was fine with it, I didn't feel obligated to address their curiosity.

The fight started when Vicky tried to kiss Nash, and he backed away from her like she had a transmittable disease. It was horrible, and I knew it, but it was terribly satisfying to see Vicky losing her shit. The reasoning was what bothered me. If I was her, I'd hate me... and that didn't sit well.

"Why does she get to go?"

Vicky's yelling had reached a volume where we could hear every word. One perfectly manicured finger pointed in my direction, and I ignored her even though I could see her out of the corner of my eye. Vicky's expression darkened while Nash spoke. It was too low to hear, but she stomped her foot and stormed toward the front doors, disappearing inside the main hall.

Nash shook his head, grabbed his bag, and everyone scattered to their seats as he stepped up into the bus. He glared at anyone who dared look his way as he trudged down the aisle to the back, where I was sitting with the guys.

"Dude, ya know how to put on a show." Myles laughed, clapping Nash on the shoulder. "I can't wait for the next one. They're the highlight of me day," he said.

"I'm sure," Nash drawled.

Nash tossed his bag down on the seat across from me. I stared down at my book, pretending to read, and tried to ignore him. He opened his mouth like he wanted to say something, but Liam dropped down beside me.

"Hello, Little Rabbit," he purred like a fucking cat. He'd never done that before and the hair stood on the back of my neck. I rubbed at my arms and Liam smirked.

Had he lost his mind? Not only did he demand no public displays of affection, but he only used that name on me when he was in Dom mode. Liam just smiled.

"Are you ready for another adventure," he asked.

Liam brought my hand up and nibbled on my fingers. My eyes shot around and landed on Nash's face. He looked like he was going to shoot his best friend. I shuddered when Liam sucked my pinkie in his mouth.

"Answer me."

I licked my lips. "Yes."

"That's a good, Little Rabbit," he growled.

"What are you doing," I asked, keeping my voice so soft that it wasn't even a whisper.

He groaned and leaned close to my ear. "Wanna piss Nash off?"

Every fucking day of my life.

Instead of yelling what I wanted to, I smirked and nodded.

"Good, let's have some fun. Take your hoodie off," Liam said as the bus started to move. Peeling it off over my head, my T-shirt pulled up with it, and heat rippled through my body as he touched my bare stomach.

"Let me help," Liam coaxed.

Liam didn't help like I thought he would, and I ended up sitting beside him in just my bra. I slid lower in the seat and stared at him wide-eyed.

"Oops," he drawled and then leaned forward like he was grabbing something off the floor. It left me directly in Nash's line of sight. We stared at one another, my heart hammering out of control.

If Liam wanted Nash to lose his mind and try to kill him on the bus than he was well on his way. Nash stared at me with the same crazed look he had yesterday. His body was tense and poised to leap across the aisle. His hand gripped his bag so hard that his hands were balled into fists. Nash's crystal blue eyes dropped to my chest, and he ran his lip through his teeth.

I glanced back, and I saw Myles watching. He looked like he was going to bust a gut from laughing. All these assholes were in on this.

Jerks. Liam suddenly sat up and I could've sworn Nash growled at him, but Liam looked totally unbothered.

"Sorry, I dropped this," he said and handed me my T-shirt. *Liar.* Snatching it out of his fingers, I tugged it over my head while Liam pulled my legs up and across his lap. He unlaced my sneakers and took them off along with my socks. Liam smiled as he noticed the little snowflakes on my toes. Myles put them on everything. One day even my laptop was decorated in intricate snowflake designs.

Liam began massaging my foot. Holy hell, he had amazing hands. "Ohhhh my," I moaned as he rubbed a spot that made my back arch.

"You look sexy, Little Rabbit, moan for me again."

He ran his thumb down to my heel, and I shuddered. This shouldn't be a turn-on, but as he switched to my other foot, he whispered for me to say his name, and I melted.

"Tell me how good it feels," Liam ordered.

"Feels incredible, Sir." He smirked, and I'd completely forgotten why we were even doing this until Nash bolted from his seat.

"Un-fucking-believable," Nash swore. "Go sit up there."

Theo laughed before he appeared and sat down across the way.

"Impressive. I thought he would last another five minutes," Theo said.

Now that Nash had stomped off, I figured Liam would stop, but he kept working his hands up my legs while talking to Theo about something to do with finance. By the time he was done with my other calf, I was nodding off. The next thing I remembered was waking up with Blake in Liam's spot and Myles sitting across from us. He smiled at me, and I returned the gesture before my eyes fluttered closed again.

OCTOBER 13 – MONDAY 11:59 PM

Ren

"Wakey, wakey, Snowflake," Myles said.

"Just five more minutes," I mumbled, annoyed at the interruption.

"We've stopped to grab food and stretch our legs."

His fingers trailed down my cheek, and I sucked in a deep breath. I glanced around.

"How far are we?"

Other than the giant golden M that made my stomach growl, I couldn't see anything to indicate where we were.

"Not quite halfway. We get forty minutes," he said, and I stretched.

I looked at my feet and someone had been nice enough to put my socks and shoes back on, but I couldn't have said who or when it happened.

Myles helped me stand, and I realized that we were alone. He wrapped his arms around me and pulled me into a hug.

"Mmm, that's better. I missed feelin' yer body next to mine."

"You always smell incredible," I said, burying my head into his warmth and taking a deep breath.

I loved all the guys, but no one had the same calming effect on me as Myles. He was my anchor, holding me steady against the crashing waves.

"I love you," I whispered, and he kissed the top of my head.

"I love ya, too, Snowflake."

Peeling away from him, I moved along the long aisle and down the stairs. I'd never ridden on a fancy bus like this one before, or even a public one, just the yellow school buses that always seemed like they were on their last legs and smelled like leather, hot plastic, and diesel mixed into one confusing scent.

Myles linked his fingers with mine as we walked inside. The overwhelmed restaurant was the opposite of the quiet night outside. There wasn't even another car in the parking lot.

"Do you mind grabbing me a number four with large fries?" I nodded in the direction of the bathroom. "I'll be right back."

"Sure. What do you want to drink?"

"Root beer, please."

The bathroom was larger than I expected and thankfully empty. I headed for the farthest stall, catching a glimpse of myself in the mirror. Man oh man, bathrooms were harsh, fluorescent bulbs and wonky glass distorting our images. It was my personal conspiracy theory that it was done so we looked like we hadn't slept a day in our lives, gained twenty pounds, and didn't have a clue how to dress ourselves. I was positive that I didn't look like death warmed over when I got on the bus. Groaning, I smoothed down the wild strands of hair that stood on end like I'd been electrocuted.

I'd no sooner locked the stall when the bathroom door opened, and a few of the swim team girls entered.

"Where is she? She's not in here, right?"

"No, she's still sleeping on the bus," someone else answered.

"What's the deal with her coming with us? It's not like she's an actual member of the team," a third voice said.

"Isn't it obvious...she fucked her way onto the bus. She's sleeping with four of the Kings," the first voice said. I stood still while my heart sped up. The thumping was loud enough that I thought they might hear.

"You're only salty because you thought Blake was going to ask you out. He hasn't given you the time of day since Little Miss Perfect came along." A new voice chimed.

"It's not fair. Four of the five Kings...can you get any more pick me?" The girl fumed and turned on the water at the sink.

"I kinda get Myles and Blake. But Theo and Liam? They're both cold and aloof. I asked Liam out once. He chuckled and walked away. Who chuckles? Asshole."

"It really is sus how they simp over her."

"She must give good head."

"Duh, she's a slut. She's fucking four guys at one time. I don't blame Vicky for acting the way she does. I'd be pissed too if my boyfriend eye-fucked another girl the way Nash does Ren."

I'd lost track of who was who, but there were at least five of them. Old hurt nipped at the back of my mind, but I wasn't the unsure new girl anymore. At some point over the last few months, I'd grown and gotten stronger. The old me would've stayed in the stall and prayed they went away, but that was Ren Davies. Now, I was Ren Mikhailov, my mother's daughter.

"You're all being way too harsh. If I had the opportunity to take on the Kings, I would jump at it. None of you would pass either because I know what thirsty hoes you are," a new voice said, and all the girls laughed.

The lock on the stall squeaked, and all heads turned my way as I stepped out.

None of them moved as I walked to the sink. I turned on the taps and washed my hands— even though I hadn't used the facilities— before acknowledging the girls.

I had picked up some habits from Liam because, with just a glance, I knew who had said what and committed their faces to memory. The guilty body language on all but one told me exactly who stuck up for me as well.

Crossing my arms, I leaned against the sink.

"Why so quiet? You all had a lot to say when you didn't think I was in here. So, let me have it. If you're going to talk shit, at least be brave enough to say it to my face."

They shuffled uncomfortably.

"Don't worry about the guys. I won't tell them what you said."

They remained quiet, and I nodded.

"Okay, that's fine, but let's get something straight. I don't care if you like me. I don't care what you call me. And I really don't care what you think of me. I know who I am. I'm a hard worker, a kind person, and a loyal friend. If that attracted the Kings, then why don't you take a look in the mirror and figure out what they didn't see in you."

Their expressions were a mix of shock and anger, but still, no one opened their mouth.

Pulling open the door, I looked at the small group and smiled.

"Oh, and I don't just give good head. It's the fucking best." I walked out and gave myself a metaphorical pat on the back.

OCTOBER 14 – TUESDAY 2:33 AM

Myles

Snowflake was doodling on my leg. Her finger swirled around, making symbols like she was creating a work of art. It felt amazing. For the first hour after the meal break she wrote in her notepad, but since then, Ren just silently stared out at the darkness.

What did she see out there? What was she thinking so hard about? What was bothering her? These questions had plagued my mind since she got back from Seattle. I'd gotten good at reading her, and she was internalizing something.

Nash was asleep in the row in front of us. I wanted to wake him up and demand to know what the hell he did to my girl. Ignoring the issue and hoping that it would right itself wasn't working. The two of them were obviously at odds. I had my suspicions but kept them to myself for now.

Taking a deep breath, I grabbed Ren's hand. She looked at me, startled.

"Sorry, I didn't know you were awake. Am I bothering you," she asked, and I shook my head.

"Nah, but yer givin' me a terrible case of somethin' else," I said, pointing at my dick.

It had been hard since she started rubbing up and down my leg. Her eyes followed my hand, and god dammit, I loved it when she looked at me with those hungry eyes. Why were we on a bus with thirty other people?

Ren sat up and kissed my cheek.

"Switch seats with me," she whispered.

The girl could've been reading an instruction manual in my ear, and it would've sounded just as sexy. Standing, I helped Ren into the aisle, then sat back down in the window seat.

"What ya doin', Snowflake," I asked as she reclined my seat.

We'd taken the last row after the dinner stop, so there wasn't as much room for the seat to lay back. Ren smiled but didn't say anything. Not even the devil could tempt me the way she did with just a look.

She ran her hand up my leg and over my cock, making me shudder. I was positive it would Hulk right out of my jeans if Snowflake kept touching me.

Nibbling her lip, Ren grabbed the top of my jeans and popped the button. My hands tightened on the armrests.

"I don't know if—" Ren placed her finger on my lips, stopping my argument.

"Be a good boy and be quiet," Snowflake whispered in my ear, and I nodded.

She needed to stop hanging around Liam. Or maybe hang around him more. I couldn't decide if I was terrified or not of this new side of Ren. There was only one thing that I was sure of...she commanded, and I obeyed. *Jump, sit, lay down, kill someone...done, I'm yours.*

Ren's hands worked methodically, and she never made a sound as she painstakingly pulled my zipper down one little tooth at a time. I glanced at Blake across the aisle, but he was sound asleep like everyone else. Thank God because staying quiet was one thing. Not showing this all over my face was another. I lifted my ass off the seat, and Ren tugged my jeans and boxers down.

Fisting my cock, I stroked it hard, needing a bit of relief. But Ren grabbed my wrist and shook her head. Nodding, I released my aching shaft and almost swore a violent blue streak as she wrapped her hand around me instead.

She graced me with the most devious expression I'd ever seen, sending shivers down my spine. Snowflake licked her lips as her silvery eyes glinted from under thick lashes. She was driving me insane as she teased me with her thumb and gentle touch. Just when I didn't think I could take any more of the seductive torture, she grabbed her blanket, pulled it up over her head, and swallowed my cock.

"Fu...." I coughed and tried to play it off as I closed my eyes and rolled my head toward the window. Not that I gave a fuck about the rest of the team, but Coach would tell the dean, and I didn't want to get banned from her room. Sneaking in and holding her all night kept me from losing my mind.

I bit my lip to keep from making another sound as she sucked on my dick and tightened her grip. It was a shame I couldn't see my cock disappearing into her mouth while she was under the blanket, but there was something fucking hot about this entire scenario. My eyes rolled back in my head as she picked up speed.

Unable to keep my hands to myself any longer, I slid them under the fuzzy blue throw and pulled her hair into a ponytail. My back arched as she took me deeper in her throat, and my hand shook, trying not to force her head down. It felt so fucking good.

The little devil began massaging my taut balls at that same time, and I lost all control. My grip tightened on her hair, and I pushed up with my hips, thrusting into her mouth faster. Ren took it all and matched me. I was so close, then she squeezed my balls, and that was it.

My body went rigid as I came. Snowflake's throat flexed and constricted as she swallowed, and I loosened my grip on her head. She pulled back but continued to suck and lick at me. Her tongue swirled around, sending ripples of residual pleasure through my body. Even though I'd just come, all I could think about was sitting her on my lap.

Fuck, if she kept bobbing her lips over the head of my cock like that, I was going to take the risk. She had a deadly power over me. I'd been blessed with the ability to stay hard, but she caused a wild and uncontrollable need to claim her until I couldn't move.

"Unless you want me to drag ya on me lap. Yer gonna need ta stop," I said, softer than a whisper.

Ren lifted her sexy head. Swollen lips, flushed cheeks, and eyes still filled with a wild desire.

"Can you do it quietly?"

I smirked. "Not a chance," I said, knowing my limitations. Quietly fucking her was out of my scope of abilities.

Her bottom lip pushed out. "That's too bad."

"Who are ya, and what did you do with me Snowflake?"

She smiled wide. "I've decided to embrace the new me. I'm done worrying about what anyone thinks," she said as I forced my dick back into my jeans. It was like battling a python once the damn thing was loose.

"I think ya should sit here and get comfy," I said, patting my lap. "Face that way." Ren turned so her back was against the glass. Smirking, I slid my hand down her stomach. "I can still make ya feel good," I growled softly in her ear, and she nodded. "Close your eyes and rest yer head against me. Pretend to be asleep." Ren nodded again as I moved the blanket out of the way so I could watch her.

She wiggled around, getting comfortable, and I groaned as her ass rubbed against my dick. If she kept that up, I would go off again.

Bless whoever made track pants. Sliding my hand under the elastic, I bit back a moan when my finger grazed the wet patch on her underwear. My cock jerked in my jeans, and I sucked in a deep breath, trying to keep my own needs in check.

Moving the lace out of the way, I rubbed her clit, and she gripped my hoodie. Blake moved in my peripheral, and I knew we were caught. He stared at us, and I smiled as he mouthed, *"That's fucking hot."* He shocked me when he pulled his dick out and stroked himself as he watched.

"Blake's awake," I breathed in her ear, and her eyes opened. Ren peered over at Blake and writhed in my lap. If this kept up, we were looking at a full-on orgy in the back of the bus. As if Ren read my mind and agreed, she lifted her hips and pushed her track pants down so Blake could see me playing with her pussy.

His eyes glazed over with lust as my fingers moved. Ren was panting and clinging to me while trying to stay quiet. Blake looked like he was struggling to stay in his seat, and it was a good fucking thing that it was him and not Nash. Poking at Nash was fun, but there was no way in hell he could resist her like this.

Snowflake bit my hoodie and moaned, "Faster." The desperation in her tone made me quake. Her hips pumped up into my hand, and each time she moved, she ground down onto my cock. I was close to erupting in my jeans, but I didn't care. Out of the corner of my eye, Blake's movement accelerated. We'd been together with her so many times that I knew his facial expressions almost as well as I knew Ren's signals. Right on cue, Ren arched her back and came all over my hand.

Closing my eyes, I unloaded with her. *Fuck, fuck, fuck.* I wanted to yell and flip her over to fuck her hard, but that would have to wait.

Panting, she slumped in my arms. I pulled my fingers from her sweet pussy and sucked them into my mouth. She always turned bright red whenever I did that, and it fueled my lust.

Smirking, I looked over at Blake, who had collapsed in his seat. He'd gotten his T-shirt pulled up in time, but just barely. I might've laughed if I wasn't all sticky myself. Cleaning up wasn't high on my priority list at the moment.

Snowflake adjusted her pants and curled up in my lap like a cat, falling asleep instantly. Kissing her temple, I held her tight. I hadn't even realized how much I needed some quiet time with Ren.

Getting away from school, Lawrence, and Owen, along with all the other pressures of senior year, was refreshing. After the asshole showed up at Wayward, I'd been edgy and on high alert. I held my girl a little tighter, never wanting to let go.

"Ya make me soul sing," I whispered in her ear. "I love ya, Snowflake."

I looked out the window into the darkness. No place felt entirely safe anymore. There were dangers all around us, but here, with Ren in my arms, I could breathe.

OCTOBER 14 – TUESDAY 11:45 AM

Nash

Fuming was not a strong enough word for the insanity taking over my mind.

Princess had slipped under my skin almost as soon as she arrived at Wayward. But having tasted her, knowing how she felt, and hearing the sweet sound of her screaming my name was agony.

She was a witch. That was the only explanation for the thrall she had over me. I'd joked about it with her and teased the guys about her pussy being magic, but...fuck my life. Now, I was the fucking addict, and I couldn't stand it. Begging, in general, was not in my repertoire, and begging for sex was out of the question.

Ren was smiling and talking to Coach like they were old pals, and he hated everyone. While I should be focusing on my warm-up laps, getting used to this pool, and concentrating on the competition tomorrow, my mind replayed last night.

The reflection of Myles and Ren in the glass had given me a mirrored, ghostly view, but it was enough. I'd almost snatched her away from him when she moaned his fucking name and came on his fingers. I was dangerously close to killing my guys over her.

"Are you nervous about tomorrow," Alicia asked. I blinked and looked down at her, confused.

We never spoke. In fact, the girls on the team avoided me, and with good reason. I'd fucked most of them at some point and left them just as fast. That was while Vicky and I were together and before Princess arrived and corrupted all of us with her...fucking niceness. Fuck her and her sweet personality, and sexy smirk, and feisty attitude, and that hot little body. Shit....

"You talking to me," I asked, glaring at her.

She swallowed, and her eyes got rounder. "Um...yeah. I just thought I'd be friendly."

"I'm not friendly."

She looked around and licked her lips, and I knew what this was really about. She opened her mouth, but I held up my hand.

"Don't bother."

"But...you don't...."

"I do, and I'm not interested in fucking you. Now, go away and leave me alone," I growled.

"Wow, she really does have a leash on all your cocks."

"What the fuck did you just say to me," I yelled, and the entire pool turned.

I took a menacing step in her direction. The impulse to wrap my hands around her throat and hold her under the water coursed through my veins. The deadly rage simmering in my blood daily wasn't being caged today.

Alicia backed up, terrified, and with good reason. We were off-property. For all she knew, I could snap her neck and leave her behind without a single consequence. That wasn't entirely true. We were away with a school event. There would be consequences, but she didn't need to know that.

"I asked you a fucking question. What the fuck did you just have the nerve to say to me?"

She backed up fast and fell into the pool with a splash as I loomed over her. Coach was on his way over, but he wasn't stopping me from delivering a message.

Vicky, and her public displays of cuntiness, were rubbing off on everyone. The sheep had gotten way too fucking bold lately. I was squashing that right now.

Alicia surfaced, sputtering and eyes wide as I squatted at the edge of the pool.

"You ever speak to me like that again, and you'll be taking your last breath. Don't fuck with me. I know your family, and I know how precious your little brother is to you. But you and they mean nothing to me. I will wipe you all out and sleep soundly. Understand?"

"Nash," Coach said from right behind me, but my eyes were locked on Alicia's horrified face.

"Do you fucking understand, Alicia Sutton? Or do I need to get in the pool and help you?"

She shook her head aggressively. "I understand. I won't say anything like that ever again."

"Collier," Coach said, more insistent this time.

Standing, I eyed our entire swim team in the pool. I wasn't leaving until they had gotten the message.

"If any of you so much as breathes or looks in my direction in a way I don't like, you will find out why I'm still the King of the school. Do I make myself clear?"

Some spoke, others nodded, but they all responded, girls and guys alike.

"Good."

"Nash Collier."

I spun on Coach, feeling absolutely feral, and he shuffled back. If he pushed me....

Ren touched Coach's arm. "Can I talk to Nash for a minute?"

"Um...." Coach glanced at her and then up at me. My hands were balled into fists, and a part of me wanted him to get in my face. My jaw cracked as I ground my teeth.

"Please," she said.

Coach hesitated, and I didn't blame him. My guys inched closer, ready to defuse shit if I lost it completely. I glared at them, but unlike everyone else, they ignored me.

"Okay," Coach said reluctantly and stepped out of the way.

Princess grabbed my hand, and I tried jerking away. She interlaced our fingers and hung on like a little koala as her nails dug into my hand. It was impossible to get free without hurting her, and fuck...that bite of pain redirected my rage to another part of my body.

Ren pointed at the guys as we walked past.

"Don't follow us."

Those assholes stopped right where they were. Princess was a fucking witch who had captured all my pieces. Before her, they would've flipped me off and followed anyway. What the hell had she done to us?

She practically dragged me to the far end of the change area before yanking open the storage room door.

"You sure you want to be in a small, lockable space with me right now," I growled as she flicked on the light and locked us inside.

"You going to hurt me?"

"Define hurt, Princess."

She set the clipboard she'd been carrying around down and glared at me.

"You know what I mean."

"Honestly, I don't. Everything I do ends up hurting you." She rubbed her face. "You know it's true."

"What I know is that you're out of control and ready to tear someone apart. What's going on?"

"You know what's going on," I said, backing away before I hauled her into my arms. My hands tingled with the memory of her skin.

"Oh my god! Just give me a straight answer."

Ren stepped into my personal space, and her addictive scent overpowered the strong citrus smell of the cleaners in the room.

Thud, thud, thud.

My heart pounded, and the sound echoed in my head.

"Fine. This is your fault. I'm like this because of you. You're driving me fucking insane. Do you think I don't know that you and Liam were fucking with me? You think I didn't hear you and Myles right behind me last night?" I ran my hand through my hair. "You're testing my fucking patience."

"I don't care what you know or what you heard. I'm with them, not you. What we do is not your concern," she said.

"You're mine," I said as anger dripped from my tongue. I held out my arm, flashing my Princess tattoo. There was no logical reason for it, just an intense compulsion.

"You can tattoo my name all over your body, but it still doesn't make me yours. That's all in your head."

"Fuck!"

She glared at me, her eyes cold as stone.

"You had me. I gave myself to you. Then you opened a trap door and tossed me away. You threw it all in my face. So don't stand there acting like I've wronged you. I won't curb how I am with my boyfriends because you can't deal with the shit you brought on yourself. Either you're with me and the rest of the guys, or you're with her. Choose what you want, but stop taking your anger out on everyone around you. You're better than that, Nash."

My emotions were all over the place, and I couldn't decipher any of them other than the white-hot anger burning me up.

"I can't figure out how to get rid of you."

"You're already rid of me. You're the one who keeps sneaking into my room, hunting me down in the gym and the art room. Or do you mean to kill me?"

"Yes."

"You want to kill me?"

"Sometimes, it's all I can think about, Princess. I have fantasies of my hand wrapped around your pretty little throat," I growled, hoping she'd back the fuck up and lock me in here. I didn't trust myself to be around anyone right now, and definitely not her.

But of course, Princess did the complete opposite. She grabbed my hand and clasped it around her neck.

"Then do it. You want me gone so badly, do it. You'll find a reason and a way to kill me at some point. So get on with it. I refuse to hide from you like everyone else. I won't cower in a corner like you're hoping. So, kill me. Finish this now, and you're free of whatever hold you think I have over you."

Her skin was tantalizingly soft under my fingers as I tried to pull my hand away.

"Have you lost your mind?"

"No." She pressed in closer, forcing me to step back until I was the one trapped against the wall.

"Back off, Princess."

"Or what?"

It would be so easy. I'd killed much larger men, and they fought for their lives. Ren stood there watching me, and the thought of her death made me feel sick. Her pulse jumped under my fingers, and I tightened my grip. But her eyes...her beautiful, silver eyes held no fear.

"You're crazy," I said to her.

"Maybe."

My lips crashed down on hers and I lifted her onto the washing machine in the corner.

"Fuck you, Princess. I hate you so much for doing this to me."

"Good, I can't stand to be in the same room as you," she snapped back and wrapped her legs around my waist.

The kiss was a battle. We pawed at one another as our tongues fought for control. A second, a minute, twenty minutes, I had no idea how much time had passed when we finally broke apart, gasping for air.

"I haven't touched her," I blurted out. Ren cupped my face, and I closed my eyes. "I haven't touched her since we broke up, at least not sexually. Threatening to kill her...well, that's a different story."

"Why are you doing this? Tell me why you're marrying her?"

"I can't. I can't say anything, but I will soon. Please just...keep me from going crazy."

"You want to have sex?"

"Well, I don't want to grab cleaning supplies and start scrubbing. Yes...you said you were mine. So be with me."

Princess gently pushed me back and hopped off the washing machine. She looked down at my bulging cock.

"That's quite the issue you have there."

"Funny." I reached for her arm, and she stepped away.

"You want me? Break your engagement with Vicky, or tell me what the fuck is going on, Nash. I will not be played by you again. You have a World Cup qualifying race tomorrow. So pull your shit together and get back out to the pool."

Ren unlocked the door but didn't walk out. She stopped and turned to face me.

"Don't fuck this up, Nash, you're so close to your dream.

Millions of swimmers will never get this close. Don't toss it away over whatever the hell this is."

The door closed, and I was alone. Stumbling back into the wall, I realized I was shivering.

She was right, but so was I. My body was eating me alive as my need for her clawed at my brain. Concentrating on anything else right now was impossible.

There was only one thing to do. I stomped out of the storage room and straight into a shower. The cold water rained down as I pulled my cock out. The frigid spray hit my back and helped cool my rage as I stroked myself into submission. Ren's annoyingly sexy mouth and tongue starred in the fantasy running through my head. It didn't take long before everything pulled tight, and I came in a mad rush, groaning.

"Fuuuuuuuccccck."

"Aren't you a sorry sight," Liam said from behind me.

Tucking my dick back into the jammer, I shut off the water and turned around to face him. Liam leaned against the tile with his arms crossed as he stared at me.

"Don't start with me, Liam. I'm not in the mood."

He shrugged. "I'm not starting anything. Your father called your phone. I answered and told him you were in the middle of a sprint. He wants you to call him back."

"Fuck. What the hell does he want?"

"No idea. But he was pissed that I didn't pull you out of the pool to talk to him."

"Not surprised. My father hates that I won't give it up. But it's good that you refused," I said. "I think he's starting to see just how little control he has on us."

"Agreed. I have to say that I genuinely thought you were going to fuck her in here. I'm glad I didn't bet on it. I would've lost my shirt," Liam said.

I growled. Swear words like honey were on the tip of my tongue. "Trust me, it wasn't for a lack of trying."

"You ever going to tell me what the fuck is going on?"

Staring into his eyes, I knew that Liam would force my hand one way or another.

"Give me until Halloween. I'll tell you then."

"Fine, Halloween it is."

With my cock and Liam dealt with, I left the locker room. It was time to find out what the hell my father wanted, but I would've given anything to be locked in the storage room with Princess all over again.

Chapter 40

Ren

What the hell did one wear to meet family you never knew existed? I'd brought the best of my dressy clothes and still was at a loss.

Finally, meeting my mum's side of the family—the ones who didn't want me dead, at least—was exciting. But now that the moment was almost here, my nerves were out of control. Twice, my lunch had tried to make an appearance. But I fought it down.

The simple black dress I now wore would have to do. I stared at my reflection and took a deep breath. Focusing on the next task, I managed to get the black eyeliner in place and created a light, smoky look.

"You look beautiful, Little Rabbit."

Liam's voice made me jump, and I almost drew a black mascara streak up the side of my face. I glared at him in the bedroom doorway.

"Thank you for almost blinding me," I said, and he smiled.

"Told you we need to work on this jumpiness."

"Can we not work on it tonight? My nerves are shot. How did you get in here anyway?"

Liam walked up behind me and, without a single touch, made me shiver. He looked so hot in his suit, and I took an extra second to let my eyes wander.

"Myles gave me the key you gave him. He was easy to bribe."

He teasingly ran the tips of his fingers down my bare arms. The touch was featherlight but the heat he created and the pressure in my chest from the pounding of my heart were opposite in comparison.

Liam lowered his head to my neck but never took his eyes off mine. I gasped as his lips touched the side of my throat before he nipped at my ear, sucking the little diamond stud into his mouth.

"Don't think that I don't know what you and Myles did on the bus," he whispered in my ear. "Naughty, Little Rabbit. I told you what it costs me to see you with them."

"And I told you...they are part of the package."

"Yes, but you also said you wouldn't rub it in my face."

I rolled my eyes at him in the mirror. "Technically, I didn't." A shudder raced down my spine as he wrapped his hand around my throat.

"Don't roll your eyes at me, or your ass will be sore for dinner." I licked my lips.

"I thought you and Theo were asleep. I thought everyone was asleep," I said and swayed as his finger rubbed back and forth over my racing pulse.

"If you're awake, then I'm awake. Remember that. I'll be sitting with you on the way back."

"Is that so?"

"Oh, it is, Little Rabbit. I'll teach you what can really be done in a bus seat."

"Are you trying to one-up Myles?" I smirked as I stared into his cinnamon eyes.

"I don't need to try. I know I can. Besides, Myles relinquished his seat because he foolishly bet against me earlier and lost."

"Are you guys always going to compete like this?"

"Probably until the day we are six feet under, but that's half the fun. Mmmm, I really want to bend you over. But we don't have time, and I came in here for another reason."

Liam pulled a long velvet box out from inside his suit jacket.

Gently plucking it from his hand, I stared at the black lid. I knew what was inside. But was I really prepared to put this on? Liam didn't push or say anything as he waited for me to choose this...to choose him. I swallowed down the lingering nervousness and cracked open the lid.

"Oh my god, Liam."

Nestled in the silky folds of the jewelry box was a stunning choker necklace no wider than my baby finger. It was entirely encrusted with sparkling blue diamonds.

"You were serious."

"Always. I don't joke about this sort of thing. I wanted it to be something you would feel comfortable wearing all the time while giving me what I need."

I looked up at him. "And what do you need?"

"You," he said, melting my insides. Tilting my head up, he touched his lips to mine. "Always you. Turn around, and I'll put it on."

Lifting my hair out of the way, I turned, and he took the box. It was a good thing he did because my hands were shaking. Once the collar was in place, I ran my hand across the sparkling blue stones that reminded me of the sky on a bright summer's day.

"It's stunning. I don't know what else to say other than thank you."

Facing him, I looked down.

"What's wrong?"

"I didn't get you anything for your birthday, and I've been too nervous to ask how your initiation went. I feel bad about that."

He smirked. "Don't worry about my birthday. I have everything I need." He tipped my head back and ran his thumb over my lip. "Or want. As far as my initiation...I'm going to talk to you about that after dinner. If I play my cards right, not only will I get my initiation taken care of, but you're going to help me."

"Me? Won't Lawrence be pissed?"

"Who says he'll find out?"

I smiled. "And you trust me enough to help you?"

"I wouldn't ask you otherwise. Now come on, let's see if we can get the rest of this crew on the move."

"They really are slow."

"Very," he teased, making me laugh.

We wandered down the hall to the next room and our smiles faded as we opened the door. The tension in the room was thick, like heavy smog.

"How the hell did he know we were here in Cali?" Myles snarled.

"Because I told him. It would be an issue if he called me to come in, and I hadn't told him."

Myles tossed his arms out to the sides. "It's already an issue. What the hell do ya mean he wants ya to negotiate for Devin's release?"

"He thinks that if I get Devin back, then he can regain control of your father," Nash answered. "He's probably right, but that's beside the point."

"There is no controlling me da. He showed up at the school willing to accept the Curators coming after him. How can Lawrence think that getting the devil freed is going to make things any better?"

"I don't know. Maybe he plans on just killing them both, but it doesn't matter. I can't get him released even if I wanted to. Not only will Nathaniel laugh at me, but Devin knows too much about us and what happened."

"Shite," Myles swore and turned around. He froze when he saw me standing there with Liam.

"Mind telling me what you've all been keeping from me? And don't bother lying," I said, taking in their guilty faces.

"Snowflake...."

"No, don't you dare Snowflake me. We are supposed to be in this together. I may not be a King, but I think I've proven myself to be trustworthy. I hate secrets, and you all are keeping way too many from me," I said, hitting Nash with a glare. He looked away, and I shook my head.

"I told you it was a bad idea to keep this from her," Liam said. I was shocked that out of all the guys, he was sticking up for me. "She's either in, and we trust her, or she's not, and we don't. Take your pick."

Myles sighed and leaned against the dresser. "Nash found out that Devin was trying to harm us. He captured him and handed him off to Nathaniel."

"Nathaniel. My cousin that we're meeting tonight?"

"Aye."

"Wait did you know who my family was when you did this," I asked Nash, and he narrowed his eyes at me.

"Of couse, you'd think that. No, I didn't. That was a fuckcd up coincidence." He crossed his arms and looked out the window again.

I believed him. "So why Nathaniel?"

"He has a small prison and knows how to handle people like my brother. Da has been losing it ever since. He's recently gone right off the deep end. He slaughtered an innocent family in Ireland because he thought they were conspiring against him. From what I've been able to gather, they were having a drink and talking when Da grabbed his gun and started shooting. Killed them all, the wee ones, too."

"Jesus."

"That's not the worst of it." He bit his lip and ran his hand through his hair. "When you and Liam were away, he snuck into Wayward and wanted me to hand you over. I woke up with a knife to my throat."

"I know. Nash told me." Myles's head whipped in Nash's direction.

"You told her?"

"Yes, because she needed to be aware of the danger," Nash said, and for once, I fully agreed with him.

"You should've been the one to tell me, Myles. You swore to me that you'd tell me anything that you could. This wasn't something to keep secret."

"I know. I know, but I didn't want ya to worry. We got it handled and have a plan to stop him. But now Lawrence wants Nash to talk to Nathaniel and get Devin back."

"Well, that's not happening," I said, and I meant it. "Not after what he's done to you. Whatever cell he is rotting in, he can stay there."

Myles's lip twitched up. "Aye, I agree, but Lawrence is getting edgy with my da on the loose. He's causing a lot of unrest, which makes Lawrence twice as dangerous. He's set me and Nash the task of finding my da and killing him."

"Oh, just a small thing then. Alright, so the answer is that we hand Owen over to Lawrence instead of Devin. That gets rid of both monsters. How do we get Owen?"

"Naw, you're not getting' involved, Snowflake. It's one thing tellin' ya and another havin' you help," Myles said.

"That's not up to you. If I'm in, then I'm in. So, tell me how I can help?"

"There is one way that won't put her in danger," Nash said from his spot by the window. "But we can discuss this later. Our ride is here."

"Tell me first. What can I do?"

Nash looked at me, his blue eyes all business tonight. It was a big change from earlier at the pool.

"How good are you at pretending to be kidnapped," he asked, smirking.

"Where's the rope?"

The guys all smiled while Liam tightened his hold on my hip. For the first time since I got involved with Myles, I truly felt like I belonged with the Kings.

Chapter 41

Ren

Wow, this vehicle was fancy. The stretch SUV could've easily held three times the amount of people. The guys were laughing and chatting as they ate hors d'oeuvres and sipped their drinks. All except Nash. Sitting at the far end of the limo, he hadn't moved in ten minutes.

He looked like the boss, staring out the window with his elbow on the door and finger touching his chin, in his car with his men and the weight of the world pressing on his shoulders.

I hated that my heart hurt and worried so much about someone who callously caused me pain, and yet...there was a part of me that understood him. Liam said he was scared. I didn't think Nash knew what the word meant, but when I looked at him—and he wasn't trying to mask what he was thinking—I could see it. Freaking Liam.

Smirking, I pulled out my phone and scrolled down to his name.

> R: What are you thinking so hard about? Sit like that for too long, and someone is going to paint you.

Nash dug into his pocket for his phone and then glanced up at me, smirking.

> NASHOLE: Only if you're the one holding the brush.

For such a little comment, it hit like Cupid's arrow. I almost tossed my phone back into my clutch. Dangerous. He was dangerous to my heart, my sanity and my soul. The definition of insanity was doing the same thing over and over, expecting a different result, so apparently he'd already corrupted one of the three.

> Ren: I'm not sure you could hold still that long.

> NASHOLE: Are you naked while painting me? If you're naked, then no, but otherwise, you'd be surprised what I can do.

I shook my head but couldn't stop smirking at my phone.

> Ren: You're ridiculous.

> NASHOLE: Maybe, but you were the one watching me. Careful, I might think you're starting to forgive me.

R: I noticed you. That's different. Watching is like stalking. I'm definitely not stalking you.

NASHOLE: You can stalk me right into my bedroom If you like. I'll even leave the door unlocked just for you.

R: Sounds unsafe. You never know who is prowling around. You could end up with a sleepwalking Myles in bed, spooning you.

I glanced up and pressed my lips together to keep from laughing as he grimaced at his phone. Nash looked up at me and shook his head.

NASHOLE: You haven't answered the question.

R: You didn't ask a question?

NASHOLE: Yes, I did. You know what I'm talking about.

R: Maybe you should ask a doctor.

NASHOLE: A doctor? Why the hell do I need a doctor?

R: To check out that itchy and annoying rash.

NASHOLE: What the hell are you talking about? I don't have a rash.

Texting with Nash was always so much fun. I couldn't believe how much I'd missed these insane chats with him. But seeing his facial expressions was priceless.

R: Sure you do.

NASHOLE: No, I don't.

R: Pretty sure you do.

NASHOLE: I swear to God, Princess.
Don't make me march across this limo.

R: That would be ridiculous. I can picture
it now. You all mad, stomping, but having
to bend over like you're in a Hobbit house
while you rant about not having a rash.
Please do it. I want to see what the
guys say.

I smiled at him across the way and waited. He smirked and laughed.

The guys turned to look at him in varying states of confusion.

"What? It was a funny reel, carry on," Nash said, and I had no idea how I didn't bust a gut laughing.

NASHOLE: Okay, no more games.
Answer my question and tell me where I
have a rash.

R: Your rash is called Vicky, and you need
a doctor to have your head checked for
agreeing to marry her. I'm concerned that
you want to be miserable for the rest of
your life. You are a mystery, Nash Collier. I
just can't figure you out.

R: As for forgiving you…I'm not sure how
I feel about anything. You purposely
messed with my head, Nash. I don't take
that lightly.

He tapped his chin with his phone and locked eyes with me. My heart raced while I waited for his response.

NASHOLE: I didn't purposely mess with you. It just seems that way, and Vicky's not the one I want.

My cheeks heated, and it felt like he was right beside me. I looked down at my phone and read over what he said...ten more times.

R: Do you like dogs?

NASHOLE: Um...sure. Where did that come from?

R: This is me changing topic.

He smirked.

NASHOLE: There is no escaping me or this conversation.

R: I don't know what you want me to say.

NASHOLE: Say you forgive me for being a dick.

R: Which time?

NASHOLE: LOL! Fair, but I think you know which time I mean.

R: You keep poking at me like you want me to be okay with you marrying Vicky. I'm not. I'm not okay with it. There, I admitted it, but I still can't be with you in any form. I just can't.

NASHOLE: Look at me.

R: Really? You're ordering me to look at you from across a limo?

NASHOLE: Just do it.

Fuck...why did I start this text chat again? I forced my eyes up from my phone and they locked with his. Stupidly, I wanted to cry. Everything from our night in Seattle came back and clawed at my heart. I tried looking away.

NASHOLE: I said look at me.

R: Why are you doing this? Can't we just tease one another like we normally do?

NASHOLE: Because I need you to look me in the eyes and see that I'm telling you the truth. I didn't set out to hurt you. Give me until Halloween, and then I'll tell you what you want to know.

His eyes seemed so sincere, but...God, this was difficult. What was right or wrong? Was he telling the truth or just a fantastic liar? When did kindness and offering second chances turn into becoming a doormat? Taking a deep breath, I sank deeper into the comfortable seat.

NASHOLE: Say something.

R: You want to tell me at your grand opening? Is that why you were so insistent that I come with you?

NASHOLE: Yes, but it's also your birthday.

My heart stopped, and I glanced up at him again.

> NASHOLE: Yeah, I asked Myles. This is the only time I'm going to beg you for anything, so eat it up. Take a screenshot or something. Please, give me till then, and don't shut me out. I meant what I said. You're mine. I meant it that night, despite what I said in the morning.

Closing my eyes, I couldn't believe I was contemplating throwing myself into the crashing waves again. The likelihood of being smashed off the rocks was high, and yet....

> R: Fine, but Nash...if you do the same thing to me again...I won't be as forgiving. I'm not a malicious person by nature, but I'll make sure you rot in hell.

He smiled wide.

> NASHOLE: Fuck, I love your fire. It makes me so hard.

I lifted a brow at him.

> R: I'm being serious.

> NASHOLE: I know, and fair enough. Now, put a smile on your face. You're about to meet your family.

I looked out the window and realized that we'd just pulled through a massive set of gates. The guards manning it reminded me of those at Wayward. Blacked out sunglasses, and most likely armed to the teeth under the unassuming suits.

"Wow."

It was the only word that came to mind as we pulled up in front of a mansion that could've passed for a castle. It was so huge. Who needed this much space? What the hell did you do with it?

"Are ya ready, Snowflake?"

I looked at Myles and nodded. I was as ready as I was ever going to be. My mind blanked, my heart raced, and my stomach did an elaborate gymnastics floor routine.

All the vehicle doors opened at the same time, and one of the guards held out his hand to help me out. His face was hard as stone, but unlike the rest of the guards he wasn't wearing sunglasses, and his eyes were kind.

The home—if you could call a mansion that—was right out of an episode of *Lifestyles of the Rich and Famous*. The front doors opened, and my heart stopped beating. Kaylani squealed and bounded down the stairs with a pair of stunning black dogs right behind her.

She ran at me like a blonde steam engine, and in a blink, the fear fell away as she wrapped her arms around me.

And it finally hit....

I have family.

OCTOBER 14 – TUESDAY 6:59 PM

Ren

Kaylani pulled back, her face as bright as a ray of sunshine when she smiled.

"I wanted to tell you soooo bad last year."

"Wait...you knew who I was?"

She nodded. "We were under strict orders not to reach out for your safety. It was killing me to see you at school all the time and not say a word. I'm so sorry. Please forgive me."

I wanted to feel betrayed, but the more I understood this world, the more I knew what she meant. An order to remain quiet was serious, especially when someone's life was on the line. Understanding it didn't stop me from wishing she had told me.

Before I could answer, one of the dogs nudged my hand, and I looked down. Its midnight black coat shone in the sun.

"Well, hello there."

"She likes you. That's Hailey with the ruby collar, and Holly has the amethyst collar."

I raised my eyes to the man speaking and swallowed hard. My guys were all tall, but this man was a walking mountain.

"I'm your cousin Titus," he said, offering a hand that dwarfed mine. Titus held it gently, with no need to prove his toughness. His calm demeanor didn't quite fit his look or the family's reputation.

Another man with unnerving onyx eyes stepped up beside Titus. He smiled and stared at me before stepping forward.

"You look so much like your mother. It's crazy. I'm Nathaniel," he said, hauling me in for a hug. I expected to be terrified. The guys talked about Nathaniel like he was the Grim Reaper, but his excitement to see me was shocking. "I loved your mom," he said before stepping back. "Last time I saw her was at her wedding to Christov," he said, with a hint of a growl and obvious disdain. "I was only seven at the time, but she had a way of making everyone feel special and seen. I'll always remember her."

My eyes filled with tears. "Thank you."

Meeting people who knew my mum and loved her...was priceless to me. I glanced over at Nash and the guys, who were giving me space. No matter what he'd done, the fact that he pulled whatever strings he needed to make this happen for me...meant the world.

"Get out of the way. It's my turn," a woman said with the warmest smile. "Oh, Sweetie, Nathaniel is right you look just like Yuliana, so beautiful. I'm your great aunt Helena," she said, pulling me into another hug.

And there it was...the confirmation that my mother had been using an alias and I'd never known.

"Hi."

It was all I could get past the emotion clogging my throat.

"Oh, no, please don't cry."

I waved at my face, trying to keep the tears at bay, when a yell—with that thick Irish brogue I'd know anywhere—broke the silence. Fiona ran down the stairs, and the tears faded as I laid eyes on her happy face and flaming red hair bobbing around her in wild waves. We collided and hugged, squeezing one another.

"I never thought I was going to see you again. How are you," I asked.

"Aye, same. God, I've missed ya. Everyone has been grand, but our talks kept me smilin'. I've been so cut off."

Pulling back, I looked her over. Fiona was as stunning as any wildflower. She reminded me of the rarest, most vibrant bloom in a forest with no comparison.

"How are your parents?"

She lifted a shoulder and let it drop. "Alive...we're grateful for that." Fiona pulled away and walked over to Nash, holding out her hand. "I can never thank ya fir what ya did. Me family owes our lives and allegiance to ya. Whatever we can do, we will."

"I appreciate that," Nash said, returning the gesture.

"Well, now that all the loud and obnoxious ones are out of the way."

The most arrogant face I'd ever seen greeted me when I turned around. That said a lot, considering I spent time with Nash and Liam, and we couldn't forget Vicky. His piercing, ice-blue eyes screamed *asshole*. He held out his hand with a dramatic sigh.

"I'm Ronan, the heir to this family."

"Oh yes, the heir, how could we forget? Next time we'll hire trumpeters and a squire to announce your grand entrance," Nathaniel mocked and I pressed my lips together. He was really growing on me.

Ronan glared at his brother before his eyes traced my body. "Too bad you're family," he said, his lip lifting. I yanked my hand out of his and stepped away.

"Lucky for me, I am," I sniped back, and he smiled.

"Oh, I like her. Can we keep her," Ronan asked, and I saw my guys stiffen out of the corner of my eye. He must have noticed it, too, because he waved his hand dismissively at them. "Relax, I'm only having a little fun. Everyone is so fucking sensitive these days."

"Shut up, Ronan. Don't disrespect your cousin."

An older man, who had to be Dimitri, slowly walked down the front steps. He carried an authoritative air, demanding respect and compliance. Dimitri looked to be in his early sixties and well-built. His salt and pepper hair only added to his distinguished look. It was the fierceness in his eyes that evoked caution. He would shoot his mother if it benefited him.

Ronan grumbled but backed up. I straightened my spine as Dimitri stopped in front of me. He stood there staring at me to the point that it was uncomfortable. I glanced around, hoping for a signal of what to do.

Dimitri's eyes softened just slightly, and a single tear rolled down his cheek before he swiped it away.

"I'm Dimitri," he finally said and held out his hand.

"It's nice to meet you," I said, and his lip twitched.

"You look just like your mother did at the same age. It's like using a time machine to get a glimpse of my past. I was sorry to hear what happened to her."

I turned his hand over and stared at the polar bear tattoo. So many nights, I'd laid in bed after the attack and dreamed of this tattoo.

"Do you know who in the family wants me dead," I asked bluntly, and Dimitri laughed.

"How about we eat dinner first? Then, we can talk conspiracies and business," he said, releasing my hand.

"It's not a conspiracy."

He paused and looked me up and down, seeming surprised that I dared to speak out of turn. I didn't care.

"The night we were attacked, my mum locked me in a panic room. The men tried to get at me and got close to the cameras. I watched the entire thing. One of the men had a polar bear tattoo on his hand. That tattoo," I said, pointing. "You're the head of the Mikhailovs in North America and I have a feeling that nothing goes on without your knowledge. So, I'll ask again. Who in the family wants me dead and why?"

"Are you accusing me of something?"

"Father, I think Ren is politely inquiring if there is any reason, even if only for her safety, that you would keep your suspicions about her attack...quiet," Titus said.

How did he do that? He managed to take what I said and turn it into a perfectly political question that didn't come off like an accusation.

"Yes, that's exactly what I mean. Please, Dimitri, if you know anything...I watched them murder her. The least I can do is find who did it."

"And do what," he asked.

Kill them.

It was my immediate response, but would I really pick up a weapon and shoot someone? The police had no record of any wrongdoing, so I couldn't have them arrested. I glanced at my guys. Could I live with myself if I asked them to do something like that?

"I...I don't know. But it's constant torture living with questions that I can't answer."

Dimitri crossed his arms and shook his head at me, and in a blink, I felt like a very small and disappointing child.

"Let me explain something to you—that despite your time at Wayward, you've not learned—this world is not fair. I feel for you. What you went through was, I'm sure, very traumatic. It's nothing compared to what all of us have lived our entire lives. This is a dog-eat-dog environment. The most powerful survive, the weak are destroyed, and we live every day with the knowledge that we are responsible for many deaths. Everyone, no matter who they are, is a threat. Families fracture all the time. New alliances are made, and this tattoo...." Dimitri held up his hand. "Means nothing."

I blinked and stared at the polar bear crest, not understanding.

"Yes, this represents our family, but thousands of men...relatives, soldiers, and wannabes mark themselves with the Mikhailov crest. The man you saw could easily be an imposter, a guard who defected, or someone from your mother's ex-inlaws. But I'll tell you this. I have not heard any rumors of any Mikhailov here or back home in Russia wanting you dead. My brother, Vadin, is an arrogant asshole, and I can't stand to be in the same room with him, but he would not kill his grandchild no matter how much his daughter pissed him off."

"So, you know that my mother angered my grandfather?"

"What I know is that dinner is getting cold, and we are standing outside where even the trees have ears. I won't discuss this any further. I would like to get to know my great niece, but if this is the only reason you came here, then you can get back in the limo and show yourself out."

My heart sank as Dimitri walked away with Ronan by his side. Helena followed in their wake but looked over her shoulder with sad eyes. I was left standing there, staring after the head of the house with so many mixed feelings.

Titus looked down at me. "Do you really think it was someone in the family who killed your mother?"

I shrugged. "I was so certain until this moment. Nash already assured me it was none of you. But there are still so many I don't know. I just thought he would want to help me. I didn't mean to start a fight."

Titus and Nathaniel shared a look.

"That wasn't a fight. That was nothing more than a tiny spat in this house. If he was angry, he would've pulled his gun,"

Nathaniel said, and my eyes grew wide as I pictured Dimitri holding a gun to my head. "If you really want to know. I will find out for you."

"But your dad said...."

His already black eyes darkened.

"Fuck my father and what he said. We don't see eye-to-eye on anything anyway, and he holds no power over me. I'll get you whatever information I can find. Unlike my father, and despite my rather course reputation, I believe in strong family ties. You can trust me. You'll always be safe with me and my wife Savannah."

"With me as well," Titus said.

"Thank you both. He could be right, and it leads nowhere, but... I want to know why my mum lost her life. I can't explain why I feel like there is more to this."

"You just can't shake it," Titus said.

"Exactly." I held my hand out toward the Kings. "The guys have been trying, but we keep hitting roadblocks."

Nathaniel smirked. "That's because you don't have the connections back home yet. Something you might want to consider is having a coming out party."

"But...I'm not into girls."

Nathaniel laughed along with everyone else. I had no clue what he was talking about.

"What my brother is so eloquently not getting across is that it's time you announce you're a Mikhailov. Anyone after you is banking on no one knowing or caring about some random girl's death. So, whether it is a family member or not, the larger the spotlight on you, the harder it is to kill you. This life is a double-edged sword. In this case, you should use your last name to your advantage. Garner clout and a following, for example."

"A following? I...I'm not looking to lead anything or anyone."

Kaylani walked over and wrapped her arm around my shoulder.

"Cousin, you have five guys who already are," she said, smiling. I looked over at Myles, Blake, Theo, Liam, and Nash and didn't see them as followers...only Kings.

"My point is...I will find out for you. And I always get what I want. Just ask my wife," Nathaniel said.

"Ha, you're only saying that because she's eight-months pregnant and can't kick your ass right now." Titus laughed.

"And yet, I still got her to marry me and knocked her up twice, didn't I?"

"You're impossible," Titus said.

"I'm also right," Nathaniel said.

They reminded me of Myles and Blake bantering, and it set me at ease.

"Okay, can we cut all the sad stuff now? How long are you in town? Want to go shopping or to the spa? We can eat at all the fanciest restaurants. I'll take you to Nathaniel's clubs and show you around. Ooh, we can go out on a party boat. What do you say," Kaylani asked like she was permanently stuck in fast-forward.

"I vote shoppin', and ya can count me in," Fiona said. "I need some Ren time, so no hoggin' her."

"Dad? Are you coming?"

Standing in the doorway was the cutest little boy. I knew right away he was Nathaniel's son. They couldn't have made a carbon copy more alike.

"Oh, do any of you speak Italian," he asked, full of hope.

"Cutter, what did I tell you about harassing our guests?"

His little lip pushed out, but Blake came to the rescue.

"I do," Blake said, and Cutter's eyes sparked as he smiled wide.

"Really? Will you sit by me?"

"Cutter...."

Blake stepped forward.

"It's okay, I would love to. Helps me brush up on it. It's really no bother," Blake said to Nathaniel.

Even though kids were so far down the list of wants in my life right now or the next few years, it didn't stop the warm and fuzzy feeling as Cutter raced down the stairs and took Blake's hand. They immediately started talking in Italian like they were old friends.

As we walked up the steps, Myles stopped Nathaniel.

"Can Nash and I speak to ya for a minute," he asked.

I knew it was about Owen and Devin, and I hated that Myles would face his brother after everything Devin had done. Leaving them to their business, I stepped into the house. No matter what Myles believed, this would tear him up. Owen didn't deserve Myles as a son. Both he and Devin deserved to rot six feet under for the hell they put him through.

OCTOBER 14 – TUESDAY 7:38 PM

Ren

As I laughed at Blake and Cutter going back and forth in Italian and asked and answered questions around the table, I felt...full.

Growing up, it had always been the same small cast of characters for any occasion. Me, Mum, Dad, Lizzy, Lizzy's Mum, and Nadia. Sometimes, it was three of us or four. Then later, with Mum's cancer treatments, it had been the two of us. Not that I minded. You couldn't miss something that you never had, but being around my extended family was a completely different experience and...I liked it.

A whole other world and people had just opened for me.

Nathaniel was brash, stoney, and said whatever he wanted. But it was easy to see his love for Savannah and Cutter. It blew my mind that Savannah had been an FBI agent, and I was dying to know how she ended up married to the son of a mafia boss. Cutter was insanely cute, and I wanted nothing more than to put him and Lip in the same room and see what chaos ensued.

Titus was quiet, his dogs laying just as quietly behind him. He was this ultra calm presence.

There was a very distinct family rift. But I really appreciated that whatever it was had been set aside to make tonight special.

Helena had every dish under the sun made for us, and it was still coming as tray after tray of dessert came from the kitchen. I kinda felt bad for the guys. They were competing tomorrow and only ate very tiny amounts. Helena spent most of dinner scolding them for not eating more.

"Psst...." Kaylani leaned over Fiona and caught my attention while everyone else was arguing over the best whiskey. "Are you sleeping with...." She looked around. "All five," she whispered and held up her hand. My face burned hot with embarrassment, but she smiled, and Fiona laughed. "Girl...hell yes," she said, holding out her fist for a bump.

Laughing, I gave her what she wanted and then turned to Fiona.

"Are you staying here in California even once it's safe for your family?

Fiona popped one of the incredible-looking pastries in her mouth and shrugged.

"I din't really know. I'm enjoyin' school here, and there's nothin' really fir me back home. But I miss me ma and da. I'll do a visit fir sure. What about you? What are ya doin' after graduation?"

That was a good question and one I hadn't thought much about since I arrived at Wayward last year. I'd been so certain with the direction of my life and now I had no idea.

"I'm still working that out. There's a lot to consider," I said, and Fiona nodded.

The guys loss was my gain, and I happily took a slice of the chocolate cake that looked divine. I happily took a bite of the moist cake and listened to the constant chatter around me.

"Lilya dear, how are you enjoying Wayward," Helena asked. It took me a second to realize that Helena was speaking to me, until everyone went quiet and looked at me.

"Oh...Sorry, I'm not used to being called Lilya. Everyone calls me Ren."

"No worries dear."

"Honestly, when I first arrived, I couldn't have gotten out of there fast enough." I glanced around at the guys, Kaylani and Fiona. "But now...now, it feels like home."

"Nonsense, home is with your family. You should come live here in Cali when you graduate. We have lots of job opportunities. You can take your pick," Dimitri said.

"Thank you, but I prefer to earn my way into a position. I like to know that I deserve what I get."

"Lilya, don't be fool hearty. We all still work hard, and there is nothing wrong with leaning into your family name."

"Maybe this isn't the best time to discuss trying to recruit Ren. Especially, considering the state of business these days. If anything Ren should come work for me, Kaylani and Titus," Nathaniel said, and it was like someone dropped an iceberg into the center of the room and sucked the air out.

"Actually, Ren is being modest," Liam said, jumping in before Dimitri could respond. He grabbed my hand on the table and squeezed. "We've started an investment banking firm with Theo, and she's already landed some large clients for us."

I had absolutely no idea what the heck he was talking about, but when he looked at me, I smiled. He couldn't have picked another topic...any topic? I knew nothing about investment banking. Liam brought my hand to his lips and kissed my knuckles.

"Also, we'll be getting married after graduation."

"What," Myles and Nash said together and then looked at one another. All I could think was that we had dissolved one argument to start another. Myles might lose his mind and jump on Liam if he kept this going.

"Yeah, sorry guys...we've been keeping it quiet," I said, playing along and praying to God that Myles caught on. I wasn't worried about Nash. He just looked shocked. Myles was ready to blow a gasket.

Theo wrapped his arm around Myles's shoulders. "That's incredible news. Congratulations," Theo said, raising his glass of wine.

Myles glanced at him and then back at me before sighing. "Aye, how wonderful," he said, but couldn't have sounded more unenthusiastic if he tried.

"Well...I'm glad to see you have chosen a good pairing for a marriage contract. Something that my children should take note of," Dimitri said.

I wanted to groan and hide under the table.

"Okay, enough of that," Helena said as she stood and dinged her glass with a knife. "I would like to propose a toast." *Oh, thank God.* I wanted to run around the table and hug her. "I'd like to start off by welcoming Lilya back into the family. It has been a long time coming, and I know that it's been a painful road for you, my dear. We are extremely happy to have you reunited with those who will love and protect you. Yulianna was a light in this world, and she has certainly passed that along to you. Hold your head high, my dear. Your mother would be proud," Helena said.

There was no stopping the tears as they trickled down my cheeks.

Ronan stood, and I thought he was next to toast, but he shook his head.

"Okay, I'm just going to come out and say it. We have nothing on the Mancini's when it comes to dramatic family dinners." Dimitri looked caught between, pissed off and shocked, as he stared up at Ronan. "When I was there last year, not only did Romeo beat the shit out of someone else's wife for trying to suck him off, but then her husband kicked her ass and made her sit all bloody at the table for the remainder of the night—before that Gio spanked his fiancé on the dining room table for mouthing off. Oh, and I got offered a marriage contract to this fourteen-year-old girl named Alex who goes to Wayward. Then she started screaming about some guy named Myles."

We all looked at Myles, who sat there with his mouth gaping.

"Wait...no...are you Myles?"

He held up both of his hands. "Hand to God, I never slept with or touched her. She just started hangin' around my lacrosse games one day," he said, completely horrified and making us all laugh.

"Well, I wouldn't go to Louisiana any time soon," Ronan said, laughing as he left the table.

This was not how I expected dinner to go. It had been a long time—well before Mum got sick—since I had so much fun at a meal. Dabbing away the last of the tears, I looked up, wondering if she was watching and happy that I reconnected with those she trusted.

OCTOBER 14 – TUESDAY 8:33 PM

Liam

Just when I thought I'd seen the worst family dynamics possible, the Mikhailovs took it up another notch. It was like Dimitri looked at Lawrence and smiled as he said, "Hold my beer."

Reading a room was easy for me, but in this case, it gave me so much information for going forward. Nash wanted to know who he could trust and who he should stay away from.

There was a very distinct divide in this family, and as dinner progressed, it became glaringly obvious that half the people sitting at the table were only here for Ren. I would've also put money on Helena being the one to call for a favor, despite Dimitri's crying act outside.

Did I doubt the emotion he'd shown? No. It was genuine, but so was the rift down the center of this family. Dimitri was too arrogant to set that aside for Ren, but Helena...she would.

Ronan, who I was quick to dislike, was the heir to his father's throne. He would stick by Dimitri's side no matter what the fight was about. Ass kisser? Maybe. It seemed more opportunistic. Whatever way the wind blew best determined his course.

Aaron was seated at the table when we came inside. He was another cousin, but from Dimitri's younger brother, who died in a car accident. Helena and Dimitri took Aaron in at seven and raised him. If there was a Switzerland in the group, it was him. Aaron had an important job with Dimitri, but Nathaniel seemed to be his closest friend.

Kaylani worked for Nathaniel and was obviously upset with her father about something, but it was easy to tell she still loved Dimitri despite his flaws.

Helena was the peacekeeper. She wanted tonight to be special, and the stress and worry of complete chaos breaking out was in her eyes. So far, everyone had been on their best behavior. Her wringing hands did make me wonder how many times a gun had been pulled at dinner.

The last three people at the table, if you didn't count Cutter—who was genuinely a cute kid and not yet touched by the dark insanity of our world—were Titus, Nathaniel, and his wife, Savannah.

This dynamic...was the most intriguing.

Titus wouldn't even look at Ronan. It was as if his brother simply didn't exist. He spoke to and answered any direct question from Dimitri, but the responses were formal, cool even. It was obvious that he didn't want to be here, and when Dimitri asked where Fawn was this evening, I thought Titus would grab a knife and leap across the table. His eyes had hardened, and the tension turned dense like fog. Shockingly, when Titus spoke, his voice remained calm like he was unfazed. He said that she was in the middle of exams and couldn't make it but sent her apologies to Ren. I didn't know who Fawn was, but now...I wanted to find out.

Nathaniel and Savannah were quite the couple. I understood the tension between them and Dimitri immediately.

Savannah had been an FBI agent, and it was obvious that no matter what she did, Dimitri would never trust her. From what I could tell, despite whatever had transpired between them, she and Nathaniel were happily married. They had one son together, and Savannah was eight months pregnant with their second child.

It was also just as evident that the mistrust and hatred ran in both directions. I was dying to know what Dimitri had done to cause the disdain in Nathaniel's eyes. I knew from rumors and the tiny bit of interaction I had with Nathaniel in the past that he wore his emotions on his sleeve, which made him an easy target at the poker table. If he was pissed, you knew. If he wanted you dead, you went missing. He had the hardest time playing nice at dinner tonight.

Nathaniel and Savannah were there for Ren and only Ren. The moment we left, they would be gone.

This was also news to me. The last I'd heard, the Mikhailovs all lived on the property, under this roof, but in different wings. That was no more. When Dimitri talked about families divided and fracturing all the time, I wondered if he was talking in general or was making a point about more than just Ren.

If that was the case...then who were the new alliances, and could we take advantage of the divide? I'd side with Nathaniel and Titus over Dimitri and Ronan any day. I didn't trust the other two as far as I could throw them, but I needed Dimitri's position for my plan. Now that dinner was over and he was a few drinks in, it was time to make my move.

Leaning closer to Dimitri, I smirked. "Mr. Mikhailov, I'd like to speak to you about an opportunity to make some easy money and have a bit of fun while we're at it."

He polished off his drink and grabbed the bottle. "Is this a conversation for the cigar lounge?"

"I'll leave that up to your discretion."

It didn't really matter to me where we were or who heard, but he seemed the type that liked a good mystery.

"Interesting." He pushed his chair back and stood. Surprisingly, he didn't wobble or waver like I expected after drinking three-quarters of a bottle of whiskey.

I nodded to Nash and followed Dimitri out of the dining hall and up a set of stairs to his Man Cave, as Ren called them. This one room was bigger than all our father's lounges put together. How many people did he host in here?

"Would you like a drink," Dimitri offered.

"Thought you'd never ask," I said, and he snorted.

"Yes, my wife doesn't like to serve minors. I prefer not to start a fight."

"Completely understandable. I'll have whatever you're drinking."

He went over to the bar in the corner and grabbed two fresh glasses. After a generous pour, he brought them to the leather couches and offered me a glass and a seat beside a crackling electric fireplace. We were in California, and it was warm out, so this struck me as bizarre, but it did offer a certain level of unexpected ambiance.

Dimitri was easy to pin down. He liked to be in control, loved to feel like every great idea was his, and would stab you in the back if things turned against him. But...he was also the only way I was getting into the game. So, I waited for him to speak.

"Alright, you've intrigued me. What do you want to talk to me about?"

I sat back and swirled my drink around, letting the firelight catch off the golden color.

"A high-stakes poker game is being held here in Cali on Thursday night—for the very elite only. I'm sure you're aware of it?"

"I am," he said. "I'm allowing them to host here," he said, making sure to let me know his position and power.

"Are you attending?"

"I hadn't decided yet. Why? Do you want in?"

"I wouldn't decline an invite," I said, smiling, and he laughed.

"Do you really think you have the chops to take on these players? We aren't talking small sums of money. Do you have the million buy-in?"

"I do, and I'm pretty confident that I can walk away with the pot," I said, sipping my drink.

"You do seem confident. But how much of that is youthful exuberance and bravado? If you lose and then have a youthful tantrum after I extend an invite, it will reflect poorly on me. Why would I take that chance?"

I smirked at the word *youthful* that he made sure to use twice.

"What if I provide compensation for the invite? Regardless of the outcome, and I assure you there will be no youthful, outbursts."

He chuckled deeply, a move meant to unnerve an adversary, but I wasn't intimidated. I smiled and waited for Dimitri to stop posturing.

"You're very interesting, Liam. I like your style." He slid forward on the leather chair, and I knew I had him in the palm of my hand. "Present your offer."

"Name your amount," I countered, and his eyebrows shot up.

It was widely known that Dimitri played for more than money. He'd won property, rights to deals, and even daughters—that he used and sold again, from what I'd heard. He wasn't exactly a trafficker, but he rode a razor's edge at times.

Dimitri currently had three mistresses that he kept at condos in different parts of the city. Each was at least a forty minute drive from the house, which most wouldn't notice, but I did. Everything mattered. His businesses, although still successful, had taken a massive hit when Nathaniel pulled his legitimate operations a few months ago. The reasoning was unknown, but I'd find out.

He was as arrogant as Lawrence and, in some ways, twice as deadly because he had the extra power and influence with the Head Council to destroy anyone who owed him.

That was where Lawrence had fucked up. He was so busy opposing the Council that he pissed off the man holding his debt. That had created an opening for Nash to align with Nathaniel, who was all too happy to bolster his income and enter a long-term arrangement.

Our world was like an onion. For every layer peeled, there was another. Families were either in debt or collected. We were near the top but not at the highest point. At the end of the day, Lawrence owed the Mikhailov family.

His interest in Ren was clear now that we knew her mother's lineage. Marrying her gave him an equal right to a seat at the table. He would instantly peel off the last layer of the onion.

She must be protected at all costs. Lawrence couldn't get his hands on her.

"Alright, I'll get you into the game. I want half a million, win or lose. If you don't have my money, then you'll pay me back in other ways."

I drank down the rest of the whiskey and set my glass aside.

"You underestimate me. I'll give you a million." Standing, I buttoned my suit jacket and smiled at his shocked expression. "I always play to win. Oh, and Dimitri...Ren will be attending with me. If you hear of anything shady, I'd kindly ask for and expect a warning. It'll be a shame if something happens to her."

He narrowed his eyes at me, probably wondering if that was an accusation. It wasn't, but I wanted him to know that I was watching everything.

Ren didn't know it yet, but from what I'd dug up, it was Dimitri who helped Yulianna escape Russia. The only question left was, why? I had my theories, but I played my cards close to the vest and never jumped the gun on going all-in.

"Have a good evening, Mr. Mikhailov. I'll meet you at the Rosemont Hotel at eight o'clock sharp."

"How do you know where it's being held? Those emails are only sent to invited members."

I smiled. "A player never reveals the ace he's holding. Have a good evening."

Before he could question me further, I walked out. Step one was done for my initiation. Now, I needed to win it all, and it was a good thing I brought my lucky rabbit with me.

Chapter 44

OCTOBER 15 – WEDNESDAY 3:10 PM

Blake

Now, this was my kind of vacation. Well, it wasn't really a vacation, but any time away from school and all the insanity still felt like we'd escaped to paradise. Kaylani said it was cool out, but in comparison to the coming snow where we were from, the bright sun and sandy beach were hot.

Ren and Kaylani might be cousins, but they were as opposite as night and day. Where Ren was fun and sweet and a lot more reserved, Kaylani didn't need anything or anyone to have a party. Her energy level was dialed up to max at all times. Ren and I had already shared a few disbelieving looks.

"Are you having a good time? This must be kind of strange for you," Ren said.

I rolled my head in her direction. Today had been perfect. After the races I had this morning, we grabbed a bite to eat before chilling at the beach near the competition pool. The rest of the guys still had one more race each, but I stamped my get out of jail free card.

"I'm great. Why would this be weird for me?"

Ren pointedly looked at Kaylani, who was having a dance party with Fiona with daiquiris in their hands. She had even managed to guilt a couple of the guards into dancing with them. I thought I'd seen it all, but two girls in bikinis and two men who looked like they stepped out of a mob movie dancing on the sand were new.

"It doesn't bother me. Remember, I used to go to wild parties all the time. They are tame in comparison."

Ren cocked her head as she stared at me, and I hated that I couldn't see her eyes through the dark sunglasses.

"Do you ever miss it? I know you said the whole partying and playboy scene wasn't really you, but was there any part of it you liked?"

Shrugging, I sat up and swung my legs over the side of the lounge chair to face Ren.

"Sure, I like a good party, but they were also a trigger for me. The stress, the drugs, the insecurity. It was a cocktail of toxic issues for me. I would only go to see friends that I don't get to often, but the risk...." I looked at the ocean and the waves slowly lapping at the shore. "It's too much right now. You can thank my very expensive therapist for helping me see that," I teased deflecting. Ren saw right through it and shifted closer, putting her hand on my knee.

"Are you still struggling?"

"Depends on the day. Most of the time, I'm fine, but I guess this is what they mean that you're never really free. I was stupid, thinking that I could control it and that I wouldn't get addicted. You know?"

"You're so far from stupid, Blake," Ren said, gripping my hand.

"Maybe, but I was arrogant. It won't be me. I only need a little. I can stop anytime. So fucking cliché, but I believed it. Now, I don't dare touch a beer with the guys. Stupid or not, I feel like an idiot."

"I wish there was something I could do to help." She smiled, and I laughed.

"You're kidding me, right?"

"Um...."

"Ren, you saved my life. You've been unbelievably supportive. There is nothing else you can do. This is my demon to battle." Leaning closer, she met me halfway, stopping just shy of kissing me. I smirked and lifted her sunglasses so I could see her eyes. "I love you."

"I love you," she said and then kissed me.

My heart sang when she took control and poured what she felt into the connection.

"You could warm me on the coldest of days and burn me quicker than any sun. I would let you scorch me to the ground for just one more kiss," I whispered.

"Hey, lovebirds. Do you want to get going? We have shopping to do," Kaylani yelled.

Now she noticed us.

Ren nipped my lip and kissed me softly before looking at her cousin.

"I guess we better," she said and stood, grabbing her towel.

Bang!

Leaping from my seat, I grabbed Ren around the waist and dove to the ground. I blanketed her with my body, trying to make us as flat as possible.

"Are you hit," I asked frantically. Blood pounded in my ears as I looked around.

"No, I'm fine," Ren said.

The guards who protected Kaylani and Fiona had their guns out as we searched for the source.

"Where did that come from," I asked.

"I think it was a car backfiring in the lot," Goran, the guard, said.

"Stay down until we know it's safe," I told Ren. She nodded.

When no one ran at us, and there were no shots, we slowly stood. The guards by the limo waved and gave the all clear, but Kaylani stayed on the ground. Goran spoke to her softly, while she shook her head and her eyes filled with tears.

Ren shifted to go to Kalyani and Fiona, but I wrapped my arm around her waist and pulled her into my side.

"Give her a minute. I think she's having a panic attack," I whispered in Ren's ear.

Fiona and her guard walked over as Goran led Kaylani to the shoreline.

"Is Kaylani alright," Ren asked.

Fiona shrugged. "I've never seen her like that," she said.

We stood quietly and waited for them to return, but the look on Goran's face told me that Kaylani needed to go home.

"I'm sorry," Kaylani said. She hugged Ren without any further explanation before trudging off to the parking lot.

"We're taking the SUV back to the house. You can carry on to the dress shops. I'll catch up once Kaylani is safely home," Goran said.

"Is she okay," Ren asked.

He nodded. "She will be."

We watched Goran march away and open the SUV door for Kaylani before Ren lifted her gaze to mine. The sorrow in her eyes was unmistakable.

"It'll never end, will it? There will always be a threat, no matter what we do. Owen, Lawrence, some gang next week, they'll keep coming. I'll just have to get used to this."

I swallowed and didn't want to answer this question.

"No...it won't end. You just become desensitized."

She sighed and grabbed my hand.

"Do you still want to go shopping? I promised myself that I wouldn't let fear control me," Ren said, and I nodded.

"Count me in," Fiona said.

Taking a second, I soaked in the beauty of this place. Most people saw nothing more than sun and sand, but for me, it was just another city of sin. It could drag you under and drown you just as easily as the ocean a few feet away. The rest of the world was oblivious to what went on under their noses every day. The wars waged on their streets and in their politicians' seats. They preferred to be blinded by the beauty, living in the Matrix as long as their zen state wasn't disturbed.

That was what really separated us from the rest of society—what separated Ren from the pack. We didn't sit on the sidelines watching as others played chess. We chose the cold, harsh reality that we were all pieces on a much larger board, and every move was strategic. Only the most cunning survived.

I'd gotten lucky. In the mad chaos that had threatened to suck me under when I was at my weakest, a little snowbird soared into my life and carried me away on her wings.

"Are you sure you're okay," Ren asked, and I smiled.

"Never better," I said and kissed her forehead.

OCTOBER 15 – WEDNESDAY 8:33 PM

Myles

"Ya know, if you were wantin' ta get kinky wit us, ya could've just said," I teased.

Nathaniel chuckled in the front seat while Nash and I rode in the back, with hoods covering our heads. It was the only way we would get to see Devin. Nathaniel had demanded that his prison location remain a secret. Not even a shred of light filtered through the black material.

We'd seen a different side of Nathaniel at dinner. He was more than the dark tyrant rumors. But there was no doubt in my mind that he would slit our throats if he decided we were a threat. I kinda liked it and definitely respected it.

"Trust me, if I wanted to get kinky, you'd know it. And you would see me coming," Nathaniel answered.

"Yeah, that's not comforting," I mumbled, and could almost feel Nash shaking his head beside me.

Nerves made me jittery, and when I was jittery, I used humor to cope.

When we had loaded Devin into Nathaniel's vehicle last January, I thought that I'd never have to see him again. It took time to work through my emotions, and some days, my mind could still turn pretty dark. I lived each day walking through a minefield of trauma. If it wasn't one thing setting me off, it was another. I could hide it, push it away, and try to forget, but today was not one of those days.

Seeing my brother, who'd abused me and had set out to torment me any chance he got, was a trigger. I hadn't realized just how comfortable I'd become not having Devin around and with Da traveling so much. My knee bounced in time to my pounding heart.

We came to a stop, and there was the distinct rattling sound of large gates opening.

"You can take your hoods off now," Nathaniel said.

The SUV parked, and I couldn't get the stuffy material pulled off fast enough. It wasn't yet dark, but the sun had almost set. The bright orange rays made the tops of the trees look like they were on fire.

"What is this place," Nash asked, eyeing the massive home that looked like any other beachfront property.

"This is the Triangle because anyone who goes in never comes out. And just like the Bermuda Triangle, no one will ever find them," he said, turning in his seat to look back at us. "Myles, you do know that I'm never setting Devin free, right? I understand the situation with your father, but no matter what he does, I'm never releasing your brother."

"Good. I don't want him to ever get out of here. Yer free ta torture him however ya want."

"Alright then, what are you hoping to gain from seeing him?"

"We need your help to deliver a message," Nash answered. "My father is a persistent asshole. He will try and negotiate for Devin or attempt to buy you off. Ultimately, he'll piss you off and ruin the relationship that we have set up. I can't allow that. We need a firm statement that conveys your position on Devin's freedom."

Nathaniel smirked, his black eyes fucking eerie in the darkening car.

"Let me get this straight. You want a response to his request, and a little note with some flowers isn't going to cut it?"

"Only if the flowers were dipped in blood," Nash countered.

"Interesting, I kind of like that. But I get what you're saying. Well, let's head in, I have an idea."

Nathaniel got out, and Nash looked at me. He didn't ask if I was going to be okay, which I appreciated, but I nodded to him none-theless to ease his mind.

Pushing open my door, I was hit with the scent of saltwater coming off the nearby ocean. I loved that smell. I'd always wanted to live near the water with the sound of waves lulling me to sleep at night. Glancing around, I whistled low under my breath. You could just make out the gates we'd driven through. Tall trees lined the drive-way, and guards were stationed everywhere. You couldn't walk twenty feet without spotting another one.

Stepping into the house behind Nathaniel and Nash, I stared at the wall of screens that covered the property and the prisoners. Mikhailov soldiers watched the video feeds and patrolled the cells.

Nathaniel stopped and looked at us before pointing around.

"When I mentioned creating a private space, Nash. This is what I meant. Everything in here and on the property is state-of-the-art. Nothing can penetrate these walls. I had them specially reinforced and designed with multiple layers for sound proofing and to prevent thermal imaging. There are drone blockers and cell phone jammers as well as cameras on every square inch of the property. There is not a single foot of space that isn't covered by a camera. No one leaves or arrives without my permission. I only have my most trusted men here, other than Goran and Ivan, who are my personal guards."

"I'm impressed," Nash said. "Did you design everything yourself?"

"No, I had help. You need the name?"

"I do. I have two spaces to outfit, and any of my current contacts would alert Lawrence."

"I'll give you the information before we leave."

Nathaniel looked at the screens, and I followed his sightline. I spotted Devin right away. He was pacing his cell and pulling at his hair. When Nathaniel's eyes met mine, a sickening feeling washed over me. There was regret or maybe pity in his gaze. It was hard to tell, but I knew what that meant. My brother had been spilling what he'd done to me. My determination didn't waver as I stared at Nathaniel.

"Alright then, let's go."

He placed his hand over a security panel, and the large metal door hissed and swung outward. We took the stairs down to the lower level and passed through more security doors and guards. This place was more secure than the Vatican. The men down here were dressed all in black, and the weapons strapped to them were intense. Knives, guns, and a couple of them even had swords on their backs. I'd never seen anything like this, and I thought I'd seen it all when it came to armed protection.

The floor was a soft grey and matched the walls, but everything else was thick, clear plexiglass. We passed a cell where a man I didn't recognize sat on the floor, sobbing. The next few were empty, and then, just like that, there he was.

Devin didn't notice me. He paced in a circle, his shaggy hair hanging in his face with his head bowed, mumbling too low to be heard. The satisfaction of seeing him in distress and the sadness pulling at my heart that it had come to this twisted into a sharp pain in my chest. Flashes of my life reared their ugly head. I wanted to shoot him and cry at the same time. He was my older brother, and he was supposed to protect me. Instead...as my mother said, he was born with the devil in him.

He glanced up before continuing his one-man parade as I stood in front of the glass. Then he stopped and turned around. Devin's furious glare found mine, and neither of us moved as we stared at one another. He was likely picturing my death, while I wondered if things could've been different if Owen wasn't our father.

"Can he hear me," I asked, not looking away from my brother.

"Yes, he can," Nathaniel answered.

"Well...I have to say, ya look like a bag of shite."

"And whose fault is that," Devin asked, taking a step closer.

"Yers, actually."

My hands were stuffed in my pockets to stop the shaking as my adrenaline spiked. Even behind the glass, I felt Devin's rage and knew what he would do to me if he were free. I was far from easy pickings, but it didn't stop the old reaction. I hated to feel so fucking weak still.

"Bullshit. I'm here because of you."

I shook my head. "Yer delusional. All I ever wanted was to have ya be a real brother to me. Instead, ya treated me worse than the rats ya caught and killed. At least ya gave them a swift death. But here ya are, a starvin' rat, and ya chewed off yer own tail. That's what landed ya in here, brother, not me."

Devin ran at the glass, yelling like a banshee, his face twisting into the monster from my childhood. It took all the strength I had not to flinch as he collided with a bang. His fingers clawed at the thick barrier.

"Da said he could train you, but Ma filled your head with mush. We should've killed her sooner."

My body tensed, and I snarled at him.

"Don't you dare mention my ma," I growled.

Devin's maniacal laugh echoed through the cells. He hauled off and punched the glass, then pointed at me.

"I should've smothered you when you were born. I dreamed about it," he yelled. "I fucking still dream about it."

Sighing, I looked over my shoulder at Nathaniel. He raised an eyebrow at me.

"Expecting something different," Nathaniel asked.

I could hardly hear him over Devin's fists pounding as he screamed, "I fuckin' hate you. I wish you were dead."

"I guess I hoped for a bit of humanity, but Ma was right...." I looked at Devin again and had no idea how we could be family. "There is no fixin' the dark that eats at his brain."

Nathaniel made a motion I didn't see, but whatever it was, my brother knew what was coming. His eyes grew wide, and he ran for the back of the cell.

"No, no, no, don't let them take me. Please, let me out of here," he yelled. He tried to climb or maybe push through the steel wall. It was hard to tell what the hell he was thinking.

Six guards walked over, and Devin's screams turned high-pitched as they pulled out black batons. They seemed standard until you noticed the end was a taser—like in sci-fi movies. The men cornered Devin, and as he tried to bolt for a narrow gap between them, he was taken down to the floor, his body convulsing.

"Where do you want him," one of the men asked.

"Take him to the torture room," Nathaniel ordered.

I watched as Nathaniel slowly removed his suit jacket and handed it to a guard. It was hard to believe that not that long ago, he was a senior at Wayward—just like us. Watching Nathaniel was like holding up a mirror and asking to see myself in ten years.

"You don't care, right," Nathaniel confirmed as he rolled up his sleeves. I shook my head.

"We don't care," Nash said.

"Very well." Nathaniel snapped his fingers. "Get me a small, long-distance container."

"You don't have to watch this," Nash whispered as he gripped my shoulder to hold me back from following Nathaniel into the next room.

"Aye, I do. This'll be the last time I ever see him, and I need closure."

As we stepped into the torture room that Nathaniel mentioned, I made the decision that I would never do anything to piss this man off.

Chains decorated the walls, and every sort of saw, knife, pliers—and things I couldn't even put a name to—were neatly displayed or lined up on a table. Devin hung from the ceiling in the center of the room, reminding me of a puppet. The guards locked his ankles in floor shackles as Nathaniel walked over to the array of knives but ultimately chose a jagged tooth saw.

Nathaniel moved like he didn't have a care in the world. If you plucked him out of this room and dropped him on the beach, you'd say he was out for a casual stroll. He tapped the flat edge of the saw in his hand as he circled my brother, who was still passed out.

"I'm going to give you a warning before I do this," Nathaniel said as he cut the orange jumpsuit off Devin's body. "I know men like your fathers. Mine is not much better. But there is one thing they all have in common."

"What's that," Nash asked.

"They don't do well being backed into a corner. Right now, even though there is chaos, they both think they have options and the illusion of control. Once this is done, Owen will slip further into the deep end."

"Trust me, he was already there," I said.

Nathaniel smirked.

"No, you only thought he was there. You take away all hope from a man like him, and he becomes twice as dangerous. Just be careful what you create. Not even Dr. Frankenstein could control his monster."

Reaching into his pocket, he pulled out sniffing salts and put them under Devin's nose. It took a minute, but then he jerked a couple of times, and his eyes snapped open. He lunged at Nathaniel in a fruitless effort to kill him or run away. This was the first time I saw real terror in my brother's eyes. Stupidly, the look called to me because no matter what he said or did, he was still my flesh and blood.

But that didn't mean I was going to stop whatever came next.

"Myles, come here for a minute," Nathaniel said, tapping Devin's chest with the saw.

"What are you planning on doing with that," Devin asked as I walked over.

"Oh, don't worry about that. Myles, I think you should say goodbye to your brother. Let him know how you truly feel about everything he did to you."

I licked my lips and looked at Devin.

"What are you going to do, baby brother?" The bastard was chained up and he still mocked me and laughed.

My hand clenched into a fist, and I let Echo claw to the surface and take over. The first hit felt so good when his head snapped to the side. A droplet of blood at the corner of his mouth fed the beast inside of me. Left, left, right, right, right, uppercut. My fists flew, and

I felt his ribs crack. Devin cried out in pain as I landed punch after punch until I was panting and stepped back to see his face beaten and bloody.

Grabbing his jaw, I forced him to look me in the eyes.

"This is almost the happiest day of me life...almost. Meeting Snowflake will always remain in my top position. The best part is I know that'll drive ya crazy. After all the shite ya did, I'm gonna walk away wit a smile on my feckin' face."

He would never be the monster under my bed again. I grinned and felt nothing but relief in watching his final moments.

"I want ya to know that I'm gonna kill Da, and then I'm never gonna think of either of ya ever again."

Rolling out my shoulders, I looked at Nathaniel, who seemed pleased with my work.

"Thanks, Nathaniel. I appreciate the thought."

"You'll never be free of me, baby bro. I'll be in every corner, and you'll remember what it was like for me to be your first for...ev-er-y-thing."

Devin sounded out the last word, and goosebumps rose on my skin. That hit hard like he knew it would. At any other time in my life, I would've been crippled on the spot as memories paralyzed me, but no more. I gave him nothing. Not a flinch or a batted eye as I stared pure evil in the face. The cruelty rolled off him, and he no longer tried to hide the insanity that lived in his soul.

"Ya may have stolen me firsts. Anyone can do that to a defenseless child. That dinnie make ya special. Yer a dime a dozen." Devin's smile began to fade. "For however many minutes or days Nathaniel lets ya live, I want ya to know that ya never broke me."

Devin snarled and jerked toward me, making the heavy chains rattle.

"He's all yers."

Nash subtly brushed my arm with his when I stepped back. I soaked in the little bit of comfort he offered. My body was weak from relief, but also the effort it took to cut off the last of my bond. To truly step away and be free.

"I'm grand," I whispered, and he nodded.

What I said to Devin was true, no longer just empty words. The shackles that he had placed on my mind as a child unclipped and fell away—along with any lingering hopes or dreams that we could've been different.

"Usually, I love having guests to torture. It's how I work out my daddy issues." Nathaniel smirked. "But I think I'm going to enjoy watching you die so much more."

"Please don't kill me," Devin begged. "I'll do whatever you want. I'm a loyal soldier, and I'm deadly. Put me to work."

"Tempting...but I prefer not to be looking over my shoulder for the knife coming for my back," Nathaniel said.

Wasn't that the truth?

Nathaniel stalked around his naked prey before suddenly snatching Devin's cock. His screams bounced around the room even though nothing had been done yet. Nathaniel's entire demeanor shifted in a blink. The teasing was gone. His face darkened into a man I never wanted to meet in a dark alley, and they called me Echo.

"Your brother may never think of you again, but I will, Devin. I'm going to think of all the times you begged me to stop, of the pain-filled screams ringing off these walls, and of all the secrets you spilled with your blood."

Nathaniel pulled hard on Devin's cock, stretching it out. I cringed when the saw was placed against his skin while my cock tried to disappear up into my body.

"No, no, no, please, no. Anything but that, please."

A wicked smile pulled at Nathaniel's mouth.

"Look me in the eyes as you scream. I like it."

Nathaniel moved slowly like it was a hundred-year-old oak he was sawing through. Devin thrashed and wailed like the demon inside him was leaving his body. Blood pooled on the floor and slid down the drain, disappearing like this never happened.

I'd never seen my brother cry. Not once over anything, but tears streamed down his face as Nathaniel made the last cut and held his prize up in front of Devin's face.

"Tell me, how does it feel to know that this will be the last thing your father sees of you?"

Incoherent words tumbled from his mouth, along with drool.

"Fine, don't tell me. Box," Nathaniel said.

A guard that I'd forgotten was even in the room stepped out of the corner and took the saw before handing Nathaniel a black container with a lid. Opening it, he laid the cock inside like a delicate piece of jewelry before shutting it and holding it out to Nash.

"Keep it closed. It will remain cool for three days so that it doesn't rot on you before you can hand it over."

Nash took the box and tucked it under his arm.

"A finger would've been fine," Nash said, making Nathaniel laugh.

"Sure, but this provides a more dramatic finish for you. I can give you his balls, too, if you like?"

"Nope, this is good. Just thinking about traveling with his cock like a pet is more than enough," Nash said, and we all chuckled.

"It's kind of disturbing that ya have boxes like that lying around."

Nathaniel smirked but didn't elaborate.

"Whatcha gonna do wit him?"

"That's for me to know. But I promise you'll never see him again," Nathaniel said.

That was all I could really ask for at the end of the day. Devin had passed out. His head swung low, sweat and blood ran down his body, and for the first time in my life, I felt nothing when I looked at him.

Nash grabbed my shoulder, and I met his stare.

"Blood doesn't make you brothers. We choose our family, and I choose you."

My eyes filled with tears, and I blinked them away.

"Yer a fuckin' asshole. Ya just wanted to see me cry."

"Maybe," he teased.

But Nash was right. Some ties were solidified by a force much stronger than DNA. Only people who had been through hell and back as they protected one another to survive could fully understand. Bonds forged in war were different from any other. That was what we were in—one long battle from the time we were born. I knew we would win, and I would stand by Nash's side forever.

OCTOBER 16 – THURSDAY 7:50 PM

Liam

While the rest of the swim team was celebrating the many medals we walked away with, I had bigger fish to fry. It had taken hours of fighting with Myles to iron out the details for tonight. The guys would hang out nearby in case of trouble, but they wouldn't be attending or stepping a single foot into the hotel. Unless Ren or I called them and for no other reason.

I'd already reserved a suite and told Myles and Blake that they wouldn't see Ren for the rest of the night. That had gone over like a lead balloon, but too fucking bad for them. I knew that shit like this would be an issue, but Ren was clear with her boundaries, so here we were. That meant I needed to establish a few boundaries of my own.

Ren sat next to me in the limo, her eyes downcast and hands in her lap. She was living, breathing, walking sin, and I was keeping a tight hold on her tonight. Damn, Blake knew how to shop. The silver dress that she'd gotten was so short that if any more were missing, her ass would be hanging out. The low scooped front gave a very seductive view of her breasts. Adding the strappy heels, straightened waist-length hair, and the collar I'd given her, she would have every man in the vicinity drooling. Ren and her outfit were my secret weapon to throw whoever I could off their game if need be.

After doing my homework, the only player who worried me was Romeo Mancini. He was conservative and didn't take large risks when it came to betting. I'd won far more than he'd lost, so he was my target...learn him, and I could definitely take the room.

Ren looked up at me when I laced our fingers, and her eyes betrayed her nervousness.

Leaning in close to her ear, I whispered, "It's going to be alright, Little Rabbit."

She nodded but didn't say anything, and I brought her hand to my lips for a kiss.

"Do you believe me?"

"I believe in you. But I don't trust any of these men. They all sound...."

"Dangerous," I finished for her.

"Yes. I doubt they'll play fair. This game is too important for something shady to cause you to lose. I hate the idea of Lawrence making you do something else."

"They may or they may not, but either way, I know what I'm doing. Besides, I'm a little dangerous," I growled in her ear and nipped at her soft skin.

She shivered, and...fuck...I was really starting to like that. Everything between me and Theo had always been supercharged, but Ren was...complex, and her body was incredibly sensitive. So much so that a single breath across her neck made her moan and her eyes flutter closed.

I did it just to see, and sure enough, Ren wiggled beside me, closing her eyes as a soft moan escaped her lips.

"You're making me want to fuck you right now, Little Rabbit. I'm going to ravage your sexy body tonight." She turned her head and bit her lip. "Don't do that unless you want me to follow through."

Ren's eyes searched my face as she slowly released her lip, which wasn't much better. Her shimmering collar stood out against her skin and all I could think of were the games I had planned for after I took everyone's money.

"We won't be returning to the other hotel tonight. Myles and Blake will have to learn to cuddle one another," I said and smirked.

"And what about Theo?"

"He'll meet us when I text him that we won," I said, smoothing the front of my suit jacket. Teasing her was turning me on, and I needed to take a moment, or I would put her on her knees in this limo.

I cracked my neck and growled at Ren as she slid her hand up my leg.

"Oops, did I touch you," she teased, and I grabbed her chin, bringing her face to mine.

"Do you want me to fuck you in here?"

She didn't answer right away, and I could feel her modesty warring with her desire. Taking her hand, I placed it over the bulge in my pants.

"I'm ready, are you? Do you want the driver to hear you scream as I make you come in the back of his car?"

Ren clenched her legs.

"I'm...not sure I'm ready for that, but you make it very tempting," she said, and I smiled.

I looked at my Rolex. We had exactly twenty-one minutes.

"You're bad, Little Rabbit. You need a lesson in patience." Spreading my legs, I pointed. "Get on your knees. You're going to fix the problem you created," I ordered, and she glanced at the dark dividing glass. I gripped her throat, and she gasped as I forced her to look at me. "I said, get on your knees. That wasn't a suggestion."

"Yes, Sir."

I dropped my hand and undid my jacket, belt, and pants as she got into position. If we had more time, I'd teach her exactly what I wanted. But, as it was, we were pushing it.

Her eyes were glued to my cock as I pulled it out and tipped her chin up.

"You have nineteen minutes to make me come. If you don't, you're going to get your first real punishment after the game. Are you up for the challenge?"

Her eyes flashed as she reached for me.

"Yes, Sir. Just don't touch my hair. I didn't spend an hour straightening it for you to turn it into a rat's nest before the event. After...you can do whatever you want."

"Deal."

Fuck, she was adorably feisty. But there was no way she'd get me to blow in under twenty. Then...she did something that no one had ever done before. Ren wrapped one finger around my balls and another around the base of my shaft like a double-holed cock ring. She tightened her hand and finger as she slid her mouth over the head, and I couldn't stop the groan. Shit...who the hell taught her that?

Ren rolled her eyes up to mine as she swallowed all of me.

"Fuck...."

She just might prove me wrong. That would be a first. I never entered a challenge I couldn't win.

But fuck me, she had a talented mouth, applying the perfect

amount of pressure to create that ache in my cock. I took a deep breath as she picked up her pace.

My entire body tuned in to the sound of her moans and the soft slurping as she sucked. The feel of her tongue and lips rubbing against the sensitive areas of my dick and the smell of her perfume that was seductive all on its own. Add in her sexy eyes, and my collar around her neck, and my normally perfectly in control temperament was quickly slipping away.

Itching to grab her hair but thinking better of it, I slid my hands down a little lower and gripped the edge of the seat. My cock hit the back of her throat every time she bobbed her head.

"You...have...five minutes," I said through gritted teeth, my entire body tensing as I tried to hold off a little longer.

Just a few seconds past the mark and I could come, and still punish her. If I didn't get this release, then all I'd be able to think about was laying her on the poker table in front of everyone.

Ren let go of my shaft and balls at the same time, sucking harder and faster. Her fingers pressed into my hips, and the surge of the blood to the tip of my cock was instant. A deep rumbling growl escaped my lips, and I swore as she snuck her finger under my sack and pressed on a highly sensitive spot of mine. Fucking Theo, telling her all my weaknesses. I was tanning his ass tonight. That thought, and Ren were all it took to send me over the edge.

"Fuck, Little Rabbit, I'm coming."

She didn't slow, and I thrust up into her mouth as I came. Ren didn't seem the least bit fazed. She sucked everything that I had to give down and then licked my cock clean. Slumping into the seat, I ran my knuckles down her cheek.

"That was very good, Little Rabbit."

Ren licked her lips and climbed up onto the seat. Opening her purse, she pulled out a package of gum. I grabbed Ren's hand and dropped my mouth to hers. My release was still on her tongue, and I instantly wanted to go again.

"Don't open that package. I want to taste myself on your lips all night. You're mine, Little Rabbit. Mine, and every time my tongue touches yours, I'll be reminded of what I'm going to do to this fucking mouth after the game."

"But I won. I should get to choose what we do," she said.

"That would be true...but you broke the rules first and touched my leg. So, I won."

Her sexy silvery eyes narrowed into slits.

"You set me up."

"No, I merely remember the rules and play by them. Something that you struggle with," I said, tucking my cock back into my pants and making sure I looked presentable.

"You're slick, Liam," she said, pushing her lip out seductively.

We pulled into the hotel parking lot, but before we came to a stop, I nipped at the side of her neck.

"It's not me who will be slick before the end of the night, Little Rabbit. You'll be wet and screaming my name until you can't take anymore. That is a promise."

Ren's eyes flared with a devious passion. I loved it. She was finding more of who she was every day and, with it, getting stronger.

The limo stopped, and the attendant opened the door for us. Sliding out, I offered my hand to help Ren. As she elegantly stepped out of the car and stood beside me, I felt on top of the world.

"You ready," I asked.

Those keen and intelligent eyes locked with mine.

"I'm ready," she answered, strong and sure of herself. Fuck, I loved that about her.

I looked up at the hotel and smiled as I pulled my game face into position. Holding out the crook of my arm for Ren to take, I smirked.

"You look sexy," I said, and Ren smiled. "Let's go win some money."

OCTOBER 16 – THURSDAY 7:59 PM

Ren

"Remember, you're a princess from a powerful mafia family. You don't let anyone talk down to you, and if they touch you...I'll kill them," Liam whispered as we walked through the doors of the hotel. I shivered at the tone in his voice but it was also comforting. I knew he was serious and that he had the skills to do it bare-handed.

With my arm hooked through Liam's, he rubbed his thumb over my hand. It was the most affection he'd shown me in public. I wasn't sure if it was a statement to anyone who looked our way, if it was part of the act for the night, or if it meant more. There were still parts of this relationship with him that I just didn't understand.

"You don't have to do that. I won't let anyone touch me," I said, looking at his hand, and he arched an eyebrow at me. "I'm not being sassy. I just know how you feel about public displays of affection."

Liam lifted my hand to his mouth and kissed my knuckles, putting the subject to rest without saying a word and igniting a storm in me.

The hotel reminded me of the one in Seattle, with fancy marble, gold accents, and flowers everywhere. Men in suits and women in elegant dresses milled around like they were part of the décor.

We stepped up to the elevator, and my nerves kicked in as Liam pushed the button. He needed to win this, and I had faith in him, but the other players being shady worried me even if they didn't worry him. Theo had explained that everyone at the table was a major player. Men from other mafia families, powerful businessmen, or politicians. Dangerous was all I heard when he told me—like we didn't have enough of that in our lives already.

"You're certainly prompt."

I turned to greet Dimitri, but when my eyes landed on the girl clinging to his arm, my mood darkened. She was not Aunt Helena and looked my age. She shrank back from my icy glare. My gaze snapped up to Dimitri's face, and he chuckled.

"You look exactly like your mother when she was pissed off."

"Mr. Mikhailov," Liam said, holding out his hand to shake. I wanted to smack it away.

My jaw muscle twitched, and I purposely turned my back on them before I said something ignorant. I knew nothing about his and Helena's relationship so I shouldn't be so fast to judge, considering what I had going on, but I couldn't help it. Something about this screamed mistress, which meant lying, cheating, pain, and hurt. It reminded me of when my mum was sick, and Dad had stayed out late and came home smelling like perfume.

"Have I offended you," Dimitri asked.

I didn't answer him even though I knew the question was directed at me. Liam stared at me, but anything that I said right now was not going to be nice.

"Lilya?" My nostrils flared. "Interesting, maybe I should revoke Mr. Hick's invitation this evening."

My entire body stiffened, and I turned to face my great uncle. I knew nothing about him, but I was so livid that he threatened Liam that I was ready to rip his head off.

"Why don't you go up, sir. Ren and I need to have a private conversation," Liam said, wrapping his arm around my waist and pulling me away from the opening elevator doors.

Dimitri looked at me and then Liam. "I'll meet you upstairs. Don't be too long."

As the elevator left, Liam walked us to a quiet corner. He let me go and put his arm on the wall beside me as he glared.

"What are you doing?"

"Did you see that girl on his arm? She was our age...and...ugh... it's so disrespectful. I can't believe he'd do that to Helena and in front of me. I just met him. You'd think that maybe he'd want to be a little more discreet," I fumed.

"Stop. Ren, I get that seeing him with a mistress pisses you off, but you can't let it overshadow what's really important tonight."

"So, you admit she's a mistress," I said, crossing my arms.

"Yes, but it doesn't matter who she is, and don't look at me like I'm the enemy."

I sucked in a deep, steadying breath, trying to calm the raging flames burning in my gut.

"I'm sorry. I'm not mad at you, Liam. But this is bringing up some painful stuff for me. I looked after my mum all the time because Neil was either working or doing that." I pointed in the direction of the elevator.

He sighed. "Look, I don't know if Helena is okay with the other women, but I can tell you that she knows."

My arms fell, and I searched his face.

"How do you know that?" He shrugged. *Liam's classic sign for I know, but I'm not going to tell.* "You're not just saying that?"

"No."

"It doesn't matter. My mum knew and it didn't make it better. She could hate it everytime he goes out," I said.

"You're right it could and if you want to question him, punch him in the face, or whatever else after the game, then go for it, but just remember something. You're a guest here, even if you are family. This is Dimitri Mikhailov's state. He holds a seat on the Head Council for all of North America, and your actions directly affect me, Nash and everyone else. You represent the Kings as much as we do. Besides, what he does in his personal time is not our business. It's between him and Helena. What you need to remember is that everything you say and do matters. You're a real princess, Little Rabbit. You need to play the game while your tongue is dipped with sugar, or in your case, maple syrup," he said, and I smirked. "Are you good?"

I rolled my shoulders and gathered my composure.

"No, not really, but...yes, I can do this. I promise you can count on me."

His eyes searched my face before responding.

"If you start to lose sight of your priorities, come and touch me. I'll remind you."

When he kissed me, the anger and the surrounding hotel dissolved into the ether.

"Mmm, you still taste like me. I can't wait to get you naked, Little Rabbit."

Pulling back, he held out his arm for me once more, looking totally unbothered while my brain was static. Apparently, I'd lost my ability to speak.

"I do love that look on your face."

On the ride up to the penthouse, I prepped myself to keep a calm and civil attitude. Dimitri waited in the hallway for us, and I tried to pretend that the girl on his arm didn't exist while I thought of the best way to handle the situation.

When we reached Dimitri, I plastered a gracious smile on my face and wanted to throw up.

"Sorry about that, great uncle, or is that great-great uncle? I can never keep these things straight. You caught me off guard earlier," I said, and I loved that he cringed.

Turning my beaming smile on the girl, I held out my hand.

"And you are? I'm still learning about family members, and you weren't at dinner the other night. Are you one of my cousins?"

"Lilya...." Dimitri's tone held an edge, but I continued to smile and ignored the subtle threat.

"What? Does she not have a name? I mean, if I have a cousin my age, I want to get to know her," I said, and his eyes darkened.

"I'm Candi, with an I, not a Y," she said, her voice as grating as Vicky's, just a little less arrogant. She clung to Dimitri's arm as if he was her lifeline. "And Dimitri and I aren't related. We're together."

I pulled my hand back.

"Ohhh...." I glanced at Liam and pretended to wipe sweat off my forehead. "Phew, thank goodness for that." Candi looked at me and then up at Dimitri, obviously trying to decide if I'd complimented or insulted them. "We better head in," I said as Dimitri opened his mouth. "Sorry, the ladies' room calls."

Liam didn't hold me back as I walked toward the open doors at the end of the hall. I could just hear Candi asking what I meant and if I had just insulted her as she threw a tantrum behind us.

"Was that better?"

"Much," he said, smirking.

"Are there any rules about throwing her out of a window?" He looked at me. "I'm teasing," I said, walking into the suite. "Maybe." I smiled at Liam as two guards stopped us to search for weapons.

"You definitely weren't joking, but I like it," he said before turning his attention to the woman with a tablet in her hand. "Liam Hicks and guest."

She checked our names off, and we stepped past them into the lavish room. Men and a couple of women lounged on couches while servers wove around with trays of food and drink. The centerpiece was one of those massive poker tables that you only saw on television.

"Do you know everyone playing," I asked.

"Yes, I study all my opponents before I face them."

We moved over to the bar, and Liam ordered a scotch for himself and sparkling water with lime for me. There were two half-moon tables set up, facing one another, in the middle of the sitting area with five seats each. All the other furniture had been moved and placed far enough away that it would be nearly impossible to see the players' cards unless you were Superman.

"There are two tables. Will you have to play everyone?"

Liam linked our fingers together on the bar. "No, each table plays for a single place in the final. Then those two face off for the whole pot. There is no second place, and if you walk away from the table then you lose all your money. This is an all-or-nothing event, so if you can't afford to lose, you shouldn't be playing."

"Wow, that's terrifying. I have no idea how you do it."

Liam smiled wide, a glimmer of excitement shining in his eyes.

"I love it. It's a rush. I started watching my dad play when I was still in diapers. He used to have card parties all the time, and I'd wander in and sit on his lap. I was hooked and started studying players and realized that my ability for reading people really came in handy while playing."

"So tell me this...how can you study all of these men if you've never played them before," I asked, and the corner of Liam's mouth turned up.

"There's more than one way to do anything in this life, Little Rabbit."

He winked, and my cheeks heated. I watched the bartender carefully to make sure he didn't slip anything into our drinks.

"Try and relax," Liam whispered as we walked over to the floor-to-ceiling windows facing the ocean. "You look like you're the one who wants to jump out the window."

"Not a chance. Not even with a parachute, or glider, or squirrel suit. Yes, I've seen them all, and it's still a no."

I hated windows like this. No, I hated heights in general and refused to get any closer than a few feet. Liam looked at me and smiled.

"Well, I know what we need to work on next," he said, and I shot him a glare.

"No way. Whatever you're thinking, it's not happening. Nope. Not ever," I said.

"You should know better than to challenge me. I always get what I want," he said. I believed that, but not about this unless he liked vomit all over him.

"We'll discuss it later," I said, and he laughed as a man walked up to us.

"Well now, hello, beautiful." I glanced at him and then back to Liam. Purposely waiting a few seconds before I looked back at the man.

"Are you speaking to me? Sorry, I thought you were talking about Liam. He looks extremely sexy tonight."

The man's mouth opened and then closed as I linked arms with Liam again.

"I'm Liam Hicks, and you are?"

"Nicolo Amato," he said, and Liam held out his hand. "Liam Hicks...I don't know that name. We must not run in the same circles." It was an underhanded slap in the face, and I wanted to wipe that cocky-ass grin right off.

Liam took it all in stride. If he felt insulted it never showed. "I like to keep a low profile. Your family is from Illinois, yes?"

Nicolo lifted a brow and looked Liam up and down before he did the same to me. His gaze was distinctly more appreciative as he undressed me with his eyes.

"I am. I feel I'm at a disadvantage suddenly. Not only do I not know who you are, but I didn't bring a sexy woman to distract everyone." Nicolo said.

"I'm more than a pretty face," I said, and he smirked. I held out my hand. "Lilya Mikhailov, I believe you know my family."

He shook my hand, and I assessed him—from his tailored black suit to blue eyes that screamed a truckload of arrogance and how he subtly glanced at Dimitri.

"Yes, I do mean Dimitri," I said, making sure he knew I saw the look.

"In that case, the pleasure is all mine," he said, trying to be charming, but there was enough of a shift in his personality to tell me he didn't really like my great uncle.

I still let him bring my hand to his lips. Liam tensed beside me, but I tightened my arm to soothe him.

"I'm sure it is, Nicolo. I'm a catch," I said, and Nicolo laughed.

"You're very...." He tilted his head as he studied my face. "Feisty." He smiled.

"You say that like it's an insult."

"I mean no offence." He smiled wide, but it didn't reach his eyes. "This is going to be an interesting evening." He nodded to Liam before walking away.

"Little Rabbit...."

"I know, but I'm not going to let anyone talk to me like I'm a piece of meat or talk down to you."

Liam traced his fingers down the sides of my face and tucked my hair behind my ears.

"I was going to say that I love this side of you."

"Oh...I thought I was in trouble."

"You're in trouble, but not because of that," he said as heat pooled in my stomach. "Anyone else you'd like to dress down before the game starts? This is very amusing."

"I should probably cap it at two for the night. I need to ease into this newfound me slowly."

Liam chuckled and pressed his lips to mine in a quick kiss.

"Welcome, players. I'm Harrison, and I will take care of all your needs this evening," an older gentleman said, and we all turned in his direction.

"The game tonight is Texas Hold 'em. There will be two tables of five, and each will have a banker to ensure that the game is played fairly. Now, let's go over the rules. Play will continue until only one person remains from each table. Those individuals will compete for the main pot. Withdrawal, once play is underway, is prohibited unless for an emergency, and your buy-in and winnings are forfeited. No weapons of any kind are allowed in the room. You and your guests passed through metal detectors and were searched on your way in. However, you will still be asked to raise your pant legs and undo your jackets to show us that you are not carrying before sitting down. If you have a weapon of any kind, it will then be placed in a numbered box. Cell phones are also prohibited."

Harrison indicated a woman holding a decorative metal box.

"Sapphire will walk around and collect your phones in a lead box. There will be no communication in or out of this room once play begins. No earpieces or smartwatches. Only one guard per player may remain in the room. They must be unarmed and stay on the far side of the room until a break is called."

Harrison gestured to the end of the penthouse that looked to be a mile away.

"Buy-ins are paid via wire transfer. The account information is located at your seat. Cheating will not be tolerated. If you are found cheating, you will—forfeit your buy-in, be escorted out, and be banned from any future games. Are there any questions?"

No one said anything.

"Very well. When I call your name, please come up, allow a visual weapons check, and then pick an envelope for a seating assignment."

The room was so thick with testosterone that you could choke on it. The egos squeezed in here were larger than the entire state. I watched as Harrison placed ten envelopes down on a table.

"Dimitri." My great uncle walked over and showed he was weaponless before picking up the first envelope. He opened it before going and sitting down.

"Nicolo. Romeo. Alessio." Name after name was called out. "Liam." I assumed Liam would walk up alone, but he held onto my arm as he followed protocol. I opened my purse for inspection before he picked up his envelope and handed it to me.

Tearing it open, I pulled out a piece of paper that said, *Table 2 Seat 1*, which put him at the same table with Nicolo, Dimitri, and Romeo. Liam sat down and turned over the paper with the bank routing information. Using his cell, he transferred the money and shot Nash a message that said, *We're in* before powering it off. Sapphire was waiting, and he placed the phone in the padded slot that corresponded with this seat number.

The measures taken to ensure a safe and fair game were impressive. In my head, I'd pictured some grungy factory with a rickety table, chairs falling apart, and smoke thick in the air. Apparently, I watched way too many movies.

Each player got settled into position and a feeling of dread washed over me that I couldn't shake.

Harrison stepped up to the tables with a phone in his hand.

"Gentlemen, we have had a no-show but also a late buy-in. They have offered five million for a seat. Is there anyone opposed to adding a new player?"

"The more the merrier. Only means I win more," Nicolo said, shooting Romeo a wink.

There was definitely tension between them, like two strutting peacocks. I smirked at the image of them sprouting colorful feathers and shaking their asses.

"I'm not opposed to extra money," Dimitri said.

"You never are," Romeo countered.

The contentiousness between Dimitri and Romeo was palpable. There was history there, of that, I was sure. Nash's chessboard analogy was proving accurate. But it was more like one of the multi-tier versions with multiple games on the go. Every move included all the boards, and a wrong one could mean death.

"If there are no objections, I will allow the player to enter," Harrison said.

He was like a priest officiating a wedding, waiting for someone to jump up and object...

I guess that's more like a judge in a courtroom, but it still fits.

"Are you okay with this," I whispered to Liam.

"I can refuse, but it will make me look weak. Part of tonight is to get my name out in these circles. I can't afford to look like I'm young and scared."

I nodded but didn't like it one bit.

Harrison waved to someone outside the door.

I didn't pay the newcomer any attention until a man paused right beside us. My heart stopped when I glanced up. No...it couldn't be... could it? I grabbed Liam's shoulder as the man continued to his seat at the end of our table and signaled for a drink.

"What is it? Who is that?"

Failing miserably, I tried to hide the terror.

"I think that's my real father," I whispered, shaking.

"What?"

"Christov Ivankov, well, isn't this a surprise. What brings you to my state? I don't remember issuing you a pardon to step foot on California soil," Dimitri growled as he slowly stood and confirmed my suspicion. A nervous vibrating started under my skin.

The tension in the room tripled as everyone watched the exchange.

Liam's head snapped to Christov.

"How is this possible? I thought he was dead."

"So did I."

Liam wrapped his arm around my waist, soothing me with his touch. But I wouldn't be able to stand like this all night. I sucked in a deep breath to avoid passing out.

Christov unbuttoned his suit jacket and hit Dimitri with a shit-eating grin.

"Oh, come now, old man. We're all here for the same reason."

"Are we," Dimitri asked.

My fingers dug into Liam's shoulder as Christov's gaze found mine.

"We are. Those old quarrels are just that, old. Let's play." He held his hand out toward the table. "You always did have an affinity for taking what belonged to me," Christov said.

It felt like he was talking about a lot more than money.

Dimitri eyed the table, his jaw muscles twitching before he looked at Liam and then me.

I had no idea what he was thinking or what he would do, but I prayed that he would throw Christov out. I didn't need or want to meet him, even if he did resurrect himself from a coffin.

"Fine, but this is a clean game of poker. You so much as make this about anything else, and you'll be thrown out," Dimitri said, and my heart sank.

Christov smirked, and there was a malevolence to him that made my skin crawl. I never thought I'd meet anyone creepier than Lawrence or Owen, but I was wrong. As I stared into his cold, calculating blue eyes, all I saw was the monster my mum had fled from, and he was here for me. I just knew it.

Oh God...this couldn't be happening.

OCTOBER 16 – THURSDAY 9:23 PM

Liam

Christov walking in, and the fear that I could feel coming off Ren—even though she was sitting on the couch —had thrown me off my game the first few hands. I lost, but it was probably for the best. It set everyone up to think that I couldn't handle playing with them. Meanwhile, I learned their tells and the fake ones they tried to present.

Nicolo was amusing. He rubbed his thumb with his index finger when he had a great hand and couldn't keep the scowl from his eyes when he didn't. His bluff was a double tap on the table with the middle finger of his left hand before he placed his bet.

Romeo loved his lighter. He might think that the opening and closing of the lid was random, but he had a specific sequence depending on the cards he held. It was so distinct that it mimicked Morse code for every card.

Dimitri played with his watch when he had a great hand and rubbed at his temple when he was bluffing.

No one realized they did these things, but I devoured each and every one until I could tell you exactly what everyone was holding.

Nicolo currently had a full house but was trying to play it down. Unfortunately, for him, I also counted cards. With this many players, I knew exactly what was coming on the river. After the dealer dealt the final card, Nicolo added another hundred thousand to the pot.

Christov, Dimitri, and Romeo folded, and everyone looked at me.

"I not only call but raise you," I said, pushing three hundred thousand into the center.

Eyebrows went up at the amount. Nicolo tapped his finger on the table, and I could tell he wouldn't be able to pass this up. He thought he had it.

He checked his cards once more. "Call," he said, matching my raise.

"Alright, gentlemen, show your cards," the dealer said.

Nicolo smiled as he flipped over his hand and showed off the full house. He reached for the pot.

"Do not touch the pot until all players have shown their cards," the banker scolded Nicolo.

"Yeah, hold up there, Nicolo," I said, giving him a cocky grin and loved that the comment would stomp all over his ego. I flipped my cards over to show the royal flush.

"Fuck," he growled and glared at me as I pulled the pot over.

"Better luck next hand," I said, wanting to rile him up even more.

His tells were stronger when he got angry. He wore every emotion on his sleeve like an open book.

"You're a fucking cheat," Nicolo said, bursting from his seat and pointing at me.

"That is quite the accusation," Harrison said from his perch at the far end of the table. He'd kept a very watchful eye over both games, and I appreciated it. "Do you think that we would allow Mr. Hicks to cheat?"

"No one is that fucking lucky," he growled.

If he'd been allowed to keep his gun, it would be out and pointed at me by now. He was an arrogant dick who really didn't like losing.

"Are you feeling a little butt sore and don't want to lose again," I asked, toying with one of my stacks.

"I'm not afraid of anything," he snarled and rolled up his sleeves.

Another subtle threat that didn't bother me in the least. Sweat suddenly broke out on his forehead and ran down his face.

"Are you going to sit down and play, or forfeit your buy-in and leave? Any money you have won will be distributed evenly between the remaining players," Harrison said.

"Yeah, Nicolo, what are you going to do," I asked, and smiled at him.

"Son of a bitch," he said, but his voice was a little wheezy and cracked.

He pulled off his suit jacket and tossed it on a spare chair. Nicolo's face was turning an alarming shade of red. He shook his head, and I looked around the room, wondering if someone was pumping in a poisonous gas, but no one else seemed affected.

"Mr. Amato is everything alright," Harrison asked.

Nicolo's eyes darted around the table, but he didn't say anything. He stumbled back and tripped, landing hard on the ground. We all stood and stared at him, not sure what the hell was happening.

Ren jumped up and ran over. Nicolo's lips were swelling as he pointed at his throat and tried to dig around in his pocket.

"He's having a reaction. Do you have any epinephrine?"

He nodded, panicked as he wheezed in another breath. Nicolo grabbed at his throat as he made little gasping noises.

"Move your hand," she ordered.

Under any other circumstance, I would've lost my shit as she slid her hand into Nicolo's pocket.

Ren pulled out the medication he was after, and I jumped up. Kneeling beside her, I ripped a large hole in Nicolo's pants, exposing his thigh. She popped the lid and pulled out the pen like she'd done this a dozen times today.

Nicolo tried to grab it, but Ren slapped his hand away before jabbing him in the leg with the bright orange needle. It only took seconds but seemed longer as Ren held the epi-pen. Nicolo coughed and then sucked in a deep breath.

"You made me look like an idiot," he said as she pulled out the needle.

Ren glared at Nicolo as he struggled to sit up.

"No, I'm pretty sure you did that all on your own." She tossed the pen between his legs as we stood. "A simple thank you would suffice," Ren said, but he just sneered at her.

"Not a chance. I didn't need help."

The other men in the room laughed.

"Next time, let him die," Romeo said.

Harrison signaled a guard who ran past the tables to help Nicolo stand.

"Fuck all of you. And you...you owe me a new suit," Nicolo snarled at Ren.

She picked up a chip from my pile and flicked it at him. I laughed as it hit him in the cheek.

"There, go buy one, you ungrateful jerk," Ren said.

Nicolo lurched forward, but his bodyguard held him back.

I moved in front of Ren and she grabbed my arm, stopping me.

"You're really not going to say thank you," Alessio asked, standing.

He was deeply tanned with a weathered look that screamed he'd been at one too many poker tables in his lifetime.

"Learn some manners, boy. She saved your life, and we all know what that means."

Nicolo's eyes flared with rage, but he didn't reply as he took in the serious faces. He was out of line, outnumbered, and he knew it.

"Boss...." Apparently, that one word from his guard held more power than anything anyone else had said.

Nicolo sighed and looked at Ren.

"Thanks. Now get me out of here."

We watched him leave before Harrison addressed the crowd.

"I think this would be a good time to call a break before the next hand. It goes without saying that you cannot touch the tables while play is paused."

Guiding Ren over to a far corner, I held her shaking hands.

"Are you good?"

"Yeah, just the adrenaline. Can you believe the nerve of that guy? He wouldn't even have gotten it out of his pocket in time if it wasn't for me."

I kissed her forehead and ran my hands down her arms, feeling her relax under my touch.

"What are we going to do about our other problem," Ren asked.

I didn't have to look to know that Christov was staring in our direction. If he thought for even a second that I would leave her alone, he was mistaken. I planned on following her right into the women's bathroom if needed.

"We stick to the plan. Win the pot, and play this out to see what he's after," I said.

"I'm pretty sure I know what he's after." Ren crossed her arms as she glanced in his direction. "My head on a platter."

"We don't know that."

"Don't we? This is way too much of a coincidence, Liam. Someone killed my mum, has been following me, and shot up my home...it has to be him. He's after me for what my mother did. Why else pretend to be dead?"

"I don't know, but why kill his innocent daughter?"

Our conversation was cut off as Romeo stepped up to us.

"Romeo Mancini, nice to put a face to the name," I said, nodding and his lip curled up.

"Oh, I'm pretty certain you already knew who I was. Just as I know, you're Emmett Hicks's son."

"Guilty. I didn't know you knew my father."

"I know of him, but I didn't know he raised a shark," Romeo said, smirking before turning his attention to Ren.

Ren pointed at him. "Wait...Mancini?" He nodded. "I hear you have unusual dinners at your house."

He laughed and then smiled.

"You must have been talking to Ronan. The meal he is referencing was certainly one of our more eventful dinner parties, that's for sure. I wanted to come over and assure you that, no matter what Nicolo says, he owes you a blood debt."

I liked that he didn't automatically try to hit on Ren.

"What's that," she asked.

"You saved his life. He owes you a favor. Anything you want or need at any time. He can't refuse it. Even something extreme, like you need a particular person to go missing. Refusal would lead to shunning by all the other families. I know his older brother. If he shamed his family like that, he would kill him. Everyone in this room would vouch for what you did. He's just an ignorant bastard and a sore loser."

"Thank you," Ren said.

Romeo started to turn away, then paused. "Do you two go to Wayward?"

"Yes."

"This is a long shot, but do you happen to know someone by the name of Myles?"

Ren and I looked at one another. "Why," I finally asked.

If this had anything to do with Owen, then Nash and Lawerence were going to lose their minds.

Romeo rubbed at his chin. "My future sister-in-law goes there, and she seems to have a fangirl-level-obsession over someone named Myles. I'm just looking out for her."

Ren laughed. "Is her name Alex?"

Romeo narrowed his eyes. "Yes...please don't tell me someone gave her a lighter or that she's already burned something down?"

Ren's brows drew together in confusion as she shook her head.

"I wouldn't know anything about that, but you don't have to worry about Myles."

"How do you know?"

She smiled. "Trust me, he is not a threat. I have firsthand knowledge of the situation."

"On second thought, maybe I don't want to know," Romeo said, and Ren laughed.

"The break is over. Please take your seats," Harrison announced.

We walked arm-in-arm back to the table. When I sat down, I tugged on Ren's hand. She sat on my lap, and I kissed her while we waited for the other players to be seated. I could feel the stares and broke off before Harrison asked us to stop.

Ren stood and walked over to the couch, and sat down, smiling. Meanwhile, I paid very close attention to Christov's reaction. He was certainly pissed, but was it a fatherly concern or something more disturbing? By the look on his face, I guessed option two. That didn't mean he wasn't her father, just that he was a disgusting piece of garbage.

The rounds went by quickly, and I purposely folded or lost the odd hand before reeling in twice as much.

After another hour, Alessio and I sat down for a final deal.

We'd already pushed all but a million each in for this moment. My heart was beating hard even though I was ninety-nine percent sure that I held the winning hand.

The flop showed three, nine, ten, and a queen on the turn. The dealer flipped a jack on the river.

"Possible straight. Please place your final bets," the dealer said.

Excitement flowed through my body, but I managed to keep my face neutral and my eyes on my opponent.

"All in." Alessio pushed the rest of his chips to the center of the table.

"Call," I said, matching him.

The dealer turned to Alessio, who smirked as he revealed an eight and a king. It was a hand that would win most of the time, but not tonight.

"Straight, king high," the dealer said before turning to me.

Smiling, I flipped over my king and Alessio's smile faded some. The room held its breath as I slowly turned over my second card.

"Fuck," Alessio swore.

"Straight, ace high. Congratulations, you win," the dealer said.

Ren squealed and ran at me. I stood up and caught her just as she wrapped her arms around my neck and kissed me. The thrill of the win and having her here with me was addictive.

"My lucky rabbit," I said against her lips.

"I did nothing. That was so impressive," she said and showed me her hand. "I have no nails left."

"Congratulations, son. Remind me never to play against you again," Alessio said, extending his hand.

With a firm grip, I knew that all these men would remember my name. I'd just become a much bigger fish.

A single pair of hands began clapping, and we all turned to see Christov standing off to the side.

"Bravo. Well done. But why don't we make the night more interesting?"

"No, I think I'm good," I said.

"Come now, you don't even know what I was going to say," Christov countered.

"I already know that whatever you offer, I'm not interested. But let's hear it."

Ren stiffened beside me as Christov stepped closer, his eyes vicious like a raptor as he stared at her.

"Thirty million, and all you have to do is put her in the pot, no money," Christov said and nodded at Ren.

"Not a chance. There is no amount of money you could offer to get me to accept that deal."

"What do you say, Lilya? Do you want to get to know your father?"

His voice ended with a growl that had Ren pressing closer to my side.

"No," she said, still holding her ground.

"I could have you plucked from that fancy school of yours. There is still time for me to take you back to Russia, where you belong."

It was a fucking good thing I didn't have my gun.

"Enough!" Dimitri yelled as he stepped out of the washroom. "I warned you."

Christov turned on Dimitri.

"This is still about poker. I offered to play for her. If it wasn't for you, I would have gotten to know my daughter in the first place."

Dimitri marched forward until the two of them were nose to nose.

"Maybe if you hadn't put your wife in the hospital so many times, she wouldn't have asked for help to escape your reach."

"It wasn't your place to interfere," Christov snarled.

"Yulianna was my family. I would do it a million times over to keep her away from you. And I'll make sure you never get your hands on Ren, either. Guards!" Men poured into the room. "Make sure that Mr. Ivankov leaves the country and spread the word. From this day forward, he is a kill-on-sight target."

"You piece of shit. I'll fucking kill you for what you did," Christov yelled as the guards grabbed him. Then he turned to Ren. "You're mine, and I will take you home where you belong. Whether you want to go or not."

Pulling Ren behind me, I lunged at Christov, and my fist connected with his jaw, rocking his head to the side. He was lucky that I didn't get a good angle, or he would've lost teeth. I grabbed the front of his suit and glared into his eyes.

"Over my dead body. If you come near her ever again, you'll wish you never met me."

"Get this asshole out of here," Dimitri ordered. We could hear Christov swearing as they dragged him into the elevator.

Ren stared at the door before her sad eyes found mine. She didn't have to say it. I knew she was thinking about her mother and how close she'd come to being raised by that man.

Walking over, I pulled Ren into a hug.

"I'll never let him near you. None of us will," I whispered in her ear. "I promise you. He's a dead man if he tries."

OCTOBER 16 – THURSDAY 11:44 PM

Ren

No amount of hot water could rid me of the cold feeling in the pit of my stomach. Christov's face as he glared at me had been full of malice. As if I was the one to cause all the problems in his life, and he was silently promising pain. It oozed off him and stuck to me like grime. There was no washing away the image of him—or the thought of all the things he had done to my mum.

Tears trickled down my cheeks and mingled with the stream. So many revelations tonight and all of them hurt for different reasons.

Not only was Christov still alive, but Dimitri had been the one to help my mum and me run away, and all this time, he'd been keeping the secret.

Will I ever be free from all the lies?

"Are you okay in here?"

I glanced over my shoulder to the partially open door at the sound of Liam's voice.

"Just five more minutes."

"Okay, take your time."

He closed the door, and I slumped against the wall. Tonight was supposed to be a big step toward the three of us being together. Liam had gotten us this massive suite—that was bigger than a house—and I couldn't even get out of the shower because my head was a mess.

I didn't want to be an Ivankov, and I didn't care what was on any paperwork. That man wasn't my father.

With that belief firmly in my head, I shut off the water and grabbed my towel. I dried myself and then wrapped my hair up before slipping on a pair of cute sleep clothes. I hadn't packed for anything sexy, and honestly, it didn't matter now.

Brushing my teeth, I stared at myself in the mirror, trying to find the parts of myself that resembled Christov. He was a monster...so what did that make me? Was this how Myles and Nash felt all the time? Knowing that someone so evil had helped create you. I couldn't help wondering, what if I ended up like that? Had he always been this way, or did someone turn him into what I saw?

After spitting out the toothpaste and rinsing, I took a couple of pain meds for my impending headache and left the bathroom. I wandered across the bedroom, not really paying attention to anything other than the continuous loop of vitriol from Christov. I suddenly hated how I analyzed every word from every angle.

Making my way out into the sitting area, I finally looked up. Tears filled my eyes as I gazed at the Kings. They stopped talking, and my heart swelled. Myles rushed me like a linebacker and picked me up, holding me tight. The towel fell from my hair, but I didn't care.

"I'm so sorry, Snowflake. God, I'm so sorry," he said, and I buried my head into the side of his neck as a fresh wave of tears silently fell.

Weakness wasn't going to get me anywhere, but I needed one night to process and let myself feel it all. Myles slowly lowered me to the floor and wiped the tears away. No one said anything, and I took a deep breath before facing the rest of the guys. Even with them all here, this place could've easily hosted a party. Blake and Nash sat in two of the four leather chairs while Liam and Theo were on the couch.

It was Theo who broke the silence as he patted the cushion between him and Liam.

"Come sit down. Liam was just filling us in."

"Do ya want somethin' to drink," Myles asked.

"Coffee, please."

"I thought ya might say that," he said, walking into the kitchen out of sight.

Sitting on the couch, I leaned into Theo before locking eyes with Liam.

"Thank you."

"I keep telling you what my job is," he said with a teasing smirk.

"I don't know how you and Myles do it, Nash," I said, and he looked up.

Despite the neutral expression on his face, his eyes were filled with every emotion under the sun. I'd only gotten a glimpse of what it would've been like to live in fear my entire life, and I honestly didn't know if I would be as strong as they were. My mum raised me to be, and I liked to think I was, but I knew what Christov would have done if the room hadn't been filled with people. He hadn't been able to touch me tonight, but his viciousness made my skin crawl.

"Do what?"

"Tolerate an insane parent. I...I thought I understood, but I didn't, not until tonight."

"You learn to live with it."

Nash shrugged. It was so him to brush it off, but he'd confessed that he hardly slept. I doubted that I knew even a scratch of the disturbing and evil things that Lawrence had done to Nash...or made him do.

I shook my head at him. "But you shouldn't have to. It's not right."

He smirked. "Why do you think I do the shit I do, Princess? Every move I make is to get out from under my father and to be a better leader than him. I can't just shoot him. If it was that easy I would've done it the moment I knew how to fire a gun. Sometimes, it's better to live with the devil you know than the one you don't."

"That's sad."

"It is what it is. I have no time in my day to feel sorry for myself, and you shouldn't either."

"Give her a break, Nash," Blake said.

Nash rolled his eyes and looked away but didn't argue.

"Christov is unhinged. I don't know if he was always like that, but it was obvious that if Dimitri hadn't ordered him out...."

"Then, I would've killed him," Liam said.

Not caring about the rules or punishments, I placed my hand on his, and he linked our fingers together.

"I know, but he was making a statement to Dimitri as much as he was to me."

"That's true. Christov got on his private jet, and it took off. But it won't stop him from entering the country from another location," Liam said.

Another wave of icy dread slid down my spine, and I shivered at the thought of having to see him ever again.

"Do you think he can really force me to leave Wayward," I asked as Myles walked back in with a hot cup of coffee in his hands. I took it from him, and he sat down on the arm of the couch.

"No, or he would've already done it," Nash said.

"You're sure about that," I asked, and he nodded.

"I am. I know how Dean Henry works...or as much as anyone does. The two things he takes very seriously are protecting his students and following the rules. If Christov had the right to remove you, then the dean would hand you over. The fact that he hasn't tells me that Christov has tried and failed or it was a threat to scare you," Nash said, growing visibly frustrated.

"Fuck," he growled, bursting from his seat.

"When I spoke to the dean about you coming with us to meet your family, I could tell there was something he wasn't saying. He tried to tell me, but he talked in riddles and hidden meanings. I'd bet my life that he knew Christov was close."

"Do we really think that it's him? I mean, everything that I could find said that Christov was dead."

"You think this is a look-alike," Theo asked.

I shrugged before taking a sip of the coffee. As soon as it touched my lips, I felt better. There was just something calming about it for me despite the caffeine rush.

"Do we know if he has a twin," I asked.

Theo and Blake looked at one another.

"Hadn't thought about that. I'll see what I can find."

"I hate to say this after the last conversation with Mom, but...do you think she knows anything about this," Blake asked, and Theo slowly shook his head.

"Anything is possible, but she would warn us if she knew he was around or alive at the very least, especially if he was a threat. Mom might have her secrets, but I don't believe for a second she would put any of us in harm's way on purpose."

"True."

"Although anything is possible, it's hard to fake the emotion I saw in his eyes. He blames Dimitri for you and your mom escaping," Liam said.

"It doesn't matter if he's the fucking Tooth Fairy. What matters is that he revealed himself, and we have one more enemy on the board. They are piling up, and we need more protection. The rest is inconsequential at this point," Nash growled as he stomped out of the room.

We watched him disappear down the hall.

"What's wrong with him," Blake asked as a door slammed.

"No idea. The situation with Christov is shitty, but he broke his best time at a qualifier today. You would think that he'd be happy," Theo answered.

"I'm going to go talk to him," I said, standing, but Myles snatched my wrist.

"Are ya sure that's a good idea? When he's pissed, we tend ta stay away."

Smiling, I gave him a quick kiss.

"Oddly, I'm probably the only person who can talk to him right now without getting punched," I said.

"She's right about that," Liam said, backing me up.

"Alright." Myles let go, and I followed after Nash.

There was only one closed door in the hallway and I heard his voice. I put my ear to it, but the conversation was still muffled. Nash turned from the window and looked at me as I walked in without knocking.

"Yeah, that works. I'll keep an eye out for them. Thanks," he said before hanging up the phone. "You would make a terrible spy or stalker," he said, putting the phone in his pocket.

"I'll make sure to scratch them off my list of possible job opportunities," I said, closing the door. "You okay?"

"Shouldn't I be asking you that," Nash asked, and I shrugged. "I'm fine. I just needed to make a couple calls. Dimitri is sending guards to escort us to the state line and then I have more guards meeting the bus on the other side to follow us back to Wayward."

"I'm turning into a right pain in the ass," I teased, and Nash smiled.

"Princess, you were always a pain in my ass. But now you're a pain in everyone's ass."

I laughed, but sadly, it wasn't far off the mark.

"Dimitri wants me to stay here in California. He says it's the safest place for me."

Nash scowled as he walked closer. I'd never known anyone who could flip a switch so quickly on their emotions. Dealing with Nash was like riding the fastest rollercoaster with large hills, steep drops, and sharp turns that plunged you into darkness.

It didn't matter how much I screamed—he yanked me along for the ride, and it was clear he was never going to stop.

"That is not happening," he said.

It almost sounded like a threat as he stepped into my personal space. Nash forced me to step back until I bumped into the wall. I'd already told Dimitri no. My life was at Wayward, and I refused to hide under his protection. But everything about Nash ordering me around made me want to push his buttons.

"What if I want to?"

Nash braced both arms on the wall, trapping me in place as his eyes bore into mine. My body quaked, but it had nothing to do with fear and felt twice as dangerous.

"I'm not letting you stay here, Princess. If I have to drag you back to Wayward with me, I will."

Defiance flared brightly in my chest. But before I could argue, he lifted the chain around my neck with one finger and showed it to me.

"You going to leave all this behind? Do the guys mean so little to you?"

"The guys or you?"

He smirked. "We're one and the same," he said, leaning in so his lips were inches from mine. "You're just fucking with me, aren't you," he asked, and the corner of my mouth turned up. "You're too much fucking trouble, Princess."

I gasped as his hand wrapped around my throat.

"And yet...you want me," I said, and his blue eyes darkened.

"No, I want to be free of you."

"You make no sense," I breathed out, shuddering as his lips grazed mine.

"You make me make no sense," he said.

That was the first Nash comment that I fully understood. He made me feel the same way. Nothing was logical, and yet, in some screwed-up way, we fit. I hated him and wanted him simultaneously. He drove me insane, but I couldn't stop thinking about him. His touch was as toxic to me as a poisonous flower, and yet...here I was, following him into this room where we were alone once again.

"I think I'm addicted to your insanity, Princess."

Nash nipped at my bottom lip, and I cursed myself as I slid my hands under his hoodie to touch his abs. His skin was feverish, and anyone with half of a brain cell knew this was a terrible idea. I should leave, but I couldn't get my body to move. He looked down to where my fingers grazed over his six-pack and then back up to my face.

"Touching me is a bad idea, Princess. A really bad fucking idea," he growled.

"Why's that?"

His eyes spelled out his desires. He wanted to rip the clothes from my body and fuck me against the wall, and he didn't care if the guys heard us. The knock on the door beside us broke the spell that had been cast on the room.

My heart was still racing in my chest while Nash looked ready to kill.

"Everything okay in there," Liam asked.

"No, I'm fucking killing her quietly. Give me five more minutes, and you can clean up the body," Nash said.

I tapped his arm, and Nash reluctantly let go of my throat. Ducking around him, I opened the door.

"Yes, we're fine. I think I need some sleep. My brain is loopy and I'm not thinking clearly," I said, even though I knew it had nothing to do with lack of sleep and everything to do with the king of the Kings.

Nash grabbed my arm before I could escape out the door. "Remember what I said."

Looking at his hand, I raised an eyebrow.

"Nash, of course, I'm going back. All my painting stuff is there," I teased.

He smiled and shook his head at me.

"Yes, I'm sure that's it," he said as I walked down the hall with Liam.

This was a dangerous game and I didn't need Nash or anyone else pointing that out to me. Every day I tried to remove myself from this poisonous world, only to be sucked deeper.

Maybe it was time to embrace the absurdity like everyone else because swimming against the current...was fucking tiring.

Chapter 49

Nash

I scrolled through the business reports and smirked. My father had put another five percent of Collier Enterprises up for purchase. Between my three shell companies, I'd gobbled it all up. Smoothing over the issues in Ireland would cost large sums to the families, but that was what he deserved for trusting someone as off the rails as Owen to do business for him. It was like dropping a crocodile in a pen of sheep. What the hell did he expect would happen?

My phone dinged, and I picked it up, smiling at the notification that the transfer was complete and the stock was mine. It vibrated again with a text from Mr. Genovese, who I labeled as G in my phone.

G: Is everything on schedule?

N: Yes, just as I promised. Purchased another lot tonight.

G: Good. Handcuffing him and proving you can handle your position is the smart play. Anything else you need?

N: What can you tell me about Christov Ivankov?

G: What do you want to know?

N: Is he a real threat? Dangerous?

G: Yes. Always has been.

Well, that was comforting. I waited for more, but nothing came. Tapping my chin, I thought of the next question while trying to dance around what I really wanted to know.

N: Did Yulianna really marry Christov?

G: Yes

N: Why do the newspapers say he's dead?

There was a long pause and I wished that I had waited to have this discussion in person. I'd be able to see a lot more in his expressions, but the die was already cast. Little bubbles appeared and then disappeared.

G: Who are you asking for, yourself or
Lilya?

N: Does it matter? When she wakes up,
she's going to want answers. She won't
stop hunting, which will put her in danger.
I'm trying to make sure that doesn't
happen. She's terribly annoying like that.

G: I can only tell you what I know and
then what I suspect happened.

N: Okay

G: Yulianna ran from Christov with Lilya,
or Ren as you call her, not long after her
fourth birthday. Before she left, she shot
Christov and his mistress, who had on
more than one occasion tried to kill her.
She'd managed to foil all of their
attempts while she planned her escape.

I shook my head, confusion setting in.

N: Wait…Christov wanted to kill Yulianna
and Ren before she left him?

G: At that point, it was just Yulianna.
Now, I don't know, considering I didn't
know he was alive.

Jesus Christ. I closed my eyes and sucked in a deep breath, happier than ever that the hallway was filled with Mikhailov guards.

N: Okay, so he had a few screws loose
then. I get that, but what about this
rising-from-the-dead routine? How did he
manage to stay hidden and why
appear now?

> G: I have no idea. But if I was going to
> guess, he or his family didn't want
> Yulianna or anyone else to know that he
> lived. It's much easier to hunt someone
> when they don't think you're after them.

Wasn't that the truth?

> G: I did some digging after your earlier
> call, and I found out that he's been using
> an alias. He also had a son with his
> mistress before she died.

Great, another generation of insanity, just what we all needed. I cringed. The same could be said of me and Myles, and so many others. There was hope, it was just unlikely if Christov raised him.

> N: What's the name?

> G: Yuriy Nikitovich. He and his son are in
> the US. Dean Henry assures me that he's
> not enrolled at Wayward.

Well, that answered that question. Dean Henry knew about Christov. I wanted to curse and throw my phone, but I took a deep breath and focused. That name sounded familiar, but from where?

> N: What's the son's name?

I ran through all the guys who worked for me, wondering if I'd hired this guy and didn't even know he was the enemy in disguise.

> G: Sabastian

My jaw dropped. Fucking Hawking Shores. That fucking piece

of shit. I slammed my laptop closed. I knew I hated him for more than his fast swim times.

G: You still there?

N: Yes. I know who that is. I'll take care of him.

G: Be careful, Nash. You already have enemies closing in on all sides. It might be best not to make a new one just yet.

Fuck he sounded like Dean Henry, but he was right. Before I shot him, I needed to know his plan so I could lure him into a trap.

N: I'll collect more information first.

Locking my phone, I sat there in the darkness, staring at the glowing green numbers on the microwave in the kitchen. A door opened down the hallway and drew my attention to a yawning Ren. She rubbed her eyes but didn't notice me. Slowly standing so I didn't make any noise, I crept along behind her.

Ren moved over to the sink and grabbed a glass while I hid behind the partition and leered at her like a stalker. We really needed to work with her on situational awareness. After she drank her fill, I followed her back the way she came. I was about to make my move when she surprised me. Narrowly missing her fist, I managed to grab her wrist and yanked her into my body with a waltz-like spin.

She yelped, but I clamped my other hand over her mouth and pushed her up against the wall. Ren bit my finger, and I groaned. I fucking loved it when she did that.

"Nsssh?" Came the muffled question. "I'm gonna kwill ewe," she mumbled, making me chuckle.

"You should be more careful, Princess. You never know what evil is lurking in the dark," I whispered. Letting her go, she turned around and glared at me.

"What the hell is wrong with you," she whispered through clenched teeth. Her hands balled into fists.

I shrugged and walked away. "Not even God knows," I said.

It was safer to put space between us, but Ren couldn't be a normal girl and stomp off angry. She just kept coming at you. I felt her following me and pretended that I didn't care as I flopped down on the couch.

"Fine, what are you doing awake? Let's start with that."

"Just doing a little illegal insider trading. How about yourself," I asked, leaning back with my hands behind my head.

"Something far less nefarious, apparently," she said. "Wait, it's not even four in the morning."

"Thank you, Captain Obvious," I said.

Ren looked like she wanted to leap on me. Fuck, that wasn't a bad idea.

"Do you always have to be such an asshole?"

"Do you always have to state the obvious?"

She crossed her arms. I loved her furious expression and the way her long hair draped over her shoulders. There was a sliver of light coming in through the curtain that made her hair glow. Something was wrong with my head because even that was a fucking turn-on.

"You're impossible. I give up. I'm going back to bed," Ren said, unfolding her arms.

I should've let her walk away.

But I never claimed to be smart when it came to her. I grabbed her wrist, and with a quick tug, she squeaked like a mouse and landed, straddling my lap. Gripping her ass, I pulled her closer. Ren's eyes went wide as she came into contact with my cock. I'd been hard since she stepped outside the bedroom. It didn't help that we were both wearing flimsy boxers with easy access.

"Nash," she growled at me, and I had to push aside the surging need enough to think properly.

"I know. We can't do this."

My mouth watered with her hard nipples in my face. The little peaks practically called my name as they poked through her tank top. It was painful, but I let her go, figuring that she would jump up and run away. But she didn't.

"You really need to go," I said.

Ren didn't move. Instead, her eyes roamed over my face. Incapable of keeping my hands to myself for very long, I ran them through her hair before cupping her face.

"You should go. I want you so bad. I don't trust myself," I whispered, drawing her lips closer to mine.

She didn't fight me, though her eyes called me every swear in the book. As soon as our lips touched, I knew there was no way I was letting her leave this couch—even if all we did was sleep. I'd spent countless nights awake, staring at my ceiling and thinking of her. Wishing I could go back and fix what I fucked up in Seattle.

"I hate her, Nash," Ren said. Softly moaning as I kissed her deeper, teasing her tongue with mine. "Why are you doing this? Anyone else...."

"I can't marry Vicky," I said, avoiding the emotion bubbling in my chest like a deadly pit of quicksand ready to trap us both.

"What are you saying," Ren asked, her fingers doodling on the back of my neck and driving me near crazy.

"I'm saying...I don't want her."

"That's not enough when you sign a contract, Nash."

"I don't love her."

"You don't love her, and you don't want her?"

I shook my head, and Ren licked her lips. God, that was fucking sexy.

"Are you saying what I think you're saying," Ren asked.

Her body melted into mine as we kissed. I broke away, panting, and touched my forehead to hers.

"I'm saying that I don't love her, and I can't marry her. Don't make me spell it out...."

Ren smiled before kissing me again.

My whole body tingled as she wiggled on my lap, and I slid my hands under her top and over her soft, heated skin. For so long, I'd promised myself that I would never travel down this path again. Never venture near it, no matter what the hell happened, and it had been easy. Girls came and went, but not Princess.

My mistake was that very first touch. I hadn't realized the danger the little, white-haired beauty posed. She unwittingly lured me in and was very aptly named. Lilya...like the lily-of-the-valley, she was as beautiful as she was deadly. And like a slow-moving toxin, she spread through my system until no antidote could save me. Ren moaned into my mouth and dug her nails into my shoulders. She might as well be clawing into my soul because no matter what I did or tried, I couldn't escape her clutches.

One by one, my pieces fell. My last holdout was the cold stone wall of Liam, but even he crumbled under her touch. I was left alone and longing as I bobbed along on an ice floe of my own making.

"Do you want me, Princess?"

"I'm scared to say yes," she admitted, and I knew exactly what she meant. She held way too much power over me.

Gripping a handful of hair, I peeled her off me. Her chest heaved, and I traced my fingers up the center of her body. Ren shuddered under my touch as I pushed her top out of the way and softly played over one nipple and then the other.

"You fucking terrify me. Does that make us even?"

"Yes," she breathed and then moaned as I licked a line over her ribcage to her nipple.

My cock strained in my boxers, and the semblance of control that I clung to slipped away as she threaded her fingers through my hair.

Taking a deep breath, I opened my fist, and she slowly sat up. If I'd thought for even a second that there was a way out for me...it died as her liquid-silver eyes locked with mine.

"You're mine, Princess. I meant it the first time I said it."

She picked up my arm and traced my newest tattoo.

"Will you ever tell me why you're such a fucking disaster," Ren asked.

I smirked at the question. "One day...I promise. One day."

"You better go," I said, nodding toward the bedroom she'd been in with Myles and Blake. "I don't want to be blamed for you caving and hating yourself for it."

Ren looked downright devious as she smiled, and I no longer knew if I had rubbed off on her or if she had on me.

"You'd be blamed no matter what," she said, making me smile.

My eyes rolled back in my head as she slipped her hand under the waistband of my boxers and gripped my shaft.

"Fuck," I said and lifted my hips high enough to free myself.

"Shh," she whispered against my lips.

"I don't care if they hear," I said.

"But I do."

Pulling back enough that I could look into her eyes, I tried to decipher what that meant.

"Do you not want this? If so, you need to stop touching me and run. Lock a door, maybe two."

She shook her head. "No, that's not what I mean. I want this moment to be us, no interruptions, no one trying to join, just...us. I'm too emotionally beaten right now for anything more."

Smoothing back her hair, I slowly wound it around my wrist and kissed her hard. She couldn't have said anything sweeter to my ears. I was a greedy fucking prick, and I wanted her all to myself. That was never going to happen, but for right now, she was mine. All mine.

"I'll be quiet," I said and then bit my lip.

The sneaky witch moved the flowy boxers out of the way and

positioned herself over my cock. My head fell back, and my fingers dug into her hips as she lowered the rest of the way down. She was so goddamn tight.

"Oh god, Nash. I hate you so much for doing this to me," she breathed in my ear.

"The feeling is mutual, Princess."

Ren wrapped her arms around my neck, and I slowly devoured her mouth, trying to tell her through touch all the secrets I was keeping. I couldn't just tell her how I felt, so I kissed her softer than ever before. It killed me that showing any feelings toward her put her in more danger. None of the words that should've been said between us came out. I wanted to keep things like this for as long as possible. No walls, no bitterness or anger, and nothing else mattered.

Even though it wasn't my nature, I let Ren pick the pace and shuddered every time she bounced on my dick. At this angle, I was buried so much deeper, and her whimpers of pleasure would be engrained in my brain forever.

Ren's pussy squeezed me, and her body shook as she moaned in my ear. She came around my cock, soaking me, and I wrapped my arms around her tighter as I rode out her orgasm.

"That's it...do it again...come all over me again," I growled low even as my body tensed.

Ren collapsed with her head on my shoulder as her body went lax. "I can't," she breathed.

"You can," I said and rolled us over so she was on her back.

"Oh god," Princess gasped as I fucked her faster.

"You're getting too loud, Princess," I teased, pressing my hand over her mouth. I thrust into her again, and her whole body twitched.

"Fuck you feel incredible." Her moans grew louder under my hand as I pumped into her hard enough to drive her into the cushions.

"You drive me insane, Princess," I growled and forced her head to the side so I could bite down on the soft skin of her throat. She shivered, nails digging into my bare arms, and unable to hold it back anymore, I came, groaning into the side of her neck as she came with me. Ren's body flexed up into mine, her eyes fluttering closed. There was no sexier sight.

All the pent-up anger, fear, and worry evaporated. It might only be for a minute or five. However long this feeling lasted, I was going to ride the wave. My hand slid from Ren's mouth, and she gasped but held me just as tight as when we first started.

Releasing her neck, I kissed my mark and glared at the stunning necklace that Liam had gotten her. Fucker put a collar on her. I knew what that meant, and picturing Princess on her knees while he ordered her around made me want to kill him as much as it turned me on.

"You're staying right here with me for the rest of the night," I said, pulling my boxers back up into place.

"But...."

"No fucking buts. You're mine tonight. You'll probably find a well-deserved reason to hate me tomorrow, so for tonight, you stay with me."

She snickered. "That's probably true."

Reaching for a blanket, I laid on my back. Ren wiggled down between me and the back of the couch with her head on my chest and an arm wrapped around my waist.

"You're not going to tell me that I'm a mistake in two hours, are you," she asked, making me smile.

"No. You were never a mistake. A pain in my fucking ass, yes, but never a mistake."

Princess yawned. "Okay...I can live with being a pain in your ass," she mumbled, and then I felt her relax as she fell asleep.

Mr. Genovese might kill me, but I couldn't stay away from her. I just couldn't, and I'd deal with the consequences even if it meant him putting a gun to my head. I could handle almost anything else, but not that, I couldn't lie to her, not anymore. Halloween. I just had to make it to Halloween.

My eyes grew heavy, and for only the second time in years, I felt real sleep pulling at me and sucking me under as I held Ren.

OCTOBER 23 – THURSDAY 3:15 PM

Ren

"Hey. Wake up."

I jerked awake and realized I was still on the couch with Nash.

"What's going on," I asked, blinking as I stared into Liam's eyes.

"Fuck off, man," Nash grumbled. I felt like a rag doll as he rolled me over and held me to his chest.

"It's eight-thirty the guys will be up soon. So, unless you want everyone to know about you two…you need to get up," Liam said.

"I don't fucking care," Nash groaned. "And turn off the light."

"Nash, we should probably get up. I need to tell Myles and Blake before they see this," I said, running my fingers up and down his arm.

"Let them see. I need sleep." He pulled the blanket up over our heads, and I couldn't help but smile. I'd never seen him like this before.

"Fine, act like a child. I'm not stepping in if Myles loses his mind."

"He's not going to care," Nash growled and snuggled closer. I never took Nash for a cuddler. It was another shock and revelation to my system.

"You need to get up and make sure that whatever you have planned for Halloween and...she who shall not be named...gets resolved before bringing the rest of the guys in on this," I whispered.

"Ugh...why do you have to use logic? It's too early for logic," Nash said, burying his head in the side of my neck and making me laugh.

"Technically, it's late for you. You'd normally be in the pool by now." He sighed and slowly sat up.

"Fine, I'm up. I'm up."

"Earth to Ren?"

Myles sat next to me, pulling me out of the daze I'd been in thinking about California. A lot had happened in such a short visit. Most pressing was *who* had happened. He spent every class we had together, making it completely impossible to ignore him since we got back.

"Sorry, Myles. I was lost in space."

"What were ya thinkin' about? Me, I hope," he said.

My guilt notched up a little more even as I smiled. Maybe waiting for Nash to handle whatever he needed to do on Halloween was a bad idea. Keeping Myles, Blake, and Theo in the dark felt like a betrayal to all of us.

"I'm always thinking about you," I said, and his face lit up. God I loved him so much. His amber eyes made me feel warm all over.

"I need to go talk to Mr. Martelli. I'll be back," he said, giving me a quick kiss before jumping up from his seat. Myles hadn't even reached the front when Nash moved over from the table across the aisle and sat down beside me.

"What are you doing," I asked and then sucked in a gasp as he gripped my leg.

"I don't think I can wait until Halloween," Nash said, vocalizing what I'd been thinking.

"Yeah, I was just thinking I need to talk to the guys and clear the air," I said.

Nash slid his hand up my thigh, and I almost fell off the tall stool.

"That's not what I meant. They can wait. I can't.

Glaring at him, he lifted a brow in response.

"No."

"Come on."

"No," I said again and looked around to make sure no one was paying attention. Myles was still distracted by Mr. Martelli. "It's one more week. We either tell them sooner, and you tell Vicky it's over, or we wait until your big reveal.

Instead of agreeing or backing off, Nash grabbed me by the waist and dragged me off the seat onto his lap.

"I can fuck you right now, and no one will ever know...if you keep extra quiet," he whispered in my ear. "Be a good girl, Princess, and sit on my cock. Fuck, I miss the feel of you and listening to your sweet little moans as you come all over me, " he said, and I shivered.

Nash shifted just enough that I could feel how hard he was pressing into my ass.

Jesus, I'd created a monster. He brought a whole new meaning to the saying giving-an-inch-and-taking-a-mile and yet I couldn't deny that just the thought made me wet. Damn him.

"Let go, Nash." Turning my head, I glared over my shoulder. "This is not okay until all the guys know." He rolled his eyes.

"Myles won't care. I'm pretty sure he's expecting it," Nash answered, but his grip on me loosened.

"He will if you don't pull a magic trick out of your ass on Halloween or if he thinks you've hurt me. What happened to nothing coming between you and the guys? You're placing me in a horrible position."

"Pretty sure I didn't force you into bed with me."

"Nash, so help me God. You're pissing me off, and if I lose it in here, everyone will know everything. You know what I'm getting at, eh?" I hissed under my breath.

He annoyingly chuckled.

"Fine," he mumbled, letting go not a second too soon. My feet touched the floor, and Myles turned around.

Myles wandered back to us with a big smile on his face and clapped Nash on the shoulder.

"I'm getting an A, man, and it's all because of Snowflake."

The Kings really needed to learn boundaries. He grabbed me and dipped me like we'd just finished a dance. Butterflies soared in my stomach as we kissed, but they were swatted down by the thought of keeping this secret with Nash even one more second.

As Myles pulled me back up, there was no mistaking the dark look and jealousy swimming in Nash's eyes. He crossed his arms and looked away while Myles hugged me. I wanted to throw up. What had I done? This wasn't me.

"I'm so happy for you. That means you have two so far this year," I said as he pulled back with the happiest smile on his face.

"I know, and ta think that before ya arrived, I'd been close to failing everythin'. I don't know how ta thank ya."

Myles cupped my face, and I glanced toward Mr. Martelli. He wasn't paying attention with only a minute left in class, but Myles took the hint and grabbed my hand instead.

His ring felt heavy on my finger. Fuck...Nash had turned me into something I despised. I hated lies and secrets, and now, I was the lying liar of lies.

I'd always been open and honest, especially with Myles and Blake. The first time with Nash in Seattle had been bad all on its own. I would've told them, but the hurt Nash had caused was too much. So I kept quiet to avoid potentially doing exactly what Liam was worried about—blowing up their whole friendship. But this... this just felt wrong.

The bell rang, saving me from another second of betrayal. Or so I thought...Nash grabbed his bag and was back glued to my side.

"Maybe I should get some extra tutoring. It's really hard right now," Nash said, and my cheeks heated.

I was going to kill him. But he would just laugh as I did it and roll around in the blood like a pig in slop.

"Right? I thought I was doomed. I can't believe how much harder it is. But having Snowflake's help is a huge relief," Myles said, and I wanted to smack my head.

Please don't let either of them say harder for a third time. Please, please, please.

"Well, I could definitely use some relief. Anything to alleviate this pressure," Nash said, smirking.

I side-eyed Nash, but despite the glimpses of a more mature man that I'd gotten, he hadn't changed at all. Nope, instead, Nash leaned into it even more.

He wrapped his arm around my shoulders and hit me with a pathetic pout.

"What do you say, Princess? Wanna help relieve all this pressure? The build-up feels like it's killing me."

"I think you're being dramatic," I said, and Myles laughed as I wiggled out of Nash's grasp.

"You're the one who believes schoolwork and grades are important. With everything I have going on with my dad, and his dad, and work, it's difficult to focus on anything else. It's getting harder by the second not to explode with this load."

"Help him out," Myles said, and my head twisted so fast I was positive I just gave myself whiplash.

"What?"

"We all need top scores, especially Nash. Work your magic on him like you do for me."

"Yeah, Princess, you can come help me now. I have a very important project that needs your expert touch."

"Um...I don't think...."

"Perfect, I'll grab us dinner and be back in a couple hours. I'm seeing Lip for a short visit, too," Myles said, and his smile lit up his whole face.

"It really is perfect," Nash said, the sexual innuendo thick on every word, just like the rest of this conversation, at least from his side.

It was a very sad day when I was happy to see Vicky sashaying down the path toward the three of us.

"Oh, fuck my life," Nash grumbled under his breath.

"There you are. I've been looking everywhere for you," Vicky said.

Why is everything so dramatic with her?

Nash kept walking, not bothering to stop or acknowledge her. Vicky, unable to take a hint, fell into step beside him.

"I was in class," Nash said, visibly annoyed that Vicky hadn't left. "And now, I'm heading to the dorms to study with Ren."

I'd never come so close to leaping on someone and punching them in my entire life.

"Studying with her...eww, why? You can study with me."

Vicky couldn't be this oblivious. Could she? She was either oblivious or stupid, and I just couldn't figure out which it was.

Myles wrapped his arm around my waist and glared at Vicky.

"Yer the feckin' eww," he said, and she rolled her eyes at him.

"Learn to speak English. Then insult me so I can actually understand you," she snapped back.

I held onto Myles tighter as he tensed.

"Oh shit, Nash, I'm so sorry. I just remembered that I promised Ivy I would help her with something tonight. Now you're free to...do whatever you want with Vicky."

His nostrils flared as he looked at me and then Vicky.

Good, feel that pressure. Jerk.

"Actually, my mom is back from her trip abroad. She wants us to have dinner as a family to talk about the wedding," Vicky said.

I caught Nash's eye and shook my head. I didn't understand this charade. It made no sense to me, and why was a date six days from now so important?

Mysteries I couldn't solve...top of the list...Nash Collier.

"Wait...is it really true? Yer gonna marry the insane slut? I thought that was just a joke."

"Who the hell are you calling a slut," Vicky growled, crossing her arms.

"Ya made fun of me. I thought that was what we were doing now," Myles responded with a glint in his eye.

"You do know you didn't disagree with the fact he called you insane," I asked, but Vicky acted like I hadn't even spoken.

"Enough, all of you. The answer is no to dinner," Nash growled.

Nash sounded just like I had with him. I really wanted to laugh, but a seed of jealousy had been planted. I was elated that he refused to go, but he still had a contract to marry Vicky in place...fuck, it burned my ass, which was ridiculous and ironic considering our history.

"What do you mean, no?"

"No means no," Nash spit out.

"Wow, I thought you didn't know the meaning of the word," I blurted out before I could stop myself. The giddiness I felt as Nash narrowed his eyes at me was simply no equivalent. "Oh, sorry, I didn't mean to interrupt your love fest. Carry on."

"Shut up, Davies. You're such a fucking loser. I have no idea why any of the Kings give you the time of day, let alone four of them," Vicky snarled, and I smiled at her.

"Oh...I guess you haven't heard."

Both Nash and Myles gave me a hard stare. They knew what I was about to say and didn't think it was a good idea. But Vicky would hear about it sooner rather than later, and I wanted to be the one to deliver the message.

"Heard what?"

Damn, it felt good to be on this side of the discussion this time.

"I'm not a Davies...I'm a Mikhailov. You may have heard of them," I said, and her mouth dropped.

"No way, that's not possible."

Stepping forward, I made sure she was looking me in the eyes so she knew it was the truth.

"Oh, it is. It really, really is. Why do you think I got special permission to go to California? You didn't think it had to do with Nash, did you?"

She nibbled her lip, uncertainty in her eyes.

"I could care less about all this hierarchy bullshit that you hold so dear. But if you or any of your wicked bitches come for me again, Vicky...Dean Henry will get a full report for your father. I'm sure that he and Dimitri will have a fabulous conversation about your treatment of me and what your punishment will entail."

Holding her gaze, I smirked.

"Have a great time planning your wedding."

"Nash, are you going to let her talk to me like that," Vicky asked as I marched away.

"Yeah, I am. You keep pushing her buttons, so you deserve whatever you get. And the answer is still no to dinner. I have things to do," Nash said before Myles and I were too far to hear.

"Walk me to my car," Myles asked, and I nodded.

As we got closer to the Shelby, the icky feeling in my stomach became unbearable. Grabbing his hands, I made him look at me. I couldn't keep this from him anymore. I would find a way to make him believe I was fine with Nash marrying Vicky, but I loved and respected Myles too much to keep him in the dark.

"Snowflake, are ya okay?" He smoothed back the wild strands of hair blowing around my face.

"I need to talk to you about something," I said, trying to keep the panic at bay.

"Okay, what is it? Yer scaring me," Myles said, and I licked my lips. "Are ya breaking up wit me?"

"What? No, of course not. I love you so much. I'd never break up with you. Unless you don't want me anymore."

He visibly relaxed and pulled me in for a hug.

"Thank the lord. Yer way too good fir me. I keep expectin' ya to one day wake up and realize that I'm surfing along on this ride but really don't belong."

"Stop that." I held him tighter.

"In that case, just tell me. There is nothing ya can't tell me."

God, I hoped that was true. I opened my mouth, and his phone rang.

"Shite, that's me da. Be very quiet, and don't believe anythin' I say. It's all a lie," he said.

He had no idea how ironic that statement was right now.

"Da? Ya got the picture?"

After the eventful dinner with my new family, we'd bought makeup, wide silver tape, and rope. I'd done a fantastic job applying small bruises down my arms and around my throat from a fictional fight I lost. We'd thrown some water on my face, put tape on my mouth, and tied my wrists before I'd climbed in the tub and thought about every horrible memory I could until I had cried for real. Myles had snapped the photo and sent it to his dad.

He had been sure that we'd hear right away, but it had been radio silence.

When it came to terrifying bad guys, I preferred when they were loud and annoying. Then, you knew where they were and what they were up to, at least. Owen going dark freaked me out more than if he'd texted about his plans to kill me.

I couldn't hear Owen's side of the conversation, but I could guess.

"Aye, I still have her. No, of course, no one knows. Dean Henry thinks she ran off again. Aye, she's a stupid cunt." Myles's eyes were so sad as he mouthed, *I'm sorry.*

It's okay. I mouthed back and squeezed his hand.

"Nah, no one is around. I'm out in the parkin' lot gettin' something from me car. Where are ya? I can come see ya tonight."

That was the worst idea in the world. Myles should never be anywhere near Owen ever again. But the guys never bothered to listen to me...no, of course not. Why listen to reason?

"Aye...okay. That's better. I'll meet ya then. The faster I get rid of her, the better. I don't need the likes of the Curators catchin' wind, ya know?"

Owen's swearing and yelling were loud enough to hear now, but the only two words I could make out were, *fucking* and *Curators.*

"I haven't seen Lawrence. Ya want me to give him a message?" Myles pulled the phone away from his ear as more yelling ensued. "Okay, okay, Da. Sorry, I just thought...." He shook his head, his hand balling into a fist. "Yer right, I should never bother to think."

I hated that man so much. No matter how hard Myles tried to hide it, I saw the pain in his eyes whenever Owen was involved. He'd just gotten rid of Devin, he didn't need this asshole lurking around again.

"Alright, I gotta go. The guys are headin' me way."

Myles hit end, cupped my face, and crashed his lips to mine.

"I'm so sorry for that. Can we talk later? I need to go find Nash."

"Yeah, of course, go for it."

"I love ya, Snowflake."

"I love you, too."

He ran off, and I slumped against his car, staring after him. Would he run away that fast when he found out what I'd done? Or would he chalk it up to knowing it would happen and he had already given me permission?

My heart ached as I walked back to the dorms alone. I hated myself. I could place the blame at Nash's feet all I wanted, but he was right. At the end of the day, I'd willingly slept with him and didn't say anything. That was on me, no matter how righteous my reasons were, and now I had to live with the consequences of my actions.

OCTOBER 24 – FRIDAY 9:01 PM

Liam

This was unbearable. I couldn't believe we had to take off from school for this. Lawrence came back from Ireland and demanded my swearing in take place immediately. But it couldn't be as simple as me handing over a check and then him writing in the book. No, not Lawrence.

We'd been here all day. Me, Nash, Myles, along with my father, Ethan, Ella, and every other family that Lawrence pulled into his cult of insanity. It started with a buffet-style breakfast and socializing, which wasn't too bad. Then, I had to present the money, and since I won more than I needed, I threw in extra to go above and beyond. Everyone seemed thrilled except Lawrence.

He questioned how I got the money. Asked if I borrowed it. Wanted to know if he would find the transaction in my father's books. He even implied I owed a favor to someone now. Lawrence wouldn't be satisfied until he caught me in a lie. But I wasn't lying. It all felt like a bad cop show where he was trying to frame me.

Then we moved on to lunch...and more talking. Only now, it was directed toward the future of our council. This included our ties to Ireland which Lawrence reassured everyone the issues had been dealt with and that the situation was under control. He then moved on to the Mikhailov family and how they would be increasing their required contribution by two percent next year. Nathaniel had given Nash a heads-up that this might happen. He'd pulled his legitimate businesses away from his father and Dimitri was scrambling to make up the lost revenue.

Shit got serious when Lawrence sent away all but his inner circle. He revealed that Dimitri wanted the trafficking business shut down completely because—as much of a cradle-robbing asshole as he was —he wanted nothing to do with the buying and selling of girls. I agreed with him on this, but Lawrence had other plans. He wanted to expand.

We followed him down into the lower levels of the house, where Lawrence kept his prisoners and his ceremony room. There, we found six girls chained to the walls.

Despite his invitation, no one in attendance showed the same excitement as Owen and Devin had in the past. Lawrence played it off as nothing more than a show and tell, but he was pissed, and we would pay for it another time.

The end of the school year couldn't come fast enough, and whatever plan Nash had with Mr. Genovese needed to happen because I wasn't working for him after graduation. I played nice now because my father was stuck, and Lawrence was vindictive enough to hurt my family somehow. But even I had my limits.

The chains rattled as Lawrence's guards dragged the girls to a cell for him to deal with later. It wouldn't surprise me if he sampled them himself first. I fucking despised him. No matter what, Ren couldn't end up in his grasp.

I watched the last of the girls disappear from under my red hood and hated that I was any part of this. Nash had warned me. He tried to explain the horrors that he'd seen since he turned eighteen. It wasn't that I didn't believe him, but I'd always hoped that he was exaggerating.

"Liam Hicks, it's time for you to be sworn in. Step forward," Lawrence said, sounding more deranged than I'd ever heard him.

As I stepped up to the dais, Lawrence's blue eyes glared at me from beneath a red mask. Nothing, not even that, could hide the evil that lurked in him. A skull sat on top of a book cradled protectively in his arms. I cocked my brow, knowing it was real with one look.

"Today, you are reborn. Reborn into a family not only bound by blood but by something much stronger. Bonds that can't be broken, loyalties that will never fade. Only in death will your ties to the Ord na Rithe be severed," he said.

Too bad for him that my bond was broken long ago.

"Hold out your hand."

He pulled out an ornate knife and cut across the center of my outstretched palm. If he expected me to flinch then he was disappointed because I didn't.

My father, in his long robes, stepped up beside me, holding out a chalice to collect my blood. When Lawrence deemed it enough he handed me a white cloth, and I efficiently tied it over the wound. It was a struggle not to roll my eyes and laugh as he dipped his fingers into the blood and drew symbols on my face.

"Since you were unable to offer your pound of flesh and have refused to take of the bounty that was presented to you tonight. I've decided that you will be marked to show your loyalty to the council."

"This was not agreed upon," my father said.

Lawrence backhanded him across the face so hard that his mask flew off and clattered on the stone floor. My father grabbed my arm as I took a step toward Lawrence.

"Mind your next words carefully, or you will find yourself put to death for treason," Lawrence growled.

Looking at my father, I stayed silent, and for once, I was happy he could read me so well. He nodded and lowered his head.

"My apologies, Master," Dad said.

Emmett Hicks being forced to bow down to Lawrence Collier made me sick. He was a vile human being, and I hoped he could feel the walls closing in on him. Lawrence might not know it yet, but he'd just made a grave error.

My father was one of the last holdouts keeping Lawrence well-funded, supplied, and in power. Being a loyal follower of the Collier family for generations, my father had done whatever Lawrence needed, just like his father and grandfather before him. Abandoning tradition was difficult for him, but the look in his eyes just before he lowered his head told a whole new story.

"I will suffer whatever the council sees fit. I'm loyal to you and the Ord na Rithe."

Feeding Lawrence's ego was the fastest way to get this done so we could leave. If I never had to attend another one of these fucked up gatherings, it would be too soon.

"Very well."

His arm rose, and a strange black pot was wheeled in on a metal cart. I couldn't see the man's face, but the black robes and white mask announced that he was one of Lawrence's personal guards.

The cauldron, for lack of a better word, seemed empty except for a metal rod sticking out the top. When Lawrence put on the thick leather glove, I knew what it was. Shit. I liked pain, but this....

The group behind me got restless, their robes rustling as they shifted at the sight of the branding iron Lawrence pulled free. The end glowed a vicious shade of red, and I could feel the heat as he walked toward me.

"Hold out your left arm," he ordered.

He wouldn't get me to break. If that was what Lawrence thought would happen, then he was sadly mistaken. Pulling up the sleeve of the red robe, I turned my arm over to expose the pale skin on the underside.

Lawrence held the brand in the air.

"From this day forward, I decree that all who are true devotees to the Order will receive the Collier crest. You will embrace the name that has always stood for strength and unity. It will be an honor to bear this symbol on your body."

"Yes, Master," everyone chimed.

Lawrence gripped my wrist, and I clenched my hand into a fist. When the metal touched my skin, I gritted my teeth against the sizzle and the white-hot pain. My body shook as the scent of burning flesh filled my nose, but I didn't scream or move as I stared the devil in the eyes.

He pulled the branding iron away from my skin, and I glanced at the bright red Collier shield. I thought of Nash as family, loved him like a brother, but this...this was Lawrence stripping us of our identity. Stealing our family names and making sure that we remembered who owned us. We might not be locked in cells or shackled by the ankles, but we were prisoners nonetheless.

"Today is a great day. Today marks a new beginning for the Order, reestablishing the trust between us and showing unity to the rest of the world. We will not be pushed around, we will not be passed over, and we will no longer be denied a seat at the head council table. I promise that change is on the horizon, power is coming, and I will strike the final deadly blow."

While Lawrence was grandstanding, I caught Nash's eye, and he shook his head. He knew as well as I did what this all meant.

Lawrence might be talking in riddles to the rest, but we knew this was about Ren. He was planning something else and had more up his deceitful sleeve than just marrying her. He was making a play for power.

And he was going to get us all killed.

OCTOBER 24 – FRIDAY 10:58 PM

Nash

"I really wish you would let me do this on my own," I said to Myles, but he shook his head and remained seated on my father's couch. "Fine, be annoying. But if he kills us both and you never get to see Ren again, that's on you."

Myles glared at me. "Yer not doing this alone. Besides, it's to do with my family and the shite they've caused. Sometimes I thank the good lord that Ma isn't alive to see this. As it is, I'm sure she's rollin' in her grave."

Waiting on Lawrence was torture. After Liam's initiation, he claimed he needed to test the new merchandise before it was sold, and we all knew he wasn't talking about the drugs. I wanted nothing to do with trafficking, and it made my blood boil to think he had pulled us further into that world.

Myles and I looked over at the open office door when we heard my father coming down the hall. He was smiling as he walked in. I wasn't surprised, although my stomach rolled at the thought of why...it disgusted me that I came from him.

Lawrence sauntered over to the corner and poured himself a drink before he turned and looked at us.

"I hope you have good news for me," he said.

Myles looked at me and I sighed as I walked over to the mantle above the fireplace and grabbed the *message* from Nathaniel.

"It didn't go the way I thought it would, that's for sure," I said, placing the box down on the desk.

Lawrence eyed the decorative golden M on the top that was far to nice for the purpose of the container.

"What is that?"

"Nathaniel's answer. Apparently, he doesn't respond well to prisoner release requests."

Lawrence sipped his drink and set the crystal glass on the edge of the desk. He was suspicious, and rightfully so. They could've sent a scorpion or something equally poisonous. The Mikhailovs, especially Nathaniel, had a reputation for being vicious.

"Did you explain our situation?"

"I appealed to his sympathetic side as well as his financially acute mind. But he wasn't interested in anything we had to say."

My father growled, slamming his fist down on the desk.

"Fucking, Nathaniel. I can't wait to wipe that smug smile off his face."

"Are you making a move on the Mikhailovs?" I held my breath as I waited for him to answer.

"In a manner of speaking. Let's just say that Vadin Mikhailov wasn't happy to learn that not only is his granddaughter alive, but Dimitri helped to keep her hidden from him."

I swallowed the uneasy feeling, but it just settled in the pit of my stomach.

"I can see how that would be upsetting," I said, keeping my voice even and praying that Myles kept his cool.

Luckily, Lawrence turned his attention back to the box. He

undid the metal clasps, swallowed the last of his drink like a massive shot, and opened it.

He stood still, staring down at the severed dick sitting in satin. I hadn't expected the snort and for him to start laughing. He doubled over, and tears ran down his cheeks while Myles and I stared at one another.

"I guess Owen can forget about Devin ever procreating," he said, sobering.

With a roar, my father picked up the box and heaved it across the room. It crashed into his portrait, and the glass shattered on impact. Myles ducked and covered his head.

"Son of a bitch," Lawrence snarled.

There was rage in his eyes, and my body prepared for an attack. I was used to this look. He was searching for someone to blame. But he was responsible for everything that had happened.

"This will push Owen right over the edge. How the hell am I going to get my hands on him now?"

"We still have one card to play," Myles said, standing from the couch. "He's desperate for me ta help him. He snuck into my room at Wayward the other night to see if I'd work wit him. I told him that I couldn't run away from the property but that I'd help him do whatever he wanted."

Myles danced expertly around the details, only giving what was needed.

"Fuck." Lawrence dropped his head and stared at the top of the desk. "That asshole just incurred the wrath of the Curators. Is he stupid? If they get him...fuck knows what he'll spill before they slit his throat."

"He's not thinking clearly. He's desperate, and desperation makes ya do things that ya normally wouldn't. I can lure him out like you wanted. I'm sure of it," Myles said, his hands balling into fists. "The shite he's pulled affects me and me brother. I'll happily kill him for this. Give us a little longer, and I promise we'll get him."

"Wait," I said. Myles and Lawrence turned to look at me as I crossed my arms.

"Why would you care about the Curators getting their hands on him? They don't get involved in family matters," I said.

My father stared at me as the seconds ticked by, and I swore.

"You've done something, haven't you? Something that will enrage the Curators if they find out?"

He snatched his glass off the desk and walked to the table in the corner not answering my question.

"Answer me. What the fuck have you done?"

Lawrence spun on me, violence oozing off him like it was coming out of his pores.

"I told you to watch your tone with me."

"And if you've done something that will get us all killed, then I have the right to know what it is," I countered, taking a step closer rather than shrinking away.

He had a gun strapped to that table and could pull it and shoot me before I ever got to him. But I'd never let him control me with fear again.

"I'll tell you when I have no choice, but for now, you're on a need-to-know basis. As long as we get to Owen first, then there is nothing to worry about. Now get out of my office. The two of you have ruined my evening."

Not arguing was difficult, but this was not the time. We walked for the open door, and he pointed across the room.

"And take that thing with you."

I sneered at him, my lip pulling up.

"Fuck you. Clean up your own mess," I said, slamming his office door behind us.

"What do ya think he's done," Myles asked as soon as we got in my truck.

"No fucking clue, but I need to make sure we don't get caught up with whatever the hell it is," I said, speeding down the driveway.

OCTOBER 25 – SATURDAY 6:13 PM

Theo

This was heaven. A single snowflake had yet to fall, and I wasn't complaining about extra time with Polly. Ren's arms wrapped around my waist made it even better. The only grey in an otherwise perfect fantasy was that I would never experience this with Liam. As much as he liked me on my bike, he had zero interest and would never willingly be a backpack.

Ren's grip on me tightened as I drifted back and forth in my lane, making me smile. I had taken the long route to the cabin, but the drive had been quiet, and we were just enjoying the cool, clear evening.

"Theo, do you think they'll be okay?"

Myles, Nash, and Blake were on a mission to try and capture Owen so there was no need to ask who she meant. Owen had taken the bait with the photo, and now it was time to reel him into shore. Nash had gotten permission for Ren to leave the property while Liam and I volunteered to keep her thoroughly distracted for the night, so here we were.

"I think they're smart and have put thought into this plan. They'll be as safe as possible."

"That was an incredibly political answer," Ren said, and I laughed.

"Yes, I suppose it was." Flicking on my blinker as we pulled up to a stop sign, I waited for the small line of cars to pass before pulling out onto the main road. "I guess we never really know. Anything can happen at any time, but we are as safe as we can be."

"Just this once, can you lie to me," she said.

"They're going to be perfectly fine," I said, but even I wouldn't believe me. "Look, the only things I know for sure are that Myles hates his father and loves you. There is no way that he will let Owen come anywhere near you."

"That's what worries me most. He will do something unsafe if he thinks he's protecting me. No matter what he says, I know that in the heat of the moment...he'll just react."

"True, but Nash is there, and so is Blake. Nash is the one person Myles will listen to and Blake is a great backup and able to call for help if needed."

"Just one more thing to get used to, I guess. I hate it, though—all this danger and worry. If my hair wasn't already white, it would be now from the stress. Every time we step outside, it could be the last."

"Life is like that in general. We just face different dangers than most," I said as we entered the massive S bend that led to our turn.

"Sure, if you say so," Ren said, making me laugh.

"You worried about Christov finding us?"

Checking for tails was second nature for all of us now. There hadn't been any so far, but you never knew. With a clear rearview, I pulled onto the dirt road.

"No, not really. He's just another in the line of assholes who wants to get their hands on me. He can wait in the back."

"I fucking love you."

Ren slid her hands down and gripped my legs as my blood heated thinking about tonight.

"I love you, too. I feel like we've hardly had a chance to spend quality time together," she said.

This was as good of a time as any to tell her my news.

"At least we'll be prepared for next year."

Slowing down, I eased onto the rough cabin road.

"Next year? Why?"

"I was accepted to Harvard. I haven't announced it yet, and I've been trying to find the best time to tell you." Holding my breath, I waited for her to respond.

"You...you got into Harvard?"

"Yeah."

Ren's body gently shook behind me, and I could hear her crying. Fuck, dread filled me as we cruised up the cabin driveway. We slowed to a stop, and I got off to help Ren. Tears trickled down her cheeks when I pulled off her helmet, but she was smiling. Confusion hit as she slammed into me, hugging me like I was going to disappear.

"I'm so happy for you," Ren said.

Holding her tight, I kissed the top of her head.

"I'll be honest, you don't look happy."

"I am...I mean, I'm going to miss you. And I don't have a clue where I'm going. But I'm so happy for you. How did you get in so soon?"

"I'm a legacy, and my dad knows the administrator. He took one look at my grades and accepted me. I got lucky."

Ren pulled back and glared at me as she shook her head.

"Yes, Ethan helped you jump the line, but you were getting in no matter what, Theo. You have better than a perfect average. Any school in the world would be doing backflips to have you. You've gone above and beyond with everything. You've got extra volunteer hours, and you're already working in a law firm part time."

I tugged Ren in against my body again.

"Yeah, you're right, I'm pretty awesome," I said, laughing as she swatted my arm.

Cupping Ren's face, I kissed her and let my lips convey what her support meant.

"I was really worried to tell you."

"Why?"

"Because I'll be far away for so long."

Ren shrugged. "I'm sure we can travel back and forth. Plus we'll have holidays and summer breaks. I assume you'll be clerking at your dad's firm?" I nodded. "We'll make it work."

I kissed her again and loved how she leaned into me like I was the only thing keeping her on her feet.

"I need to tell you something, too," Ren said. I turned and leaned against my bike. "Ugh, I'm sorry I've kept this from you, but...shit. I slept with Nash," she said, cringing.

Crossing my arms, I narrowed my eyes at her, and her cheeks turned bright red.

"I'm so sorry. I should've told you right away. I feel terrible," she said, looking at me with the saddest eyes. "Don't just stare at me like that. Say something, even if you want to yell at me. I know I deserve it."

"Do you really think I didn't already know?" Ren's mouth opened and then closed. "First of all, the two of you are not exactly subtle, and second, Liam has been keeping me up to date on all the dirt. What I'm wondering is why it took you so long to say anything?"

She sighed as I reached out and grabbed her arm, forcing her to step between my legs.

"Where do I start? It shouldn't have happened. Seattle was a complete disaster, I never wanted to speak to him again, and he's engaged to Vicky. I don't even know what the hell I was thinking."

"Do you love him?"

Ren crossed her arms.

"As long as you can love someone and want to stab them at the same time."

Laughing hard, I smiled at her annoyed expression.

"It's fun watching you turn yourself inside out with your feelings for him. Trust me, we all want to love Nash and kill him at the same time. You're in good company."

"Why are you taking this so well," Ren asked, eyeing me suspiciously.

"Get that look off your face. Liam and I haven't been with anyone else. We'd never do that to you. But this thing with Nash has been coming for a long time. We've all seen it as much as the two of you kept trying to deny it."

Ren sucked in a deep breath and looked down at her boots, the leather on the jacket squeaking as she moved.

"Will you be honest with me," she finally asked.

"Always."

"Am I stupid for believing him? He says that he's not marrying Vicky and that he has a plan. But I'm feeling pretty gullible right now."

"No, you're not." Ren lifted her gaze to mine. "For as long as I've known Nash when he has a plan, he follows through. He may have signed that contract, but I don't think he would've done it without having an exit strategy." I ran her ponytail through my fingers. "Besides, I've seen the way he looks at you. He's in love. Nash may not say it, but he is, so there is no way he's marrying her," I said, hoping that I was right.

My faith in Nash and his plans had never waivered before. But this seemed like a tricky situation, with Mr. Genovese being Vicky's father. He was a man you didn't piss off unless you wanted to go missing.

At the sound of the cabin door opening, Ren and I looked over.

"Hey, are you two coming in or what? Dinner is getting cold," Liam yelled.

"Yes, Sir, coming right away, Sir," I yelled back.

The press of his lips promised a hard spanking. It was my lucky night.

"We better go before Mr. Grumpy pants drags us inside," I said.

"I heard that," Liam growled, making me and Ren laugh.

Rising on her toes, she kissed my cheek. "Thank you."

Holding her hand, we walked toward the cabin, and all the earlier butterflies and excitement came racing back. I'd imagined what it would be like to have the three of us together so many times that I'd lost count. Tonight really was a dream coming true.

OCTOBER 25 – SATURDAY 7:40 PM

R^{en}

Why was I nervous? I'd been with Liam and Theo separately, so why was it so stressful to be alone in the room with them together?

Liam had prepared an entire surf and turf platter that required far more skill in a kitchen than I had. He cooked the tender beef cubes right at the table with a special burner, and all the while, the two of them talked and laughed without missing a beat.

In my head, I'd pictured us like a tricycle, but this felt more like a bicycle with one training wheel falling off.

The conversation stopped and was quiet for so long that I looked up to see both Theo and Liam staring at me. My gaze bounced between them.

"What?"

"Why are you so nervous," Liam asked.

I licked my lips, setting my fork down.

"I'm not sure. Maybe we're all just better in separate pairs."

They looked at one another in silent communication. I really hated when they did that.

"Are you saying you don't want to be with us together?" Theo looked confused.

"I don't know. I'm sorry. I need a minute."

Getting up, I walked down the hall and into the bathroom.

My head was a mess, and my emotions were worse. Identifying with a Yahtzee dice was new, but that was exactly what my insides were like. Everything was all over the place. Leaning my arms on the edge of the sink, I slumped and closed my eyes.

The door clicked as it opened, and I knew it was Liam without looking. He ran his hand down my back, and I relaxed a little with his calming touch.

"What's going on, Little Rabbit?"

I shook my head. "I don't know."

"Try."

Sighing, I stood up and stared at him in the mirror behind me. His cinnamon eyes were as soothing as his voice, but the intensity commanded me to answer him.

"I'm going to say this, but I want you to know that I don't ever want to go back."

He cocked his head and stared at me.

"Things were simpler before I came here, before I said yes to Myles, before I learned who I was, and before I got into a polyamorous relationship."

I looked up at the ceiling because I couldn't face Liam as I got this out.

"I should be worrying about what I want to do after graduation. I thought I had it all sorted, a clear plan for myself. But now...now I worry about how every decision affects someone else and have no idea what I want anymore. I'm floating around in this abyss of uncertainty with no clear direction. I'm in this relationship with all of you, my choice, and yet...I'm overwhelmed, Liam."

Pacing the small bathroom, I took a deep breath and shook out my hands.

"Things I never worried about are constantly running through my head and my heart. Will I hurt this person if I do this? Should I base decisions on what I want or vote with everyone else? Do I want to be part of this world or break away? And if I do that, like my mother did, what does that mean for me, for all of us?"

Liam grabbed my arm as I turned to walk past him for the tenth time. He slowly drew me into him and tipped my head up, forcing me to meet his eyes.

"What you need is to compartmentalize. You did it when your mother was sick and even when you first got here. School had its own box, your friendships were in another, looking after her was a third, and dealing with your father was one. You were able to handle all the moving parts because you didn't let them jumble together and cloud what you needed to do or your feelings."

"Those were easy. This...this is so much harder."

"Maybe, but life is never going to be easy. You know that. You could hide out on a beach where no one knows your name, and you'd still have responsibilities and issues. What would you do for work? Where would you live? Are you never going to worry about your friends? Are you going to stop standing up to assholes?"

Liam slid his hands down my arms until he was hanging onto my fingertips and brought them to his heart. I could feel the steady beat thumping under his skin.

"I don't see you ever being able to do that, even though it seems like the easier solution. As we've both learned, running is not the option that works. Besides, you can't keep your nose out of anything. You'll end up in trouble again," he said, and I smirked.

"Sometimes the world seems so large, and I'm just an insignificant speck that can't really make a difference and will continue to screw up." I bit my lip. "I haven't told Myles and Blake about Nash. I'm a liar, a cheater, an adulterer, and a total fraud and...."

Liam began to laugh.

"What?"

He just kept laughing, and I glared at him.

"Don't laugh at me. I'm being serious."

"I know, that's what makes it so much funnier."

I tugged my hands away and crossed my arms.

"If you're waiting for an apology, you're not going to get one from me."

"Why did I think you'd understand?" I grumbled.

"I do understand. That's why I'm not going to apologize for laughing. Little Rabbit, stop running in circles chasing that little cotton tail of yours. Let's start with the world part. Guess what? We all feel like we are insignificant and have no real purpose. No matter how in control we want to be, out there is a wild-ass jungle of billions of people all trying to run their own rat race and figure their shit out. We can't control every aspect of our lives any more than they can."

Hopping up on the counter, I sat there and just stared at him. How could he make a statement like that and seem so unbelievably calm? Like it didn't matter if a bomb dropped on us right now. Would we just go with the flow of what was next?

"Are you saying I shouldn't try?"

"No, I'm saying that you need to stop worrying about every little thing and hurting everyone's feelings. Let me use Myles and Blake as an example. You love them, right?"

"Yes."

"Okay, what does telling them about you and Nash solve?"

"I won't be a liar. I won't be hiding this massive secret from them when I swore to be truthful. That's what it will solve."

"Okay. All I heard is, it will make me feel better."

My mouth dropped open. "That's not what I said."

"Isn't it? Look, they both already said they were fine with you being with anyone from our group, right?"

"Well...yes, but...."

"No, there is no but. Okay, Little Rabbit, your lesson is understanding that you're no longer Ren Mikhailov, the princess. You've become Lilya Ren Mikhailov, the queen," he said, rubbing his lower lip.

Without even realizing it he just smacked me in the face with a memory. *Remember Ren, you were always a queen.* I'd never forgotten those words and now I realized Mum meant so much more.

"Does a queen ask her subjects if every decision she makes is okay with them? Do you think Dimitri asks for permission from his family? Do you think Ethan and Ella run all their choices past Theo and Blake?"

"No, but those aren't the same thing."

"Wrong."

Walking over to the sink where I was sitting, Liam grabbed six little balls of soap. I smirked at the little flowers that had Nash losing his mind. It was nice to see that he hadn't replaced them the moment my ass was out the door.

Liam placed one of the soaps close to the tips of his fingers, then another one almost beside it but not quite. There was one in the middle behind the two, with the remaining three in a straight line taking up the rear.

He pointed to the blue soap. "Myles."

Then to the pretty yellow one. "Blake."

The soft purple color. "Theo."

Then, to the green one by itself in the middle of his hand.

"Me. And before you ask, I'm there because I'm Nash's second in command, and...I'm your Dom."

He smirked, and I did the same. It was easy to figure out that the other two were me and Nash, but I didn't interrupt.

"This shitty looking black one is Nash," he said, chuckling. "This one at the very front is you."

"Why don't you have Nash at the front? He's your King."

"And there is no king greater than he who has an even better queen to guide his hand. Granted, this relationship dynamic is more complicated, but we all have one thing in common, and that is you... our queen. In one way or another, you complete us and elevate us to be better versions of who we are. That includes Nash. He is better because of you, and as hard as he is fighting his feelings, he will cave. When that happens, the two of you will be unstoppable."

"This is insanity. I don't have that much pull over anyone, least of all Nash. And even if I do, I don't want it. Also, that still doesn't explain why I shouldn't feel bad about not telling Myles and Blake. I'm lying by omission. I would be livid if they slept with someone else."

"Whoa, first off, Nash is not just some random someone else. All the guys, including myself, have already said we don't care if you want Nash. Hell, the whole group dynamic was agreed upon before I even got involved, true?"

"True."

"So technically, you didn't do anything that wasn't already acceptable. You don't need to make public announcements about what or who you do or when. This is not a secret you're keeping because they'll be pissed you had sex with Nash. They'll be pissed if he doesn't get out of the marriage to Vicky. Big difference. You not telling Myles and Blake until you see what happens on Halloween is a strategic maneuver to keep the peace. Is causing issues worth you feeling better?"

"No, I guess not. But I may kill him anyway if he doesn't find a way out after he told me to trust him."

Liam laughed. "I wouldn't blame you. Bottom line is that you can feel however you want, but it doesn't make your decision wrong if it betters the group. You don't have to explain yourself to anyone. You're the queen. You're my queen and one sexy little rabbit at that."

My body heated with the lust in Liam's eyes. He could melt an entire iceberg with that look. Grabbing the balls of soap, I held them all together in one neat little pile.

"I don't want to look at us like that. I want this. Equals. Mikhailov or not, I don't want to control any of you."

"And that's exactly why you'll make an excellent leader. You don't want control or yearn for power. You don't make decisions based on what will garner you more money, and you sure as shit don't care what anyone thinks of you. If there was ever someone that could be labeled as incorruptible...it is you. You have a kind and honest heart, Little Rabbit, but you also have a ferocious bite when you need it."

Pressing my lips together, I stared at the soap and still didn't like it.

"You'll always do what is right, even when it feels wrong. That's what will make you great. It'll make Nash great and turn us into a powerful unit."

"Then why does it feel so terrible?"

"Because you care. But that's where you need to compartmentalize. Just because something is uncomfortable doesn't mean it's wrong. It means you've looked at all the outcomes, and it's better not to do *XYZ* or to do *XYZ*. Look at Nash. He hasn't shared his plans. He didn't even tell us where he went over the summer or who he met. We were as blindsided by Vicky and his ties to Mr. Genovese as you were. But do you see us putting his head on a spike?" I shook my head. "Exactly, and why is that?"

"Because he's the king, and he chooses what to tell you when he feels you need to know."

"Good, now say it with me. You are the…"

I rolled my eyes at him. "Queen."

"Good, and what does the queen do?"

"Only tell what is needed, when it is needed, to whom it is needed after taking all factors into consideration."

Liam winked at me.

"See, Little Rabbit, you get it. You don't have to like it, but you get it. Also, don't kid yourself. We all keep things from you and Nash. That won't change unless you kick us to the curb. It's the simple truth. In looking after each other, we sometimes protect a secret. Understand?"

"I understand, but I feel ridiculous when you call me queen. It's totally weird."

Liam laughed. "You'll get used to it." Stepping between my legs, he took the soap and set it aside. "Do you feel any better?"

"I do, thank you. I still have no idea what I'm doing with my life, but one issue at a time."

"Compartmentalizing already, look at you. And, since that's the case, I think it's time for dessert," Liam said, dropping his lips to my ear and whispering, "I'm starting with you."

The hair on the back of my neck stood as my body lit up like a Christmas tree.

Liam was probably right about the natural order of things, but that didn't mean that tweaks couldn't be made. What was the point of being queen if you couldn't make adjustments? What that looked like…I had no clue, but there had to be a way.

Chapter 54

OCTOBER 25 – SATURDAY 8:03 PM

Liam

Ren shivered and tilted her head for me when I nuzzled her neck.

"Such a good little rabbit."

She was still tense but for a totally different reason than earlier. Placing soft kisses on her skin all the way up her throat and along her jaw to her lips, I captured her sweetness as she melted for me.

Reaching out with one hand, I turned the doorknob without looking and scooped her off the counter as it popped open. Ren wrapped her arms around my neck, and I smiled as she took control.

She didn't even realize she did it, and while it was against the rules, there was something about how it happened when we were together that didn't bother me at all.

"Looks like you're feeling better," Theo said.

Ren broke the kiss and blushed as I sat her on her feet.

"I am."

Theo stood and this was the first time I got to experience how they were together. Until this very moment, I wasn't sure how I would feel. But the way Theo wrapped his hand around the back of her neck and drew her in made me...hot.

She sucked Theo's bottom lip into her mouth, and I realized that there was absolutely nothing about my little rabbit that wasn't perfect. She was beautiful, unique, and pure.

As hard as I tried, the only flaw I could find was that she was too kind-hearted. She wanted to help everyone, and that was why she needed us. We could and would get our hands dirty, but she would keep us pushing for what was right. She wouldn't allow us to fall prey to the same greed that destroyed so many before us.

I pulled my shirt off, and Ren looked at me. Her eyes were pure fire until she spotted the bandage on my arm.

"What happened," Ren asked quietly. Her concern was evident in every feature as she reached for my hand.

"Lawrence, but I'll be fine."

I ran my knuckles down her cheek, and the corner of my mouth turned up as she glared at the bandage like she was thinking of all the ways she wanted him to die.

"Trust me. I hardly feel it, and no, I'm not showing you tonight. Erase him from your mind. Thoughts of him don't belong in this place."

"He did that yesterday? When you, Nash, and Myles were gone all day." I nodded. "He needs to be in a deep, dark hole."

"He will be, but you don't need to worry about that right now."

Walking over to the fridge, I grabbed water and then sat down in the large leather chair next to the empty fireplace and pointed my finger between the two of them.

"I want a show. Carry on."

Theo caught on quickly and kissed Ren again. He grabbed her hair and bent her back while she clung to the front of his shirt to stay upright. Fuck they were a picture. Ren's mouth hung open, and her eyes closed as Theo trailed his tongue down her throat and kissed the base of her neck. A soft moan escaped her lips as he released his grip on her hair.

It hung in long waves like an icy waterfall, and the craving to wrap it around my fist was strong. Theo slowly straightened with Ren in his arms. They looked like they were caught in the throws of a sensual dance as he took a step forward, and she took one back. He didn't stop until her back was pressed up against the wall. I licked my lips, burning with envy.

He drew her hands above her head and then followed it with her hoodie that he tossed on the couch.

"I love it when you shiver like that," Theo growled against Ren's lips.

My jeans tightened, watching his dominance over her. I'd been teaching him a little too well it seemed. Theo effortlessly took control of the entire situation. In a few moves, he had Ren standing before us in a sexy little thong and bra. Without a single word, Ren bent backward over the arm of the couch as Theo got on his knees between her thighs.

I sucked in a deep breath to keep myself in check as Theo pulled the fabric out of the way and gave me an unobstructed view of his tongue working Ren over. I couldn't see her face, but the little moans were like a siren's call to all my senses.

Grabbing the remote off the small table beside me, I hit the button for the television and flipped through music stations until I found one that set the mood. The smooth yet dark and sexy instrumental selection filled the room and added to Ren's whimpers.

"Stop, but don't move."

Theo obeyed beautifully while Ren struggled. I sipped my water and watched her knuckles turn bright white as she gripped the cushion.

"Continue."

"Oh god," Ren said.

"Stop. Little Rabbit, you're not allowed to make another sound until I say."

Her sassy attitude permeated the air, though she said nothing.

"Don't sass me," I said for good measure and then softly chuckled as she swore. It was barely audible over the music, but I caught it.

"Theo?"

He looked at me, his green eyes full of devious desire. I loved seeing this part of him alive and shining—it made me fucking smile.

"Our little rabbit doesn't seem to know the meaning of hold still or keep quiet. Please go grab the bag of toys." Theo smirked. "And take off your shirt," I ordered.

He stared me down as he grabbed the bottom of his black t-shirt and slowly peeled it off over his head. His abs were taut, his hair messy, and with the black jeans, he looked badass. Fuck me...between the two of them, I was being tested.

Theo walked out of the room, his back and ass flexing as I watched him. He returned a moment later with my black bag that had a few things I'd brought from home. He pulled each item out and laid them on the coffee table beside Ren. She couldn't tell what any of them were because I stored my toys in separate leather sheaths that were tied closed. For all she knew, they were knives, cock rings, and everything in between. The last item he removed from the bag was a tube of lube. Theo knew my preferred order and would've laid the items out accordingly. I pointed to the sleeve that housed ten different sizes of butt plugs. These weren't the exotic set that I used on Theo. This was a brand-new training set, just for my little rabbit.

We would have her together eventually, but that took time and patience. Just the thought of both of us fucking her as she screamed sent a shiver racing down my spine.

"Um...." Ren started as Theo unwrapped the black leather to show off the shiny silver plugs.

"Quiet, Little Rabbit."

Theo gingerly ran his fingers over them as he teased Ren. He stopped on the largest and smiled. Annoyed that I couldn't see her facial expressions, I took another swig of the water before standing and walking closer. Ren's hair was splayed out over the couch, her chest heaving as she stared at Theo, her face easily readable. She looked caught between excited and terrified.

"The smallest," I said, and her eyes darted up to mine.

Stepping around the table, I squatted down and smoothed some of the wild strands of hair away from her face. I saw Theo out of the corner of my eye as he pulled the tiny plug and held it in his palm.

Ren licked her lips and looked away, but I tapped her arm and pointed to my face.

"You keep your eyes on me until I say otherwise." She nodded. "Are you scared?" She nodded again. "Don't be. Theo knows what he's doing, and he won't hurt you. It will feel...unusual until you get used to the sensation." She licked her lips, running the bottom one through her teeth. "By the time you've worked up to the large size, you'll be begging us to fuck you hard, and I can guarantee that you'll be screaming our names."

"Close your eyes," I said, running my hand gently from her forehead down to her mouth, over and over until they stayed shut, and she began to take regular breaths once more. Leaning in close to her ear, I growled. She sucked in a ragged breath, and her body arched from the sensual sound that awakened all of her primal instincts to run.

While Ren was distracted, I glanced at Theo. He nodded that he was ready, and I gave him the signal as my fingers trailed down her arm to her fingers.

"Breathe, Little Rabbit, and focus on my touch," I said, tracing her stomach and up her chest between her breasts. "You're going to feel a little bit of pressure, but just relax. Right now," I said, and she shuddered. She held her breath, and the moment she released it, I knew it was all the way in. "That's it. It's in."

Goosebumps rose where my fingers had been. Every twitch of Ren's body and flinch of her facial expression told me exactly how she was feeling.

This was what got me off and turned me on more than anything. The ability to read another so easily and to inflict arousal with just a touch was powerful. Forget money and fear. This was what I craved. Possessing the skills that made another willingly hand over their body and mind to you was a rush. It came with immense responsibility, but there was nothing I loved more than holding Theo's, and now Ren's, needs in the palm of my hand.

"Continue feasting on our little rabbit," I said, and Ren jerked as Theo got to work.

Her eyes snapped open as I caressed her hard nipples, the little peaks pushing the lacy material. Ren's breathing picked up, and her plump lips begged to be kissed. As hard as she tried, she couldn't hold perfectly still. I could just see Theo's eyes between her legs and knew exactly how talented he was with that tongue.

"Don't come, Little Rabbit. If you do, I'll have no choice but to tan your sexy little ass," I groaned in her ear. "On second thought... come. My palm is itching to redden your skin and then fuck you hard."

Ren's nostrils flared, and her eyes hardened as she silently accepted the challenge head-on.

"Oh fuck, does that feel good? I bet it does. His hot tongue swirling around your clit and plunging deep inside of you," I softly said, and Ren shivered.

Inch by inch, I slid the straps of her bra off her shoulders until I was able to fold the lace away from my prize.

"Theo."

He stopped and Ren's body went slack. She'd been right there on the edge.

"Is your pussy begging for that sweet release, Little Rabbit?"

Ren turned her head, her lips close to mine, but her eyes were filled with a fiery passion that only came when your body was tormented with desire. She opened her mouth to answer, but I touched my finger to the lush, softness of her lips, shook my head, and then turned to Theo.

"Yes, Sir," he said, and my cock throbbed with those two little words that were said every day a million times. But they meant so much more.

"Grab the clit stimulator, the curved one with the vibrator attached."

Theo moved quickly to prep the toy. I held out my hand, and he gave me the remote. Ren's curiosity flared in her eyes as she watched us.

"Do you know what this is?" She shook her head. "You're about to find out. Trust me, you're going to want to come. Your body will beg you to let go. You'll ache all over and throb between your thighs, but you won't...not until I give you permission."

My little rabbit moaned as Theo pushed the thick vibrator inside her and then attached the stimulator. It acted like a miniature simulation of someone sucking her clit. As soon as it was in place, I looked at Theo and he stood.

The large bulge in the front of his jeans drew my attention. He'd gotten amazingly good at hiding the ache, but I knew he was just as pent up as Ren.

"Take your jeans off and make sure we can both see you," I said.

Theo's fingers worked swiftly on the button and zipper of his jeans. Bending over, he pulled them off and kicked them aside. He was commando, just how I liked him. There was nothing as amusing as grabbing him when he least expected it and dragging him into an empty classroom or storage area.

"Come here. I want the little rabbit to watch as you stroke your cock."

My mouth watered as his hand ran up the entire length of his shaft and back down. He would look incredible with a piercing... or two.

"You ready, Little Rabbit? You can answer."

"Yes, Sir," she panted.

Everything was already getting to her, and I wanted to see how much more she could take before breaking.

"Good girl...now keep your eyes on his cock and picture him being the one fucking you. Can you do that for me, Little Rabbit? Can you be a good fucking girl?"

"Yes, Sir," she whispered this time and then bit her lip.

Rolling her nipple between my fingers, she moaned, and I hit the vibration button. Ren's eyes popped open, and she convulsed as I added the sucking action. But the sexiest thing I'd ever seen was when her entire body bowed, pushing her breast into my palm as I turned on the self-propelled fucking feature. We were still on level one, but she was having difficulty breathing through the extreme sensations.

After a few minutes, she relaxed a tiny bit, and I upped the speed to level two. Ren gritted her teeth like she was in pain as she tried to resist the pull of her orgasm.

"Don't close your eyes, Little Rabbit. Watch Theo stroke himself while he watches you."

Ren's head rolled from side to side, sweat beading on her forehead.

"Look at him. That's a direct order."

Half-lidded with ecstasy, she gazed at Theo. The ring I'd put on before dinner tightened as my cock thickened to full size with no relief tucked inside my jeans. The throbbing was like its own heartbeat, the need ever-increasing.

"Tell me how that feels."

"So...so...so good," Ren stuttered out.

I moved out of the way and directed Theo where to stand.

"Little Rabbit, be a good girl and stroke his cock for him. Theo's arm is tired," I said, walking around to watch the toys work.

The thick purple dildo thrust in and out a couple of inches at a time as it buzzed. I slid my hands down her thighs and ran my finger through her wet lips. Glancing away from the pleasure torture, I watched as Ren's hand on Theo worked in time with the vibrator fucking her. His head was back, and his eyes were closed while the swollen tip of his dick announced that he was close to coming as well.

Ren's eyes locked onto the device when I held up the remote. She shook her head. A horrified expression crossed her face as I moved my thumb over to the little levels button.

"You still can't come...but you can yell," I said and hit the button.

"Fuuuuuuuucccccccccck!"

Ren's legs straightened and shook as the dildo went faster. "Oh god, oh god, Liam...please...please...I can't."

"You can."

I hit the off button, and she cried out in frustration.

"Don't worry about me. Lick just the tip of Theo's cock."

Grabbing the back of the couch, Theo lowered himself closer to her mouth. Watching them was as good as an aphrodisiac. Their desperation for release perfumed the air.

"Good girl. Now suck the head of his cock into your mouth and moan."

Theo's legs nearly buckled as she did.

"Excellent, keep going. I'm turning this back on."

She shouldn't expect warnings going forward, but tonight was just night one.

The toy picked up where it left off, right on level four, and if I hadn't been standing between her legs, she would've squeezed them together.

The dual moaning got louder and louder, their faces twisted in delicious agony as I undid my jeans and stepped out of them. Neither of them noticed my cock bouncing in the air as a line of precum trickled down the side.

"Stop," I said, impressed that they'd both managed to hang on, even if it wasn't by much.

Ren whimpered, and her hips bucked up like her body had a mind of its own.

"Let him go," I ordered.

Ren released Theo as I gently removed the vibrator but left the butt plug in place.

"Theo, come here."

He paused before me, and I grabbed him, crashing our lips together. He groped my shaft, breaking the rules, and I groaned into his mouth. Fuck, I loved the feel of his hands on me.

"You're going to get into trouble for that," I said.

"I'm counting on it," he growled.

"You're a lot more trouble as a switch," I said, smirking as he smiled.

"I really am. You love it, even if you don't want to admit it. Just like how you're enjoying this far more than you ever thought possible," Theo said, and he wasn't wrong.

I arched my eyebrow at him and nodded at Ren.

"Get between her legs. Fuck her and bend over. Your ass is mine," I said, my teeth grinding together.

"Little Rabbit, are you still with us, or did you pass out?"

"I'm still awake, Sir," she said, but her voice was breathless and about to be a whole lot more.

"You can come on Theo. But just know...you'll be coming a minimum of three times before the night is out."

Theo grabbed her ass, pulling her hips higher onto the arm of the couch, and sank balls deep.

"Fuck," they swore together.

Picking up the lube, I slathered myself and then spread more between Theo's ass cheeks. He hummed as I rubbed my finger around the base of the very large plug that he had put in before they left Wayward. I gently pulled it out, a little jealous that he'd ridden his motorcycle here and had felt the subtle vibration the whole time.

He grunted as the last of it slipped out. I set it aside and got into position.

"I set the pace," I commanded, teasing Theo's ass with the tip of my cock.

It was much quicker to push all the way in with the pre-prep, but I held still, enjoying the feel of him. Pulling out and pushing in, I found a rhythm that suited me. A few thrusts later, Ren screamed as she came.

Theo was shaking, but I hadn't given him permission to come yet. Wrapping my hand around his throat, I squeezed. He leaned back into me, eyes closed as his cock pumped into Ren.

"You're such a good boy. Tell me how you like that," I ordered.

"I fucking love it, Sir," he said, hissing as I picked up the pace and gripped his throat tighter. He trusted me completely and didn't fight, which fed my craving for control.

"Do you want to come?"

"Yes, Sir."

"You want your cock to release a load in her while I pound into your ass," I snarled in his ear and felt him quake against me before he spoke.

"Fuck yes, Sir."

"Then do it. Come for me."

I bit down on the skin at the crook of his neck and let loose. I fucked him hard and fast, driving him deeper into our little rabbit.

His hands dug into her ass to hold her steady, making his arms flex with the effort.

With a guttural yell, Theo came. Every muscle in his body tightened, including his ass around my cock. Ren screamed again, calling out our names. I didn't want to hold off and instead chose to enjoy the moment with them. There was plenty of time to drive them both to the edge of insanity.

My eyes closed as I came, slamming him into Ren and continuing the orgasm circle until I was drained.

Hugging Theo, I caught my breath and let the euphoric feeling flow through my body.

"I love you," I whispered. "Both of you."

"I love you, too," they said together, making me warm all over.

"That's good because I'm ready for round two," I said and smirked as my cock twitched, looking for more.

OCTOBER 25 – SATURDAY 9:19 PM

Nash

Owen couldn't have picked a shittier bar for this meet. Mulligan's was a ways down the road from my club and in the heart of the industrial district. The pink neon above the entrance flashed that they were open, but the road sign had long lost any lights and sat dark. Scanning the road, I didn't see anyone and turned my attention back to the front door.

There were five cars, four motorcycles, three pickup trucks, two stray cats, and all it needed was a fucking partridge in a pear tree.

It was an overcast night, which worked in our favor when we

made our escape with Owen. Glancing in the rearview mirror, I watched as a car slowly made its way up the road. But as it passed under the street lamp, I could clearly see a woman driving.

Myles hadn't said two words, which was rare for him. Most of the time I was begging him to shut up. His tense jaw, bouncing knee, and clenched fists told me that he was gearing up for a kill.

"Hey, before this all goes down, I want to give this back," I said, pulling the thick manila envelope from the backseat and handing it over.

"What did ya find," he asked as he took it from me like it might bite.

When Myles went to Ireland to complete his initiation, he'd spoken to some families on my behalf and gathered more support than I ever expected. One of those families, the O'Learys, had been close friends and allies with Meghan McCoy, Myles's mom.

Before he left, they handed him that envelope and told him that it had been given to them by his mother before she passed. He didn't have the heart to look inside when he got back and asked me to go through it for him.

"Mostly paperwork on shady business ventures and copies of ledgers to show that he was skimming money. Lots of things that could've been used to have your father arrested. There are also some very personal pages that I skimmed, talking about what Owen was like and how she feared for her life, but more for you and Lip."

Myles nodded and gripped the envelope tighter. Reaching out, I put my hand on his shoulder.

"There were also DNA test results. Devin wasn't your mother's son. There was no mention of who his mother was, but the results are conclusive."

Myles slumped in the seat.

"Thank the Lord. Doesn't change the fact that me da is a wanker, but at least when Devin...." Myles looked out the window. "Well, at least he wasn't me full brother, ya know?"

I nodded.

"There's more." He looked at me. "Your mother had two letters inside the envelope. I opened them to skim, but I ended up reading them fully."

This was really fucking uncomfortable.

"Okay...and?"

"She lied about some things and took the secrets to her grave."

"What? About what?"

"The first letter also had a DNA test inside and...well...you're not Owen's son."

"I'm sorry, ya wanna say that again?"

"Your father is Matthew McCoy. The letter states that Matthew never wanted to challenge your father, but when Devin started to hurt you, your mother strong-armed him into taking Devin. That's how he ended up here in the States and going to Wayward."

"My uncle is not my uncle but my da, and me da is my uncle?" Myles shook his head. "There's no way."

"Yeah, she had tests done. The second letter, well...it specifically talks about a time when Owen was really abusive, and well...Lip isn't Owen's either."

"Jesus fuck...I'm almost afraid to ask." He rubbed his eyes. "Who is his da?"

"Filip is an O'Brien, as in Ethan O'Brien," I said and watched Myles's face flow through a million emotions in the blink of an eye. "Before you lose your mind, your mother never told Ethan. Apparently, it was a one-time thing. A mistake when he was over in Ireland for work and had been staying with them for a few weeks."

Myles just stared at me like his brain was misfiring, and nothing made sense anymore. I'd warred with whether to tell him this before or after the meeting, but I'd already been sitting on it for weeks.

"Look, I know this is insane and a shock, but, on the bright side, if it's true and we tell Ethan he can get a DNA test and claim Lip." Myles just blinked. "This is a good thing. It means that Owen can never touch him again. You know what a good man Ethan is, and Ella...well, I have no idea if he told her about your mom, so that's complicated. But still, you can use this to keep Lip away from him. I don't know if you've given this much thought, but if we kill Owen...I don't know if a court would award you custody even though you're his brother, just think about it."

"What the fuck....what the fuck...what the fuck? He needs to die and sign over his rights. That's all there is to it."

"Who, Ethan?"

Myles shook his head.

"Naw, me da. If he's dead and gives me rights to Lip, then I don't have to worry, and I never have to tell Ethan or fuck...Blake and Theo...fuck me life, they're his half-brothers."

He slammed his fist against the dashboard before his pained eyes found mine.

"I can't lose Lip, Nash. I love him, and I can't let Ethan take him from me any more than that bastard I've called Da all these years."

"Ethan wouldn't do that. Breathe, man, and think this through. You don't have to say anything now, and I'll keep quiet. This is your family and your decision. But...Ethan and Ella are good people despite whatever happened. Blake is your best friend, and Theo would never hurt Lip. They already treat him like family."

Myles rubbed his face, fear over something I never even considered sitting heavy on his soul.

"Well, I guess now I know why Lip has always been so smart and not like me at all. I joked that I had no idea where he came from... fuck...."

"Hey, shut the fuck up. Lip is your half-brother, too, and once Owen is dead, he'll need you more than ever."

"I know...I'll never abandon him, even if he isn't related to me at all. But letting Ethan take him...I don't know if I can live with that either," he said.

I squeezed his shoulder.

"This secret is safe with me. I won't say anything. But Myles, if it was your son, would you want to know?" Shrugging, I opened my door. "It's almost time. We should head inside and get set up."

Myles grabbed my arm before I could slip out of the truck.

"Thanks for tellin' me and...for reading it. I...I still don't know if I can."

"Anytime. Now, you can worry about the rest of it later. Fucking celebrate that you're not this prick's son, and let's go kill him already," I said, and Myles smirked.

I put my ball cap on and pulled my hoodie up over that to completely cover the sides of my face.

Alright, Owen, show time.

OCTOBER 25 – SATURDAY 9:47 PM

Myles

Nash went straight to the bar when we walked into the dingy pub. I spotted Blake and wouldn't have known it was him if I hadn't been looking. He wore a scraggly brown wig and a thin goatee that made him appear ten years older. Walking over to a booth opposite the bar, I sat down with my back to the corner. It allowed me to keep an eye out for me da, and there was less likelihood that he would spot either of the guys.

The closer it got to ten, the more my knee bounced, and my fingers tapped on the table, but it was excitement rather than nervousness. I'd dreamed of killing him for years and always wondered why we never connected and why he hated me. Now, I knew. Maybe he had an inkling all along that I wasn't his. It really didn't matter the reason, he was an asshole my whole life, and this was it.

"Do you want anything to drink," the only waitress on duty asked. I didn't look up at her and shook my head. "You can't just sit in here. You need to order something," she said.

I grabbed the sticky plastic menu, standing up at the back of the table, and looked it over.

"Fries and two pints of Guinness," I said, keeping my voice low.

If she suspected I was underage, she didn't say anything. Just scribbled it down and walked away. I put the flyer with the six appetizers away and leaned back, making sure that I could still feel my gun. It was stupid to think it had jumped out of the back of my jeans and taken off, but its heavy weight kept me calm. As calm as one could be with the bombshell Nash had just dropped.

The door opened, and I kept my head down. Two more bikers joined their friends at the far table as I glanced up. Picking up my phone, I checked for new messages, but there wasn't anything. Shite, I didn't like this. What if he found out where Liam and Theo were taking Ren? What if he was there right now and had hurt or killed them and taken Snowflake?

I was ready to call it and jump up when the door opened again and in walked Owen. He looked around, and I lifted my arm as he turned his head in my direction.

He walked over with his hands in his pockets, which I didn't like. He could be concealing any kind of a weapon.

"Hello, son," he said, sitting down across from me. He glanced around again. "Hope ya don't mind meeting here," he said, and I shook my head.

"I ordered ya a Guinness," I said when the waitress walked over with the two beers. "Why did ya want to meet here? It's nowhere near where I told ya I wanted to meet."

He smirked. "Where's da girl?"

"Safely tied up," I said and took a sip of the dark beer. "I told ya I'll take ya to her, but I'm not givin' ya the address."

"Why, son? Do ya no trust me?"

I chuckled. "Don't take me fer a fool. Yer me da and I said I'd help ya, but I want ta know what I'm gettin' involved in before I do anythin' else."

"Yer no the one that gives out orders," he snarled, his hands clenching into fists.

"Naw, see, we're not doing that anymore," I said, and his eyes narrowed. "Devin got a say, and I want one too. Besides, I took all the risk of gettin' her out of Wayward without being seen. If they find out what I did, then I'm as good as dead. So now that yer calmer, I wanna know what the fuck is goin' on. The whole story," I said.

"Lawrence is a feckin' liar, that's what. He told me ta go have a meeting, and I no sooner sit me arse in the chair when the entire place lights up with bullets."

"So ya didn't kill the Killroy family?"

Owen slammed his fist down on the table.

"Nah, I didn't. He set me up," Owen said.

Anything was possible when it came to Owen and Lawrence. They both had killed dozens or more people over the years. I was more concerned with what Owen wanted with Ren.

"Fine, he's a prick, and we'll take care of him, but tell me...what of Ren," I asked, and his jaw twitched.

"What I choose to do wit her is none of yer business. So tell me where the little bitch is," he snarled, not paying attention as the plate of French fries was placed on the table.

Pulling out my wallet, I tossed a fifty down and put it away again.

"Fine, ya don't want ta tell me, I'll take her back to Wayward. I'm no playin' this game with ya," I said, standing.

Owen grabbed my arm and sighed.

"Sit. Lawrence says ya have news of Devin. Tell me what ya know and how I can get him back, and I'll tell ya what you want ta know."

Fucking Lawrence. He wanted to ensure my father—or uncle, or whoever the fuck he was to me—lost it. Did he really think I'd back out of this moment? I sat down again.

"How was he?"

Tapping my phone, I sent him the photos I'd taken of Devin while Nathaniel tortured him. As a bonus, I added the pic of the open box with his severed cock inside. I stuffed a few of the fries into my mouth as Owen opened the text. His lips pulled up into a snarl, and his eyes darkened.

"You were there, and ya didn't do anythin'?"

"What was I gonna do? That place is a fortress. Didn't know where I was going and didn't have a choice but to watch," I said, eating a few more fries.

He hit the table again, and people took notice.

"Bollocks, that's all ya did. I bet ya sat back and laughed. I bet yer in this with Lawrence, aren't ya," he asked, his voice getting louder.

"I hate him," I said. "Why would I work wit him?"

"Ya hate me, and yet here ya are," Owen said.

"I don't hate ya. I just never understood why ya hated me," I growled back.

It might not be the truth now after all he'd done, but it had been true. At one point, all I wanted was for him to love me.

"I couldn't figure out why ya considered me worthless and Devin perfect. You've made yer thoughts of me very well known. All I wanted was yer approval, for ya to look at me the way you did him." I sat back and crossed my arms as I glared at him. "Fine, ya want the truth about Devin...I didn't care if they killed him or what they did. I couldn't have saved him if I wanted to, but I didn't want to," I said, and Owen's eyes narrowed.

"Is he still alive?"

I shrugged. "Don't know, and I don't care."

His fists clenched, and he snatched the beer off the table, chugging it like we were at a frat party. Owen wiped his mouth with the back of his hand and slammed the mug down.

"So yer not working with Lawrence?"

"Naw, never. Come on, let's get out of here, and I'll take ya to Ren," I said, standing once more.

He didn't stop me, but Owen smirked and poked me in the chest as he rose to his full height.

"Is that so?"

"Aye, why do ya keep askin'?"

He pulled a switchblade out of his pocket, and I stepped back as he clicked it open.

"Then tell me, son. Why is Nash's truck parked down the street? Did ya really think I wouldn't notice it?"

"Hey, I don't put up with that shit in my bar. You want to fight, then get the hell out," the bartender yelled.

I looked over to see both Nash and Blake moving slowly into position behind Owen.

"Honestly, yeah. It's a nondescript, black truck parked between two others. This tells me that you were sitting outside watching and saw us park. Besides, Nash is not Lawrence."

Nash inched closer, trying not to draw his attention.

"Always so quick, ya are. It amazes me that ya never put together that I hated yer stupid face because you weren't mine. I never loved ya," he said, and I snapped.

Not giving a fuck about the knife, I swung at him and clipped his jaw, forcing him to step back. Owen glared at me while I let all my hatred show in my smile.

"Good, then it brings me even more joy to tell ya that Devin is nothin' more than fish food. I watched every glorious second of his death. He asked for ya the whole time. Too bad ya never got the chance to say goodbye."

Owen roared and lunged at me. I grabbed the arm holding the knife, but he yanked his wrist and shocked me with a kick in the gut.

I hit one of the tables as I stumbled and landed on my back with the air knocked out of my body.

I clutched my chest, gasping as I watched Nash dodge the knife that Owen was wielding like a small sword. Blake got in a shot but gave away that there were three of us, and the blow wasn't enough to knock Owen down.

He staggered to the side and screamed as he swiped at Blake. Owen narrowly missed slicing him right across the face. I rolled off the table, trying to catch my breath, and watched in horror as Owen lunged for Blake again. Nash jumped in and blocked the strike as the blade carved through his jacket and hoodie to cut open his arm.

"Ahhhh," Nash yelled.

I grabbed my gun, aiming, but the bartender fired first. His shot went into the ceiling from a shotgun that deafened us all. I jerked and ducked as he pumped it to reload.

"I said get the fuck out of my bar," the bartender yelled, pointing the gun at us this time.

Owen was the first one out.

"I got him," Blake said as he tore open Nash's jacket.

Running after him, I caught sight of Owen as he streaked around the side of the bar. My adrenaline pushed me faster than ever as it thrummed through my body. We were both sprinting down the center of the road and I was gaining when a truck pulled out of an alley. Owen pushed harder and grabbed the tailgate to pull himself into the truck bed. He turned to look at me as I followed after the vehicle. He smiled and waved while a coldness swept through my body.

No, he couldn't get away. He needed to die.

Taking the risk, I aimed and unloaded my clip. Six shots rang out in the night. One of them winged him. He grabbed his leg and dropped down as I watched the taillights until the truck disappeared around the corner.

"Fuck! No!"

The rage was all-consuming as I screamed over and over. He was in my grasp, and I'd let him escape.

"Myles?" I turned back toward the bar and Blake's voice. "Nash needs stitches, let's go."

I glanced back down the empty road and spit.

"I'll get you, Owen, and when I do...I'll make sure you wish you died as easily as Devin. That's a promise."

Chapter 56

OCTOBER 26 – SUNDAY 4:22 AM

Ren

Liam, Theo, and I hurried down the hallway to meet up with the guys. It was convenient not having to knock before walking into the room. Nash sat on his bed with a white bandage on his bicep, and I quickly scanned Myles and Blake for any injuries.

"Are you all okay?"

"Aye, Snowflake just feckin' pissed. That piece of shite is still out there breathing," Myles said, greeting me with a hug and a kiss on the top of my head.

"What the hell happened," Liam asked before anyone else could.

"Owen made us before it even started. I think he got twitchy when Myles wanted to take him to the location rather than meet him there or just give him the address," Nash said, glaring at his arm.

"Then my fucking father, and his impeccable timing, decided in all his infinite wisdom to talk to Owen. No idea when that convo happened, but he told him that Myles had news about Devin. I don't know if he was selling the lie or setting us up. I never know with him."

"Well, I don't need to say it, but this isn't good. Owen is a wildcard at the best of times, and now he knows he has no one to help him. He'll be looking for ways to lash out," Theo said as he sat down.

"He had help," Myles said, and we all looked at him. "I was thinkin' at first that he ran after a random pickup that just happened to pull out of the alley." He shook his head. "But the more I think about it...why didn't the guy stop when Owen was standing there mocking me? He had to have known that there was a strange man in his truck bed. It woulda been pretty fuckin' hard to miss him. I unloaded my clip at them, so I could see the driver wanting to get away, but it still seemed like a planned escape route."

"That makes this a bigger shitshow," Liam growled. "Who the fuck would help the likes of Owen? Has to be someone with nothing to lose because Owen has nothing to offer but chaos. No way to access money, no connections, no family to call on...he's alone."

Nash ran his hands through his hair.

"I don't fucking know. Maybe we should've put more effort into learning who his associates were before this. But there are only so many of us and not enough goddamn hours in a day. And now this," Nash said, pointing to his arm. "Our rematch with Hawking Shores is Wednesday, and I can't get in a pool. Fuck!"

Standing up, he walked over to the window and stared outside.

"I think our rematch is the least of our worries at the moment," Blake said.

Nash spun around, glaring at Blake, and his rage finally had a target.

"You don't care because it's not your dream that hangs in the balance," Nash growled, and the tension rose in the room as if we'd just turned up the dial on the thermostat.

"I get that this is your big dream. But I think living or dying is still more important than if you get to swim. If you're dead, you can't exactly swim. Then again, I guess it doesn't really matter if it's one of us. I'm sure you'd find a replacement," Blake shot back, standing from Liam's bed where he'd been sitting.

I'd never heard Blake talk back to Nash like that.

"What the fuck is your problem? I saved your fucking, ungrateful life tonight, asshole," Nash snarled, taking a step closer to Blake.

"I didn't need your help. I had him, and you got in the way," Blake said, pointing at Nash.

"Like hell. You didn't have him. He would've sliced your fucking neck open. Maybe I should've let that happen. You always wanted to be a martyr."

"Whoa! Enough," I said, marching forward between the two of them with my arms out. "Before you say something you can't take back."

They didn't back down but stayed quiet.

"Look this is a horrible situation for all of us, but fighting amongst ourselves isn't going to help anything. You can go back to blaming one another after Owen is caught."

Blake was the first to walk away, but I could tell by the look on Nash's face that he wouldn't be satisfied until he fought with someone.

"Guys, I know it's late, but can I get five minutes alone with Nash?"

I didn't take my eyes off Nash like that would somehow keep him in place and quiet long enough to let things remain calm. Myles touched my shoulder on his way out.

"I'll be fine, promise."

"Okay, I'll be waiting in the hall," Myles said. As the door clicked closed Nash's eyes locked with mine.

"You have a really dangerous habit of locking yourself in the lion's cage when it's pissed off," Nash said.

"Maybe because I know the lion is actually a pussy cat who wouldn't hurt me," I teased and walked toward him. His lip twitched.

"I'm not a pussy cat," he grumbled. "Besides, you said I always hurt you."

Nash crossed his arms and then swore as he pressed on his injury.

"Always, may be an exaggeration. But I'll deny it if anyone asks." He smirked. "Tell me what happened," I said, grabbing his hand.

"I saw the blade. It almost got Blake across the face while he was reaching for his gun. I reacted. I don't know if I got in the way, but Blake hasn't taken a life, not in cold blood. Axel and a few others don't count. He didn't strike the final blow."

Sitting down on the bed, I tugged on his hand, and he parked it beside me.

"So, were you worried he might get stabbed or that he'd lose his innocence?"

Nash looked at me.

"Blake is the only one of you who still has that aura. The rest of you have a shadow of death following you around."

"Well, thanks for that fucked up imagery," Nash said.

He looked away from me and sighed.

"Maybe both. Maybe I still worry that something like that could push him too far. Killing someone point blank...I don't know...I just reacted." He pointed at the door. "Not that he gives a fuck about that or what it just cost me."

"Wrong and wrong. Blake is pissed because he feels lesser than all of you and that you treat him with kid gloves. Whether you mean to or not, it doesn't change how he feels."

"I don't have time to coddle him," Nash growled.

"Nash...all he wants is for you to say he did a good job. He wants to feel like a part of the group. He doesn't want to be judged on what happened with the drugs or his overdose. At some point, you need to show him that he has your complete trust again. Otherwise, he'll continue to lash out at you, and you'll lash out at him until it's unfixable."

He shook his head at me.

"You know, you sound like Liam...a fucking cuter version, but still."

I smiled. "Well, since you trust Liam, and I sound like him, then trust me. Throw Blake a lifeline."

"Like what?"

I shrugged. "I don't know. That's something you need to figure out." I pointed at his arm. "As for this. Can you get them to reschedule?"

"The meet isn't the issue. It's the cutoff deadline for sending in my times. If I beat Sabastian then I have enough qualifying scores to submit. I can still send more, but handing them in early looks really good."

I tapped my chin and thought. "Is it just that one race?" He nodded. "As long as you don't care about the pain, pulling open your stitches and needing it closed back up again, then I have an idea."

"Okay, you've got my attention."

"You can use this special spray to keep it dry."

"What spray?"

"I'd have to look up the name for you, but when my mum had surgery, she got some to put on her incision so she could shower. It took her a really long time to heal, and she got sick of covering the wound with plastic because she reacted to the adhesive. She started using this spray instead."

"Okay, get me the name, and I'll buy some boxes."

I giggled at the thought of him having an entire room full of it, just in case.

"There are also some sports thingies that you can put on to help hold the area together."

Nash smirked.

"Sport thingies? How very descriptive of you. I'm not sure how I've never heard of it before," he teased, and I would've hit him if he didn't have a wound.

"Funny. I'm trying to help you here. I'll find that, too. How is it that I know about this stuff, and I'm not the athlete," I said, lifting an accusatory brow at him.

"Because you and Theo are obsessed with knowing every piece of useful and useless information there is."

I laughed. "That's true."

"Also, when you're a specimen like me, you don't worry about that stuff."

"Oh my god, how do you ever fit through a door?"

Nash smiled and grabbed my hand, sending dangerous little sparks traveling up my arm from his touch.

"You won't be able to train between now and Wednesday. Will you be ready?"

"I can think of a few ways to keep my stamina up," he said, his tone shifting into something far more sexual.

He leaned in close to my neck. It should've felt weird when he breathed in like he was sniffing me, but I'd gotten so used to Myles doing the same thing that it felt normal.

I quickly stood, but Nash didn't let go of my hand.

"No, Nash. We've been over this," I said.

"Yes, but that was before I was brutally injured in battle and needed comforting."

He gave me his sad eyes, and I shook my head at him.

"Okay, you need to lay off the Game of Thrones. The answer is still no, but...." I bent over and kissed his lips softly. "I'm glad you're going to be okay," I whispered. "Don't let it go to your head."

Nash shifted on the bed. "Oh, it's going to a head, just not the one you meant."

"You are impossible," I said, just as the door opened and Liam poked his head in to look at us.

"Is it safe to enter?"

"Yeah, I was just leaving," I said, tugging on my hand. Nash reluctantly let go. "I'll get you the names of those thingies."

Nash rolled his eyes but smiled.

"Night, Princess and don't worry, we'll keep you safe."

"I know."

Chapter 57

OCTOBER 28 – TUESDAY 4:00 PM

R**en**

Are you kidding me?

It didn't matter what time of day I tried calling Lizzy —she always put me straight to voicemail. I was starting to think she had me blocked. I hadn't even done anything wrong other than be concerned. If it wasn't for Nash, I wouldn't even know why she wasn't speaking to me. Now, I was torn between my concern and being angry as hell with her.

I stomped down the sidewalk outside the athletic building and tried two more times, but it rang once and went to voicemail. With a frustrated growl, I seriously considered throwing my phone for the millionth time.

"If that wasn't the sexiest little tantrum I've ever seen," Nash said, and I turned around to glare at him.

"I'm not in the mood, Nash."

He leaned against the wall, looking like a cat lounging in the sun. Nash pushed away and slowly wandered toward me.

"What's going on?"

"There's nothing you can do. I'm just frustrated." I pointed at him. "And I don't mean sexually before you even go there."

He smirked and stopped just in front of me, and I glanced around to see if anyone was watching us.

"We shouldn't be doing this," I said.

"Doing what? I'm just standing here talking to you," Nash said with the devil dancing in his eyes. "Now, this is me doing something."

Grabbing me around the waist, he turned us so that my back was against the wall. Not giving me a second to think, Nash dropped his lips to mine, and I shuddered. My head spun, which only added to the mass confusion already swirling around inside of me.

Breaking the kiss, Nash smirked at me.

"See the difference?"

"What I see is an annoying asshole who loves pushing my buttons."

"That too." He smiled, showing off his wicked, dimpled smile. "Now, tell me what's wrong."

"It's Lizzy, she won't speak to me."

My heart was breaking at the thought of her never talking to me again.

"Have you considered just leaving her alone," Nash asked, and I crossed my arms and looked away from him.

"Maybe that is what you would do if it was your best friend. But I can't. She's going through this life-altering experience, and I'm her person. I'm the one who talks to her into the wee hours of the morning. I'm the one who sits and holds her if she needs to cry and anything else she needs once she decides what to do. I mean...she's cut me off completely and...." I scrubbed away the stupid tear running down my cheek. "I keep replaying our last talk over and over, and I can't stop thinking that I pushed her too hard. Maybe I demanded to know too much. I don't know."

"I have news for you, Princess. You push, and you tell us what we don't want to hear. That's what you do, and if you stop doing that, then you stop being you."

Staring at my feet, I kicked a little stone. It was a gorgeous, warm day, and I couldn't even drum up the enthusiasm to enjoy the afternoon sun shining down on us.

"Maybe...I really am a pain in the ass."

Nash laughed. "You're just figuring that out?"

"It's not funny, Nash. My best friend is pregnant, and I'm stuck here, useless. She's blocked me out of her life." I held my hands out. "I feel completely helpless. I don't know what to do. I just...."

He tipped my chin up, silencing me as my heart sputtered all over the place.

"I'll help you, but under one condition."

"You love your conditions," I said, unable to hide the snark in my tone. "Fine, what's the condition?"

"That you never change who you are."

I'd been expecting something sexual, and all the gears in my brain skidded to a halt as I tried to process what he said.

"Not for her, me, or anyone else. Promise me that, and I'll help you get in touch with your friend."

I licked my lips. "I promise."

Nodding, Nash pushed away from the wall, and I sucked in a deep breath. He pulled out his phone.

"Do you need her number?"

Nash smirked at me. "Princess, do you really think I don't have the phone number for every single person you've ever encountered? That guy Rylan is a dick and still wants you. I may have to pay him a visit."

There was no hiding the shock written all over my face.

"Are you a freaking stalker?"

"No, I just take what is mine very seriously. Make no mistake, Princess, you're mine."

He held out the phone for me.

"Here you go," he said as Lizzy's voice came through the line.

"Hello, is anyone there?"

I'd deal with Nash, his stalking, and his proclamations later. I put the phone to my ear.

"Lizzy, it's me, please don't hang up on me." The line was silent. "Lizzy?"

"Fuck Boo, you're...."

"A pain in your ass, I know, but I love you," I said.

She sighed and then broke down crying. Walking away, I sat at a picnic table, my eyes filling with tears as she bawled in my ear.

"I didn't want to cry," she said.

"Lizzy...."

"I'm...I'm pregnant," she blurted out, and I froze, caught between acting shocked or telling her that I already knew.

My conversation with Liam was fresh in my mind. I closed my eyes and lied by saying nothing. Something I was getting far too good at lately.

"It's okay...whatever you need from me, I'm here. I'm always here no matter what."

"I know you are...." The heartbreaking sobs coming through the line were killing me, and I would have given anything to hold her right now. "You must think I'm such a moron. You have three guys, and I'm the one to get knocked up."

It was five now, but telling her that wouldn't help anything. That was a conversation for another time.

"I don't think you're a moron. I'd never think that. Tell me every-thing, whatever you want."

She sniffled. "I've moved in with my dad."

"In Toronto?" I pinched my eyes, hating this.

"Yeah. I just got here a few days ago. I wanted to call you so badly. Every time my phone rings, I want to answer, but then I picture your disappointed face filled with pity and worry, and I can't do it."

"Lizzy, I don't pity you, and I'm not disappointed in you."

"You were about school."

"Yes, but I couldn't wrap my head around why someone with great grades and only a few months left would drop out. I knew you were lying to me and not telling me the real reason."

She sniffed again. "I'm sorry. I should've told you right away."

"It's okay, just please don't cut me out again. I...I can't handle that. I was so freaking scared," I said. "How far along are you?"

"Ten weeks."

"I hate to ask this, but did something happen with you and your mum? Why go to your dad's when you guys don't really get along."

"No, we are okay. She's not happy, but we're okay. My dad is being surprisingly supportive. We've had some of the best conversa-tions ever since I arrived. It's kind of odd. Oh, and he got rid of that girlfriend I hated."

"Jess?"

"Yeah, her. God, she was such a bitch."

"Okay, no changing topics. I know your ways, woman. Why did you move?

Lizzy sighed, and I could tell that she was gearing herself up to blurt out a lot of information at once.

I didn't want to push her too hard. Distraction was my best course of action. I tapped my fingers on the wood tabletop and picked at some of the weathered parts. Nash sat down beside me and grabbed my hand when I winced. There was a tiny sliver stuck in the tip. I wanted to pull away, but he held me firm and studied the splinter before gripping it and yanking it out. It welled with blood, and I shivered, staring into his clear blue eyes as he brought it to his mouth and sucked.

"Well...." Lizzy said, startling me out of the Nash trance.

"I decided to give the baby up, but I wanted to pick the home. I never thought I'd be interviewing potential families. It was really kind of crazy how many couples applied who couldn't have children. Anyway, the family I chose is so incredibly sweet. She's been through so much already, and they were heartbroken when they realized that she couldn't have any kids. Oh, I'm gonna cry again. These hormones are legit."

I smiled at that and tried to ignore Nash as he softly ran the tips of his fingers up and down my hand.

"Back to the story...they live like an hour away from my dad. I moved out here so they can come to all the appointments with me. Boo...seriously, if I wasn't so distraught that I got pregnant in the first place...I would say I was happy that I could do this."

"You mean that?"

"Yeah. It's really weird. This huge thing happened, and I thought it ruined my life. I want kids one day, but not now, not like this. I know that sounds so dramatic. People have babies all the time. But the asshole I slept with wanted nothing to do with the baby and blocked me. I really had to think about my options. Did I want to have it and go to court, fighting to prove he was the father? And then fight for child support or have...well, you know...I was a mess. Then I started researching online and found a lawyer close to me who specializes in helping families who can't conceive connect with someone...in my situation. It just clicked. It kinda made me feel like you."

"Me? I don't understand."

"Boo...girl...seriously. I have known you since we were six and I can't remember a time when you haven't found a way to help me, your mum, someone struggling at school, or volunteering for underprivileged kids. Even when you should be worried about yourself, you focus on finding a silver lining and helping. You're my hero."

Okay, that did it. I burst into tears, and we both cried into the phone. Despite being a blubbering mess, Nash scooted closer and turned so he could pull me into him. *Credit where credit is due.* He held me while I sobbed and rode it out, not saying a word or copping a feel. Last year, I would've said he didn't have a kind bone in his body.

"I...I—" I started, but Lizzy cut me off.

"Nope...don't say you aren't one. Heroes don't need to wear capes to inspire someone."

I bit my lip, trying to hold back the rest of the tears with little success.

"Okay, I won't."

"And don't think I don't know you don't think that it's true, but it is," she said, making me laugh.

"That was a complicated sentence. I hope this works out. You've always been a great judge of character when they don't have a dick," I said, and she gasped.

"Bitch...it's so true."

We both laughed then. I didn't move away from Nash and didn't care who saw.

"I swear, I have a radar for the worst. But they are always soooo fucking hot. Anyway, I promise I won't keep you in the dark anymore. I just didn't know how you'd take it," Lizzy said.

"You know me better than that. I'm sorry I pressed about school," I said.

"Don't be. I did drop out. But...I signed up for an online course and test on Zoom with the teachers."

That made me so happy.

"Good, I'm glad. I miss you, Lizzy. I wish I could squeeze you."

"I miss you, Boo. I'll send pictures soon. Oh...and how did you make your phone show up as my doctor calling?"

I looked over my shoulder at Nash, and he smirked.

"I don't know. That wasn't me. Maybe they were trying to call in at the same time. Technology these days," I said, shaking my head.

Only Nash would find a way to spoof a number for me. Unbelievable...and yet...I sorta loved it. Jerk.

"Oh, in that case, I better call them and make sure everything is okay," Lizzy said.

Unbelievable.

"Okay, let me know. I want to see you."

"I know, but...don't take this the wrong way, but not until after the baby is born and I'm back home. I know this is going to sound strange. But I need to do this on my own, and I'll crumble if I see you in person, Boo. If you let me, I'll lean into you, and this is important to me."

The idea of not seeing Lizzy at all while she was going through this gutted me. But I would do what she wanted.

"I get it. But if you change your mind, you know I'm here. No matter what it is or time of day, just call me."

"I will. Love you, Boo."

"I love you too, Lizzy."

The call ended, and I just sat there, staring at the dark screen for a minute before handing it back to Nash.

"Thank you," I said. "I needed that."

"You're welcome, Princess," he whispered in my ear, and I shivered. "Come on, I should watch the rest of practice."

"You mean to yell at the guys for being slow and pathetic."

Nash laughed as he stood and held out his hand.

"Same thing," he said, making me chuckle. I accepted his offer and he helped me stand. "Oh, and I have a gift for you."

"It's not another box of thongs, is it?"

"Oooh, no, but a good idea."

I rolled my eyes at him. "You really are impossible. You know that, right?"

"I do," he said as we reached the athletic building, and he pulled a door open for me.

"So, what's the gift?"

"Like I'm going to tell you when I can keep you in suspense."

Nash laughed as I glared at him.

"One of these days, Collier, I swear, one of these days."

He nudged me. "You better stop while you're ahead. You know that threatening me only turns me on, and then you'll have to suffer the consequences of your actions."

I shook my head at him but couldn't stop the laugh.

"Jerk."

OCTOBER 29 – WEDNESDAY 4:45 PM

Nash

The teams started to arrive while I waited for the spray on my arm to dry. This was the second application just to be safe.

I ignored most of them. It was my senior year, and I'd never see them after today. There was only one person with times close enough to mine who could compete at the next level.

Sabastian—who also happened to be Christov's son. What would he do if I asked about his father, Christov? Instead of Yuriy, the bullshit name he used to hide out in the US.

"Still can't believe this needed nine stitches," Myles said.

The gash started on the outside of my arm and wrapped partially onto my bicep. It was a damn good thing that I'd been wearing multiple layers. He would've cut deeper, and then I really would've been in trouble.

"Yeah, I'll be sure to get him back for it the next time I see his fucking face," I said.

"As long as I get the final word, do whatever ya like," Myles growled. "I won't rest until I've found him and he's no longer a threat."

"Who are you threatening now," Sabastian said as he dropped his duffel down on the bench beside ours.

God, how I wanted to take the long strap from his bag and wrap it around his neck. Instead, I smiled at him as I pulled up the protective bandage with Myles's help.

"Worried we were talking about you, Sabastian," I asked, and he snorted.

"Nah, you don't scare me, Nash. I know you have a reputation for being a dick, but I think all that stuff about you being dangerous is smoke and mirrors."

I chuckled as I smoothed the wrap.

"Is that so? Interesting. Well...if you're not scared of me, then you should come to my club's grand opening."

Sabastian looked at his team and then at me again. "I didn't know you had a club. Did your daddy buy it?"

"I don't need my daddy to buy my toys. Your daddy got you that Mercedes AMG GT63 in custom cherry red, didn't he? I would've gone black, personally."

I'd only told Liam who Sabastian really was. That would mean Theo knew, but Myles would've already pummeled him looking for answers and I needed to be a more covert. What did he know about Ren if anything? What did he want with Ivy? Did Christov try to enroll him in Wayward and Dean Henry blocked it? So many questions.

"You spying on me now, Nash," he asked, stepping closer.

"If you call spying, seeing you pull out of the coffee shop, then sure. You're the one who just confirmed your daddy bought it." I tapped my chin. "It's funny, though, I thought you were at Hawking Shores on a scholarship. It begs the question of how he afforded that car."

Sabastian smirked. "I see Ivy has been talking about me."

"Oh, come now, Sabastian. You wanted her to say something, or you wouldn't have mentioned the bullshit story in the first place. You were testing her. But why lie to Ivy? If you wanted to know something about me, you could've just asked. I might even have been flattered enough to sign a copy of my swim card for you. Wanna do a selfie?"

He laughed hard, and the tension that had been building as the rest of the schools and guys tuned into the conversation dissipated.

"You know, I think I might actually like you. It's too bad we're on opposite teams," he said, and I crossed my arms.

"Yeah, too bad," I said, not meaning a word of it. "The invitation stands. Bring Ivy as your date unless, of course, you plan to keep lying to her." I looked around the room. "That goes for all of you. Volatile opens Halloween night, costumes are mandatory, and no cover. Come check it out. It's seventeen and older for the night, so make sure you have your ID."

Liam, Myles, and Blake followed me as I turned and walked away. We had to keep the same roster for this race, so Theo was out.

"Hey, Nash?" I looked back at Sabastian. "Good luck."

The corner of my mouth tugged up. "I make my own luck."

Marching out, I sucked in a deep breath, feeling right at home with the heavy scent of chlorine in the air. Not getting up first thing in the morning for my swim or practicing after class had been excruciating.

As we walked along the edge of the pool to the starting area, I glanced up at the bleachers. There were only a few dozen people this time with it only being one make-up race. There was no extra fanfare for this, but I didn't care. I'd take any excuse to kick Hawking Shore's ass and get in the pool.

Princess smiled as we walked past where she was sitting with Theo, Ivy, and Chantry. I winked before looking away and then froze. Myles kept walking and crashed into my back.

"Jesus, man, what are ya doin'?"

"What the fuck is he doing here?"

I growled under my breath and stomped toward my father like a heat-seeking missile.

He smiled as I glowered at him, wishing I could drown him in the pool and solve all my problems if it were only that easy. Lawrence stood calmly, his hands folded in front of him, and I knew what he was doing. If I made a scene like I had on my birthday then I looked like the bad guy, again.

"Father, what are you doing here," I asked, keeping my voice down.

"I came to watch you swim. Can a father not want to support his only son in his passion?"

There was no one around us when I glanced back. Even my guys were keeping their distance while still being vigilant. They had my back if I needed them.

"Who is this act for? No one can hear you and we both know you have no interest in my swimming career. You haven't come to a meet since I graduated Golden Oak Prep. In fact, I distinctly remember that after I placed third, you told me that I was wasting my time and that I'd never make the Olympics, so I should get my head out of my ass. I was twelve. Way to parent, by the way. I couldn't say that then, but I can now."

He smirked, and his eyes lost the fake sweetness to show the real devil under the pretense.

"I want to make up for lost time."

To anyone who didn't know him, they would think that behind the tailored suit, soft smile on his lips, and shine in his eyes, was a proud father. But that was because they bought the lie.

"Bullshit, what do you really want?"

"I've been trying to reach you about our situation. You haven't responded. In fact, I'm pretty sure you've been ignoring my calls. No one, not even you, can ignore me."

"Don't you mean your situation?"

He smirked, and at any other time or place, I would've been sucker punched.

"No, you and Myles took on the project. I haven't heard a single word about how it's going."

"There's nothing to tell. He is proving to be more elusive than we thought," I said.

"I see."

I didn't respond. There was no winning this fight because he would always turn it on us.

"You do know that I could've sent the guards to pick you up?"

"I'm sure you could've. But I can have you barred from the property, and then you won't have the luxury of popping in for...whatever this is," I said, and his eyes hardened.

"Good thing this is just a friendly visit. Though, there was another reason...."

He sucked in a deep breath, his eyes going to the bleachers.

"There is someone else I was hoping to see, and would you look at that, she's sitting right over there. This must be my lucky day."

Lawrence left, and my jaw felt like it was cracking. It took everything I had not to grab him and drag him off the property far away from Ren. I'd been trying not to antagonize him by banning him, but now...I was tempted. He was never getting his hands on her. So help me god, I would never let him touch one hair on her head.

The guys shared the same dark expression when Lawrence sat

down beside Ren. Theo's presence was the only reason I hadn't lost my shit. Fuck, she was something. The way she straightened her spine and refused to look at him was so fucking sexy. She didn't flinch or get up and move. She silently let him know he didn't intimidate her. What I had once found annoying about Ren, might be her greatest asset.

"What is he doing here," Liam asked when I rejoined them.

"Fucking with my head, making subtle threats, and throwing the marriage contract he has with Ren around like a trophy. You know, being a prick as usual."

I crossed my arms and tried not to stare—it would only embolden him.

"He'll marry her over me cold dead body," Myles growled.

"He won't. Oh, and you're not taking Ren to Volatile's grand opening," I said.

"Why?"

"Because she already agreed to go with me," I said, smirking at his scowling face.

"Why would she agree to go wit you?" He glared at me and crossed his arms.

"She owed me a favor, and I collected. Oh, and I already got her costume. Don't worry, you'll like it."

Myles's lips pressed together in a hard line. It was way too easy to poke at him when it came to Princess.

"What are ya up to, Collier?"

He eyed me as suspiciously as I'd just done my father. God, I was so excited to see the look on his face when he found out that Princess and I slept together. He wouldn't be shocked, but he'd be pissed I didn't tell him. Fucking, priceless...I really needed new hobbies.

"Nothing more than normal. We're all going together in the same car, but I thought you should know that she'll be walking in on my arm."

I smiled at him, and he swore under his breath.

"You're an arse."

"Maybe, but don't forget it's her birthday," I said.

"It's her birthday," Blake asked, and then shook his head as we all stared at him. "Why is it that I'm always the last to know shit? You all suck."

Myles shrugged.

"I asked. Why didn't you?"

They glared at one another, and I decided that it was just as much fun, stirring the shit and watching it, as being in the middle.

"Hey, it was Liam, right?"

We turned to see the guy that Liam had saved walking over.

"I promise not to grab you today." He smiled. "And no matter what happens, I just wanted to say thanks again. I haven't been able to stop thinking about that meet."

"Not a problem, Trey. But just so you know, the lifeguards would've saved you. I'm not that much of a hero."

"Either way, you still helped me, so thanks."

Trey went back over to his team and Sabastian's scowling face. He definitely didn't like him making nice with us. I smiled at him, filing that away for later.

"Swimmers, please move to your lanes," Coach yelled.

Putting my father and Sabastian out of my mind, I focused on winning.

Myles grabbed my shoulder and grumbled under his breath.

"This will be me fastest swim ever," he said, glancing over at Lawrence, who was trying to talk to Ren, while she gave him the cold shoulder.

"You and me both."

R^{en} Either Nash had a secret talent for clothes shopping, or whoever helped him had impeccable taste. The velvet and satin felt incredible as I smoothed my hands down the front. It was the prettiest and sexiest version of Elsa's dress—complete with cape and tiara—that I'd ever seen.

The guys had banded together to make my birthday extra special and today had been nothing short of magical. I had a feeling tonight would be the same, and it all started with a call from Dean Henry.

Ivy, Chantry, and I were summoned to his office where he told us that we had been dismissed from classes and our teachers informed. As if that wasn't cryptic and unnerving, he then sent us back to our dorm room.

TWELVE HOURS EARLIER

"What do you think is going on," Ivy asked, and I shook my head as we rode up to the senior floor in the elevator.

"No idea. He's never done that before. Now that I think about it, I've never been ordered to my room ever in my life," I said, and Ivy and Chantry laughed.

"Of course you haven't, you're Ren," Chantry teased.

I was really loving this side of her. Ever since the volleyball-to-the-face incident, she'd been much more open and talkative. She stood straighter, joked more, and didn't cower when the mean girls walked by.

"Hey…I got in trouble before coming here," I said as we stepped off the elevator and froze. My heart stopped and fell all the way back down to the ground floor before restarting and racing at full speed.

Blake stood before us with a cheeky grin on his face. He was dressed like a cross between a sexy rocker and a Chippendale dancer. No shirt, tattoos displayed, his favorite black, ripped jeans, leather cuffs on his wrists, chain around his neck, and combat boots on his feet. That was all fine, but he was also wearing a bow tie and holding a silver tray with tall glasses of something bubbly.

He licked his lips as he stepped forward.

"Would you care for a refreshment? We have sparkling, non-alco-

holic champagne. It's actually really good," he said, making me smile as I reached for a glass.

Ivy and Chantry each took one, and he twirled the empty tray in his hand like a circus performer. The sweet drink tasted like a high-end apple juice when I took a sip. Blake stepped in, and I gasped. The heat from his body made me shiver from head to toe. He tipped my chin up, and all I could hear was the heavy thumping of my heart. As always, his lips hovered over mine until I took the offering, and then he took my breath away with a kiss that would curl anyone's toes.

He licked my lower lip and smiled. "So sweet," he whispered, leaving me lightheaded and confused.

"Blake...what's going on?"

"Follow me and find out."

Glancing at Ivy and Chantry, they sipped their drinks and tried to hide their smiles. Were they in on this? There was no time to grill them as Blake led the way back to my room.

Everything seemed normal until Myles stepped out into the hallway wearing an identical outfit to Blake with a tray of all my favorite treats. Fresh fruit, the chocolate chip cookies from downstairs, and even the raspberry muffins that he still picked up because he said they helped win me. It had nothing to do with the muffins. It was all him, but I loved that he randomly brought them.

"Hello, Snowflake," he said, really putting on the accent.

I nearly melted at his feet. No one could look as full of mischief as Myles. It brimmed inside of him.

"And ladies. Would you like a snack," he asked, his voice like gravel.

I needed to start carrying a fan. He held out napkins, and I smiled at the little snowflakes all over them. I chose one of the muffins and a few strawberries.

Once we each had food, he smiled and opened the door. You could've knocked me over with a feather. Our beds and desks weren't touched, but all the extra furniture was removed. In its place were massage tables, comfortable chairs, like you'd see at a spa, and portable foot baths.

The blinds had been drawn, so the room was dark, but everywhere you looked were twinkling lights, flowy sheers, and burning candles. Soft music played, and just like that, I'd stepped away from the school hallway and into a relaxing alternate reality.

"This is incredible," Chantry said, her eyes wide as she looked around.

"Totally lit," Ivy said.

Two women I didn't recognize stood in the middle of the room with Theo. He snapped his fingers, and they walked toward Ivy and Chantry while he walked toward me.

"Are you ready to be pampered?" Theo's dominant tone was thick and pressed on me like a hand despite speaking in a whisper.

"Why are you all doing this?"

One arrogant eyebrow arched. "Is today not your birthday?"

"Well, it is, but...."

He placed a finger over my lips, and the sentence died in my throat. Heat flooded my body and joined my racing heart in a competition to see which could get me to pass out first.

"Then you have your answer. So, I'll ask again. Are you ready to be pampered today?" All I could do was nod. "Good, then follow me, Shiver," he said, running his thumb over my bottom lip...and shiver I did.

I would've followed him off a cliff. We turned toward the bathroom door, and my heart sputtered again at the sight of Liam. He leaned against the door jamb, and the only thought in my mind was...holy hell.

We walked up, and I barely noticed when Theo took the drink and napkin of goodies. Liam's eyes were commanding and easily penetrated my soul without a word. There was something in the way he looked at me that made me want to drop to my knees at his feet and surrender. That was what Theo had meant. Liam's energy, aura, presence—whatever you wanted to call it—was indescribable.

"*You look scrumptious enough to eat, Little Rabbit,*" *Liam growled as he held out his steady hand while mine visibly trembled.* "*Don't worry, we're going to take very good care of you.*"

The butterflies soaring around inside of me went wild with the sexual undertones of that one simple sentence. Then, Liam closed us into the bathroom together.

"*We're going to start with a massage to relax and restore your mind and muscles.*"

He tapped my arms, and I raised them over my head for him to remove my sweater vest. Even though he hadn't touched my skin, it was so sensitive with him near me that the soft blouse I'd worn a thousand times felt scratchy. One at a time, he effortlessly undid the little buttons, and I trembled right down to my toes as he stepped behind me. All my logical brain cells that had been hanging on decided it was a good time to exit stage left.

I closed my eyes as he slid the blouse off and then unclasped my bra and used just one finger on each hand to slide it over my shoulders and down my arms before it disappeared. His hands felt large and warm as he massaged my tense muscles.

"*Lean into me,*" *he breathed against my neck, and I melted into his chest and sighed as he caressed down my sides, around to my stomach, and then up before retreating the same way.*

"*That's much better, Little Rabbit. You are such a good girl.*"

Liam might be a magician. I didn't even feel him unzipping my kilt, but suddenly, it dropped to the floor. He kissed my neck and I shuddered against him. He helped me step out of my kilt and then circled me like prey. I was overwhelmed by his energy that pressed on me like a soothing hand. Liam didn't need to speak. He pointed or tapped a body part, and I knew exactly what he wanted. He called himself a Dom, but to me, it seemed otherworldly.

He freed my hair from the messy twist on top of my head and then helped me slip into the comfiest robe. I knew Myles had picked it out almost immediately. It was a dark navy with lighter blue snowflakes all over it.

Myles was obsessed with them, or me, or maybe the imagery was so tightly wound together in his mind that he couldn't stop himself from buying everything with the design. That meant he was always thinking about me. What once would've freaked me out was now as warm and cozy to my mind and soul as this robe was against my skin.

"Alright, Little Rabbit, let's get you loosened up."

The bathroom was quiet and felt like our own little world, so it was jarring to hear the soft music when Liam opened the door. When I stepped out, I noticed that Myles, Blake, and Theo were gone. Liam must have seen my disappointment as he led me over to the massage table.

"Don't worry. They'll be back once the massages are done. We thought this was best to give Ivy and Chantry more privacy."

I could just make out someone on the other side of the temporary privacy screen. Between it, the sheers and the candlelight, they were no more than a blurry shadow.

I smirked. "That was very thoughtful. This is...incredible," I said as Liam loosened the tie on my robe, his fingers teasingly grazing my skin.

"We haven't even begun. Wait to praise us once your day is over." My lip tugged up.

"Okay," I said, even though I knew that this was going to be the most amazing day.

It would be nice to numb some of the ache of yesterday. I'd spent most of it crying, hating that I couldn't visit my mother's grave. It had been one year. One whole year of so many firsts, changes, losses, and wins, and all I wanted was to tell her about everything.

In my heart, I knew that she wasn't in some casket buried in the ground, but it would've given me a place to visit. A place to feel like I was closer to her. A place to mourn. I'd walked from one class to the next like a zombie and only made it because one of the guys was with me all day. After classes Blake had taken me for a walk. We listened to the birds while I quietly sobbed.

What they arranged for today was twice as special. It had been a long time since I had a girl's day. Mum and I used to go all the time before she got sick. The guys had planned something sweet, but for me, it held so much more meaning.

Pushing the robe from my shoulders, I stood naked in front of Liam and loved how his eyes traced my body with a searing heat.

"Lay face down," he said.

Climbing onto the table, I sighed when I felt the warming pad. I should've known Liam would be an amazing masseuse. But I realized I hadn't given him enough credit the moment he spread warm oil along my body and began to work the muscles.

Firmly and in the most delicious way, his fingers dug into my skin right where I was the tightest and worked each little ball of tension. He started with my shoulders, then moved down my back to my arms and legs. I was practically asleep when Liam squatted beside my head. I couldn't see his face, just his knees and bare feet, but I could picture the piercing look in his gaze.

"This massage is going to relax you in every way," he whispered in my ear. My relaxed heart began pounding out of control in my chest once more. "And when I make you come...you must remain silent, Little Rabbit." Shivers raced down my spine in excitement. "Not. A. Single. Sound," Liam breathed in my ear. "Do you understand?"

I swallowed and licked my lips. "Yes, Sir."

"Good, Little Rabbit. Roll over," he ordered and then stood.

Was he really doing this with Ivy, Chantry, and two people I didn't know in the room? I still couldn't see anything but shadows when I rolled over. Getting settled on my back, Liam grabbed me by the ankles and dragged me down the table until my head was on the bed and not the opening for my face. I'd almost made the mistake of squealing but pressed my lips together. Liam smirked, knowing that I'd almost gotten myself in trouble, and we hadn't even begun.

He removed the head attachment before coating his talented hands in the fragrant oil and getting to work. His face was cast in shadows as the candlelight flickered. At that moment, I decided there was nothing more erotic than Liam's intensely focused stare.

His hands ran down my body, fingers and thumbs like magic. Gently gliding them over my breasts, ribs, and hips, he slowly stoked the fire between my thighs. It wasn't humanly possible for him to know my body better than I did, and yet he found spots that lit a need in me that made no sense.

The aching in my core had me begging for more. I was caught between being the most relaxed I'd ever been and so pent up that I wanted to scream as Liam continued his slow, sensual torture.

Liam had been waiting for me to reach that point and how he knew I was there, I will never understand.

He gently pressed my clit, and I came so close to screaming that I had to bite my lip as my body bowed off the table. He kept massaging and then did it again and again, and by the time his finger slipped inside me, I was done. It took seconds while he rubbed my G-spot to push me over the cliff without a parachute. The earth-shattering quaking ripped through me, and if I hadn't gripped the bed, I would've fallen off. Dots danced behind my eyes, and my mouth hung open in a silent scream.

Of course, Liam wasn't done forcing the orgasms out in waves that made me writhe on the table over and over again. I was panting hard when he removed his finger and then smiled at me as he sucked it into his mouth.

Liam's arms flexed as he braced himself and leaned close to my ear.

"You taste as delicious as I suspected, Little Rabbit. One day soon, I'll do nothing but feast on you." He smoothed back my hair, and his eyes locked with mine. The candlelight danced like miniature flames in his cinnamon-colored eyes. With a devious smirk, he stood up straight, and I saw how excited he was.

Liam touched my chin, forcing my attention back onto his face.

"No, this is not about me. Today is only about you," he said matter-of-factly. "Now roll over again for me. The lava stones should be ready."

Standing before the full-length mirror, I couldn't get over what they had done. The pampering had been an all-day affair. After the massages, we enjoyed mani-pedis, feasted on all my favorite foods, and watched a trashy rom-com. Then, they'd brought in a professional stylist to do my hair and makeup. There were even little decorative crystals on my face, fanning the corners of my eyes.

I loved everything about today and wanted to remember it forever. We were in for a future of craziness, and we still had so many enemies, but the Kings made me feel like we could conquer anything together.

"God, Ren, you look so beautiful," Ivy said.

Turning, I smiled at her.

"So do you. You look stunning as Belle. I can't believe Sabastian agreed to go as Gaston."

"Me either, but he said he was happy to." Ivy looked downright giddy.

I had no idea why Nash invited the swimmers from Hawking Shores when he obviously hated them. But I'd given up trying to understand Nash's motives. He juggled secrets like a clown would balls.

"And I love your costume, Chantry. You make the sexiest pirate ever. Even your sword looks real," I said, and she laughed and posed for me.

There was a knock at the door just before it opened, and in walked the Devil himself.

Nash didn't bother with a costume, opting to wear an all-black suit that fit him like a glove and a masquerade mask. He looked every bit the mafia Don he was born to become. I knew from Myles that the guys would be dressed the same except for their masks. Each of them had picked a different color. Nash's was black and silver.

"I need to speak to Ren alone for a minute," he said, his exquisite blue eyes accentuated by the covering.

Chantry and Ivy slipped past him, and as the door closed, I sucked in a shuddering breath. He looked dangerous, dashing even, and I hugged my stomach as it tumbled around with each step he took.

"You take my breath away, Princess," Nash said, and my eyebrow cocked.

"Careful, Collier. That almost sounded like you caught some of those pesky feelings."

"Oh, I still hate you," he said, smiling.

"Good, because I definitely hate you," I said and felt the blush heating my face. "Thank you for the dress. It's amazing." I ran my hands down the lush white faux fur lining the edge of the cape. It was so soft that I wanted to cuddle in it, and rub it against my face.

"I'm glad you like it. I got you something else."

"Nash...."

"No, you're going to take this," he said, and my eyes went wide.

I stared at him like he'd lost his mind when he walked over to my bed and kneeled down to pull something out from underneath.

"What are you doing?"

"I stored this here for safekeeping," he said as he placed the brown-paper covered parcel down on the bed.

Walking over, I stared down at the gift and then looked up at Nash. He grabbed my hands before I could reach for it and sighed.

"Look, here's the thing...tonight, you'll understand why I

couldn't say anything to you and why I had to wait. Some of those things may make you angry."

"Oh, you are not off to a good start. Why?"

"Just...trust me. I know you well enough to know that you'll want to punch me in the face."

"Is this about Vicky? Are you stuck in the contract?"

My whole body felt like it was waiting for his response.

"No, and yes. I know how to deal with her and the contract. But Vicky is still a part of this. I'm not making sense. The point is, I really want you to remember right now."

"You're kind of scaring me."

His knuckles brushed my cheek. "Don't be. It's not like that. Just...please try to forgive me for keeping what I know from you. I don't beg and I don't normally say sorry, but I will for this, for you. I had no choice and to prove that I'm not a complete dick. I got you this." He held his hand out toward the gift. "I guess it's better to say I got it back."

"You didn't...."

With a racing heart, I reached down and pulled at the tape holding the edges of the paper together. My eyes filled with tears as I stared at my mother's painting. The same one I'd used as a bargaining chip to get Nash into the banquet. My hands went to my mouth, and shock kept the sob from escaping.

"I know you said that in the museum, it could be loved by many, but this painting is special. It was clearly made with love for you. I couldn't let you use this for me, especially with everything I said and did after."

Nash gripped my chin and forced me to look at him. Smiling, he pulled the folded, black pocket square from his suit jacket and dabbed at the tears, trying not to ruin my makeup.

"I could say I'm sorry a million times, and I know you'd never truly believe me. Believe this...I have demons, and I will always be an asshole, but I'm sorry for what I said...how I treated you, and for keeping what I have from you."

"Shut up and kiss me," I ordered.

Nash crushed his lips to mine as he pulled me against him. My head spun while every emotion swirled around like a vortex inside of me, including terror over whatever worried him.

I sucked in a deep breath as our lips parted. "Please tell me you didn't hurt Mr. Paval to get this back?"

He chuckled. "Would I do that? I mean does he really need all of his fingers," Nash teased, making me smile. God, I hoped it was teasing. "We better go, or I'll miss my grand opening," Nash said.

Plucking the pocket square from his hand, I wiped away the lipstick on his mouth before folding it and putting it back in his pocket.

"Thank you, Nash, and I will try to remember even though you've officially scared the shit out of me."

He smiled wide. "Good, I like to keep you guessing."

"I hate you so much," I said.

"I hate you more."

Chapter 60

OCTOBER 31 – FRIDAY 7:50 PM

Ren

There was an electric buzz in the air as we walked downstairs. Wayward apparently put on a Halloween bash every year, and the music was pounding from inside the cafetorium while students and teachers alike milled around in costume. Dean Henry stood out from the crowd, standing near the office door, his face passive but his eyes watching everything. He nodded to us as we passed.

"Do you think he ever unwinds or goes home, for that matter," I asked, curiosity getting the best of me.

"Who, Dean Henry?"

"Yeah. I mean, everyone else is having fun tonight, and he looks… sad."

Nash looked back. "I honestly don't know with him. Just when I think I have a read on him, I realize that I don't. He could be married with ten kids or live under the floor like a troll, and I don't think we'll ever know."

"Maybe, but I kinda feel bad leaving him here," I said.

"Princess, the dean is not a lost dog. He'll be fine. If he wanted to party, I'm sure he would. Besides, I don't think my new club is the best place to take him out for a bonding sesh, you feel me?"

"I didn't mean to invite him tonight. Never mind," I said as Nash pulled open the door.

"Nash, wait up. I'm ready."

We both froze and turned to see Vicky jogging across the foyer in her costume. She was dressed as a Roman goddess and looked stunning.

"What the hell are you talking about," Nash asked.

I was caught between stepping through the door or staying put and watching the chaos. I chose to stay put. Nash had asked me to trust him.

"Your grand opening. It's tonight, right? Everyone has been talking about it, and it would be the perfect time to let everyone know about us." Vicky looked at me, her lips pressing together. "I'm your…."

"Stop…just stop. The answer is no, Vicky," Nash said. Vicky's face turned an alarming red, and like a pot near boiling, I could see her rage simmering. "I didn't invite you for a reason."

"But…I don't understand. Why does she get to go," Vicky asked, her finger pointing at me. "What the hell, Nash? Why the fuck are you acting like such an asshole?"

Nash's face darkened as she yelled at him.

"If you don't start treating me better, I'm going to call my father," she roared.

Everyone nearby turned to stare at the unfolding drama, including Dean Henry. He shifted toward us, already on alert. Vicky was at least consistent in her love for public showdowns.

Nash made a vicious sound under his breath, and for just a second, I genuinely feared for Vicky's life. She might not see it, but it was in his eyes. I grabbed Nash's arm before he did something stupid.

"Then call your daddy like a cry baby, Vicky. I'm sure he'll love to hear how you made yet another scene in front of Dean Henry this time," I said, nodding toward the man.

Vicky didn't take the hint.

"Shut up, and stay out of this," she snarled at me while staring at my hand gripping Nash's arm.

She was far too consumed with her jealousy and rage to use any of the sense God gave her.

"If you were smart, Vicky. You'd walk away."

"You walk away, bitch," she snapped. Nash tensed, and my hand tightened.

"Give me a minute first," I said, and she crossed her arms.

"Why do you want to be with Nash so badly?"

Her eyes narrowed.

"No, I'm serious. If someone treated me the way that he treats you, I wouldn't stand for it. But you keep coming back for more. That's not love, Vicky. Allowing that behavior makes you look desperate and useable. Don't let anyone treat you like you're worthless. I may not like you. In fact I despise you as much as you do me, but even I can see that you deserve better than that."

"Don't you tell me what to do. You're not the one engaged to him while he flaunts another woman in my face," she said, and she had a point.

"That's enough," Nash said. "Call your father, or don't call your father. I don't really care at this point, Vicky. You're not coming with me, and if you even think about showing up on your own, you will not be granted entry."

"Fuck you, Nash," she said and stormed off.

I looked up at Nash, and he sighed.

"This will be sorted by tomorrow, I promise," Nash said, knowing that as much as I loathed her, I really hated being in this position more.

"Swear it to me," I said.

"Do you want me to pinky swear?"

I glared at him, and he smirked.

"Fine. I swear on my life that this will all be sorted by tomorrow."

Nodding, I stepped outside and sucked in a deep breath as I stared at the sexiest sight I'd ever seen. A stretch limo sat idling at the curb between the SUVs I'd seen multiple times now. But it was the four guys dressed in matching black suits with masks on that made me melt. How in the world had I gotten this lucky?

Nash held out his elbow. All we needed was a red carpet to complete the fantasy.

"Fuck, Snowflake, ya look beautiful," Myles said, stepping forward and wrapping his arms around me.

"Hey, back off, McCoy. She's my date for the night," Nash said.

Myles rolled his eyes.

"I'm stealin' a dance later. He can go feck himself," Myles whispered.

"I can still hear you, asshole."

"I don't care. She's my Snowflake, not yours," he said, getting into the limo.

That was something else I couldn't wait to do tomorrow. I was done hiding this thing between me and Nash. No matter the outcome of tonight, I'd find a way to say what needed to be said and keep the peace. Liam and the rest of the guys might be okay with omitting or lying, but it wasn't me, at least not when it came to relationship stuff. We needed trust, and right now, I'd broken it.

"Come on, Ren, get in here. This limo is incredible," Ivy yelled, and I smiled.

I couldn't remember the last time I was so excited for my birthday.

OCTOBER 31 – FRIDAY 8:45 PM

Ren

Holy shit.

I'd only been here once, and the last time I was here, nothing had been done to the outside, and the inside was a construction site. Now, it looked like a completely different place.

Nash had taken the old architecture of the area and incorporated it into the design. A brand-new stone face had been erected with modern black accents to give it a chic look. He replaced the small crappy windows with eight-foot tall panes draped with black sheers.

Through a veil of mystery, you got a peek at what was going on inside, still privy to the debauchery while you stood in line. It definitely made you want to be part of the action.

The parking lot had been redone, and Nash must have bought the overgrown parcel next door because it was now part of the club. Over the massive windows, built right into the rock, was glowing red neon letters spelling *Volatile* which stood out like a beacon.

He'd gone all out for the opening. Spotlights, velvet ropes, and an actual red carpet running from the drop-off area to the front door. It was as if he'd taken a fancy club from the heart of New York and plunked it in the outskirts of Portland.

"Jesus, Nash. This is stunning," Ivy said, her mouth hanging open like the rest of us.

"It really is gorgeous," I said, smiling at him.

"I couldn't have done it without my guys, they made it happen," Nash said as the valet opened the door.

"Well, whoever did what...it's incredible. I can't believe it's the same building."

Nash got out and offered me his hand. Taking a leap of faith, I slid mine into his.

There was no fanfare or flashing lights from paparazzi, but the excitement in the air and the very long line to get in gave the club that vibe.

Security guards weaved through the crowd, standing out in their black suits among the party goers in costume. People were dressed in everything from the classics, like a vampire, werewolf, or zombie, all the way to Beetlejuice, a Minion, and Fortnite characters.

"Oh my god. I feel so special," Ivy squealed from behind me as we walked up to the front doors.

It was easy to feel that way, surrounded by the Kings.

Morrison stood at the door, looking like he'd been recruited by the secret service, complete with the black suit and earpiece.

"Morrison. All good so far," Nash asked as we stepped inside where it was loud with music and club chatter.

"So far, but the night is young. The guards are diligent and the built-in scanner around the door was genius," Morrison answered. He pointed to the glowing red strip that looked like regular LEDs. "It went red when you walked through the door."

"Perfect," Nash said.

Ivy smiled at her dad, and as soon as we started to walk away, she greeted him. I couldn't hear what she said with all the sounds around us.

We moved as a unit down the hallway to a door on the left and entered another world.

"Wow."

"You like it," Nash asked, practically yelling in my ear.

"This is incredible."

The inside matched the outside perfectly. Reclaimed barn board on the walls complemented the black marble floors. The long bar with glowing red lights felt upscale yet still fun.

"Are all these people even allowed to have alcohol," I asked, and Nash laughed.

"You would be the person to ask that right away. I'm running some all-ages and over-twenty-one nights once we are up and running. All the fancy bottles are just for show, and all the fruity drinks are alcohol-free. I don't want to get shutdown my first night."

"Let me show you to our section," he said, holding my hand as we weaved through the crowd.

They'd kept the building's original design with the wall divisions but only to create alcoves for specialized entertainment. In my head, it felt like fingers jutting off of the main room at the back of the club.

We walked from one fantasy into another. Each was slightly different but still offered comfortable seating, a small dance floor, and a show. In the first section, aerial dancers hung suspended from the ceiling by silks. The second one felt like a horror movie with performers on stilts dressed as monsters moving through the crowd. The third space we passed through had a darker, sexier vibe, with male dancers making girls scream. They were appropriately wearing the iconic *Scream* masks.

There were five unique areas in total before we reached an opening with velvet ropes and guards stationed outside.

"This is the VIP area," Nash explained as the guard moved the rope. "Normally, it can be divided into three spaces with walls that pull out from the back to provide privacy. For tonight, I kept it reserved for us and no one else."

"There's Sabastian," Ivy said, pointing as she smiled. "I'll be back," she said and darted off, dragging poor Chantry with her.

"Don't trust him," Nash breathed in my ear.

I watched Ivy as she danced her way through the crowd to the group I'd seen at the swimming competition.

"Why? What do you know?"

"Not enough to say for sure. But he lied to her about not having money," Nash said, and I narrowed my eyes as I glared at the guy.

"Why?"

"No idea, but he has a three-hundred-thousand-dollar car. You don't have that and claim to need a scholarship. So either his family came into a large sum of money recently, or he's a liar."

"I'm going to go order drinks. What do ya want, Snowflake," Myles asked, and Nash laughed.

"You don't need to go up to the bar when you're in here."

He walked over to one of the tables and picked up a tablet. Holding it out to Myles, he tapped the screen, and the *Volatile* logo flashed across the front before it brought up the drink list.

"Well, shit...look at that."

"I'll take something blue," I said.

"On it." Myles bit his lip as he started searching which made me smile.

"You've thought of everything," I said as Nash led me toward the tall windows.

"I tried to. But I wouldn't have been able to make this happen without Liam and Nora. They really came through, and if you need anything, Nora is wandering around here somewhere, keeping everything in order."

"I'm good, but thanks."

I looked over my shoulder at the guys. Liam pulled out a deck of cards as they sat down in the plush leather chairs.

"Do you ever feel left out? Like you're part of the group but still an outsider."

Nash followed my line of sight and smiled.

"It can be lonely at the top. But someone needs to be looking out," he said.

"Like the sheep herder watching over his flock," I teased, making him laugh.

"I guess you could look at it that way. The biggest difference is that I'm always planning the next move. My guys don't do that. Not to the same extent anyway."

We stood there silently our arms just barely touching as we watched the crowd outside and the cars driving past. For the first time, I felt the weight.

"Why don't you walk away? Just leave the insanity behind and start over," I asked, and Nash was quiet for a long time.

"Because I was born into this life. It's all I know. In this world, we can either run or fight to survive." Nash locked eyes with me. "I don't run."

I thought about what he'd said as we looked out the window. I wasn't born into this life, and yet I understood him...I understood all of them. I felt the draw to protect as surely as if they were families that I was responsible for, when in reality...I didn't know where or how I fit into the puzzle. Liam called me their queen. But the queen of what? I might be a Mikhailov, but that was nothing more than a name. What did it really mean?

Reaching out with my pinky, I linked it around Nash's. He glanced at me but didn't say anything as he tightened his finger to hold mine.

Chapter 61

OCTOBER 31 – FRIDAY 8:59 PM

R^{en}

Tears streamed down my face from laughing as Myles spun me around on the dance floor. I twirled until Blake caught me, and the insanity continued. At least Blake had rhythm and actually danced with me. Myles was like a dying chicken flapping its wings around, but I wouldn't have him any other way. Blake and I laughed as he swung his suit jacket over his head.

"I better stop him before he does a full striptease," I yelled, and Blake nodded, laughing.

I signaled to Ivy and Chantry that we were sitting down before I grabbed Myles's flailing hand and dragged him off the dance floor. Nash, Liam, and Theo were in a very intense game of War when we entered through the velvet ropes. Theo and Nash refused to play poker with Liam, and I couldn't blame them. I screamed as Nash snatched me around the waist when I walked by and unceremoniously hauled me down onto his lap. Myles almost fell on top of us both.

"Feck man, yer a ballbag," Myles growled.

"I told you. Princess is mine for the night," Nash said.

I bit my lip to keep from laughing as Myles cursed like a sailor before grabbing the tablet and ordering another pitcher of water and some fancy fruity drink. Nash's phone vibrated, and he tensed up when he looked at the screen.

"What's wrong," I whispered.

"It's time," he said, and I narrowed my eyes at him.

Before I could ask him what he meant, he whistled. The guys turned, their smiles fading as they looked at his face. Nash slowly stood and set me on my feet.

"I need the VIP area."

"What," Liam asked, leaning forward. "But...."

"I'll explain later."

Liam looked as suspicious as I felt.

"That's all we get lately. Later, it's always later," Blake said.

"Guys, please. I don't know what's going on either," I said, and everyone slowly stood like they had lead in their pockets.

Myles held out his hand for me, and Nash shook his head.

"No, Ren stays with me." That got another round of uneasy looks.

"What is Mr. Genovese doing here," Theo asked.

We all turned to see the Don of Dons making his way through the club. I'd only seen him that once, but he was as intimidating as I remembered. People moved out of his way—and the dozen guards following him—like a wave.

"That's who you're meeting with," Liam asked.

"Yes."

"And you don't want us here?"

"Not yet." Nash looked at Liam. "You'll know before the night is out."

I thought for sure Liam would argue, instead he nodded as he headed for the rope. Theo, Myles, and Blake followed, but they each gave Nash a look that promised he wasn't getting out of here tonight without telling them everything.

Mr. Genovese walked up the steps, and the guys ducked their heads in respect and greeting. I had no clue why Nash wanted me here for a meeting with Vicky's father, but a little warning would've been nice. Was he breaking off his engagement to Vicky with me here? That seemed like a recipe for getting us shot on the spot.

Only one guard stayed with Mr. Genovese, but when he lifted his finger, the man stopped and stayed by the rope.

"Nash, it's a pleasure to see you again," he said, and all I could think was that Nash was going to hold me in front of him like a shield.

"Likewise, Mr. Genovese."

"Please, we are past that. You can call me Edmundo."

I remained quiet, watching the two of them and feeling like Liam as I analyzed every shift in their body language. As his eyes that reminded me of a winter storm found mine, I swallowed hard and held out my hand.

"Mr. Genovese, it's a pleasure to meet you under more social circumstances," I said and his lip curved up before he chuckled.

He shook my hand, and a calm feeling washed over me. He might be intimidating but there was a kindness in him that I could just sense.

"You look beautiful, *fiore mio*," he said, and I glanced at Nash.

My Italian was rusty, but I was pretty sure he just called me my flower. If he was a perv and Nash had found a way to sell me, I was going cut off his dick.

"Come, let's talk," Mr. Genovese said.

Nash led us to the chairs closer to the window and away from those partying. My heart hammered as we sat down. Everything about Mr. Genovese oozed power and sophistication. Even the way he unbuttoned his jacket before sitting looked like a sign of authority.

Nash was nervous, and that made me more nervous than anything else. He was never worried but he looked like he wanted to run from the room. That told me that whatever he'd done was bad... really bad.

I really want you to remember right now. Please try to forgive me for keeping what I know from you. I had no choice.

"Why don't we get to know one another a little bit," Mr. Genovese said, and I wanted to snarl at Nash. I glared at him as I burst from my seat.

"Did you find some loop-hole to sell me? Is this what you meant when you said you'd get me out of the contract with your father? How dare you," I growled.

"Ren...."

I pointed at him, seeing red. "No wonder you didn't want the guys to hear this. They'll never speak to you again. But that's nothing compared to what I'm going to do. You're lucky I don't have a weapon on me."

"Ren...." Nash tried again.

"All that talk of caring about me. Meanwhile, you're no better than your father. Selling me off to the highest bidder. Is that how you got the money to pay for all this?"

"Ren, it's not like that."

"Really? Ohhhh, that's right, you had no choice. Screw you, Nash." I looked over my shoulder. "I'm sorry, Mr. Genovese. I'm sure you're very nice, but Nash had no right." I moved to leave and get the hell out here, but Nash jumped up. "Get the hell out of my way, Collier. Don't make me put you on your ass in front of Mr. Genovese because I will do it."

Mr. Genovese's laughter sounded rich and deep. When I looked back, he was bent over, laughing so hard that I paused, and my anger took a momentary timeout. I glanced up at Nash, and he was shaking his head.

"You didn't sell me, did you?"

He pressed his lips together and shook his head. "Nope."

"Well, you certainly have your mother's fire," Mr. Genovese said.

I turned around and stared at him.

"My mother?"

He smiled and there was a look in his eye that I recognized. Gasping, I grabbed my purse and found my phone in a mad rush to pull up the information about my mother. I thumbed through the pictures until I found the one I needed. My eyes went back and forth from the old, grainy photo of my mum with a man that I'd never been able to identify to the Don sitting in front of me. Hand shaking, I slowly held out my phone. Mr. Genovese took it and smiled, his eyes warming as he touched the screen.

"That's you, isn't it?"

He handed my cell back and then gestured to the small love seat beside where he was sitting. Nash and I walked over and sat like we were on autopilot.

"Yes, that's me. A very long time ago now. We were seventeen," he said.

"Oh my god, you...you knew my mum."

"No...I loved her. I still do. She is part of my soul and always will be," he said, and my eyes stung with tears.

"I don't understand."

"So much lost time," he said.

Mr. Genovese sat forward on his seat and held out his palm. As soon as I placed my hand in his, he ran his thumb over my knuckles.

"I met Yulianna when we were ten, and from the first moment I saw her, I knew I wanted to marry her. I didn't care that we were children. When we turned eighteen, I would make her mine. Unfortunately, your grandfather had chosen someone else for your mother."

"Christov?"

He nodded, his eyes darkening.

"Christov is a bastard. A violent and evil piece of shit that I thought was dead. Now that I know he's alive, I'll be swift to rectify the situation. He hurt her...and I can never forgive myself for letting that happen."

His eyes filled with so much contained rage that I feared for whoever faced him.

"Did you stay in touch with her, Mr. Genovese?"

I was so excited to speak to someone who knew my mum for so long and obviously loved her fiercely.

"A little bit, yes. Please call me Edmundo or Eddie. Maybe...one day something else..." he said cryptically, and reached into his jacket pocket and pulled out a letter. "I couldn't give this to you until your eighteenth birthday," Eddie said, holding it out. I looked at Nash, but his face gave away nothing.

Taking the envelope, I tore it open, and like confetti, a handful of pictures fell out onto my lap.

"Oh my god."

They were all pictures of me or me and my mum. Tears ran down my cheeks as, one at a time, I set them on the small table beside the couch. The last one stopped my heart. It was my mum holding me, but it wasn't Christov kissing my head. It was Eddie.

My hands were shaking so badly that I couldn't open the paper. Nash reached out and grabbed them.

"Hey...look at me." I lifted my eyes to his. "Let me."

Nodding, I let him take the letter and unfold it.

My Beautiful Baby Girl

If you are reading this, then I'm no longer with you. No matter where I am or what has happened, I want you to know that I love you. I've loved you with my whole heart my entire life, and I would do anything to protect you.

There are so many things I wish I'd told you. When I learned I was pregnant my heart was filled with so much joy. You have always been my queen, and I can't believe you're already eighteen. From the second you were born, you lit up the darkest room. Never lose that, baby. It's your superpower.

You'll need it to safeguard your future from the evil that will try to claim you. You see, being my daughter comes with danger, and dear Lord, that scares me for you. But when I look at you I see the strongest person I know, and I was blessed to be your mother.

I made a promise that on the day you turned eighteen, you'd learn the truth. Some of this will be very difficult for you to understand why I hid it from you, but just know that it was never done with malice. All I wanted to do was protect you for as long as I could. I can only pray that you'll understand and, one day, forgive me for keeping this from you.

We were born into a world filled with twisted lies and vile secrets. Keeping track of them is impossible.

Around every corner is someone who will betray you, but some will love you and die for you.

What I tell you next is a story about a love so strong that it couldn't be broken, no matter the costs.

I, Yulianna Mikhailov, was born into a powerful Russian family. When I was eighteen, I was forced into a contract to marry a man I loathed and who hated me just as much. His name was Christov Ivankov. I swore that I'd get away from him because my love for another was too strong to let go.

You, my amazing daughter, are not Kayleigh Ren Davies or Kayleigh Ren Ivankov. You, baby girl, are the princess shared by two of the most powerful families in the world. You are Lilya Ren Genovese. Edmundo Matteo Genovese is your father.

Nash stopped reading. I covered my mouth as I stared at my biological father. A man I never knew existed. His face was neutral, but his grey eyes held as much pain as was gripping my chest.

"It's okay, go on," I said.

I realize this will be hard to accept and I wish with my whole heart that I was there to explain it all to you. Eddie and I fell in love when we were very young, just children really. But from the first moment I looked into his eyes, I knew. I felt it in my soul that he was the one.

We wished for a fairytale life of princes and

princesses that was solely made for movies. In reality, our paths are chosen based on money, power, and
control.

At that time, Eddie's family was not what it is
today. Eddie fought to become the Don of Dons. He
fought to increase his family's status and their holdings. He fought so that one day, we could be
reunited, and no one would stand in our way.

My father chose Christov. His family had political influence in the Russian government. I was only
eighteen. Eddie had less to offer then, and no matter
what I said, your grandfather wouldn't change his
mind. That was the end of it. I was engaged, but
my heart couldn't be caged by my father's or even
Christov's rage.

I refused to be told who I could love. What
Eddie and I had was...special. It was unbreakable,
and by the grace of God, Eddie loved me and all my
crazy just as strongly as I loved him. We burned
brightest together. Nothing and no one could stop us.
I want you to know that you were conceived out of
love, and that is all that matters. We wanted you so
much that we were willing to risk losing our lives to
make it happen.

Please don't blame Eddie for staying away, that
wasn't what we planned. At the time it was too
dangerous for us to remain together. We were young
with no money, power, or influence. We would've been

hunted, and my father, your grandfather Vadin, would've killed Eddie. So I waited until I could run with you safely.

When I left Christov, things happened that destroyed my chance of going straight to Eddie. Instead, I took you into hiding and chose to give you a life that I never had. I wanted you to grow up just like any other kid.

That meant hiding you from Eddie. I didn't dare let anyone know where we were, and it broke my heart every single day to do it, but as I said, I would do anything to protect you.

Fate is strange, and at one of my art shows in Vancouver, Eddie walked in as a buyer. We stared at one another in complete shock. He had no idea where I was, and I didn't know he was coming. My heart beat again at the sight of him. He'd spent years searching for us, and I should've died for what I'd done to him, to us. A lesser man would've killed me and taken you, but Eddie told me he still loved me. He understood why I hid and forgave me. We stayed together in Vancouver for the night and I've never cried so hard as when I left the next morning.

You were only eleven, and we decided then that we would keep this secret until you were eighteen. I wanted you old enough to hear the truth, understand it, and then make your own choices. Eddie and I promised that, as tempting as it was, he would not reach out until your eighteenth birthday.

But, baby girl, please know we didn't do it to hurt you. We so badly wanted you to grow up without fear, rules, and politics clouding your every move. We let you grow your wings and fly. Most of all...we wanted you to be happy.

I'm so, so sorry that I'm not there in person to tell you this, but I know Eddie is, or you wouldn't be reading this letter. Just in case something happened to me, I sent your father this envelope to keep safe until your birthday. I'm sure you're hurt and angry, and you have every right to be. But when you're ready, I am begging you to please give Eddie a chance to be in your life. He is more than a good man. He is a great man. You're so much like him, and I couldn't be prouder of the woman you're becoming.

I love you, my baby girl. I always have, and I always will, no matter what.

I love you too, Eddie. My heart has only ever beat for you.

Take care of each other.

Mum

Nash folded up the letter and pulled the last piece of paper out of the envelope. Even through my tears, I recognized a birth certificate.

I ran my fingers over our names and slowly raised my eyes to Edmundo's. Now that I really looked, I could see myself in him.

"I'm sorry I missed so much of your life, *fiore mio*. Every day without you and your mother has been excruciating,"

Edmundo placed his hand over his heart, and I didn't know what to feel. Shock blocked everything else.

There was so much to say, and I didn't know where to start.

"I—"

Bang, bang, bang, bang!

Nash grabbed my waist and threw me to the floor, using his body as a shield.

Crash!

The club was suddenly so loud. It sounded like a war zone as the window we'd been sitting near exploded and rained down on us. I screamed, covering my ears and squeezing my eyes closed as images of the night Nadia was shot flashed in my brain.

"Get her out of here," Nash yelled.

I didn't know who he was talking to and fought back when unknown hands and faces I didn't recognize dragged me away.

Everything happened fast, but it felt like I reached for Nash in slow motion as he pulled a gun from under his jacket and fired out the window. Men in black suits surrounded me, blocking my view.

"No, no, let me go," I yelled while fear raced through my body. The guys were in there. My guys. "No, I can't leave them," I cried, but there was no fighting the wave of muscle, and they weren't listening to me.

My ears rang in the sudden silence as I was dragged outside into the cool night.

"Get in the car, sir, I'll head back in with half the guards," one of the men in black said.

Being tossed into the back of a limo was not how I saw this night going. The door slammed, and the wheels squealed as it fishtailed. I plastered myself against the small back window, my hands clawing at the cold glass as I pictured everyone that I loved dying.

"Let me out of here. I can't leave them," I said and looked

around to see Edmundo sitting near me. Glaring at him, I pointed. "Take me back,"

The car sped down a side street, and I fell over.

"My men will keep your friends safe," he said.

I pushed myself up and tried to make him understand.

"They're not just my friends. I love them. I can't leave them."

Just the thought of one of my guys dying or even Ivy and Chantry made me sick to my stomach.

"I need to protect them," I said, and the words sounded ridiculous out loud. It didn't matter though. All I could think was that we needed to turn around and go back.

Edmundo crossed his arms. "And how would you protect them?"

I opened my mouth, closed it, and swore as he called me out on exactly what I'd just been thinking.

"Then give me a gun. Nash taught me to shoot."

"Great, I'm happy he did that. You should know how to use a gun. But have you ever been in the middle of a firefight?"

"No, but...."

"Oh, so you don't know how to control your fear, or your breathing, or anything else. Shooting cans off a fence is very different than a life-and-death shootout, where any mistake can kill you or someone else. My men train for this every day and have lived through many firefights. Let them do their job. The answer is no. I'm not taking my daughter, who I just reconnected with, back to be involved in a gun fight. You're a princess, not a guard."

"God! This is so frustrating. I can take care of myself."

"Be angry with me all you want. It won't change the fact that I'm not turning the car around."

His phone rang, and he picked it up.

"Marcus? Okay, okay, I'll tell her."

He ended the call and looked at me. Fear lanced my heart and made me lightheaded. Did I want to hear what he would say next?

"The shooting has stopped. There are many injured and few

deaths. Your friends from the table are alive. My head of security is riding with three of them to catch up with us. One stole a motorcycle, and the other stayed behind. That's all I know."

Slumping in the seat, I tried to gain control of my breathing as the car flew down the road. I could picture everyone in my mind. Nash stayed behind. Theo stole the motorcycle, and Myles, Blake, and Liam were together with Edmundo's guard Marcus. Dear God, I wouldn't have been able to handle it if they'd died. Losing any one of them would be like losing a limb.

"What about Ivy and Chantry?"

He lifted a shoulder. "Marcus didn't mention them. Once we are safe, we will find out."

"I can't believe this," I said, shaking my head. "Just when I think there is no possible way my life could get any crazier, my real father shows up on my birthday, and I'm running from bullets."

My hands trembled in my lap, and I looked up at Edmundo, who was sitting quietly and staring at me.

"So, you're my father...my actual father. I feel like I have far more than normal," I said, and he smirked.

"I'm sure you do. Yes, you're my beautiful daughter and I hope that you'll allow me the chance to get to know you," he said.

"I'd like that. I have so many questions still. I don't even know what to ask first, but I'll start with...do you know who was shooting at us?"

"No, I don't know. I didn't see, and as far as I'm aware, none of my enemies would be so stupid."

"Not even Christov? He's a threat," I said.

Edmundo's dark grey eyes locked with mine, and his massive hand clenched into a fist.

"Not even he is so stupid, but I will find him, and I will crush every bone in his body until he prays for forgiveness. He'll regret ever laying a finger on your mother. That I can promise you."

The wheels screeched as we skidded around a curve, and the glass divider lowered.

"Sir, we have a serious problem," the driver said, his voice frantic.

My heart rate spiked all over again. He looked in the rearview mirror, and there was terror in his eyes.

"What's wrong," Edmundo asked.

"The brakes are out. I can't stop, and we're gaining speed."

His foot was thumping the floor as he tried to brake repeatedly. The world raced by when I looked out the window. Oh, dear God.

"Put it in neutral and use the emergency brake," Edmundo said, and then grabbed me, pulling me into his side and holding me tight.

"It's not working, and I think we also lost the power steering. They must have cut multiple fluid lines."

Dread flowed threw me, followed by the understanding that we could all die. The gun shots and being dragged out of the club had all happened so fast that my brain took a minute to catch up to the reality. But this...this I understood.

A new terror gripped me as I pointed at a pickup truck pulling along side us. The man driving wore an evil mask of insanity, and even though the windows of the limo were blacked out, it felt like he was staring directly into my soul. I would know that malicious face anywhere. It was Owen. I'd dreamed of killing him for what he'd done to Myles.

Before I could get out the words, he smiled and weaved away from us. I watched him crank the wheel, and the truck slammed into the side of the limo. We skidded sideways violently, the back end swaying as we hit the gravel on the shoulder.

"Leave it in neutral, and as soon as we are under twenty, throw it in park," Edmundo yelled and then looked at me. "Just hang on, I've got you."

Edmundo wrapped his arms around me tighter. I grabbed him, my hands balling into fists as I gripped his suit and buried my head against his chest.

We began to slow, but I screamed when a shot rang out, and our driver's blood splattered the windshield. He slumped forward on the steering wheel, and the car jerked, throwing us around the back like rag dolls. Owen rammed into us again, and the metal bowed, making a crunching sound like a beer can at a frat party.

Then there was confusion, and my hair stood on end as if we were flying. We lifted off the seats and hovered in the air like gravity had ceased to exist, but unfortunately, we were not that lucky.

Crash, crunch, thump, thump, thump, bang.

The limo's frame twisted and screeched as we hit the ground and rolled. I was ripped away from Edmundo, but I could still see him reaching for me.

"Dad!"

Our fingertips brushed before we were pulled apart, and then... there was nothing.

OCTOBER 31 – FRIDAY 9:43 PM

Myles

The same truck that I'd chased after the night we tried to capture my father sped down the street and squealed as it turned the corner. The shooting might have stopped, but chaos had erupted. The glass windows had exploded inward with the gunfire, and everywhere I looked, people lay injured and bleeding. Others were crying or screaming as they huddled by walls or behind furniture. A few were dead, their eyes sightless as they bled out on the floor. This was a goddamn disaster.

"Fuck, fuck, fuck," I said, dodging people as I ran for the VIP area where Ren and Nash had been.

One minute Mr. Genovese's guards were here and then the shooting stopped and they all seemed to vanish. Sirens were already loud in the distance. This was a huge fucking mess, and yet all I cared about was making sure my Snowflake was safe.

Liam, Theo, and Blake ran out of another section of the club together where Ivy and Chantry were huddled with Sabastian and Trey. I had just started up the stairs when Nash skidded to a stop with one of Mr. Genovese's guards. Nash looked us over and visibly relaxed.

"Where's Snowflake?"

"With Mr. Genovese, his guards put them in his limo. This is his head of security, Marcus. He stayed behind to help us handle the situation. The cops will be here any minute."

"Wait, so you're saying she's alive?"

Nash nodded, and I leaned forward on my knees, taking a deep breath and rubbing a hand over my heart. For just a moment, it felt like it had been ripped from my chest.

"That was me da. I don't know who the guy was in the back with the AK, but I saw him get shot," I said.

"Yeah, I got him," Nash growled. "This is a fucking nightmare. I'll stay here and talk to the cops," Nash said as Morrison jogged over after checking on Ivy. "Morrison, what should we do?"

"It was a drive-by, and there are a lot of witnesses to back that up. But we need to get rid of your guns," he said. "They'll take them as evidence, and if you've ever used them or plan on using them in the future, they will have a ballistics record on file."

"Okay, give me all of your weapons. I'll take care of them in case you guys get stopped trying to leave. Go with Marcus and get the hell out of here. He'll take you to Ren. Then we'll deal with Owen because, so help me god, I'm going to tear his intestines out of his body with my bare hands and strangle him with them," Nash snarled.

"Git in line," I said.

"My truck is out back. The keys are above the visor, take it," Nash said. I handed over my gun before running for the exit, followed closely by the others. But I jumped in the driver's seat.

"I'm taking that," Theo said, pointing to a motorcycle parked on the road with the helmet on the seat like the driver would be right back.

"Do you know whose bike that is," Liam asked.

"Nope, and I don't care." Theo peeled off his suit jacket and tossed it in the truck before running for the motorcycle. I let him do his thing and pulled out, following the black rubber marks of tires that had been left behind.

"Where are we heading?"

Marcus sat in the passenger seat, staring at his phone.

"Veer right here," he said.

The truck wasn't happy with the sudden jarring movement.

"The road forks up here and turn left," Marcus said.

"This is a strange way to go," I said.

"The main road was blocked off back there. It said construction," Liam answered from behind me. I hadn't even noticed. I'd been so focused on following Marcus's directions.

"Are you tracking them," Blake asked.

"Yes. They are on this road but a bit ahead of us and traveling fast," Marcus said.

There was a loud roar, and in a blink, Theo blew by us like we were sitting still, shaking the truck.

"Fuck," I said, gripping the steering wheel tighter. "Does he have a death wish?"

"Trust me, Theo knows what he's doing," Liam said, far calmer than I felt.

When the road opened up on the straightaway, I floored it. The engine revved as the miles clicked higher. My car could handle this speed and more, but I'd only driven Nash's truck a few times and never at top speed. I had to ease off the gas a little as the engine complained. It wouldn't do us any good getting stranded at the side of the road.

"There's the rest of my team," Marcus said, pointing at the red taillights ahead of us. Theo had caught up with limo as well.

I squinted my eyes and stared at the oncoming lane of traffic.

"Is that arse in the wrong lane," I asked, weaving over slightly to see a pickup running parallel with Mr. Genovese and Ren.

Everyone leaned forward to see and what happened next felt like it was right out of an action movie. The piece of shite smashed into the side of the limo.

"What the fuck?"

Nash's truck lurched forward when I hit the gas. Theo was weaving behind the pickup that had just hit the limo like he was trying to get its attention. The motorcycle swerved again, and I recognized the battered tailgate. There was an unmistakable flash of a gun going off, and the limo jerked toward the edge of the road.

"No, no, no."

My worst nightmare came alive in front of me when my da crashed into Ren's limo, and it soared through the air and off the road.

"No!"

The scream ripped from my throat as we helplessly watched it hit the ground and roll. Tires flew off, a door went flying, and the trunk popped open before the stretched car was torn in half as it crashed into a tree and came to a stop. Smoke rose in the air as the SUVs in front of us hit their brakes. Men jumped out and ran for the crash.

The pickup truck fishtailed as I reached where Ren had gone off the road. My brain completely shutdown with panic. I jumped out of the truck, but Liam grabbed me before I could run, slamming me against the side.

"Let go of me," I roared and tried to pull away.

"Look at me," he said, shaking me. "Whatever happened down there, happened. I have the most medical training. You need to help Theo get your father. That was him in the truck and he cannot escape." I looked around and wanted to throw up. Terror was eating at my insides. "Seconds mean the difference between life and death. Do you understand me, Myles? Get your father. Don't leave him to just Theo. I'll take care of her. I promise."

As much as it killed me, I knew he was right. He let me go, and I hopped back in the truck, the tires spinning as I raced off after Theo.

"God...." I squeezed the steering wheel as pain wrapped itself around my beating heart and threatened to stop it forever. "Please, help her. You can't take your angel home yet. Please don't take her, I'm begging you. If you need to take anyone, take me. I hand myself over to you, but please not her."

Owen...I'd lost sight of the truck and needed to focus on getting to Owen. Violence that had only ever filled me once before coursed through my veins and helped push the fear aside enough that I could think.

Pulling out my phone, I hit Nash's number.

"Kind of busy here," he said.

"The limo was run off the road," I said, and it was dead silent.

"What?"

"I don't know if they're alive. I'm after Owen. He did it. Theo's on a motorcycle following him, and Liam and Blake are with...." My breath hitched as I swallowed the wail of pain down. "She has to be okay, Nash. I...."

"Listen to me...she'll be fine."

"You don't know that."

"What I know is that we don't have time to think of the worst-case scenario. Track Theo's cell. He should have it on him. I'll send backup. Once you get that fucking piece of shit, take him to the warehouse. I'll talk to Morrison so I can get the hell out of here and keep you updated. Myles...think positively. Princess is strong, and she'll fight, so don't stop fighting for her."

My teeth clenched tight, and my jaw cracked as I let the rage fully take over my mind until only one thought filled me: Find Owen. He wouldn't get out of this alive.

"I'll git him," I growled.

"I know you will," Nash said and hung up.

One memory at a time rose like the Devil's hand to show me my past. The abuse that never stopped. The mental games that he used to try and break me. The broken bones, knife wounds, and threats he used to keep me scared. The vile sound of his laugh as he made me cry or scream. It all fueled me, filled me, and made me who I was right this moment.

Owen wanted to tear my heart from my chest. But I would rip open his rib cage and smile as I squeezed his black heart. I'd make sure he was staring into my eyes as the light faded from his for hurting my Snowflake.

Chapter 63

Nash

"Morrison, I need to go."

"What about your statement?"

"Tell the cops I'll come by the precinct tomorrow." I ran for the door and then skidded to a halt, remembering I'd given Myles my truck. "Shit," I yelled and looked around. "Nora, I need your car."

"Okay." She ran into the office and came back, throwing her keys at me. She pointed out back. "I'm parked on the street."

"What's wrong," Ivy asked.

Sabastian stood beside her, playing the doting boyfriend role well, and I didn't dare say anything in front of him.

"I don't have time right now," I said and ran out the back.

Nora's glowing orange car was easy to find on the street. It was the same fucking color as a hunter's vest with black trim and tinted windows.

"What the fuck," I growled, getting into the Charger. There was even a little stuffed tiger hanging from the rearview mirror.

I pulled up Liam's phone and set my GPS, then called Merlin. I hadn't spoken to him other than to set up payment and shipping route protection, but I needed him now. The first fucking thing I was doing when the club started making money—if it ever did after this —was to hire bodyguards. I was sick of borrowing and begging people.

"I'm surprised to hear from you. Thought you'd have your hands full with that mess at your club," Merlin said, not bothering with pleasantries, which was fine with me.

"I need your help."

"I'm not getting involved in whatever that was about. We deal with enough heat from the cops as it is," he said.

"I want to speak to your president."

"You speak to me. That's how this works."

"Fuck! Merlin, I don't have time for this. The fucking piece of shit that just shot up my place ran the woman I love off the fucking road. I don't know if she's going to live. I need your help. I'll pay you whatever you want. I don't care."

"Jesus. I'm sorry. Why didn't you just say that? Where do you want us?"

I slumped in the seat, my heart hammering out of my chest.

"I'll call you back as soon as I know what hospital. We're also after the guy who did this."

"Say no more. Point us in the direction, and we'll go after him. No one goes after a man's old lady and gets to breathe another day."

Merlin hung up the phone, and I'd never been so happy about an alliance. The word around town was that the new President, Snake, was a real hard ass and an asshole, but he was fair, honest and a loyal SOB. Our few dealings so far had backed up those claims. Right now, I needed all of that and the MC's manpower.

Flashing lights blinded me when I crested the next hill.

"Jesus Christ," I whispered as I saw the limo folded around a tree.

It was burning in a blaze as tall as the treetops. Firefighters stood in the field trying to put it out, and I couldn't breathe. The air refused to move. Braking hard, I willed myself to get closer, but for the first time in years, I was terrified. It was like waiting outside of Mya's house all over again and knowing that no matter what I did, nothing could stop the pain. The sadness would engulf me.

My phone rang and I hit talk without looking to see who it was.

"Yeah," I wheezed out.

"Nash, it's Liam, you okay? You don't sound right." There was a siren blaring in the background.

"Just tell me if you got her out before it exploded." My body shook, and I pinched the bridge of my nose.

"Yes, we did. That's why I'm calling. We're on our way to St. Margaret's Hospital." I glanced down at my phone, and sure enough, the dot was moving. "I'm following the ambulances. Mr. Genovese and Ren are both unconscious and in bad shape, but they're breathing. The driver is dead."

My forehead hit the steering wheel as I sucked in a shaky breath. Taking my own advice for Myles, I swallowed down the fear and made a three-point turn to go around the accident.

"I'll meet you at the hospital. Have you heard from Myles?"

"No. So you know it was Owen?"

"Yes," I growled. "I spoke to Myles. But I haven't heard from him since. Owen will die slowly."

"We all want that," Liam said, his voice uncharacteristically filled with emotion.

"I'll be there as fast as I can," I said, ending the call.

I'd always pictured killing my father first, but not anymore.

"Hang on, Princess, please hang on."

OCTOBER 31 – FRIDAY 10:36 PM

Myles

Theo was the only reason we still had a chance to get to Owen. Horns blared as I weaved around traffic, following his taillight. Luckily, Owen's truck wasn't as fast as the rocket Theo was riding.

He'd taken the cutoff for the freeway, but the ramp was closed and now we were speeding down the service road. Theo looked over his shoulder when I closed the gap between us. We were heading for a more rural area. I leaned over and opened the glove compartment, but there was no gun.

"Fuck," I muttered as I flashed my lights and rolled down the window.

Theo slowed a little and dropped back beside me.

"I'm going to run him off the road," I yelled, and Theo nodded.

The truck roared as I pulled past Theo. The driver's side broken taillight flickered like an SOS, but there would be no help coming for Owen now. That death certificate had been filled out years ago, but tonight, he'd signed and dated it.

His face glowed from my headlights when he glanced in the rear mirror. It was just a flash, but there was fear in his eyes, and it fueled my soul.

I aimed for that corner, and his truck jolted as we collided. He tried to brake, but I kept my foot down, and smoke rose into the air. Easing off a little gave me a few feet to floor it again.

This time, Owen's pickup swerved, but he managed to keep two wheels on the pavement. I didn't give him time to recover and came for him again. The massive front grill of Nash's truck crushed in the bed as I pushed the back end off the shoulder.

"Fucker," I swore as he turned toward the open field.

Nash's truck soared over the low edge as I chased him down. Theo was in my rearview, following on the sideroad. The field was rough, the truck was bouncing hard and almost hitting my head off the roof.

"Yer not gettin away," I growled.

He was aiming to get back on the road. Just as he started up the embankment in front of Theo, I slammed into the tailgate, and it was enough to launch him across the road with me following right on his ass.

An ancient maple stood proud in the ditch on the other side. I veered left, but Owen had too much momentum to miss it completely. The passenger side of the pickup crumpled in as he collided with the tree. The force stood the truck up on its nose, crushing the roof and popping open the driver-side door, ejecting Owen. A body flew out of the bed and landed in the grass like a ragdoll.

I was out and stalking toward Owen as Theo ran down into the ditch. Owen's leg from the knee down was twisted the wrong way, so he was using his arms to pull himself on the ground toward a gun. As he reached out, I stepped on his hand and squatted in front of him.

He laughed and spit blood as he looked up at me, his eyes wild.

"I hope dat cunt of yours is dead," he said.

My fist connected three times with Owen's face. His bones cracked under my knuckles before Theo pulled me off.

"He's mine," I snarled like a rabid dog.

"You're right. He is, and he will be. But we need to take him somewhere secure and get to the hospital. Liam texted. Ren is alive but in critical condition and is being rushed into surgery. Something about swelling in her brain. Is he worth not being by her side?"

I stopped fighting and stared down at Owen.

"Naw, he's not."

Theo let me go and ran to Nash's truck. He opened the back door and dug around before pulling out zip ties and duct tape.

He bound Owen's hands, while I made loops for his legs and smiled when I cranked them together, pulling his twisted leg sharply.

"Ahhhhhh!"

Owen's eyes snapped open from the pain, and before he could spew any more crap at me, Theo slapped the tape over his mouth. I stood but stumbled back and fell on my ass.

"What's wrong," Theo asked as he kneeled beside me.

"I'm just lightheaded."

"The adrenaline is wearing off. Just breathe for a minute," Theo said, and I looked up at him.

"What if she doesn't make it? I can't live wit out her. I can't."

Theo smacked me across the face so hard that my head snapped to the side, and I fell over into the grass. I glared at him and sat back up.

"Get your head out of your fucking ass. I know you love her. We all love her. You don't think I'm fucking out of my mind with worry right now?"

He pushed me, and I fell over again but caught myself before I hit the ground.

"I know better than all of you what this surgery means. But spiraling won't help anyone. Do you really think Ren would sit here crying if the roles were reversed? No, she'd be doing everything she could to help until she passed out from exhaustion."

Theo pointed at Owen on the ground, staring at us.

"I need your help to get him in the truck. Ren needs us to be strong for her, so listen the fuck up. You're going to get your ass up off the ground, then stop letting your mind fuck with you—because that's what that fucking prick wants—and help me."

Theo leaned in closer and snarled at me as he lowered his voice.

"If you don't pull your shit together, then so help me, I'll tie you up beside that piece of shit, and you can ride in the back with him. It'll be a real father-son bonding moment for you. Then, I'll let Nash deal with you. But I promise you, that I won't ever let you step foot in that hospital because you won't deserve to be by Ren's side. Do you feel me, brother?"

I'd never seen Theo so enraged. His green eyes were filled with a level of insanity that I didn't even think he was capable of, and yet it was exactly what I needed to hear.

"Aye, I feel ya," I said.

"Fucking fabulous, now get up," Theo ordered.

Who the fuck was this guy? He was a totally different person.

Theo stood and held out his hand to pull me up.

"Thanks."

"Don't thank me. Do your job and help me, so we can get the fuck out of here and be with our girl."

Giving Owen one last look, I swept away the trauma he'd caused me time and again. He wouldn't beat me...not ever again.

"Aye, let's git the fuck outta here."

NOVEMBER 1 – SATURDAY 1:00 AM

Myles

My entire existence, before Snowflake came along, had felt like a lifetime trapped in *Groundhog Day* hell. An endless repetition of horror and pain. I died over and over again on the way to the hospital. Every time I got close to slipping off the cliff of despair, I remembered what Theo said and pulled myself back again.

Snowflake was my everything. Imagining a world without her was not just bleak. It was nothing.

We went straight to the ICU waiting room, garnering stares as we ran by people. I spotted Nash first as he paced the plain beige hallway like the Grim Reaper. He looked up when he heard our approach.

"Tell me," I said.

He licked his lips and looked between us.

"She's still in surgery. They're doing a craniotomy to relieve the pressure in her brain. She hit her head in the crash."

My legs shook, and I stumbled to the side, but Nash grabbed me and pulled me into a hug.

"We don't know anything yet. They said it could be three to seven hours. It's barely the three-hour mark." I nodded as I clung to him.

"She can't die."

"She won't. Princess is tough as nails."

"This is all my fault. I let Owen get away. I had him in my grasp at the bar, and I let him escape. If I'd just takin' the shot."

Nash held me tighter.

"If it's your fault, then it's my fault, too. I was so focused on the wrong things. I should've known that he'd try something like this."

Nash pulled back and gripped my shoulders.

"She's going to be okay." He looked at Theo. "You good?"

"As fine as one can be," Theo answered.

Nash led us to the waiting area, where six bikers had taken up spots around the room. He'd messaged saying some were showing up at the warehouse to help us out, but I hadn't expected to see them here, too.

"Don't worry, they're just extra protection. We don't know if Owen was working with anyone else or it was just him and the guy in the back of the truck," Nash said.

I knew we had a deal with the Lost Souls, but hadn't realized it extended to guard duty. Then again, I never asked.

"Here, I took a pic of that guy for ya," I said, handing Nash my phone.

He looked at the photo and growled.

"That's that fucking dick Hammer who was working with Devin."

"The one who shot at you and Liam in the warehouse?"

"Yeah, I'll let the Lost Souls guys know they don't need to keep looking for the prick."

Nash took my phone and walked over to the bikers as I sat down between Theo and Blake.

Why was everything in here so depressing? Every hospital I'd ever been in—and I'd seen my fair share—was all the same. White or beige floors, walls, and doors. The only break in the monotony was the dark blue chairs and the framed scenic images on the walls.

Blake's leg bounced fiercely while his eyes were open but unfocused on a part of the floor. I knew that look. Not giving a fuck who saw us or what they thought, I grabbed his hand and laced our fingers together. He jumped in surprise and looked at me.

"Yer my brotha, and I won't let ya sink," I said to him as he locked eyes with me.

"You're my brother, and I won't let you sink either."

Sitting back, I focused on the wall clock, watching the second hand slowly circle until an hour passed and then another. When the door to the surgery area opened, everyone jumped up. I hadn't even noticed that Ethan and Ella arrived.

"Hi, I'm Doctor Boyd. Who is here for Ren Davies," he asked.

"We all are," Nash answered.

"Alright then. Ren made it through the surgery and is stable. The next seventy-two hours will tell us a lot more. We will be monitoring her very closely. Before you're allowed into the room, you should know that she's intubated and we are keeping her in a medically induced coma to let her brain recover. So don't be surprised by all the equipment. Its purpose is to monitor and keep her comfortable."

"A coma, Jesus." I ran my hand through my hair.

"It's common after a head injury. It will allow her brain to heal in a resting state," Doctor Boyd said.

"Will she be okay? Will there be lasting effects or deficiencies," Ethan asked, and I wanted to punch him for even thinking that, let alone saying it out loud.

"We won't know anything definitive until she wakes up. I can say that she took quite a hit to the left frontal lobe." Boyd touched his head to demonstrate the location. "We are most concerned with Broca's aphasia, but like I said, it is too early to tell."

"What is that? Broocias apphassia," I asked, stuttering over the words I'd never heard before.

"Broca's aphasia can affect many things but most commonly speech. She could struggle with articulating words, expressing needs and wants, and having difficulty naming items or with anything repetitive. But that doesn't mean she doesn't know those things or who you are. She will require therapy to get back to where she was before the accident if that is the case. There is also a good chance that she will have temporary amnesia, which is very common after an accident. Again, we won't know the extent of any of these until she wakes, but I must implore all of you not to push her. She needs to remember on her own."

I sat down and put my head in my hands as Snowflake's smile danced behind my eyes.

"Ren suffered several bodily injuries as well. Three cracked ribs, lots of bruising, a dislocated shoulder, her ankle, and a wrist that we reset. A slice on her arm needed five stitches, but none of these were serious or life-threatening. It's a miracle, really. Are any of you here for Edmundo Genovese?"

"You can tell me and him," Nash said, pointing to Marcus.

"Are either of you family?"

"Can you come with me for a second," Nash asked quietly, and the three of them moved far enough away that I couldn't hear them.

Nash's face was serious as he stood there with his arms crossed. Marcus looked like he would kill the doctor if he didn't start talking.

"What do you think that's about," Blake asked, and I shook my head.

"No idea."

They spoke quietly for a few minutes before returning. I was really hoping that Nash hadn't threatened the doctor who just operated on Ren's head.

"A nurse will be by to let you know when Ren is in her room and ready for visitors."

Doctor Boyd gave us a tight smile and walked away.

"This isn't fair. It's just not," I said as tears stung my eyes.

Ella sat down beside me and pulled me into a hug before she turned to Blake and did the same with him.

"She has the kindest heart. She doesn't deserve this."

Ella grabbed my chin, her eyes firm before she started to sign.

Ren will be fine. But she may need our help, and I don't know a group more capable of helping her recover than all of you.

"What if she has what the doctor mentioned," I asked.

Then, we will help her learn to speak again, but there are many ways to communicate that don't involve speech. I'm talking to you right now and not using my voice. Do you pity me?

"Naw, of course not."

Ella nodded. *She's a fighter and will work hard. Help and encourage, but don't ever pity her. She'll hate that. Understand?*

"Aye."

Ella hugged me again, offering comfort, but it didn't stop Owen's smug face from entering my mind. My hands balled into fists. By the time I was through with him the Devil himself would congratulate me on a job well done.

Give me the fire. I would burn in hell to see him suffer for eternity.

NOVEMBER 4 – TUESDAY 11:11 AM

Nash

At nineteen, I had lived ten lifetimes of pain, or so I thought. These last three days, while we waited for the doctors to wake Ren, had taught me that no matter how bad I thought things were, there was always another low.

Vicky's presence at the hospital was a headache we didn't need. I thought for sure Myles was going to kill her when she started screaming that this was all our fault. She had no idea how right she was, and guilt was slowly eating me alive. I let Marcus deal with her but ensured that she never came near Ren's room.

Everything was pushed to the side. I blew off school, my father, and—after updating Dimitri on the accident and her condition—I'd turned off my phone. I couldn't deal with anything else.

Outside the hospital chapel, I paced the hallway until I finally worked up enough courage to open the door. A statue of Jesus was at the front, surrounded by candles. Some were burning while others sat waiting for someone to light them. Stained glass covered a small window and felt oddly right for the space. There were only eight wooden benches for seating.

Taking a deep breath, I stepped over the threshold and found myself on my knees in front of the statue.

"I haven't spent a single day believing in you," I said, glaring up at Jesus. "Why would I when you've never helped me? If you exist, you know what my father has done. Things I can never share, things I never want to think about but claw at me every day. You allowed that. Why?"

Shaking my head, I looked down at my blood-coated hands while my heart hardly beat from the scars.

"I understand why you would forsake me. I don't understand how someone who is supposed to be this all-powerful, all-forgiving being could allow this to happen to a girl who is the walking embodiment of what you preach."

Looking back up, I implored again.

"Why her?" The statue didn't move. "Tell me, make this make sense."

A tear rolled down my cheek.

"Because this makes no sense to me. You want to torture someone, then torture me. My soul is already black. I can take it, but hasn't she been through enough? Leave her alone. I'm begging you, just leave her alone."

"Have you considered that the reason she's alive is because he was there in that car with us?"

When I turned, Mr. Genovese sat in a wheelchair just inside the door. I hadn't even heard it open. He slowly rolled closer until he was beside me. We sat there, but I didn't respond. He seemed to accept my silence for an answer.

"My mamma used to say, Edmundo, the good Lord will not always show his face, but you will feel his hand when you need it. I didn't really understand that most of my life." Edmundo looked away from the statue and stared at me. "Nash, I'm not going to tell you to believe in a god that you are obviously struggling to understand. But what I do know is that we went off the road at sixty miles an hour. The car was torn in two and exploded. We should be dead. Instead, we were thrown clear with really minimal injuries." He gripped my shoulder. "There were wings in that car. How many wings have been around you when you needed them?"

I just stared at him, not sure what to say.

"Come on. Vicky will be back shortly, and I want to see Ren."

Nodding, I stood.

"Do you want me to push you?"

"Sure, I'm not too proud to say that this is a hell of a lot harder than it looks."

Turning the wheelchair around, I pushed Edmundo to the door and hit the automatic button. As I waited I looked back at the silent statue that still held all of it's secrets. Edmundo might be right or full of shit. The only thing I knew for sure was that this world was a fucking disaster and I didn't see it getting better anytime soon.

Reaching Ren's door, I walked in, and the chatter died down.

"Guys, can you go grab something to eat for a bit? I'll watch her and let you know if there's any change," I said.

Liam nodded, stood, and stretched.

"I could use some food," he said, letting me know that we still needed to talk from his look on the way out. I'd gotten a reprieve with the accident, but I wouldn't be able to hold them off for much longer.

The rest of the guys followed, glancing at me and then Edmundo as they left.

"Are you going to tell them who I really am," Edmundo asked as the door closed.

"Yeah, once Ren wakes up."

The door opened again, and two nurses walked in.

"She is doing very well, so we are going to extubate her now," the one that I knew as Rosie said. She'd been the nurse on duty the night Ren and Edmundo arrived and it didn't feel like she ever went home.

"What does that mean?"

"We're taking her breathing tube out. She's trying to breathe on her own, which is great news."

Hope filled me as they began to work.

"Will she wake up right away?"

Rosie looked at me.

"She could, but it could also take an hour. Sometimes more if her brain decides it needs the extra time. Be patient. I know it's difficult, but so far, she is progressing exactly the way we would want to see. Better than infact."

I smirked. That was so Princess. Even unconscious she was kicking ass. I sucked in a deep breath, my heart pounding hard.

Come on Princess, wake up.

Ren

There was a loud bang, and I looked up from playing with my dolls. Mommy ran into the bedroom, and I jumped as she opened my closet door and pulled out my suitcase.

"Mommy? What are you doing?"

"We need to go away, baby."

"A trip?"

She smiled at me. "Yes, a trip." She pointed to my toys. "Grab your favorites, but only a couple."

"Okay."

Standing, I smoothed my dress like I'd been taught and walked over to my toybox. I grabbed Mr. Bunny, who I couldn't sleep without, and my coloring book with crayons.

Mommy put the suitcase on my bed and began filling it. I'd never seen her like this before. She seemed...scared, and there was a black and blue mark on the side of her face. She stuffed the suitcase full and put my coloring book on top.

"Why don't you hang on to Mr. Bunny?" She smiled. "Here, put on your jacket, baby, it's cold outside."

"Is Daddy coming?"

"No, Daddy is too busy to go on this trip," she said, and my lower lip pushed out. He was always too busy. "It's okay, baby, we are going to have a great time. It will be our secret adventure."

"O...kay," I said and put my arms through the jacket.

Mommy locked the suitcase and bent down to zip me up. I could see her face easily now, and I touched the black mark.

"You're hurt."

Mommy smiled wide.

"I'll be fine, I walked into the door. I'm so clumsy," she said, but I pressed my lips together. I'd walked into the door before, and it hurt, but I didn't have a mark like that. "Come on, baby, we have to go, or we're going to miss our flight."

I sucked in an excited gasp. "We're going on a plane?"

"Yes, isn't that exciting?" She grabbed my bag and then my hand. "Let's go."

We walked out of the room, but Mommy was walking faster than normal, and it felt like she was dragging me along behind her.

I tripped on the stairs going down, but Mommy held me up so I didn't fall on my face.

"It's too fast," I said.

"Sorry, baby, we need to be fast or no trip, no plane."

Reaching the bottom of the stairs, we ran past Daddy's office, and I saw a hand on the ground behind his desk. No, Daddy needed us. I tugged away from Mommy.

"No, Lilya."

I ran around the desk, and Daddy was lying on the floor with a puddle of red water around him. Mommy grabbed me and picked me up.

"No, Mommy. Daddy's hurt."

She didn't say anything as she ran out of the house.

"Mommy, put me down. Daddy needs us."

I struggled as Mommy tried to buckle me into my seat.

She grabbed me by the shoulders.

"Daddy will be fine. Trust me, baby, he is playing a game."

I knew she was lying, but Mommy never lied to me.

"Please, baby girl, I need you to listen and trust me. Okay? Can you do that?"

I nodded, not wanting to upset Mommy anymore as tears fell down her cheeks.

"Okay, Mommy."

She clipped me in, closed the door, and ran back into the house before coming back with my suitcase. She put it in the passenger seat beside her, and we drove really fast out of the driveway. I held Mr. Bunny to my chest, running his soft ear over my face.

It was snowing a lot. I couldn't see the houses or any cars as we drove, but Mommy didn't slow down.

"Shit."

"Mommy, you said a bad word."

She looked in the mirror at me. "I know, I'm sorry ba...Ah!" Mommy screamed as the car started to spin. It was almost like a fun ride, and I lifted my arms. Then we hit something hard, and that didn't feel good.

"Ouch," I whimpered, my lip trembling.

"It's okay, baby, it's going to be okay. I'm calling for help." There was a ringing in the car, and then a man answered.

"Hello?"

"Uncle Dimitri, it's me, Yulianna. I need your help."

Nash

"I need to move up my timeline," I told Mr. Genovese as we waited for Ren to wake up.

"My father will want me to start doing his dirty work more and more with Owen gone. The deeper he has hooks into me, the harder it will be to get away later," I said, leaning on the bed and gently running my fingers up and down Ren's arm. "I can only tell him to fuck off so much before he will find other ways to force me to do his bidding." I looked at Ren.

"Nash, I understand that, but certain things need to be in place first. You're almost there, don't rush. That's when we make mistakes. We will take extra precautions going forward."

Edmundo was right. I knew that, but I also knew my father. Lawrence wouldn't let me ignore him for much longer. He would know about the accident by now and who was in the car. Sighing, I let my hand fall beside Ren's.

"Nash, I know that this is a difficult question, but I have to ask it."

Looking up, I locked eyes with him.

"Did you sleep with my daughter?"

A cold sweat formed all over my body, and I swallowed hard. "Yes, Sir."

"So you broke my trust already?"

I would rather be trapped in a room with a thousand FBI agents over this one man.

"Yes, I did...twice," I said and his eyebrow rose.

My mouth ran dry. This was it, he could have me dragged out of here and killed or cancel our deal. The moment I slept with Ren it was null and void.

"You knew the consequences, went behind my back, did the one thing I asked you not to, and then kept it from me. Give me one good reason why I should trust or believe a single word that comes out of your mouth."

My heart was in my throat, while he sat there calmly. His question felt like a knife hanging over my head. I looked away and stared down at Ren.

"Because I was already in love with her. I wish I could say that I'm sorry it happened, but I'm not."

I had now confessed this to two different people and neither was who I expected. I looked up and locked eyes with Edmundo again.

"I love her. I have no other excuse."

Edmundo sighed and looked away. He was quiet for a long time and I didn't dare move.

"Alright, our deal stands. But before I speak to Vicky, I need to know. Will you honor the contract you signed no matter what happens from this day forward?"

Swallowing the lump in my throat and gazing at Ren's beautiful face, I gave my answer.

"Yes, of course, I will," I said, and then jerked when Ren's baby finger touched mine.

I grabbed her hand and stood as her eyes began to flutter.

"She's waking up," I said, and Edmundo rolled his wheelchair closer.

Ren's intoxicating, silvery eyes finally opened, and my heart began to beat again. She turned her head and looked at me. I smiled before pushing the button for the nurses.

"She's awake!"

Love the characters? Want to know more? Then be sure to check out:
    Next Book In Kings of Wayward Academy - Queen's Gambit
    More about the Mikhailov Family - Protective Phlox
    More about the Mancini Family - Driftwood Daffodil
    More about the Lost Souls MC - Malice

Editor's Note

Where do I even begin? This book has left me completely shooketh. All the pieces have fallen in spectacular fashion, but as we well know, Brooklyn Cross thrives on our tears. There is still much of Ren and the King's story to come. Ren now has more family than she knows what to do with.

And speaking of the Mikhailovs...

Official Proclamation of Ownership:

Here ye here! An official claim has been requested and accepted for Mr. Nathaniel Mikhailov. The lucky woman is none other than the amazing Laura Reads Too Much. She can henceforth claim sole ownership of Nathaniel. May you live happily ever after, and remember to back my claim on Myles McCoy, always.

Several official claims have been made in recent weeks. If you feel inclined to claim a man from the Brooklyn Crossverse, all I require is eternal acceptance of my claim on Myles and your pesky little soul...

Brooklyn Cross does not approve this message.

Thank You

Thank you to all those that decided to pick up this book and read it. It is only with readers continued support that Indie Authors, such as myself, are able to keep writing which is why your reviews mean so much to us. If you enjoyed this book, please consider leaving me a review.

ABOUT THE AUTHOR

Writing is not just a passion for me. It is a lifeline to my sanity.

I have always loved writing but suffer from severe dyslexia and short-term memory retention issues. I struggled in school while I worked every night on re-training my brain.

I was frequently treated like I would never succeed, and I found myself putting my love for writing on a shelf.

Even at the age of six, I found it easier to communicate with animals than people, which was a big reason why I was drawn to dressage horseback riding. I remained focused on my passion for riding until I had to step away from the competition world for personal reasons.

Today, my desire for writing and storytelling has been rekindled. I have published multiple books and will never let anyone or anything hold me back again.

I am a proud romance author who offers my readers morally grey heroes, a ton of spice, epic journeys, and redemption stories.

-Follow Your Dreams-

Brooklyn Cross